There was time **those final moments.**

Marti, still bound, was able to roll herself onto her side. From that position she used the fingers of one hand to write in the dirt. She prayed the darkness would cover the word, that it wouldn't be seen until the police arrived.

She prayed for other things, too. For the souls of her dead mother and father, for her own soul, for that of her friends. She prayed for the child she had given up so many years before. And when her killer dragged her to the makeshift cross and lashed her to it with rags so tight they cut into her skin, when it dawned on her what he planned to do, she even found it in the long-lost depths of her soul to pray for the person who was doing this hideous deed.

But even as Marti prayed, she knew it was far too late for that. The mother of God didn't come around much anymore.

MEG O'BRIEN

SACRED TRUST

ISBN 1-55166-586-7

SACRED TRUST

Copyright © 2000 by Meg O'Brien.

MIRA and the Star Colophon are trademarks used under license and registered in Australia, New Zealand, Philippines, United States Patent and Trademark Office and in other countries.

Visit us at www.mirabooks.com

Printed in U.S.A.

This one's for Emily Hope

ACKNOWLEDGMENT

No book is written in a vacuum, and I would like to thank some of the people who helped me throughout the writing of *Sacred Trust*, either in technical areas or in providing support in a variety of ways.

Many, many thanks to:

The Carmel Police Department, and especially Officer Joe Avila, who generously took me on a ride-along and provided me with invaluable insight into the workings of the Carmel PD. If there's anything in this book that's incorrect about local law enforcement, it's not his fault, but mine.

Al & Pat Tracy, of Tracy's Kenpo Karate Studios, for advice and technical support in writing the Kenpo scenes. Your generosity in reading those excerpts and assuring me of their authenticity is most appreciated. Special thanks to Pat, good friend, for her ongoing online support.

Cathy Landrum, invaluable friend and research assistant. As always, Cathy, a fabulous job—especially regarding crucifixion and the inner workings of the Catholic Church after Vatican II. I couldn't have made it through without you.

Merrill Leslie, for being a sensitive Carmel landperson who left me to my endeavors and only showed up when I needed her—a writer's dream.

The Carmel Il Fornaio coffee group, especially Nancy Baker Jacobs, who offered friendship, advice and support in the darkest of times. One must not, of course, forget "The Master of the Game," Robert Campbell; "The Curmudgeon," Bob Irvine; and "The Young Turk," Bob Norris. Thanks for the great talks, the advice and for being there every day. Oh, and Jeannie?—keep up the excellent artwork. Sol? Not to worry—the Sol in this book bears no resemblance to you, other than his name. I'd never accuse you of being a lawyer.

My editor at MIRA, Amy Moore-Benson, whose excellent direction and editorial skills are beyond compare. Thanks for your faith in me and in this book.

Last but not least, special thanks to my son, Greg, whose wise advice as a reader and writer in his own right, helped me to iron out the plot for *Sacred Trust*. I must also acknowledge that the ideas for the trepan scenes sprang from his dark, twisted, writer's mind. Guess the nut doesn't fall far from the tree.

Part 1

Land of Milk and Honey

Mishne 13: "Indeed, the blessing of an abundant and profuse nature will cause them harm, by allowing them to slumber in the bosom of idleness...or to fall into evil ways."

1

MARTI

He grabbed her in the lot of the supermarket in Seaside, grabbed her from behind as she was stepping into her car. He shoved her face forward into the back seat, then blindfolded, bound and gagged her before she ever had a chance to see him.

She thought it must be a him because of the strength it had taken, trying to fight him off. Not once did he let her raise her face off the vinyl seat, his hand and knee pressing her down so hard she thought she would smother.

He took her keys, and she heard him lock the back door then slide into the driver's seat. He drove forever, it seemed, and she wondered if they were on Highway 1. Along the way she tried desperately to remember every detail, counting three stoplights, three red then greenish hues making their way through the blindfold. If I can remember light and sounds, *she thought,* I might be able to tell the police where he took me.

At that point she still believed she might live to tell the police. He might rape her, then let her go. Rape would be terrible, but it was something she could find *a way to live with, just as the women she'd been interviewing tonight had found a way.*

It wouldn't be easy, she knew. But if God were with her, if all her old saints were with her, she could do it.

Silently, she began to pray the words of the Memorare, *words from the early days that took no effort but tumbled over and over from her mind like a mantra:* Remember, oh most gracious Virgin Mary, that never was it known that anyone who fled to thy protection or sought thy intercession was left unaided. Remember, oh most gracious Virgin Mary, that never was it known that anyone who fled...

When the car came to a stop, the prayer did as well. And when he dragged her from the car and shoved her to the ground, tearing her clothes off piece by piece till she was naked, she tried to scream and plead through the gag, ''Please don't hurt me, don't hurt me.'' But then he began to beat her, and she knew the flogging for what it was—an old familiar ritual when gently done, but now powered by the seeming hatred of a demented soul. The leather thongs had small metal balls attached to their ends, and he brought the flagrum down full force, first on her breasts, then, as she tried to squirm away, on her back. She felt the blows cut into the outer tissues, felt the capillaries break, then the veins. She knew when the blows reached into the muscles, when arterial blood began to spurt and her skin to hang in strips.

Smothering would have been a blessing, was her only coherent thought. If only she had smothered and had it done with.

Marti Bright never got to tell the police the many details she stored away that night. Not the way his hands felt on her mouth, the musty paper smell, nor the scuffling sounds he made after the flogging as he dragged her to the place on the hill.

She didn't get to tell the police the way he wheezed and coughed with the effort it took to kill her, high, piercing sounds that were almost like that of a woman. Or the way she knew, finally, why this was being done to her. The why, if not the who.

There was time for only one thing in those final moments. Marti, still bound, was able to roll herself onto her side. From that position she used the fingers of one hand to write in the dirt. She prayed the darkness would cover the word, that it wouldn't be seen until the police arrived.

She prayed for other things, too. For the souls of her dead mother and father, for her own soul, for those of her friends. She prayed for the child she had given up so many years before. And when her killer dragged her to the makeshift cross and lashed her to it with rags so tight they cut into her skin, when it dawned on her what he planned to do, she even found it in the long-lost depths of her soul to pray for the person who was doing this hideous deed.

Finally, as the nails punctured her palms, the prayer she screamed silently into the gag became, Mary, mother of God, save me. Please, oh, please, Mary, save me.

But even as Marti prayed, she knew it was far too late for that. The mother of God didn't come around much anymore.

2

ABBY

Nobody believes me now when I tell them that I, Abby Northrup, of all people, used to be a nun. They look at my *Better Homes and Gardens* house, the "perfect" marriage I had before Jeffrey screwed me over—or, more precisely, screwed that bimbo over—and they laugh.

But it's true. I used to be a nun. Oh, I was only seventeen when I entered, and I never took vows. When I left the order at eighteen, people asked me why. Trying to be funny, I said, "I decided I liked boys more than girls." That was true, too. But only half the truth. Because at Joseph and Mary Motherhouse, at eighteen, I loved Marti Bright more than anything in life.

Marti was one of those eighteen-year-old women who seemed ageless. She might have lived a lifetime before she was five. She was kind and funny, generous and giving. She spent hours in the motherhouse chapel, praying till her knees were scarred. Her face was peachy, like the cliché, and her eyes huge and dark. She had a musky scent that I loved and later identified as Pacquin's hand lotion, and there was such an aura about Marti Bright, we gave her the nickname "Shining Bright." In later years, after we both left the convent—"leapt over the wall," as they said in those days—Marti became a photojournalist, and the nickname stuck: *Shining Bright.*

They called her that on the news this morning, when the best friend I ever had was found crucified on a hill in Carmel. The newsperson droned unthinkable words over the car radio as I drove recklessly to get to Marti, shock and horror vying for room in my heart. "A world-renowned photojournalist, Marti Bright would forget, in third-world countries, that she was there on assignment. Several times her cameras disappeared while she fed rice and water to starving children. Dave Arnott, you knew her. Tell us something about this woman they called Shining Bright."

A male voice had taken over, heavy with sadness. "Marti was more than beautiful. She had a beautiful soul. More than once she was found crouching in the dirt, her khakis covered with mud. 'Cameras can be replaced,' she once told this reporter, 'but not the grasp of a child's fingers on yours as you siphon the tiniest drops of water or food into a starving mouth. Not that particular moment, or that particular child…'" Arnott's voice had trailed off, and the first newsperson had finished simply, "Marti Bright will be sorely missed."

I stand looking at my old friend now, her naked torso swinging slightly in a brisk wind, exposed for half the town to see. Her wrists have been bound to the makeshift cross with some kind of cloth, and there are large, thick nails through her palms. Her beautiful dark hair has been cut as if with a blunt knife; its ragged edges are plastered to her skull by the rain. Blood is pouring down. There are bruises everywhere, and odd, peppery cuts all over her abdomen and breasts. From this angle I cannot see how her back has been stripped of flesh, though I've been told this is the case.

The worst of it, however—the absolute worst—are the words "I LIED" painted garishly in red across her chest.

Soon the national media will be here, but for now the stringers push forward for close-ups—not for the local television stations or papers, which might have the taste not to show them, but for *Hard Copy,* the *Inquirer,* and that ilk. Even an old Cesarean scar is hot news, the faint, smooth line from belly to pubic hair glistening beneath pelting rain and the storm-darkened sky. Till now, no one in the press has known that Marti had a child, nor has her family, or most of her friends. She never married, never seemed interested in a family, only her work.

I knew, however. I was there by Marti's side fifteen years ago, I saw the child lifted from her womb. I stood holding her hand, tears streaming down my cheeks along with hers. There was a time when Marti kept no secrets from me.

That has changed of late. It must have, I think, staring numbly at my friend before the sheriff's investigators cut her down. With the incessant *click click click* of cameras all about me, I think that something major must have changed. Because of all the secrets Marti told me over the years, she never once told me who in the name of God might have hated her so much, they could have done such a God-less thing.

The cross upon which Marti's thin, battered body was nailed and strung is planted deep into rain-softened ground above the Carmelite monastery, not five minutes from my house. This side of the hill is bare of trees, and on a good day I might have been ambling along Highway 1, on my way to breakfast at Rocky Point, and seen her here. Until the rain began, however, the fog was heavy in Carmel, visibility less than a block or so either way.

I struggle to keep my composure as they lay my best friend on a sheet of black plastic in the cold rain, the medical examiner poking and prodding into places she never would have allowed him to touch if alive. As if to escape the ugly scene, my mind swoops back, way back, and I wonder how it is that such things come to be. There we were twenty years ago, Marti and me, two women with high hopes, thinking we could do anything, go anywhere, and that even if one day we became old women pushing walkers around in a nursing home, we would at least have bright, golden memories to warm us till the day we died.

I don't know what happened to Marti's dream. But was it my fault, I wonder, the death of my dreams? Did I cling too much to the past? Was there something in me that wished to be back in that time when love seemed so pure, so good, rather than the way it was with Jeffrey?

Even now, months later, it sickens me to remember the way I found my husband with that bimbo on the sheets I had only that morning laundered, her breasts dangling over his chest, him gobbling them up like a starving orphan while that poor pitiful part of him that, to my knowledge, hadn't functioned for weeks, stood ramrod straight, poking into every opening in a way I'd long since tired of it poking into me.

By then my marriage had come down to doing other things that pleased Jeffrey, like adding Bounce to the dry cycle so the sheets wouldn't scratch his sensitive skin. If I'd known what he was doing with *her* while I was at the office struggling to come up with a witty new column, I'd have dumped a bottle of Drano into the wash.

Damn Viagra, anyway. That's what started the whole thing.

Not that I really cared. I'd given up loving Jeffrey long before, and who can blame him for seeking solace in the hills, even if those hills were made of boundless pasty-white flesh?

So, yes, I caught the dream, then threw it away. But wouldn't you know, there are still the damned penances to pay. Not Hail Marys nor Our Fathers, as in the past. That would be too easy an out. For my penance I have the fact that, even though Jeffrey is still around, still sleeps on a couch in the house to keep the rumormongers at bay, there is another memory now, one less warming to take into that time when I'm shuffling along a cold corridor with people who wear bibs and shout for help, though they know not where they are.

And, oh, Marti. You who were so shining bright. Where have you been, and who have you been with, that you should end up this terrible way? You can't be dead, Marti. Can you? Surely you will rise up and laugh any moment now, teasing, ''The joke's on you this time, Abby! I finally got you!''

I would give anything if the joke were on me. Anything at all.

''Abby.'' Ben Schaeffer, detective on the Carmel P.D., stands beside me. His brow is furrowed, his hazel eyes dark with sympathy. ''Sorry. I know you were good friends.''

I nod, though my neck seems as stiff and unbending as my mind, which will not wrap itself around this terrible thing. ''Thanks for talking the sheriff into letting me through the lines. How much longer do you think it'll be?'' I clear my throat and try to steady my voice. ''Can't they cover her up or something? It's not right, her lying there on the ground like that. And the damned rain won't stop, it just keeps coming down and down and down—''

Ben puts a hand on my arm. ''Steady, Ab. It shouldn't be too much longer. I'll see if I can do something to speed things up.''

I watch his tall frame move with authority toward the coroner and the two sheriff's deputies hovering over Marti. Several yards behind me, pushing against the yellow crime line, are the eager photographers and reporters, some of whom are co-workers. One, Billy Drubin, stands with his hands stuck in the pockets of a drab raincoat, his shoulders hunched.

''Hey, Abby, what'd you find out?''

When I don't answer, he says, ''You're not covering this for your column, are you? How come they let you inside the line?"

I walk over to him, knowing he won't leave me alone unless I do. The others are watching us, picking up every word we say. If I talk to Billy, I tell myself like someone in a dream, the rest will go away.

"Marti's a good friend," I say. "I've known her for years."

"Geez, that's rough, Abby. Sorry. What happened? They got a clue?"

"No. It's too soon."

"Are you on it?"

"For *Round the Town*? Hardly."

"Even so, if you knew her..." He takes a crumpled pack of Marlboros out of a pocket, taps one out and lights it. His match sputters, and within moments the cigarette is soggy from the rain. He leaves it dangling from the corner of his mouth. "Hey," he says, "why don't you talk to me? Tell me all about her. The inside story, things we don't already know, I mean."

I look at him, wary suddenly. "What inside story, Billy?"

His pale blue eyes are bright, avid. "Well, you know, there've been rumors. She was pretty famous for a while, the top of the heap as far as photojournalists go. So what happened? Why did she disappear all of a sudden? Hell, Abby, no one's seen her around for months. And what's that 'I LIED' all about? And the scar on her belly?"

I stare at him, wondering how I ever got to be part of this ravenous mass of vultures called "the press."

"I have to go, Billy."

"I mean, if you were that close," he insists, tossing the cigarette to the ground, "you must have some idea where she's been. And what she's been up to."

Anger seeps into my zombie-like state. It is, perhaps, the first glimmer of reality setting in.

"Dammit, Billy, drop it! I don't know!"

Turning back, I see that the small group of men surrounding Marti has begun to disperse. Ben is still there, talking to the sheriff and Ted Wright, the coroner, and a body bag is being zipped over the bruised and battered torso of my friend. A sharp pain hits me in the gut as her once-beautiful face disappears inside the black plastic. Tears flood my eyes.

Ben looks at me and strides through the mud in my direction, his jeans and running shoes becoming splattered with thick brown goo. He puts a comforting arm around my shoulders, and I lean on him only slightly, more aware now of the media and what might show up in the evening news.

"Will Jeffrey be home tonight?" he asks quietly.

I shake my head. "He's in Washington."

"My place?" Ben asks even more quietly. "In an hour?"

I hesitate, nodding toward the coroner's van, into which Marti is being loaded now. "Don't you have work to do?"

"The sheriff's in charge out here. And there'll be a countywide task force." He looks at his watch. "I have a couple of hours."

Once, I would have gone with Ben out of reckless abandon, even revenge. *What's sauce for the goose.* I was still angry with Jeffrey then. Now my husband

and I barely talk. We live under the same roof out of expediency, pretending at marriage while leading vastly separate lives.

My only thought at the moment, therefore, is to feel Ben's arms around me. To slip between his cool, familiar sheets and forget.

Thank God for Ben, the safe one, I think. In all the madness of Jeffrey's unfaithfulness, Ben has been here, a good friend, steadfast as the day is long. He's the one I can trust not to betray me. Ever.

"I want to see her again," I say, my voice thick with sorrow. "I never really said goodbye."

"I'm sure that can be arranged." Ben stands behind me, his arms wrapped around my waist, the two of us staring out his living-room window at the leaden sea.

"Where is she now?"

"She'll be at the coroner's office for a while," he says. "An autopsy, you know."

I shiver. The coroner will take his bloody knives and saws and cut into my friend. He will break her breastbone to get at her heart and carve out her stomach to get—

"Can I see her before they do all that?"

"I'll check, okay?"

He lifts my hair, planting a light kiss on the back of my neck before going to the telephone in the kitchen. Across the breakfast bar I see him pace as he talks, the long cord wrapping around his slightly thickening waist. Though Ben is tall, and was gangly as a teenager, his fortieth year has found him with what most charitably might be called love handles.

I've always liked them; they give me a secure feeling, something to hold on to when the world goes topsy-turvy all around.

I can hear the kinds of grunts he usually makes when talking with others in law enforcement. *Right, yeah, sure, fine.* They seem to have their own language, an abbreviated one for talking on police radios that carries over into everyday life.

Coming back, he says, "Tonight, around ten. They should have her...she should be all right for you to see her by then."

He is trying to be careful, but I know what he means: my friend won't be in pieces. At least, she won't look that way.

"Hey, hey," he says softly, pulling me into his arms. "It'll be all right. I'll go with you."

Gratefully, I put my arms around his neck and stand on tiptoe to kiss him. One hand pulls me toward him while another pushes my blouse aside and covers my breast, squeezing it so hard I can almost feel pain. I am instantly aroused, everything in me screaming to know that I, at least, still live and breathe.

After that, he needn't do a thing. I am all over him, my passion swinging from tender to nearly vicious, and he allows me that, knowing the anger and hopelessness that sit in my heart, the utter futility and rage.

Spent, we lie naked side by side in Ben's king-size bed. A tall, wide window frames a Carmel Highlands scene that has been painted by ninety percent of the artists in town: charcoal cliffs, emerald pines and hillsides dotted with seven-figure homes. Beyond them lies a cerulean sea with wild waves crashing.

Ben's home is simple, a bachelor's hideaway. The view, however, can take one's breath away.

Ben sighs and stretches. "That was quite a work-out, lady."

"You know it."

"Feeling better?" He pulls me to him.

"Well, I haven't got much energy left for anger." A cloud crosses my mind. "Not right now, anyway."

He turns on his side to face me. "You're thinking of tonight. You don't have to do it, you know."

"See her? Yes, I do."

"What can it accomplish?"

"I can say goodbye."

"I thought you did that out on the hill."

"It's not the same."

He takes my hand, which lies on the pillow between us. "You want to talk about it?"

I start to shake my head, then pause. If there were ever anyone I could tell about Marti, it would be Ben. And I need to get it out, all those old memories, the pictures of those days that have been surging through my mind since I saw her hanging there.

"It started out as one of those silly schoolgirl crushes," I say, licking my bone-dry lips. "Marti and I went to the same high school, Mary Star of the Sea in Santa Rosa. It was an all-girl school, and neither one of us was self-confident enough to flirt with boys. So when they came over from St. John's, say, for sports events or dances, we both sort of stayed in the background while the other girls fell all over them.

"Marti was into journalism, and so was I. We worked on the school newspaper together and became friends. Marti was the brighter star, however. She was the one who championed all the causes, from ending global war to preserving the planet. She wrote articles for the paper, gave speeches and marched for peace. I pretty much tagged along behind."

I pause. How to tell the rest of it? Even to me it isn't clear how everything happened, right to this day. "In our senior year," I continue, "we talked about what we wanted to do with our lives. The nuns were pushing us to become nuns, of course—they always did in the Catholic schools. But it wasn't till our senior year that either of us considered it seriously. We knew we wanted to give our lives to a larger cause, so to speak. We just didn't know what."

Licking my lips again, I swallow against the bile rising in my throat, the morning's breakfast of scrambled eggs tasting like copper now. "The thing is, neither of us felt inspired by what was going on in the world. The eighties were almost upon us, and we could see the writing on the wall. The self-indulgence, the materialism. And there was...oh, I don't know, a coldness about the world. It was getting too big, and it seemed that people had stopped caring about people. We felt—foolishly, of course—that everything that was ever going to happen had already come and gone. The two big wars, Vietnam, the hippie era. More than anything, we figured the world was going to pot, no pun intended, and we didn't want to be part of it."

I brush my hair back from my forehead, which is still damp from the exertion of making love. "So we were running away, I guess, more than anything else. And there was one nun—Sister Helen—who kept urging us to enter the order she was in. She had us cleaning out votive candles in the school chapel and pressing altar cloths. You name it, we got caught up in it. 'Serving the Lord' came to look so much better than making our way in a world we didn't feel much a part of, anyway."

"In other words, you found an acceptable way to drop out?" Ben says gently. With one big, rough finger, he strokes my arm.

"Something like that. Marti, of course, was always more outgoing than I. But she was also idealistic. Giving her life to God was the ultimate sacrifice, the noblest of all goals. She felt she could make more of a difference from within the walls of a convent than from without. Through prayer, and so on."

I look at Ben, wondering if he thinks the two of us ridiculous. But he isn't smiling that odd little smile, the way he will sometimes when he's thinking something critical and doesn't want to say it.

"Go on," he urges.

"Well, come September, we both entered the novitiate at Joseph and Mary Motherhouse, up in Santa Rosa. It was great fun at first, an adventure like none we'd ever had—wearing the black postulant's uniform and veil, getting up at dawn and praying in the chapel, even scrubbing floors. We loved every minute of it. But then one of the nuns caught us alone together, just talking, you know, and she reported us to the novice mistress. Joseph and Mary was behind the times, and the rules hadn't been loosened up after '62 and Vatican II, the way they were in some motherhouses. Special friendships, the novice mistress informed us, led to trouble—in other words, lesbian relationships. They were therefore *verboten*. We were ordered not to see each other anymore, and in fact were allowed only to spend time with other postulants in groups of three or more. There was never a moment when we could simply be alone and talk."

"That must have been tough," Ben says, "after being so close through high school."

"It was awful. Maybe it was the forbidden aspect of it. Or just plain loneliness, like being away at camp for the first time. All I know is, the more they told us we couldn't see each other, the more we suddenly had to. We even broke one of the strictest rules, that of all-night silence, to meet in the choir loft when everyone else was asleep. Then one night, our friendship, just as the novice mistress had warned, became something else. We didn't do much, just held each other's hands and kissed now and then. Neither one of us had sex in high school, we were both virgins, but the more time we spent alone together, the more this…this *feeling* grew between us. The funny thing was, it all seemed so perfectly natural. And it didn't take much more than a kiss to make us happy. I remember Marti's lips…"

I pause, blushing.

"What?" Ben urges me, smiling. "What about Marti's lips?"

My blush deepens. "Oh…they were harder than I thought they'd be. More like a man's lips, you know?"

He takes my chin in his hands and kisses me, long and hard. "More like this, you mean?"

When he doesn't stop, and in fact lays his body completely over mine, I pull back for a breath, laughing. "Wait a minute. Don't tell me you're jealous."

He raises his eyebrows in an exaggerated expression. "Jealous? Me?"

"You." I poke him lightly on the nose with my finger. "You're the one who wanted me to tell you."

He sobers and falls back, lying on his side again. "I meant that. Tell all."

I sit and reach for the glass of ice water I brought earlier to the bedside table. The ice is melted, and the water tastes like chlorine. But it wets my lips, which helps. Seeing Marti drained of blood, my own seemed to drain away as well. That was hours ago, but inside I still feel like old parchment that has begun to crumble. Even making love with Ben has not changed that, only added a touch of moisture, a small ray of hope that one day I might be myself again.

"Marti," I remember with a small smile, "was usually the instigator when it came to breaking the rules. She was the brave one. When some of the other girls wanted to sneak out during recreation at night and go to the woods to smoke, Marti was right there with them. In the lead, in fact. Sometimes I tailed along just so I wouldn't seem too square. Not that I smoked, never liked it even then. The thrill of breaking the rules was enough for me."

I reach up, adjusting the pillows behind me so I can sit. "Finally, when we'd been caught far too often, and the usual penance of prostrating ourselves on the chapel floor for twenty minutes while reciting umpteen Hail Mary's didn't work, they got Sister Helen to come from the high school to talk to us. Besides being our teacher in high school, she was our sponsor into the convent, and she was livid when she found out what we'd been doing. Sister Helen was a nun from the old school, and she still wore her long black habit in 1980, even though most nuns in active orders were in civilian dress by then. She said she had worked too long and hard to receive her habit and wasn't about to give it up."

"And did she give you a whuppin'?" Ben asks, stretching out on his back with his hands laced behind his head. "Or a whack on the knuckles with a ruler? That's what my teachers at St. Thomas's used to do."

"Neither," I say, turning to rest my head on his shoulder, my fingers by habit stroking the wiry brown hairs on his chest. His arm comes around my shoulders and pulls me close. "She just told us in no uncertain terms how disappointed she was in us. She said if we'd had any respect for our vocations, we never would have behaved so abominably, and in fact she was convinced now that we didn't even have vocations and shouldn't become nuns at all."

"Ouch. What did you and Marti say?"

"Not much. But Sister Helen was right, and we knew it. We didn't even have to talk about it. The next day we met in the hallway outside the novice mistress's office and went in there together to tell her we were leaving."

"How did the good Sister Helen take that?"

"I don't know. I never saw her again. I went home for a few weeks, then moved down to Berkeley, to college. Marti went East to school. We kept in touch, but I think both of us felt bad, like we'd wrecked our one chance to do anything really great, or at least selfless, in the world.''

I pause, thinking. ''On hindsight, we may not have wanted to see each other for a while for fear we'd be reminded of our failure. I know that personally it took me a long time after that to get back into the world, so to speak.''

''But you and Marti have been in touch over the years.''

''Yes. That year in the convent faded, and we got back together.''

I see his look. ''As *friends,*'' I emphasize. ''In fact… ''

''What?''

I shake my head. ''Just an old memory, that's all.'' Maybe when Marti has been gone longer, I can tell him about her baby.

Sighing again, I reach for the glass of water and drink deeply.

''So, are you shocked?'' I ask Ben.

''That you had a schoolgirl crush on Marti Bright? No, those things happen. It's more like I'm intrigued.''

I throw my pillow at him. ''You men! You love the idea of women being together, don't you?''

I have meant only to tease him. But a shadow falls over his face, and I remember too late that I've hit a sore spot.

Darcy, Ben's ex, had a wild affair with the owner of the Seahurst Art Gallery in Carmel, Daisy Trent. When Daisy ran off with several artists' money and

Darcy ran after her, all the way to Paris, Ben was left to pick up the pieces. The scandal was in the papers for months, and Ben—for some reason he's never felt it necessary to explain—made reparation to the artists for the money Daisy, his ex-wife's lover, stole. This all occurred before I met him, and he doesn't like talking about it.

"Sorry," I say.

"That's okay." But the playful mood is gone.

After a moment I wonder aloud where Marti's funeral will be and who will arrange it.

"She didn't have family?" Ben asks.

"A brother, as I remember. They weren't close."

The phone rings next to the bed. Ben lets it ring, but then the machine comes on and a male voice says tersely, "Ben, it's Arnie. It's important. Pick up."

Ben groans and reaches for the receiver. Grunting a hello, he listens. At one point he frowns and looks over at me.

"What is it?" I ask when he hangs up. Arnie, I know, is a fellow cop on the Carmel P.D., and a friend.

He hesitates.

"Ben?"

"Uh, Arnie talked to Sheriff MacElroy. He says it looks like Marti was dragged from a car to that place where they found her. There are signs of a struggle in the brush off to the side. Marti—or someone— scrawled a name in the dirt there."

I sit up, and for some reason I can't explain except that I feel suddenly exposed, I hold the sheet against me, covering my nakedness. "Really? What name?"

Instead of answering, he gives me a funny look. "Abby, when was the last time you saw Marti?"

"I don't know, months ago."

"Can you be more specific?"

"Sure. Around three months ago. August, I think."

"She lived in New York City, right?"

"Yes."

"Do you know why she was here?"

I shake my head, perplexed. "She was doing a magazine piece about the homeless, and I think she was talking to people at the rape crisis center in Seaside. Why?"

"You saw her frequently when she was here?"

"A few times."

"Did you and she have an argument?"

I stare at him, turning cold. "Ben, what the hell is going on?"

He slides out of bed and begins to dress. A wall seems to build itself between us. "I tried to reach you several times early this morning before I finally got hold of you, Abby. Where were you?"

"Out walking Murphy along Scenic," I say, becoming angry now at his tone. "Why?"

He doesn't answer.

"Ben, why are you suddenly sounding like a cop?"

Dragging a dark green blazer out of the closet, he puts it on over khaki pants, then a tie. When he stands before me again he is all-business. The wall is complete. "Abby, I've been working Homicide fifteen years. There are certain patterns you come to look for. And when someone who's being murdered scrawls a name in the dirt… Look, I'm not saying it's always the case. But one thing we're taught as cops is that it's most likely to be the name of her killer."

There is a small silence, during which I wait for the other shoe to drop. Still, I'm no dummy. I already know what the shoe is. "So Marti wrote my name…Abby. Right?"

"Better get dressed," my lover says. The one who would not betray me. Ever.

He doesn't take me to the station on Junipero in handcuffs, but he does take me there. He has to, he explains as I dress. Somebody there wants to talk to me, he explains further in the car.

He won't tell me who that somebody is. But Ben, in the blink of an eye, has changed. I feel somehow I've lost two people this day.

Which is ridiculous, I tell myself. Ben is still with me. He helps me out of the car, as my knees are weak. He sits me in a quiet back office of the small station and asks me if I'd like coffee. I nod, and he goes to get it for me, setting the cup before me with one sugar and plenty of cream, the way he knows I like it.

If a man cares enough to remember the way you take your coffee, it's not all bad, I think.

Meanwhile, my mind races. Why would Marti have written my name in the dirt? Who wants to question me about it? The sheriff? I know the Carmel P.D. facilities are often used by the sheriff's department, as well as other investigative agencies. And, though Ben will be part of the task force that investigates Marti's death, the sheriff's department has jurisdiction over the area where she was found.

Ben has placed me on one side of a long table, halfway down it in the middle. He takes a seat at a far end, along with Arnie Lehman. Both men sit silently, their arms folded, faces wooden masks. This frightens me more than if they'd put me under a bright light and tortured me with thumbscrews.

I wonder aloud if I should call a lawyer. Ben gives me a quizzical look but doesn't say a word. Arnie assures me quietly that I haven't been charged with anything. He looks at the closed door, then raises a skinny arm to check his watch. He sighs, stretches. Ben rubs his face with his palms.

Just when I think I can't stand another moment of this, two men in dark business suits walk in. One is taller than the other, with sandy hair. The second man is older, his face lined, hair gray. Rimless glasses hide his eyes, and both men's expressions are bland, giving up nothing.

"Ms. Northrup?" the taller man asks as my eyes turn his way. I nod.

"Special Agent Mauro," he says quietly, extending a hand that holds a thin leather wallet with a badge affixed to it. As he flips it open I see the words *Secret Service* on a card, with Special Agent Stephen Mauro's name and likeness beneath them, along with a seal.

"This is Special Agent Hillars," he says.

The older man nods. They take seats directly across from me, and I'm almost relieved. *Thank God it's only the Secret Service,* I think, for surely this has nothing to do with me, after all. So far as I know,

I haven't been passing counterfeit money, nor have I plotted against the president of the United States.

At the same time, part of me is certain I'm about to be arrested for some horrible crime I cannot remember committing. It is a schizophrenic moment: What did the other Abby do that this one has blocked?

"First, we would like to thank you for coming here today to talk with us," Agent Mauro says politely. "We understand this is a difficult time for you."

I'm tempted to point out that I didn't have a choice, but a warning glance from Ben makes me opt for keeping my mouth shut.

"I...your welcome," is about all I can manage.

"We'd like to ask you a few questions about Marti Bright," Agent Mauro continues, taking a small pad and black pen from an inner pocket. "Ms. Northrup, I understand you and Ms. Bright were close friends?"

The agent seems to choose his words carefully, and beneath his steady gaze I feel like a deer pinned down by a gunsight.

"Yes, we were friends."

He nods. "We need you to tell us everything you know about Marti Bright. How you came to know her and for how long you knew her, how often she came to the Monterey Peninsula, the last time you saw her, who her other friends were, who she might have been involved with over the years—intimately, that is—and—"

"Wait a minute." I can't help interrupting, as my

mind is reeling. I wet my lips. "Some of your questions I can answer. Others, I don't know."

"I'm certain you'll do your best," Agent Mauro says blandly. Agent Hillars leans forward slightly. His voice surprises me. He is thin, ascetic-looking, and I'd expected the tone to be clipped. Instead, it is soft and full, a Southern marshmallow.

"We are very sorry to trouble you at this time, Ms. Northrup. We understand you have suffered a loss. We felt, therefore, that the kindest way to do this would be to question you here. If you would prefer, however, we can talk in a more official setting."

The subtle threat in his words shakes me a bit. "I...no, it's not that I don't want to cooperate, it's just..."

I'm beginning to feel again that I need a lawyer. Not only that, but my gut says I need to protect Marti. I decide to tell them only the things they probably already know, or can find out through public records.

"Let's see..." I say thoughtfully. "Where did I meet Marti?"

I tell them how we met in high school at Mary Star of the Sea in Santa Rosa, and how we then entered the convent together at Joseph and Mary Motherhouse. Basically the same things I told Ben earlier, though leaving out the kind of relationship Marti and I had all those years ago. This I keep to myself, glossing over it under Ben's watchful, knowing eye. He doesn't contradict me, and that, at least, is a relief.

Agent Hillars moves restlessly, and Agent Mauro

frowns as I'm telling them how Marti and I left the convent together and then went our separate ways to college. "She was always the more earnest student," I babble, "winning the best scholarships, getting the better grades, while I just sort of muddled through—"

"Might we move ahead, please?" Agent Mauro interrupts. "Ms. Northrup, I would like you to tell us about the time when Ms. Bright first began to come to the Monterey Peninsula." Beginning to write on his notepad, he adds, "That would be fifteen years ago, correct?"

"More like fourteen," I lie.

He stops writing and looks at me.

"Up till then," I add quickly, "we had only telephone contact and an occasional meeting in New York City, when she would fly in for a few days on business. If I could take the time, I would meet her in New York for a day or so of shopping and shows."

"And you never saw her here until fourteen years ago?"

"Never," I say firmly.

Agent Mauro studies me a long moment. I stare back, unflinching. He looks down at his notes, and when he lifts his eyes I get that deer-in-a-gunsight feeling again.

"Ms. Northrup, you and Ms. Bright had a relationship at one time that was closer than simple friendship, I understand."

My face turns hot, and my glance flicks to Ben. "Where—"

"Did I learn that? Let me put my cards on the

table, Ms. Northrup. We know quite a lot about you. Where you went to school, what your grades were from kindergarten on, and the fact that you have a genius IQ you've seldom bothered to use."

"I—" Stunned, I shove my hands into my pockets, trying to hide their slight shaking as Mauro continues. Out of the corner of my eye I see Ben watching me, a thoughtful expression on his face.

"We have names of your friends through high school," Mauro continues, "the fact that you were class president not once but three times despite being somewhat of a rebel, the unfortunate state of your marriage at the current time..." He pauses. "And, of course, your relationship with Marti Bright."

I am speechless. Appalled. I have heard about the long arm of the law, of course, and how thorough it can be. But that they have this kind of information on me is unthinkable. Who have they talked to?

My anger grows, and I no longer think to be careful. "If you know all this, why the hell are you here asking me questions? Why don't you go back to your *informants* and ask them?"

"Ms. Northrup," Agent Mauro says calmly. "There are certain...shall we say, 'holes' in the information we have been given."

"Imagine that." My voice is icy. "Something the Secret Service can't find out about someone."

"For instance," the unflappable Mauro continues, "who did Ms. Bright see when she was here on the Monterey Peninsula?"

"See?"

"Friends, associates. She must have had a reason for coming here."

The older man, Hillars, leans forward slightly again. I am alerted to the fact that my answer to this is important. They are setting a trap. But for who?

"Mr. Mauro, pardon me, but you've obviously done your homework. You must know Marti wrote and photographed several stories here and in Santa Cruz about the homeless. She won awards for those stories—they weren't exactly hidden in a drawer somewhere. Again, why are you asking me things you already know?"

He smiles, though there is no warmth in those gray eyes. In fact, they are so flat and cold they remind me of a pit bull sizing up its next meal. "I suppose you might say I'm more interested in *why* Ms. Bright came here so often over the years, not that she did. Why here, when there are so many other cities with these problems? In fact, bigger cities with bigger problems?"

"Maybe she liked the weather," I snap.

"Or maybe she was having an ongoing liaison here with someone," Mauro says smoothly, not skipping a beat.

"A what?" I am momentarily startled. Then I can't help laughing. "A *liaison*? You mean an affair? Good God. You don't know as much about Marti as I thought."

Mauro narrows his eyes. "Why do you say that, Ms. Northrup?"

"Because Marti was all-business. She didn't have time for liaisons, she didn't care about anything but her work."

"Are you speaking of just lately, Ms. Northrup?

Or was she that way when she was here fifteen years ago, as well?''

I have purposely told him Marti did not come here until fourteen years ago. Did he forget—or is this part of the trap?

The only thing I'm sure of now is that it's time I took a stand. Rising, I say firmly, ''Agent Mauro, I need to go home and feed my dog. If you don't have some sort of subpoena in your back pocket, I'm not answering any more questions—until, that is, you tell me what this is about.''

Mauro looks at Hillars, and a question seems to pass between the two men. Hillars gives a microscopic shrug. Mauro closes his notebook and slips it back into his inside coat pocket. Both men stand, and Hillars gives me a look that seems to border on either anger or contempt. I can't be sure, as it's quickly gone.

Mauro, courteous as ever—on the surface, at least—extends a hand. ''Thank you very much for your cooperation, Ms. Northrup. We may need to talk with you further. If so, we'll be in touch.''

I accept the hand and am rewarded when he drops mine after a brief clasp. He is clearly irritated with me.

Good. Whatever he brought me here for, he didn't get.

A heavy silence fills the room after they leave. I turn to Ben, my voice as cold as my hands. ''I'd like to go now.''

Ben looks at Arnie, who shrugs. ''I've had enough excitement for one day.''

Ben nods. Standing, he walks around the table to

my chair. The tie comes off. So does the jacket. The shirt sleeves are rolled up, and he smiles.

The wall comes down. Or so he thinks.

He is, after all, a man.

Ben pulls his black Explorer to a stop in front of my house.

"Just let me come in with you," he says for the second time. "I just want to be with you, Abby. You shouldn't be alone."

I jump out and speak through the open passenger-side door as my hand prepares to slam it. "No thanks. I prefer to be alone."

"Goddammit, Abby, I had to cooperate with them! I would think you'd be grateful, for that matter."

"Grateful?" The amazed tone in my voice says it all: what I am feeling, thinking, remembering about that cold office, that cold chair and the cool, unemotional presence of a man I had only hours before made love to, allowing questions that were slanted to make me give the Secret Service of the United States some piece of information that might, for all he knew, incriminate me.

"Yes, dammit, grateful!" he says. "If you'd been Jane Doe off the streets, you think it would've been that easy? Maybe you should spend some time finding out what usually goes on when a suspect is being questioned."

He clamps his jaw shut. Too late.

"*Suspect.* You're calling me a suspect now. Damn you, Ben. It's my name, right? My name in the dirt where Marti died. Is that what this is all about? Did the sheriff call in the Secret Service? Or did you?

How else would they even know about me? And what the hell does the Secret Service have to do with any of this, anyway?''

''You know damned well I didn't call them,'' he says. ''You should also know that if Arnie hadn't called me—if he hadn't told them you and I were friends—it could have gone a whole other way.''

''And you should know that you are one son of a bitch, Ben Schaeffer.''

I slam the door. Ben grinds the gears of his Explorer, pulling away from the curb. As I turn to my house, my heart, which is heavy, lifts momentarily at the thought of walking through the door and having a big ball of canine fluff jump into my arms.

Woman's best friend—her dog.

3

Murphy isn't at the door waiting for me, the way he usually is. While that worries me a bit, there have been times when he's sneaked out with Frannie, my part-time housekeeper, and she hasn't taken the time to find him and bring him back. Frannie has a family at home to feed at night, and she's often in a hurry. Murphy doesn't stay gone for long, at any rate. He likes keeping an eye on me, like a mom who thinks her toddler, once out of sight, must be up to no good. I figure he'll show pretty soon.

Dropping my purse on a table in the hallway, I head for the kitchen, seeking a glass of wine. The kitchen sparkles in the late-afternoon sun, not only from Frannie's cleaning but from sunlight on the sea. Tall windows look out on the Pacific Ocean from every room. A million-dollar view, people have called it. Six million would be more like it, in today's market. For this—a house that cost less than a hundred thousand to build twenty years ago.

I have been envied for my house. Most of the homes in Carmel have names rather than addresses. Mine is called *Windhaven*. A major movie was filmed here in the fifties, and you can see *Windhaven* on the movie channel at regular intervals.

There is less beach now, of course, as the shoreline's been eroded by recent storms. But the house and its view have been photographed by *Better Homes and Gardens, Sunset* and *Architectural Digest.* When Jeffrey and I were first married we moved here and opened *Windhaven* for tours during the Christmas season. That was before Clint Eastwood won his run for mayor of Carmel. Jeffrey, who dabbles in real estate, but whose obsession is politics, was working with Eastwood's advisors pre-campaign, and we had tons of friends then—artists, writers, actors, politicians. We decorated with holly garlands and strung lights on everything, including the stately pines along the drive. A wild patch of lawn stretches out from the terrace of *Windhaven* to the cliff, and along the edge of the cliff are Monterey pines that Jeffrey and I planted as windbreaks. In terms of trees they are still infants, yet already they lean to the south from the north winds that buffet them all winter long. If one were to look carefully, one might detect how Jeffrey and I lean, as well, from the buffeting our marriage has taken over the years.

At what point, I wonder, taking a wineglass from the rack beneath the top cupboard, does a marriage begin the downward slide? At what point does it go from holding hands while walking, eyes meeting across the room in a secret, knowing smile, and an occasional embarrassing gush, "Jeffrey is everything to me"? When does the steady feel of aloneness set in for good, not just now and then? And when the distaste for flesh once loved and sought after?

It is, I think, a question—or whole slew of them—that only a decent glass of Seven Peaks can answer.

I reach into the double-door refrigerator and pull out a bottle of my favorite Chardonnay. Opening it, I fill my glass and decide to take the whole bottle to the living room with me. What the hell, it's been a rotten day.

And there is still the coroner's office to come. I glance at my watch and note that it's not even five o'clock, and I can't see Marti till ten. What am I going to do with the next five hours?

In the living room I sit in an overstuffed chair, staring out the window. Not at the sea, which only makes me feel more alone, but in the opposite direction, at the street. People walk by on Scenic, many of them with their dogs. I am irritated that Murphy isn't here. Why did he have to run off today of all days?

No. The real question is, *Why did Marti have to die today?* That's the source of my anger, not Murphy. Not Ben.

Why is my friend dead?

And who would have had reason to do it in just that way? The hideous makeshift cross was crafted, Ben said, of four-by-fours from a house under construction at the bottom of the hill. Who had the strength to drag those four-by-fours to that spot far up the hill, nail them into a cross and then plant them in the ground—much less with Marti's weight added to them?

Who would have been evil enough to paint those awful letters on her chest? And the final, inevitable question—why is the Secret Service involved?

The more questions I come up with, the less answers there seem to be. Nothing works today. Not sex, not wine. Chilled, I set my glass down and cross to the fireplace, laying paper and kindling, then logs. I strike a long match and watch the fire catch then build, warming my face. Sinking to the floor, I sit beside the only heat I've found this day. Outside, the rain begins again. I hear it strike the copper chimney flashing, the pitter-patter growing to a pounding, like nails, like nails in a cross, like nails...

It is only now that I am able to think about the rest of it, the thick, blunt construction nails tearing through her palms, the blood from them draining through the strips of cloth that held her wrists and ankles in place. But the alcohol has loosened everything I stuck way back there and had hoped to forget.

Huddling on the rug before the fire, I allow my body the fetal position it's been wanting all day, and at last the tears come. There's no one to hold them back for, now. There are perks when one lives virtually alone. One can cry anytime, and there's no one around to hear.

Sometime after six I awaken from the stupor I'd cried myself into and make my way around the house, closing blinds and turning on lights. I wonder again where Murphy is and am more worried now than irritated. This isn't like him. A blend of German shepherd and chow, he has a huge appetite, and by five-thirty he will usually come loping along the street and up the path, looking for food.

I miss his being here. Murphy is the one thing that got me through the worst of the bad times with Jeffrey. He has the pointed face of a shepherd, but around the neck he looks like a lion, especially when he sits in a lion-like pose at the top of the stairs, which he does every night, outside my bedroom door. A born protector, he won't leave that spot till I head downstairs in the morning.

Going to the phone, I call Frannie, my house-keeper, at home. When she picks up, I hear children in the background, a big, noisy house full of laughter and good times. As often happens, I feel a pang of jealousy. I think Frannie knows this; she looks at me sadly sometimes, aware that, though I have more money, she has more love. This should create some sort of balance between us, but it doesn't. "Money," I heard Frannie tell a friend on the phone one day, "might make a nice down payment. But it sure can't beat a good man."

"Frannie, did Murphy get out when you were here today?"

"No," she answers between calls of, "Get off that, right now, young man! Didn't I tell you not to walk on the tables?" Her youngest, Billy, has Attention Deficit Disorder. His favorite pastime is performing circus-like stunts on the furniture, when he isn't jumping from the loft in the living room.

"What's wrong? Isn't Murphy home?" she asks. "He was there when I left."

"Are you sure? I don't see how he could have gotten out. Did you close the door tight?"

"Of course," she says, then, "No! I said absolutely no cookies. Dinner's just about ready."

I hear the exasperation in her voice, as it is building in mine. If Frannie is half this distracted when she's here, I am thinking, it's no wonder Murphy got out.

"Abby," she says, "maybe he's up in the attic, sleeping. I did go up there just before I left, with some things I wanted to store away. Maybe he was up there and I didn't realize it and locked him in."

"That's probably it," I agree, relieved. "I don't know why I've been so worried about him. Just a feeling, but you know how it is."

"Sure. I do that with Billy. He drives me to distraction, but just let something the least bit odd happen, and I'm a crazy lady."

We both laugh. "Well, thanks. Sorry to have disturbed you."

"That's okay. Let me know, though, will you? I'll sleep better when I know you've found the Murph. Oh, and Abby." She lowers her voice. "I heard about that awful thing on the hill today. She was a friend of yours, wasn't she?"

"Yes."

"God. I'm so sorry. Are you okay?"

"I will be. I guess it takes time."

"That's for sure. When I lost Will...well, you know."

"Yes."

Frannie has a boyfriend now, but I remember how long it took her to get over the loss of her husband, and how much his traffic accident haunted her, making her unable to drive for weeks. She needed the money she made cleaning, though, and I arranged my schedule on cleaning days to pick her up and take her home at night. The time we spent in the car together helped us to bond. We became friends.

"So, anyway, let me know."

"I will, Frannie. Thanks."

Hanging up, I head immediately for the attic. Something about this still doesn't feel right, however. If Murphy were in the attic, he'd have barked when he heard me come in, or at least be whining by now for dinner. There is something wrong, something terribly wrong.

My worries prove to be founded when no Murphy comes barreling from the attic as I open the door on the second-floor landing. Still, I go up there, remembering that once he fell asleep for hours on a pile of old winter blankets.

Flicking the light switch on the wall at the top of the stairs, I stand in a narrow pool of light. One of the bulbs on the two-bulb fixture has burned out, and only a small area is illuminated, a circle of perhaps five feet around. It has the effect of spotlighting me, while the rest of the attic remains in the dark.

I fold my arms tightly around myself as wind creaks the eaves. Old movies fill my head, and I imagine that someone watches from a dark corner, waiting to do those same things to me that have been done to Marti. I tell myself I am being silly, that my fear is only a hangover from seeing Marti that terrible way, an image that will probably forever be imprinted on my brain. Forcing myself to speak, I call out for Murphy. "Here, boy. Where are you? Murph? Are you up here?"

No answer.

Another creak of wood, this time from the far end of the attic, where I can't see a thing. "Murph? Is that you? Murphy, come here!"

My voice is shaking now, and I can't decide

whether to go to the end of the attic and look, or run. Damn! Why didn't I bring a flashlight?

Because there was no reason to think I'd need one. That other bulb wasn't burned out the last time I came up here, I'm certain it wasn't. I look at the light again, squinting, and for the first time I see that the bulb has not simply burned out, it has been removed.

The old celluloid scenes roll on: a heroine tiptoes down the stairs into a dark, dank cellar with a candle, electricity out because of a storm, thunder crashing, the killer waiting for her at the bottom, knife upraised. I hear myself yelling silently, "No, don't! Don't go down there, dummy! How stupid can you be?"

God, I hate those movies.

There is no alternative, however. If Murphy is here he may have been hurt. Or he could be sick.

Too sick to whimper?

Could be.

Trembling with every step, I move toward the dark end of the attic, waiting for a blow to fall at any moment, for someone to jump out and strike me dead. My hands reach out to feel in front of me, like a person blindfolded in a child's game. There should be nothing in the way. I remember clearing an aisle through the assorted suitcases, electric fans, hanging garments and boxes of old books.

My hand touches a form before me in the aisle. I feel the shape of shoulders, neck. I scream.

My other hand swings out wildly to strike whoever it is, while the first hand is still warding him off. Then I'm swinging with both hands, punching, kicking, going for the eyes with my thumbs.

There are no eyes. No eyes, no head.

I am seeing Marti on that cross, swinging, and here in my attic someone has hung a body with no head. I begin to scream, over and over, the sound low in my throat, like a growl, and then I am on my knees. In a tiny, still-sane corner of my mind I remember an earthquake-disaster kit I put together and left on top of a trunk. Scrambling on my hands and knees I go for it, reaching the trunk and fumbling. The kit is right where I left it, and next to it is the backpack with pepper spray and a heavy-duty flashlight. I whip out the pepper spray, then the flashlight. Pressing the rubber button on the light, I pivot around. The headless body in the aisle is illuminated. A dress form. A sewing mannequin from my downstairs sewing room. It has indeed been hung from the rafters.

It feels as if all the bones desert my body at once, and I'm left with nothing but weak, jellied flesh, not enough to stand on. Part of me wants to laugh.

The other part wants to kill Frannie. She must have brought this up here, knowing I never use it anymore. But she knows better than to put things in the aisle. I've told her to leave a path free so I can get around more easily. Why the hell didn't she remember this, for God's sake?

I hear myself, inner voice rising to a crescendo, and finally I do laugh, though the timber's a bit feeble. I'm beginning to sound like Frannie when she rants on about Billy leaving his toys all over the place. And, of course, she hung the dress form from the rafters to keep a path clear, just as I asked her to. I realize now that the form is not directly in the aisle, but off to one side.

Rising unsteadily to my feet, I put the pepper spray down and point the flashlight toward the dark end of the attic, where the noise had come from. There is nothing there. Only the pile of blankets I thought Murphy might have fallen asleep on. The bright beam slides across their white dust-proof cover. No Murph. No murdering intruder. Nothing but cobwebs and old memories.

Hanging alongside the aisle is my wedding gown in its protective cover. On the floor next to it are two cartons of photograph albums from the early days with Jeffrey. Next to them are two Seagram's cartons full of spiral-bound notebooks I used for my journals till a few years ago.

I turn away, truly worried now about Murph. If Frannie didn't accidentally lock him up here, where in the world is he? This has never happened before.

Downstairs again, I stand in the big center hallway and think. Maybe the cellar door got left open and he sneaked in there. It's a small cellar, holding only the hot-water heater and furnace, so it doesn't take too long to check out. The light is bright at the foot of the stairs, and one glance though the open door at the top tells me Murph isn't there. While I'm wondering what to do next, my doorbell rings.

Puzzled, I go into the foyer and turn on the porchlight, looking through the narrow window next to the door. It's nearly seven now, dark, and my neighbors and I have an unwritten rule between us not to visit without calling first.

Through the window I see someone I have never seen before, a young man with a shock of blond hair, in his early twenties, perhaps. He is dressed in jeans and a green windbreaker, and holds a leash. Murphy is at the end of it, head bowed, tail between his legs.

I am so glad to see him, I yank open the door and don't immediately answer the young man, who is asking, "Is this your dog? Somebody at the house next door said he was."

That Murph is my dog becomes immediately obvious when I reach down and throw my arms around him, and he—relieved, I imagine, not to be yelled at for escaping—laps my face, neck, hands and then my face again.

"Where did you find him?" I ask finally.

"Down on the beach near Eighth Street. He seemed lost, but I thought maybe he belonged to somebody along Scenic, or at least close by. I've been checking at every house along the way that had somebody at home."

"I don't know how to thank you," I say, still stroking Murphy's head and holding him close.

Up till now, the young man has not been smiling. At this point, his expression hardens. "Well, I've got two dogs myself, and I know I wouldn't want either of them wandering around. Look, there is one thing…"

I stop petting Murph and stand, thinking the kid probably wants a reward. "Of course. Let me give you something for your trouble."

He shakes his head. "No, not that. I need to ask you about this."

Reaching down, he pulls the light brown fur apart on Murphy's back so that the skin is clearly visible in the illumination of the porchlight. There, scratched into the skin as if by a needle or pin, the edges still bloody, is the letter A.

Murphy whimpers, and for a moment, my vision goes dark. "Oh, God. Oh, God." My stomach, still half-queasy from this morning with Marti, lurches, and my legs go weak. The kid holds a hand out, and I grab it to keep myself from falling.

"Sorry," he says. "That's why I took so much trouble to find the owner. I thought maybe he or she had done this, and if so, I didn't want the dog going home to more of the same."

Squatting back down, I take Murphy's face between my hands and talk to him as if he could answer. "My poor baby. Murphy, who did this to you? Who did this?"

"His head and tail were down like that when I found him, like he'd been beaten or something, and then when I was petting him I saw this…" His voice trails off again. "I can see it's a surprise to you."

My sorrow is replaced with anger. "Of course it is! I can't even think who in the world could have done such an awful thing."

They are almost the exact words I said to Ben earlier, about Marti. In the next moment I'm filled with fear. There's got to be some kind of madman on the loose. Two such terrible acts in one day? That's one too many for coincidence.

And the A. What can it mean? First my name on the hill where Marti died, and now this, here, on Murphy?

It has to be someone who knows me, who knows Murph is my dog.

That thought is the most chilling of all.

The kid stands watching me with my arms around Murph and seems satisfied that he's okay. I ask him if he'd like to come in for coffee. He shakes his head.

"Thanks, but I've got to be somewhere. I'm just glad I found you. It took a while, you know? You might get some ID for his collar."

"But I—" Reaching down, I check Murphy's collar. "His tag was on here this morning."

The kid shrugs. "Maybe it fell off."

"Are you sure I can't give you something for your trouble?" I ask. "You really went out of your way."

Shaking his head again, he gives Murphy a pat on the head. "Bye, Murph. Take care."

Halfway down the path he looks back. "You take care, too, okay? This is a pretty weird thing. There's no telling what somebody would do. Somebody who'd do this kind of thing, I mean."

My hand tightens on the door. "I know. Thank you. I really can't thank you enough."

I watch him walk through the arbor gate, with its many twinkling white lights. A fairy-tale scene, I once thought. It now occurs to me to add, "By the Brothers Grimm."

I take Murphy to the kitchen, where he gulps down food as if he hasn't eaten in a year. That, I think, is a good sign. While he eats I try the vet, though I know from experience they're closed at night. I get the machine that tells me they'll be open at eight in the morning, and a night number to call if it's an emergency.

When Murph is finished eating, I cleanse the letter "A" on his back carefully with water and a clean paper towel, to get a better look at it. The wound is more superficial than I first thought, and his spirits seem to be returning. I decide not to drag the vet back to his office this late; the morning will do. After spreading antiseptic lotion on the wound, I take Murphy into the living room. There I hold him on the couch, his head on my lap, till he falls asleep.

Briefly, I consider calling the police. But everyone at the station knows me, and they would tell Ben. I don't know if I'm ready to talk to him yet.

I sip my wine, now warm, and try to sort out the multiple shocks of the day. Only now do I become cognizant that Murphy still wears the leash the young man was holding him with at my door. I wonder where it came from. He did say he had dogs of his own. They weren't with him, however. Does he make a habit of taking walks on the beach with a leash in his pocket?

Whatever, I should return it, I think, as upon closer inspection I see that it's real leather and probably expensive.

There is only one problem. I never did learn where he lives, or even his name.

At nine-thirty that night I dress in jeans and a warm sweater and boots for my trip to Salinas and the coroner's office. Murphy sleeps soundly in the living room by the hearth.

When I leave, I close and lock all doors carefully, to prevent any further mishaps. In the morning I will talk to Frannie again. Clearly, Murph got out somehow when she was there. Did she simply not notice? Or was she afraid to tell me? I can't imagine that, though I have to examine the possibility.

At ten-ten I stand alone, looking down at Marti. Her body, on a cold steel autopsy table, has been covered with a sheet to the chin. Even her head, from the hairline back, has been covered, leaving me to wonder what horrors lie beneath the rough white draping. The smell sickens me. A combination of chemicals and death, I imagine, though I've never actually been this close to anyone dead before. Thank God, I think, it isn't what I've read about, or seen in the movies, when a body has been left undiscovered for days.

Just seeing my friend like this is bad enough. In death, her skin is smooth and pale; she doesn't look a day over eighteen. That, and the sterile white sheet, bring to mind our "cells" at the motherhouse, twenty to a dorm room. White sheets hung from a foot or so below the ceiling, separating each cell, or cubicle, giving the appearance of a hospital emergency room. Inside each cell was a bed and a small wooden stand of drawers for our clothes.

"Remember, Marti?" I say softly, my lips curving into a slight smile. "Remember the time you stuck hundreds of veil pins all over my bed?" The pins with their round black heads studded the white bedspread, and I had to remove each and every one before I could lie down and go to sleep that night. It was Marti's revenge for my having short-sheeted her the night before.

Silly practical jokes, and even sillier because we were eighteen, supposedly grown. At twelve, they might have made sense, but...

"We were still so young at that age," I whisper.

"So naive. When did we stop having fun, Marti? And why?"

Children, some say, are pure spirits when they come in, full of joy. Emotions like fear, sadness and guilt are built into them as they grow. By the age of seven, children are determined, at least by the Catholic Church, to have reached the age of "reason." That's when, in effect, they take on the guilt and sins of the world. Each year from then on finds the child growing more serious, taking on more "burdens."

Marti and I must have been late bloomers. We still had some fun left in us when we went off to Joseph and Mary. Both of us came from families that had loved and supported us, given us every chance to explore our lives and what we thought we wanted to give, as well as get. My mother was, and still is, a seemingly happy-go-lucky Irish woman, a bit plump and not more than five feet tall. My dad, a retired salesman, loves her to distraction. He calls her his little "butterball," and he takes care of her and protects her as if she were made of glass. That's because, he says, she's really "laughing on the outside, crying on the inside," like the old song. She carries old sorrows, he tells me, that she never shows anyone and won't talk about, not even to him. My mother's favorite expression is a cliché, but still true: "Smile and the world smiles with you, cry and you cry alone."

Marti's parents, both of them gone nearly twenty years now, were different from mine; a bit distant, though just as supportive. Her mother was a literary genius, hailed in the forties for her innovative style of writing and showered with awards. Her father was an artist, also said to be a genius. They died together, recently, in a plane crash in Central America, on their way to help children who had been orphaned there during a catastrophic storm. The entire world grieved when they died.

I can't help thinking, now, that at least they weren't here to see their daughter murdered. Life does have its small blessings.

Behind me, a door opens and closes. I feel a draft on the back of my neck. Big, familiar hands cover my shoulders, and I lean back to rest my head on Ben's chest.

"I didn't know if you'd come," I say.

"I thought you would call me."

When you had time to cool down, he means.

"I might have," I say, "but something happened."

He turns me around, and I see that he's worried. Deep lines run from cheek to mouth, and his forehead is creased. Poor Ben. From photos I've seen he was handsome and carefree at eighteen. He's still handsome now, at least to me, but it's as if that snapshot of the eighteen-year-old has been sharpened by a unique new photo process called Life. His forehead is so creased from worry, it will be permanently so by the time he's fifty, and his eyes have taken on an intense, cautious look.

"What happened?" he asks me. "Are you all right?"

"I'm fine. It's Murphy."

His eyes narrow. "What about Murphy?"

"He got out today. Somebody did something to him."

"What?"

"They, uh…carved the letter A into his back."
My voice catches. "Into his skin."

He puts his arms around me, holding me against
his chest. "Holy shit. Abby, what the hell is going
on?"

"I don't know." I push him away, afraid that if I
start to lose control, I'll never get it back. Turning
to the autopsy table, I say, "I don't want to talk
about it now, okay? What have they found out about
Marti?"

He shoves his hands into his pockets, as if not
knowing, now, what to do with his arms.

"It'll take a while to run certain lab tests," he
says. "But Ted says she didn't die from the nails in
her palms. Death by crucifixion can take days, and
whoever killed her apparently didn't want—"

He breaks off abruptly. "You sure you want to
hear this? It can keep for now."

"No, tell me. I want to know."

"The ultimate cause of death, at least from what
Ted can tell without toxicology results, was blood
loss from an injury to the brain."

"What kind of injury?"

He looks uneasy. "I think I should let Ted tell you
about that. Okay?"

"I…okay."

Again he hesitates. "Abby…those odd tiny
wounds on her body. You saw them?"

"Yes, they were all over her front."

"They're on her back, too. I guess I told you.
Anyway, the coroner says it looks like she was

beaten with a whip of some kind. Something with small metal balls on it.''

"Dear God." I look at Marti and my eyes tear, thinking how much she must have suffered. "Ben, what if she was alive, even with the nails in her palms? She must have been alive while she was being beaten. What if she saw and felt everything?''

I reach out to touch Marti's cheek. It is cold as an ice floe, and I remind myself that this is only her shell. Marti isn't here. She won't be, not anymore.

The absolute finality of her death hits me then. Before this, I have been cushioned to some extent by shock. Now the fact that I will never talk to my friend again, never laugh with her again, that she won't be at the other end of the phone when I call, or leaving messages on my machine, smacks me in the face like a rock.

Ben puts his hands on my shoulders once more and steadies me while I cry. My tears fall onto the white sheet like so many tiny veil pins, though there is no joke now, no responding laughter, no love.

Ted Wright, the coroner, enters the room. A pale, slight man with intelligent blue eyes, he gives me a careful look.

"I asked Ted to talk to you," Ben says, "but only if you want him to."

I dry my face with the back of my hand. "I want him to."

Ted clears his throat, obviously uneasy. Though he deals with death and mangled bodies on a regular basis, he is a kind man, I know.

"Don't worry, Ted. I won't fall apart on you."

His eyes behind the steel-rimmed glasses are filled with sympathy. "I'll try to keep it simple," he says, standing beside me to look down at Marti.

"The first thing, and one that struck me as odd right off, is that certain rituals seem to have been observed. Not only the crucifixion, but the scourging—"

He looks at Ben, who nods and says, "I told her."

Ted begins again. "I've done some reading about this, and the killer seems to have deliberately mimicked the kinds of crucifixion deaths that existed in ancient times, including a scourging with a whip. A flagrum, if you will. Such flagrums were constructed of leather thongs with small lead balls at the end of each thong. It is said Jesus of Nazareth and others condemned to crucifixion were scourged in this manner until they were nearly dead. Only after this were they nailed to a cross."

He sighs and removes his glasses, wiping them on his sleeve.

"Ted, what is it?" I say.

Putting the glasses back on, he shakes his head. "I've never seen anything like this. I'm sorry, Abby. My guess would be that this is some sort of execution-style killing. Possibly to silence your friend, or to send a message to someone else. Perhaps even revenge for something she did. The words that were painted on her chest, in fact, would seem to confirm this."

Ben tightens his arm around my shoulders, and Ted says, "Are you sure you want me to go on?"

"Yes," I respond in what sounds amazingly like my ordinary, day-to-day voice. "Go on."

I want to know everything, suddenly. I want every word burned into my brain so that when and if I ever meet up with the monster who did this to Marti, I will feel perfectly justified in killing him.

"Her back...the skin on her back," Ted says, "is in strips. And the fact that her feet were nailed to the cross, that she wasn't simply hung on the cross with strips of cloth, is significant. In reported cases of crucifixion, the very act of hanging—without the feet being affixed to the cross, that is—would cause death to occur rather quickly from suffocation. That is, provided the victim didn't die first of cardiac failure, blood loss or dehydration. The weight of the body on the cross pulled the arms upward, causing the pectoral and intercostal muscles to be stretched. This led to hyperexpansion of the lungs and an inability to breathe. The victim would attempt to raise himself with his arms to relieve the pressure, which caused muscle spasms. Unable to hold himself in that lifted position, he would die very quickly."

I close my eyes briefly, but to steady myself, not to ward off the picture. Ted's recital is working. My anger is growing.

He shakes his head sadly, looking at me, then down at Marti. "In your friend's case, as I've said, her feet were nailed to the cross. I find this significant. In ancient times, when the feet were nailed, it was done primarily to lengthen the victim's suffering. It gave the victim something to press against—to raise himself against, rather than using his arm muscles. In that way, he was able to breathe momentarily. He would alternate between slumping to relieve pain on the feet and then pressing against his feet, in order to breathe again. The pain caused by pressure on the nailed feet, of course, would have been terrible. Eventually the victim, who in many cases began this terrible ordeal with loss of blood, became too exhausted to lift himself any longer. The respiratory muscles became, you might say, paralyzed. Which led to suffocation and death."

He sighs. "This is a simplification, of course. There are other medical details…fluid buildup in the lungs and perhaps the pericardium, hypovolemic shock… I could go over these with you, but—"

Ben shakes his head, and this time I agree. I wonder if I'll ever be able to forget this, even if Marti's killer is one day caught and put to death. "Thank you, Ted. This is enough."

Then I remember something Ben said earlier. "Just one thing, Ted. Ben told me you thought Marti had actually died from a brain injury. Not suffocation?"

He takes several long moments to answer. "Without having seen the results of her toxicology tests," he says with obvious reluctance, "which will take a bit of time, that is my best guess."

"Are you saying she died from a blow to the head?"

Ted looks at Ben, obviously miserable about having to do this with me. I would take pity on him, but I need to know everything.

"Please, tell me," I say.

One of Ted's hands goes to Marti's forehead. He brushes it gently, as if brushing back her hair, though it's hidden under the white sheeting. "As I said, I've done some reading about ritual murders, in particular religious ritual murders. What I found on your friend... Abby, have you ever heard of trepanning, or trephination?"

"I don't think so. It doesn't sound familiar."

"Well, a trephine is a surgical instrument with sawlike edges. It's used to cut disks of bone from the skull, in medical practice. The cult of trepanning, or trephination, however, is something else. It's been around, off and on, for thousands of years, and seems to be making a comeback now, if you will. Followers of this cult believe that drilling a hole into the top of one's head where the soft spot, or fontanel, was at birth brings a person a feeling of bliss—the greatest high one can experience."

"Drilling a hole? You can't mean they do this to themselves?"

"That's precisely what they do, I'm afraid."

"Ted, that's...it's sick."

"I agree. However, there does seem to be historical evidence that this has been practiced by thousands of people over the centuries. Some believed it would help mental illness, headaches, epilepsy. Others claimed it gave them special mental powers. In your friend's case..." He pauses.

"You don't mean somebody did this to Marti," I say, shocked.

"I'm afraid it looks that way, Abby. I found a hole the size of a quarter had been drilled into her skull, probably by a corkscrew-like object, such as a trephine."

Seeing my expression of horror, he stops, waits a moment, then continues. "Unfortunately, the instrument used went too far—into her brain. There was

massive bleeding, and I suspect this is what ulti-
mately caused her death. As I've said, I can't be sure,
of course, without further tests and examination. But
I suspect that whoever did this did it after nailing her
to the cross.''

I look down at Marti again, imagining the scalp,
then the skull, being drilled through, the horrible pain
she must have experienced.

I try to swallow, but there is no saliva, only bile
in my throat, and I am shaking. "God, Ted. Why
would anyone do such a thing?''

"My best guess,'' he says, "is that it fit with the
religious aspect of this murder. According to reports
I've read, priests once performed this act to release
evil spirits from people who were thought to be pos-
sessed.''

I lean back against Ben, my legs too weak to support me much longer. The bile is in my mouth now,
and I fear I'll vomit. Reaching for a Kleenex in my
bag, I hold it to my mouth.

Ted's glance slides from me to Ben. "You should
take her home, now,'' he says. "Abby, again, I am
very, very sorry. Try to get some rest. Put this out
of your mind for a while.''

"Put it out of my *mind?* Ted, how can I? Who
would have done this to Marti?''

"I can't answer that, I'm afraid. Your friend was
a well-known personality in her field. People like that
sometimes make strange enemies.''

I can't imagine Marti ever having made an enemy.

I turn to Ben, anger taking over. "How long, do
you think, before you get this monster?''

"I don't know, Ab. Carmel—the council, city administrator, angry residents—everyone wants this solved, and quickly. The task force is working on it already, including the sheriff's department, the police departments of every city on the Peninsula, and of course—''

He breaks off. *The Secret Service,* he was going to say. But he didn't, and I'm guessing that's because Ted is here. Ben is supposed to keep the Secret Service's involvement quiet, apparently.

"I can promise you one thing," he says, his expression grim as he looks down at my friend. "I'll do everything I can to find out who did this, Abby."

I let him lead me to the door, but midway there I turn back.

"Ted, you didn't say. Was Marti...was she raped?"

He shakes his head. "I've found no evidence of sexual attack, Abby. No, everything about this points, as I said, to an execution-style killing. It was the style that counted, I'd guess—perhaps the shock value of the terribleness of it, not the actual cause of death."

4

I leave Ben outside in the parking lot, climbing into the Explorer and again promising to find Marti's killer. It is a comforting promise, though I fear that's all it is. I wonder how long it will be before they start questioning me again.

We haven't talked further about the name "Abby" at the crime scene, or the letter A carved into Murphy's back. If that seems odd, I attribute it to Ben's haste to get back to the station and the case.

At home, I tend to Murphy first, cutting open a capsule of vitamin E and rubbing it gently into the wound on his back to hasten the healing. Still feeling numb, I double-check doors and windows, making sure they're all locked. Taking a cup of hot chocolate upstairs, I undress for bed, putting on a pair of warm pajamas. Murphy plants himself outside my door, as usual, at the top of the steps. After a few minutes I call him in with me, patting the bed and urging him to lie beside me. Careful not to touch the sore spot beneath his fur, I position my arm around him, seeking to comfort us both while we fall asleep. He licks my hand and looks at me with eyes that seem full of questions for which I have no answers. Sighing, he lies back down.

First thing in the morning I call the vet and he

tells me to bring Murphy in at one. I settle him down on a blanket by the fire, fix myself some breakfast, do the dishes, throw some clothes in the wash and sweep the side patio. Then I call Frannie to let her know Murphy's been found, and tell her what was done to him. She is horrified, and we commiserate about that a few minutes. Finally I call Ben to find out if they've made any progress on the case and if there's any word about Marti's funeral. The one thing I forgot to ask Ted was how soon he'd be releasing her body. Ben isn't in, and the woman at the desk assures me she'll have him call me as soon as she hears from him.

After that I don't know what to do with myself. All this activity has had only one purpose—to keep me from brooding about Marti. It can't help things to sit and mourn. Yet, what's the alternative? To head out on a white charger? I would give anything to be able to avenge my friend's death. If I knew who killed her, I would probably, at this moment, do him in with my own bare hands. I just don't know where to begin.

If only she had talked to me about her life more recently, if only I had made more of an effort to be with her, to find out what was going on with her. If only, if only, if only. Could I have done more?

I turn to writing to get my mind off things. It doesn't seem to help. At the computer in my study, I try to come up with next week's column, but my mind won't work. I feel as if I'm sleepwalking, and finally give up struggling for the witticisms my readers have begun to expect, all the funny and sometimes caustic observations about life in Carmel that residents and tourists alike seem to enjoy. Instead, I toy with the keyboard, typing out Marti's name and then the letter A, over and over, like some kid scrawling her boyfriend's last name after hers in a geography workbook: *Annie Smith. Annie Smith Jones. Mrs. David Jones.* Everywoman's dream...to get that ring, marry that man.

In this case, the occasion is not a wedding but a funeral. Though what the difference is, I swear I don't know. For me, they both seem related to death or dying.

Well, then, write a piece about weddings.

I write that down and follow it by wondering if old memories still cling to the fabric of our wedding gowns. If I were to go up in the attic and put mine on, would I feel the happiness I felt on my wedding day?

I remember an old movie with someone who donned an antique wedding gown, which took her back to another time when she was someone young and in love.

I stare at the screen and wonder why Marti never married. Was it because of the baby? Did she feel it wouldn't be fair to have a happy married life, having given up the child that could (or should) have been a part of it? The "should" would be Marti's; she would think that way, not I.

And so I'm back to "Shining Bright" again. Finally I close this exercise in futility and open my journal file, which I keep under the word *Dervish* in a hidden document that only someone wise in the ways of computers could find. The path is so obscure as to be Chinese in nature, the point being to keep it from Jeffrey's prying eyes.

Which can't be as hard as I make it out to be. Jeffrey doesn't understand much about computers; he has secretaries for that. Assistants, really, but he won't call them assistants or even allow them to classify themselves as such on a résumé. To do so would dilute, he has said quite openly, his own position of power.

When the file comes up I see that my last journal entry was six months ago, just after I caught Jeffrey with the bimbo. Since then, I haven't had the heart to put my life down in black and white. My feelings have been too embarrassing, even humiliating.

When I was a child, I used to pray, "If I should die before I wake, I pray the Lord my soul to take." Later on, in my twenties, I fell hopelessly in love with someone for three years, and took to this writing of journals. Absolutely everything went into them, every foolish, futile longing. When it was over I had a corrugated Seagram's carton three feet by three, bulging with spiral-bound notebooks from the drugstore that were filled with largely unreadable ramblings, scrawled in blue ink from a ballpoint pen. For years, I toted this damn box with me every time I moved, like a turtle unwilling to shed its shell. I'd go zooming down a freeway with this stupid *thing* in my trunk, scared to death I'd be killed by some idiot suffering road rage and my survivors would end up reading all that dross. I couldn't let go of the dross, however, neither the journals nor the man. Thus my nightly prayer became, "If I should die before I wake, I pray the Lord my journals to take."

Now I know that there are more ways of dying than one can conceive. Further, there are days when there is no Lord, or at least he's checked out for the day.

Jeffrey came along after that three-year journal-writing madness, on one of those Lordless days. My heart still had a hole in it, and my car still had that box in its trunk. I just didn't think about it so much anymore, thoughtlessly shoving it aside to make room for groceries every Friday night. Then I met Jeffrey. And a whole new literary era began.

Because heaven was closed that day, I fell head over asinine heels in love with Jeffrey Northrup, right off the bat. And because I still believed in journals, I spread the craziness of our lives across the clean pages of a bright new book, as if making up the bed of my heart with fresh new sheets. In the beginning, I wrote down all the "I know he really loves me" stuff and the "I'll die if he doesn't remember my birthday" madness.

The irony is, Jeffrey is dead now, not I. Oh, he walks and talks. But for me the funeral took place six months ago.

I met my husband sixteen years ago at the Pebble Beach Golf Club. I was down from San Francisco having lunch with a couple of other women, all three of us in our early twenties. They were friends of mine and secretaries, as Jeffrey would say, though they did all but run Monterey for their employers. I was working as a reporter for the *San Francisco Chronicle,* and had a pretty good career going. I'd come down for lunch on a day off and to soak up some sun.

Jeffrey was at the club that day playing golf. At

two hundred dollars a game, that set him far above us. But he came in all sweaty and smiling, especially when he saw us. Not that he knew us. Jeffery, I later learned, always smiled at good-looking women.

I counted myself among them, at that time, the good-looking women. I had dark hair that fell to my shoulders in shiny waves, and huge brown eyes. There was something exotic about me, I'd been told by some. Not that you could prove it by me. I still had those mental tapes from childhood, the ones that said I couldn't do anything right, my hair looked like a rat's nest, and I'd never amount to much.

How I got those tapes, where they came from, is a mystery to me still. Certainly not from my parents, who supported me in every way. Sometimes I think those beliefs, running over and over in my head, came with me from another life, that I carried them in when I was born.

Which presumes a belief in reincarnation—something I'd rather not think about. The very idea of having to do all this over again and again and again makes me cry, at least on those days when it doesn't make me laugh.

Jeffrey made me laugh. At first, he said truly funny things, a born comic who never made it onstage but went, instead, into politics and business. Then, later, he made me laugh in another way. Oh, I know I shouldn't have. But he'd come into the bedroom stark naked with that—that appendage sticking out ten inches if it was one, like some old-time romance writer's "flaming sword," and he'd look at me with those sultry eyes and rasp, "You really want it, don't you?"

And I couldn't help it. His hair would be wet from the shower, black curls clinging to his forehead, and my eyes would travel from that to the green eyes I had once loved, the aristocratic nose, the chest a thicket of graying black hair, and I'd laugh.

Largely, I'd laugh because by then I knew I wasn't the only woman Jeffrey used that line on. We'd been married ten years, and good old Jeffrey had cut a swath a mile wide through the women of Carmel with that flaming sword. The very idea that I'd still want either him or his impressive appendage was ludicrous. So I'd try to muffle the chuckles, but, well…

Several times I thought Jeffrey might hit me when I laughed. He never did. Instead, he got his revenge by taking away my child.

The vet gives Murphy a couple of shots and, after voicing innumerable questions about the letter A, declares him on the mend—physically, at least. Murphy still has a sad, hound-dog-look about him. I take him home and find Frannie waiting for us, though it isn't her usual day to work.

"I couldn't believe it when you told me what happened," she says, her hazel eyes worried under the mop of red hair. She gives Murphy a hug. "Are you okay, fella?"

He doesn't seem ready to be touched, backing off from her and giving a slight growl, which stuns me. Never have I seen Murphy behave this way.

"The doctor said he might be touchy for a while," I offer by way of apology.

Frannie nods and follows me into the kitchen. "I

swear to you, Abby, I don't know how he got out. I was sure he was inside when I left.''

"Well, he's a sneaky little guy. When he gets it into his head to bust loose, he does have his ways.''

"That's true," she says thoughtfully. "Remember the day he ran out while I was bringing in groceries? I thought he was up in your room all the while. And one day he scooted right past you when you came in, and you had to run halfway down Scenic to catch him, him with his tail wagging all the way.''

We both laugh at the ordinariness of Murphy's escapes, carefully skirting the truth—that this is not one of those ordinary times, and the letter carved into my dog's back only proves it.

"It's hard to keep track of him lately," I say, waving a hand around the kitchen. "There are too many places in this house for him to disappear to, especially now that Jeffrey's not here half the time.''

Frannie shakes her head. "You should sell this place. Cliff said he could get at least three times what you bought it for sixteen years ago.''

Cliff, her new boyfriend, is a local Realtor.

"And go where?" I say. "Out to the valley? Into a condo? I'd miss the ocean too much. Besides, I've always liked this place.''

Frannie casts a look around. "You've got a great view, I'll say that. But if I were you, I'd be nervous alone here at night.''

"Nervous? Why?"

"You don't know? You haven't heard it?" She clamps her lips down as if wishing she hadn't said anything.

"Heard what, Frannie?" I am only half smiling.

"For heaven's sake, you're not buying into that old ghost story, are you?"

"Hell, no. I'm talking about something much more earthly than that. Last week, when I was up in the attic—"

She breaks off, turning away.

"What about the attic? Did you hear something?"

Her green eyes flick my way. "Why? Did you?"

"Frannie, stop it! Just tell me. What did you hear?"

"A noise," she says. "Just a noise, that's all. It took me a while to get up the courage to go up there. And when I did, there wasn't anyone there."

"That's odd," I say. "I heard a noise, too. It scared me half to death."

Her eyes meet mine, widening. "What do you think it was?"

"Now that it's daytime and the sun's out? I'm inclined to believe it was a squirrel."

"And last night?"

"Last night, I was certain it was that guy in the movies with the hockey mask, lurking in the shadows to grab me."

She wraps her arms around herself, shivering. "I kind of thought that, too. Abby, you should get out of here. Cliff says—"

Cliff, I think, is angling real hard for a sale and a commission.

I change the subject. "Frannie, did you take the second bulb out of the light fixture? There's only one in there."

"No. I thought you did that. I could hardly see

my way around, and I meant to go back up with another bulb, then I forgot. Sorry.''

''Never mind, I can do it. But if you didn't take it out, who did?''

''Jeffrey?'' Frannie asks, shrugging.

''He hates going up in the attic. Says it's—''

''Stuffed with a lot of worthless junk that makes him sneeze,'' she finishes for me, grinning. ''That's why I put some of his favorite things up there every time I clean.''

''You don't!''

''I do,'' she says complacently. ''It wasn't very nice, what he did to you with that floozy.''

Ben calls around six. ''I need to see you. Can you meet me in town?''

''I could, but why don't you come out here?''

''Town,'' otherwise known as ''the Village,'' is only a few blocks away, but I'm already in my comfortable sweats and don't feel like dressing again.

''You know I don't like coming there,'' he says.

''Jeffrey's hobnobbing with the president. He won't be home till the weekend.''

''Even so.''

Ben is hoping for a promotion to chief of police when the current chief retires. But for all its artists and writers, Carmel is basically a conservative town, and Ben worries about gossip. An adulterous affair in his personnel folder wouldn't impress the town council or those on the board who might appoint him.

''I don't know why you don't divorce him and get

it over with," he says, not for the first time. "Throw the prick out."

"I already did throw the prick out. It's the rest of him I can't get rid of."

He laughs. "No, seriously—just do it."

"You know I promised I'd stay till after the election in November. My freedom will be my Christmas present."

"I still don't get it. My gut feeling tells me Jeffrey is up to something, and it doesn't have anything to do with his position as primary mover and shaker in the reigning party. Any idea what it might be?"

"In politics? Who knows? He says he's worried that any scandal in his life could rub off on the president, and he doesn't want to take any chances, given the moral climate of the country these days—the backlash that's carried over from previous presidential capers."

"Abby, just how close is he to President Chase?"

"They're thick as thieves from what I can see. Jeffrey's one of the few men in the country who's on the phone with him several times a week. And he's virtually running his campaign for reelection. From behind the scenes, of course."

"What about Jeffrey himself? Does he have aspirations to run for office?"

"Not at all. He looks upon politicians as drones, or rather chess pieces he can move from here to there at his whim."

"Abby, divorce isn't all that scandalous these days. And he only works for the president. What makes you think Jeffrey isn't making you stay with him till after the election just so he can live in the house?"

"Yeah, like he has such a good time here now."

"Then it's something else. Maybe he wants you back."

"People in hell—"

"Want ice water," he finishes for me. "I know. So meet me for dinner, okay? At the Red Lion?"

"You mean the Britannia, or whatever they're calling it now?"

"Yeah."

"You want to have dinner with me in public? Good Lord, man, are you on drugs?"

"Nobody there will care. It's not like the Mission Ranch, for God's sake."

I sigh. "Okay, but—"

"But you're already in your sweats and you don't feel like dressing. One more reason for the Red Lion—the Britannia, whatever. I'll meet you in the pub."

"Why not the Bully III?"

"I'm already at the Red Lion."

"But the Bully III has the best French dip in town."

"You won't eat much, anyway."

I sigh. "You know me too damned well."

"How's the Murph?" Ben says once we're settled at a table in the Red Lion, now the Britannia, by the fireplace and have ordered drinks. The Britannia pub is a place where locals hang out, sort of a Cheers bar, and just about everyone in here knows us. It amazes me that Ben's willing to be seen with me here.

"Murphy?" I say, answering his question. "He's not too bad. Snappy, though."

He frowns. "Have you heard anything more about how that might have happened?"

"No. The kid who brought him home said there wasn't anyone else around, so I haven't gone out asking."

"Still, I think I should talk to him. Maybe there's something he saw, but didn't realize its importance. Did you get a phone number?"

"No. I wish I had. He put his own leash on Murphy to bring him home and forgot to take it back. It looks expensive. Possibly even custom-made."

"Why don't I take a look at it? If it was made by a local artisan, I might be able to track the guy down."

"Okay. I'll get it to you."

"We've found Marti's brother, Ned, by the way." Ben smiles a thank-you at the waitress, who sets down our drinks. "He's coming out here to arrange the funeral."

"That's what I called you about earlier. You got my message?"

He nods, taking a deep draft of his Sierra Nevada pale ale. "I thought we could talk here instead of on the phone."

I toy with my Chardonnay. "When is Marti...how soon can it be?"

"At the end of the week, Ted says. He thinks the toxicology reports will be pretty much routine, and he's put a rush on them to get them out of the way as soon as possible. He's doing it for you, he says. He likes you."

"Ted's a sweetheart. So's his wife, so don't get any ideas. But back to Marti's brother. He wants the funeral here? I'm surprised."

"I take it he feels that's the most expedient way to do it. Financially, that is. I also got the impression he and Marti didn't get along."

"That's true. She didn't talk about him much, and I can count on the fingers of one hand the times I saw them together."

"You don't know why they might have been estranged? If they were?"

"No. But he's a lot older. Ten years, I think. Maybe he resented having a new baby around when he was the only child for so long."

I sip my wine, and Ben looks at me with a teasing light in his eyes.

"Great hairdo," he comments, remarking on my quickly pulled-back ponytail. "And I love the beaten-up running shoes. Pure Carmel."

"Well, I need to be fleet-of-foot when I'm around you."

He lifts an eyebrow. "I can't imagine why."

"Perhaps because you asked me here to interrogate me," I say.

"I could have done that at the station."

"Oh, so you brought me here to woo me? Gee, I thought we did that at your house, not in public."

When he hasn't an answer to that, I sigh. "Okay, so just get on with it. What do you want to know?"

He sets the heavy glass of ale down on the table. The fire crackles beside us, and I'm starting to get too warm, which is what I get for not layering. At the bar the patrons, mostly locals, carry on easy conversations with one eye on the television on the back wall.

"I want to know about Marti's baby," Ben says. "That's one thing you forgot to mention, Ab—the reason for that Cesareian scar."

"I didn't forget," I say, shrugging. "I just promised her I'd never tell anyone."

"But she's—"

"Dead now. Yeah, gee, you know what? I know that." I frown. "It's just hard. Anyway, why do you need to know about that?"

"I'm not sure yet. I just have a feeling it's got something to do with the reason she died."

"You do, huh?"

Ben's "feelings" are something I've learned not to ignore. He's known for his intuitive skills, not that he's like one of those fancy profilers on television. He just thinks things through better than most, while seeming not to move ahead much at all.

Besides, wine has always loosened my tongue. It doesn't take much on an empty stomach.

"It was a long time ago," I say after we've ordered food. "Back in the eighties. Marti had been working in Central America a lot, so I didn't see her much. One day she showed up at my door, already in labor. It was shortly after I'd married Jeffrey."

"She came here? To Carmel?"

"Right. I tried to get her to tell the father about the baby so he could help her, but she was adamant. Said it would be better for everyone concerned if he never knew. She wouldn't even tell me who the father was."

"Maybe he was married," Ben says.

"Maybe."

"What did she want from you?" he asks.

"Only to stand by her, I think. Her parents had been killed a few years before in a plane crash in Honduras, and except for Ned, that left her pretty much alone in the world. She never had much time for making close friends, with all the traveling and the kind of work she did."

"So you were with her throughout her labor?"

"Yes."

Ben is silent a moment. "What did Jeffrey think of all that?" he asks finally.

"He never knew. He was away when it happened, and Marti swore me to secrecy afterward."

"Still…wives usually tell their husbands things they keep secret from others, don't they?"

"Not in this case."

He doesn't push, and I don't have to tell him how little I trusted my husband, even that early in our marriage.

"One thing I don't get," he says, shaking his head. "How could she have covered up her pregnancy? Wasn't she well known by then?"

"Yes, but Marti was always very thin. She was able to hide the fact that she was pregnant, she told me, for the first six months. After that, she took a sabbatical from work and went off to some cabin in the woods."

"A cabin in the woods? Sounds kind of rough."

"Marti was used to difficult conditions. She was also very strong."

"Where was this cabin?"

"I think she said in Maine. A friend loaned it to her."

"Where was the baby born?"

"Right here in Monterey."

"At Community Hospital?"

"Yes."

The waitress sets our plates before us, and Ben toys with the hot turkey sandwich, mushing it around on his plate. "Another thing I don't get, then, is how she managed to keep the birth of this child a secret for so many years. Especially if she had it in as public a place as CHOMP."

CHOMP, the Community Hospital of the Monterey Peninsula, is high-profile because it's the initial hospital visiting celebrities go to for care.

"First of all," I say, "she never went anywhere for prenatal care. Marti was into alternative methods of healing, and she knew her body really well. Also, when she went in to deliver the baby, she went through emergency. And paid cash."

"Cash? That must have set her back a lot."

"I helped her," I say, shrugging.

"Ah. That explains it."

He tastes the sandwich and makes a face. I knew he wouldn't like it; Ben loves turkey like a Pilgrim, but hates gravy with too much pepper in it. Besides, they'd made it with toast. He prefers mushy white bread.

"Still," he says, "with computers being what they

are, or were even in the eighties, you'd think there would have been a record of the birth.''

"There was a record. For a Maria Gonzalez, from Salinas. You know how many Gonzalezes there are in Salinas? Marti told them she was here in Carmel working as my maid when she went into labor."

"And she passed? As Hispanic?"

"She had brown hair, brown eyes, and she was dark from all the years of working as a photojournalist below the equator. Plus, she spoke the language. She passed."

The truth is, most busy doctors and hospitals don't really look at people as people, anyway. Especially when they're named Gonzalez and have no insurance.

"I confirmed that she was my housekeeper," I say, "and the closest thing she had to family."

"And, of course, since she—or you—paid cash, no one asked too many questions."

"Right. We figured this would be better than if she went to the county hospital. She'd have had a harder time disappearing into the system there, given the way the government keeps an eye on things. And she might not have had as good care."

"Your wiles continually astound me." Ben shakes his head, turning his attention to a hot, chunky slice of garlic bread.

"Send it back," I say.

"Huh?"

"Send the turkey san back. Tell them the gravy's too heavy on the pepper and you don't like it on toast. They'll give you something else."

"Nah, I don't want to bother them."

"They're good about those things here, they'll fix you whatever you want."

He pushes the plate away. "I'm not really hungry, anyway."

"We should have gone to the Bully III."

He gives me a look. But truth be told, I'm not hungry, either. When the waitress comes by again and asks how things are, we tell her they're pretty good. She takes our plates away and brings us another round of drinks, which suits me just fine.

After dinner we walk south along Sixth Street till we come to the park with the sculpture of an elderly man and woman sitting on a bench side by side, like an old married couple. He wears wingtips, she an old-style hat. The sculpture was donated to the city by an art gallery, after much dissension as to whether or not it was good enough to be put there. Which goes under the heading *Only in Carmel*.

"You know what pisses me off about them?" I say.

Ben looks at me with obvious surprise. "These old people? What?"

"They look perpetually happy. Nobody's perpetually happy."

"Well, maybe they give us something to aim for," he says, defending the bronze duo.

"Hmmph."

"You know what you are?" he says. "A curmudgeon. A thirty-eight-year-old curmudgeon."

"Gee, thanks. I love being compared to William F. Buckley and Andy Rooney."

He puts an arm around my shoulders and pulls me

down to a bench across from the old couple. There he nuzzles my neck.

"Careful now," I say. "What will people think?"

"It's dark here. Besides, nobody's looking. They're all satiated from their own dinner and wine, and they're heading back to their inns to make love by a nice cozy fire."

"Sounds like a plan to me. Are you finished interrogating me yet?"

His lips slide up to mine. "I guess I could think of a few more fine points to explore."

"Well, get on with it, then, young fella. I'm aging pretty fast."

"Feeling better?" Ben asks as we begin walking again, along Ocean Avenue. Most of the shops are closed, but brightly lit restaurants line the block. At one count, probably not the latest, there were eighty-seven restaurants in the square mile of Carmel Village, and more than a hundred art galleries.

"Better?" I ask. "Could you clarify?"

"Than you were when you were sitting at home alone, thinking."

"Oh, that. Sure. You've wined and dined me like all get out. Why wouldn't I feel better? Like a fattened calf, in fact."

"Funny, you don't look like a fattened calf."

"Yeah? Then why do I feel like some ax is about to fall?"

"I never can fool you, can I?" my lover says.

"Just remember that. So, what is it?"

"I didn't quite tell you everything."

"I never for a moment thought you did. Okay...so what is it?"

"Mauro and Hillars. They want to talk to you again."

"Oh, God." I groan, holding out my wrists as if for handcuffs. "What a way to end a day."

He contains a smile, but I see it toying with his lips. "Not now. I just wanted you to know that they mentioned it. Said they'd be in touch with you."

"Ben, what the hell is going on? Why the Secret Service?"

"I don't know."

"Don't give me that."

"Abby, I swear, they won't tell any of us what they're doing here. Between you and me, it's driving me nuts. I thought maybe when they talked to you again, you might get some clue."

"Ah, I see. And share it with you?"

We resume walking, and he takes my hand and tucks it into his pocket. "I thought you might. We do share a few good things, don't we?"

"A few." Halfway down the block I pause, adding, "We're gonna share a whole lot more if you don't stop doing what you're doing to my fingers."

"It's my new interviewing technique," Ben says.

"Well, guess what? It's working."

For the first time in the five months we've been together, Ben comes home with me. And, of course, it's the one time Jeffrey decides to return early from a trip.

We are under a nice warm comforter in my bedroom—the one only I sleep in now, though Jeffrey still shares the closets. A fire is crackling, and the French doors to the bedroom deck are open a few inches so we can hear the waves beating on the shore. There is soft music playing.

Even so, I hear my husband's footsteps on the stairs. No way to miss them, after all these years.

Ben and I are both naked, and our clothes are strewn all over the floor, so there's no time to grab something, throw it on and pretend we're having a council meeting. Though I hear there are Carmel council members who have done just that, over the years.

As Jeffrey walks in, I sit up, pulling the sheets to my neck and playing for time. "You're home early," I complain loudly, hoping to put the blame on him for catching us.

He takes in the scene with one glance.

"Well, if I'd known you were entertaining, I'd have called ahead," he says mildly. Despite his attempt at indifference, I could swear his graying George Clooney hair is bristling—like a lion's when he finds a strange male in his lair.

Ben, for his part, struggles to maintain his dignity—a losing battle, given that he's lying naked next to another man's wife. I can hear the wheels rolling: Do I get out of bed and run into the bathroom while they duke it out, or do I grab my clothes and make a fast departure out the door?

Ben hates confrontation of the personal kind. Give him a gun and a perp, and he's a whole other guy.

"Stay where you are, Ben," I say firmly. "It's not as if this is something new for Jeffrey, after all."

I feel him sliding down under the sheets inch by inch.

"Hello, Ben," Jeffrey says. "How's the bid for promotion going? I hear you're up for chief."

The threat to expose us is obvious. Whether Jeffrey will carry it out while I've got him and the bimbo as collateral is doubtful. Still, he must swagger a bit.

"It's going fine," Ben says in a conversational voice that makes me proud. He has apparently decided to pretend he's standing in our living room, dressed in a tux. "How are things with you, Jeffrey?"

"Fine, fine." Jeffrey heads for his walk-in closet. "Well, you two go on with what you were doing. I just came back for clean shirts."

Ben and I look at each other. Jeffrey gets his shirts. He stops at the bureau for cuff links and takes his time finding them. Ben and I are motionless in the bed, sheets to our necks, barely breathing.

"I'll be off now," Jeffrey says a hundred years later, making his way to the door. He stops only momentarily on the landing as Murphy growls again. We hear his footsteps going down the stairs, then his car leaving.

Ben groans and throws the comforter over his face. His voice comes muffled from under the pillowy down. "If he tells anyone, I'm a goner."

I crawl under the covers and reach for him. "Well, then, young fella, I say we make hay while the sun shines. Let's see, what have we here..."

5

Marti is buried in a small Catholic cemetery south of Carmel, along the road to Big Sur. The burial site is on an old Spanish estate, and I have learned through Ben that the owner, Lydia Greyson, came forward to offer it. She would be honored, she said, to have Marti laid to rest along with her own ancestors. In addition, she pledged that Marti's grave would be well protected from curiosity seekers, behind the high adobe walls of the estate.

Who this woman is, or why she has offered a family burial plot to Marti, I don't know. I can only suppose she must know Marti's brother, Ned, or at least have talked to him, as he would have had to agree to the arrangements.

A long line of black cars and limos winds southward along the twisting road. There are places where one can drive only fifteen miles per hour in the best of weather, and the best of weather has not graced us today. Fog creeps in on great big elephant feet, clomping up from the sea and over the road, where it smothers the hills.

Jeffrey drives our black Mercedes, and we sit quietly beside each other, steeped in our individual thoughts. Ahead of us, in a limo, is Ned, whom I've never really met, despite the few times I saw him years ago with Marti. When we were in high school, Ned was away in college, and when we went to Joseph and Mary, the most he ever did was show up on visiting Sunday once or twice.

With Ned are two women veiled in black. One seemed slightly familiar at the church, in the way she carried herself, but there was no way of knowing who she might be. Family, surely, to be veiled that way. This surprises me, as I had thought all of Marti's other relatives had passed away.

Behind us are limos filled with local residents, some of whom want only to be part of history. A great many, however, genuinely came to offer their respects to Marti. This show of affection stuns me. Even though I have always known how much my friend was loved, she has reached many more people with her photographs and stories than I'd realized. In the church, the words *Shining Bright* were whispered often among the pews.

Bringing up the rear of the cortege are local and international reporters. Everyone who could possibly commandeer a limo or car has become part of this today, including famous anchors like Jane Pauley, Tom Brokaw, Katie Couric. Our local congressman was at the church, as well as more than one senator, and I wonder briefly what Marti would say about this fuss. Would she be gratified? Or embarrassed? My guess is a little of both.

"Hmm? What?" Jeffrey says.

"I didn't say anything."

"You made a noise."

"I was smiling."

"No, you made a noise." His voice is cool, though

his hands tighten on the steering wheel. "A snort, unless I miss my guess."

"Well, if anyone knows my snort, it would be you, Jeffrey."

"Not only am I far too familiar with it, but I'm rather certain I know what you're snorting at now, as well."

"No doubt you are."

"You think this is all too much, all this attention paid to Marti."

I look at him. "And you? What do you think, Jeffrey?"

"That you are far too cynical. It's your worst failing."

After a moment of silence I can't help it. I snort. "Well, at least we know it's not *your* worst failing, Jeffrey."

My husband stands beside me, his arm linked through mine supportively as photographers snap more photos of us than of Marti's grave. "I told you they didn't split," I hear one of them say, not bothering to keep her voice down, while another murmurs, "She looks like she's holding up better than him."

It's true that Jeffrey doesn't look well. His eyes are strained, his face gaunt. I would feel sorry for him, but I'm guessing that exercise, not illness, is at fault for this. Most of Jeffrey's life energy is sucked dry these days by his frenetic attempts to stay young and firm for the bimbo. The old platitude does hold true: After a certain age one must choose between the face or the ass. The fact that I've added a few pounds as ballast helps to plump out any wrinkles that might threaten to emerge as I move closer to forty, while Jeffrey lifts the weights, runs the miles and hurtles recklessly toward the sea of romance and early cardiac arrest.

On the other side of the coffin from us are the two women in black with veils over their faces, and Marti's brother, Ned. His face is somber, though his mouth twists in what might be rancor at the priest's words: "To you, oh Lord, we commend the spirit of this woman of utmost virtue and unfailing faith. We ask your angels to carry her swiftly to that High Place where you reside, to guide and keep her throughout her journey home..."

My eyes meet Ned's, and I am shocked by the look of hatred he sends me. Within moments I shiver and am forced to look away. I can still feel those cold dark eyes on me, however, and the emotion behind them. Searching my mind, I can think of no reason for it, and after another moment I give a mental shrug and go back to listening to the priest. He is saying the prayers of the dead, and the two women next to Ned are making the sign of the cross. As the service ends, one steps forward to toss a handful of dirt onto the lowered coffin. She draws the black veil from her face and looks directly at me. I am shocked to see the now-aged but unmistakable face of Sister Helen.

It has been twenty years, but not a day has gone by in the look that passes between us. I am still the novice, she the angry and disappointed sponsor of my and Marti's ill-fated gift of our lives to God.

The other woman draws her veil back, as well—a

stranger with short, steel-gray hair. No one I have ever met before. Sister Helen turns her gaze from me and speaks softly to her companion, who nods and walks slowly back toward the line of waiting black cars. Sister Helen moves toward me.

"Good morning, Abby," she says, the gravelly voice still strong and just as intimidating. She is in civilian dress, a black suit, stockings and shoes, which further surprises me. Years ago she swore never to stop wearing her habit.

The look she gives me is one I remember, though—stern and unyielding. I feel I've done something wrong and, as if in a time warp, I look down quickly to see if I've got my white postulant's collar on backward, or if my black oxfords have come untied from too much racing along the halls.

Is there a run in my black hose? Did I spill gravy down my front?

The glint in Sister Helen's eyes tells me she knows exactly what I'm thinking and is enjoying every moment of my discomfort.

"A sad day," she says.

"Yes," I agree. "A very sad day. I'm surprised to see you here, Sister. How are you? How have you been?"

She doesn't answer but continues to appraise me. An awkward silence ensues.

"Did you, uh…did you and Marti keep in touch all these years?" I try.

"We spoke now and then," she says noncommittally.

I wonder why Marti never mentioned being in contact with Sister Helen.

"Are you still in Santa Rosa?" I ask. "At Mary Star of the Sea?"

"Hardly."

Her tone is bitter, and I don't know what to make of that.

"You've retired?"

"I suppose one might say that."

I'm at a loss.

"And you, Abigail?" she asks.

It has been years since anyone called me that, which oddly adds to my discomfort.

"I live here now. In Carmel."

"Of course you do. And why not?"

This time her tone annoys me. "What do you mean, Sister?"

"I mean, Abigail, that you always land on your feet. Despite the cost to others."

Her hostility astounds me. It is as if, in her mind, my breach of promise to become the Bride of Christ occurred yesterday.

We face each other, two women with far too much to say, and too many years behind us to say it.

At this moment Marti's brother comes to stand behind Sister Helen, placing a hand on her shoulder. "Helen?" he says. "We're ready to leave."

She gives him a brief look and turns back to me. "You know Marti's brother, Ned?" she asks with what seems to be studied courtesy.

"No, we've never met."

Up close I can see that Ned Bright is handsome, in a rather old-fashioned, Jane Austen–novel way. His face is thin, like Marti's, composed of elegant angles and lines. The brown eyes, enhanced by long lashes, can only be described as lovely.

I extend my hand to shake his, but he doesn't take it.

"It's you who killed her," he says. "When all's said and done, it's you."

I am stunned. "That…that isn't true!" I can only manage, as a third-grader might. "Marti was my best friend!"

"You were never a friend to my sister."

I look at Sister Helen for help, for support and confirmation that none of this is happening, but she turns away.

"I'm ready to leave," she says crisply.

Ned takes her arm and they walk together, joining the other woman at one of the few remaining cars. I stare after them in bewilderment and shock.

Feeling newly bereft, I ache to be at home with my dog, my books, my bed. It has been only four days since Marti died, and every moment has been packed with grief woven tortuously with brooding attempts to figure out what happened.

I wonder when the Secret Service will be on me again. *I've done my best to throw them off the track, Marti. Ben's the only one I've told about your son. With any luck…*

Suddenly, to stand on yet another foggy, rain-soaked hill when my friend is no longer here, and then to be told she was not my friend, is more than I can stand without breaking down.

Looking around for Jeffrey I find him schmoozing with a group of people we know, as well as several strangers. I watch my husband shake hands, nod, smile, laugh and generally act as if he's at a political clambake. Sighing, I turn away, thinking to walk back to our car and wait for him.

It is only now I see another man, standing fifty feet back from the burial area, under a row of eucalyptus trees. He seems about my age, tall and rather frail. A stiff breeze has sprung up, pushing the fog into my skin, and just as I tighten my black cape around me, the man seems to huddle into a navy blue windbreaker. My path takes me closer to him, and I see that he holds in one hand a bunch of pink roses.

Something about this is familiar. Déjà vu. Where have I seen this scene before?

Then it comes to me: *Tommy. Tommy Lawrence, from high school.* A boy from St. John's, a nerd whom none of the girls liked. He once gave Marti a tiny bunch of pink roses. He met her at the bus stop one morning, his face hot, hands shaking. While a group of our classmates stood by and snickered, Marti thanked the boy warmly, pushing her then waist-length hair from her face. She pressed the roses later and kept them between the pages of a history book.

"He gave me more than these roses," she explained to me. "What he did took a lot of courage, and that deserves to be honored."

Remembering, I walk toward Tommy, stepping up my pace. He sees me and glances away, as if not wanting to make contact. He is still shy, I think, and I smile to put him at ease. Drawing close, I can make out tears in his eyes. His cheeks are wet as if several have already fallen.

"Tommy," I say. "Tommy Lawrence. How are you?"

"Hi, Abby."

"You remember me?"

He gives a shrug. "Sure. You were Marti's best friend."

"But we never even talked. How did you know?"

"I guess I knew a lot about Marti. Back then, anyway."

Of course. He was obsessed with her. In the end, a simple gift of pink roses turned into hanging outside her house at night, following her to school in the morning and being outside on the steps when classes let out. What for Marti began as mild embarrassment later turned into a case of nerves—even fear.

"I never meant her any harm," he says now, as if reading my mind. "I just wanted to be around her."

"Tommy, you frightened her," I say. "If you didn't want to hurt her…"

"Why did I do it?" He shakes his head. "I guess I couldn't help myself. It was like we were always meant to be together, from the first time I saw her. And when she thanked me for the roses I gave her that day, I thought I knew it for sure. She kept saying she only wanted to be friends, but I told myself if I could just show her I really cared, she'd like me, too."

It was a story old as the hills. Do enough nice things for someone, be good enough to them, and they'll learn to love you. How many people with hopeless crushes cling to that belief—before reality sets in?

"She did like you, Tommy," I say gently. "She just wasn't interested right then. You know?"

"Yeah. Yeah, I guess you're right." A lock of brown hair falls over his forehead, bringing back the image of that young boy. "Pretty stupid, huh?"

He smiles at me, and his whole demeanor changes. "But I've grown up. I no longer lurk outside women's houses." He looks down at the pink roses, and sadness settles over his face again. "I just wanted to bring her flowers."

Sympathy for the young boy who, at least for a short while, brought a smile to Marti's face, makes me take his free hand. "C'mon. I'll go with you."

His grateful glance is enough to make me glad I decided to do that. We cross the lawn to Marti's grave, where Jeffrey is still holding court. Too bad, I think, he didn't bring champagne and hors d'ouevres. The party would be complete.

But I'm too used to this sort of thing, and too jaded about Jeffrey's shenanigans, to invest much energy into being annoyed. I figure karma will get Jeffrey in the end. Or somewhere.

I stand with Tommy Lawrence as he takes a single pink rose from the bouquet and drops it onto the coffin of the woman he once loved from afar. The rest of the bouquet he puts beside the grave site, with the others. When he turns back to me I see he is weeping again.

"I know it's been years," he says, wiping his eyes with the back of one slender hand. "But it's like it was only yesterday."

"I know," I say. "I've been feeling that same sort of thing. Everything from back then seems so immediate somehow, as if we've warped right back into that time."

He smiles. "Thanks for understanding. Can I drop you off somewhere?"

I shake my head. "My husband..." I motion toward Jeffrey.

"He doesn't look like he's ready to leave," Tommy says.

"No, he doesn't, does he?"

"I have a couple of hours till my plane leaves. Let me buy you a cup of coffee. To thank you," he adds quickly. "I don't mean anything by it. You don't have to worry."

I smile to let him know I'm not in the least worried. Thinking for a moment, I realize that no one from the funeral mentioned getting together for coffee and food afterward. Unless Ned and Sister Helen were doing that, and the other woman with them, it seems that Marti—once cold in the ground—is to be forgotten.

"Let's go back to my house," I say. "Jeffrey will be along eventually, and he'll probably bring people with him. Meanwhile we can have coffee and sandwiches. How's that? You can follow me in your car."

"Sounds great," he says. "But I took a cab here."

"Then you can come with me."

"Great," he says again. "Thanks."

As we walk toward the Mercedes, I turn back to wave at Jeffrey and motion that we're going ahead— he'll need to grab a ride. His return wave is automatic, the smile fixed and bland. I doubt he even knows I'm leaving.

Ben does, though. He's been standing by the line of cars on the drive, with his partner, Arnie, throughout the ceremony. Even closer to the graveside I've seen a couple of detectives from the sheriff's department and the police chief from Monterey. No Secret Service, however.

Ben lifts a brow at me as I pass him to get to my car, though he doesn't speak, probably because of Tommy. I know, of course, why they're here. Ben and Arnie were in the back of the church during Mass, earlier, then followed the funeral procession on the long trek down Highway 1 toward Big Sur— the unmarked brown police car sticking out like a sore thumb behind all the black limos. "The Brown Turd," Ben calls it. Unmarked, though absurdly known to every crook in town, it's Ben's favorite car, and to the consternation of his fellow officers, he refuses to give it up.

The reason he, Arnie and the sheriff's detectives are here today is because it's common knowledge, according to Ben, that the murderer often turns up at the funeral of the murdered.

I wonder if they've pegged anyone yet. Anyone besides me, that is.

"This place is fabulous," Tommy Lawrence says as I rinse out the coffeemaker and pour beans into the grinder. "Haven't I seen it somewhere? Like in a magazine?"

"You may have," I admit, a trifle embarrassed. "It's nice, but old," I add, as if in apology for having so much. "There are a lot of things going wrong with it suddenly."

It has occurred to me that Tommy's shirt collar, though clean, is a bit frayed, and his dark green pants are thin in the knee.

He is standing by one of the casement windows looking out onto the side patio. "You're right," he says, wiggling the window frame. "The screws holding this on are loose. Anybody could get in here. I hope you have good security."

"I've got Murphy," I say. "You may have noticed he hasn't left my side since we walked through the door."

I look down at Murph, who thumps his tail.

"Is that because I'm here?" Tommy asks.

"Probably."

"Well, I hate to tell you, but he doesn't act much like a watchdog. More like a happy-go-lucky puppy."

"You think so? Try something," I offer.

"Try something?"

"Like taking my arm, as if you're going to do something to me."

He looks embarrassed, but does as I ask, gripping my upper arm. Murphy is on his feet immediately, growling, teeth bared.

Tommy drops his hand. "Okay, okay," he says, backing off and laughing. "It's okay, boy."

Murph doesn't back down till I tell him to, and Tommy looks at me, amazed. "Geez! You've really got him trained."

"No, that's the funny thing about it. He's not trained at all. Just naturally that way. You can even pet him, and the worst he'll do is lick you to death. Just don't try anything with me.''

Tommy leans down and tentatively pats Murph on the head, stroking his fur from head to back.

"What's this?" he asks, feeling the rough spot where the vet cut back the hair to treat the wound on Murph's back.

"He had a little mishap," I say, not wanting to talk about it. "He's all right now."

"A mishap? This looks like more than a mishap. Poor guy." Tommy parts the fur to try to see the wound better, but Murph growls low in his throat, telling him in no uncertain terms to back off.

Tommy settles on his heels. "Poor guy," he says again.

Within minutes the coffee is ready, and I take down two cobalt-blue mugs and fill them with the steaming brew. Handing one to Tommy, I lead him into the living room. Murphy trails behind.

"Let's sit here by the window," I say. "The sun's coming out at last."

As we settle in, he asks, "Can we talk?"

"Of course. I thought we were."

"No, I mean about Marti."

I wonder if he knows how it happened. What was done to her. It was in all the papers, on all the news. But is he going to ask for details? I'm not sure I'm up to that.

"I just wondered," he says, "if you know what she was doing all these years?"

I look at him over my cup, surprised. "Marti was a photojournalist. You didn't know? She traveled all over the world with her work and won several major awards."

"No, I'm aware of all that. What did she do with her life? Her personal life? They say she never married, never had a family. What did she do all those years?"

I look at him sharply. "I don't know, Tommy, why do you ask?"

He seems to tense up. His hands, which are long and thin, wrap around the coffee mug as if to stay warm. "Curiosity, I guess. I mean, I've wondered if she was happy. If she ever…you know, loved anyone."

I set down my cup. "You still cared about her," I say softly. "All this time, you never got over her."

He shakes his head. "I couldn't just forget her. You don't, you know…forget the first person you ever loved."

"But, Tommy, it wasn't really a relationship. She never returned your feelings."

He seems about to say something, then clamps his mouth shut. Tears brim his eyes. "It doesn't matter," he says finally. "You don't stop caring just because the other person…" He shakes his head, wiping at his eyes with a thumb.

"I think she was happy," I say gently. "As happy as anyone could be who's devoted to her work and doesn't have time for relationships."

"So she was never in love?"

"I…I didn't say that. I think she was. Once."

He straightens and looks at me sharply. "With who?"

"I don't know."

"Then how do you know—"

"I just do. Can we leave it at that, Tommy?"

He falls silent. Then, "Just one thing. She had a baby, right? That's what they said on the news, that she'd had a Cesarean operation."

Sighing, I stand. "Tommy, I can't talk about that. Besides, I think I hear Jeffrey coming into the garage. And there are cars pulling up in front. Time to play hostess." For some reason, I feel relieved that my husband is about to walk through the door.

"Sure. Sorry if I pushed. I'll leave."

"No...look, I didn't mean that. Please stay." We walk back into the kitchen. "How long do you have till your plane leaves?" I am thinking another hour at the most.

"Actually, till about ten tonight."

"Ten? But it's barely past noon. I thought you said a couple of hours."

He grins. "That was only because I wanted you to think I'd be leaving soon. That way I figured you wouldn't feel you had to entertain me. I was going to buy you some coffee, if you let me, then go for a walk on the beach and maybe get some dinner somewhere."

I can't help but be impressed with his honesty. But then, the boy I remember always was honest about his feelings. As Marti said, it took a lot of courage for him to even approach her the first time with those flowers. And it's rare to find people who carry their feelings out in the open, where people can see them.

Besides, it feels good to have someone here who knew and loved Marti. In the past hour or so, the pain has eased a bit.

"Well, if you've got all that much time," I say, "I think I'll just lasso you and put you to work." I hand Tommy bottles of white wine from the fridge and reds from the wine rack in a niche by the pantry. "Take these into the living room, will you? Set them on that sideboard over by the fireplace. And then get yourself back in here, boy. You can help with hor's d'ouevres."

"Those cute little hot dogs in crescent rolls?" he asks, grinning as he crosses the room.

"Pigs in a blanket? Hah. I doubt Jeffrey..." Remembering that Marti loved pigs in a blanket, I shrug. This could be, at least in my head—and maybe in Tommy's—her party, after all.

"Oh, why the hell not? Pigs in a blanket it is."

"Hoo, boy," Tommy says.

Jeffrey's party turns out to be the typical last-minute affair. I have never known when he would invite people over, and I've always understood that this was my job, part of why he married me—to have a hostess. I've even gotten rather good at it.

Once having performed my usual duties, I stand with Tommy Lawrence in the dining-room area, safely away from the hullabaloo in the living room. People have come just as they dressed for the funeral before noon, in toned-down blacks and grays. Still, there are more diamonds, emeralds and rubies in my living room this afternoon than at Tiffany's and Cartier combined. Most of the conversation revolves around politics, the stock market and golf, and I've heard every story there is to be told over the past ten years. People forget what they've said to whom and tend to repeat their victory tales. Personally, I prefer to listen to Frannie, who cleans for most of these people and delivers me tidbits that give me laughs and get me through the day.

For instance, Frannie has told me how, as she was on her way to clean Cynthia Slyke's kitchen, scrub her floors and wipe pubic hairs out of her tubs, she passed Cynthia on the drive, and Cynthia—leaving for tennis in her tan and chocolate Mercedes convertible—waved at her and warbled, "Bye-bye, dear! Have fun!"

"Fun!" Frannie ranted while telling me about it the next day. "And me seven months pregnant with Billy! It's a wonder he wasn't born with a burnt nose from all the Clorox fumes, or with the cord wrapped around his neck, all the bending I did for that airhead!"

Not all of Jeffrey's guests are idiots, of course. There's Harry Blimm, president of the Seacoast Bank of Carmel, who comes over to me now, taking my hand. He pats it with his chubby one. "I'm so sorry about your friend," he says. "We'll miss her terribly."

"We?"

"At Haven House, that is. She was our strongest supporter." He shakes his head sadly. "I tell you, she leaves a hole we have little hope of filling."

I feel stupid, as I don't know what he is talking about. "Haven House?"

"Our shelter for the homeless," he says. "In Seaside. You didn't know?"

I shake my head.

"There are so many women and children in the

shelters now,'' he says. ''Marti came and talked with them several times. She seemed to have her own private agenda in choosing Haven House for volunteer work. Never would talk about it, though.'' He peers at me curiously. ''I don't suppose you might know?''

''No, I'm sorry, I don't. This is all news to me, Harry. I do remember she was doing several pieces about the homeless, as well as rape victims. She flew out here several times for that.''

''No, no, no, this was something entirely separate from that. Marti never took photographs at Haven House. The women's and children's privacy were everything to her.''

''I see. Exactly what did she do at Haven House, then?''

''Simply talked with women, held their hands, cried with them. A beautiful soul.'' Again he flicks a look at me. ''I'm surprised you didn't know.''

''I am too, Harry. And how do you know about all this?''

''Well, I am on the board of Haven House, you know. Have been for twenty years.''

More news. I wonder, briefly, where I've been. Head in the sand? Too absorbed in my own difficulties to worry about others?

After that Harry wanders off, and later, when everyone is well soused, I see our esteemed bank president dancing with his wife's red hoop earrings on, and one of my colorful Spanish tablecloths wrapped around his waist. His bald head glimmers under the crystal chandelier in the living room, and everyone stands around clapping in time to the music and Harry's tomfoolery.

There was a time when I would have cheered him on, as well. Now I know too much. Harry is in Jeffrey's pocket, and a very deep pocket it is.

There is nothing, I think, that moves the world like cash. Unless it happens to be blackmail.

Tommy Lawrence joins me in the kitchen.

"You sure work hard at all this," he says as I start to clean up. "Don't people like you have maids?"

I laugh. "What do you know about people like me?"

"Not much, I guess."

"That's what I thought. The truth is, I like doing the scut work for parties. It gives me a means of escape, so I don't have to socialize so much."

"You don't like socializing?"

"Tommy, Carmel is a small town. I've known most of Jeffrey's friends for years. Let's say I'm jaded, okay?"

"And then there's the way you look at him..." Tommy says, shaking his head.

"Him who?"

"Your husband. Like he's a stranger. It's none of my business, of course, but don't you two ever talk to each other?"

I sigh. "Only when we must."

"Oh."

"Yeah, oh." I finish loading one of the two dishwashers and turn to face him. "You don't mind asking personal questions of people, do you?"

He grins. "Sorry. I'm always curious about what makes people tick. I don't think I told you—I'm a writer."

"Really?" Somehow this doesn't surprise me. It fits the picture of the shy young man with the bunch of pink roses. "What do you write?" I ask, feeling sure he'll say poetry.

"Novels. Thrillers, actually."

"Thrillers! Are you published?"

He looks uneasy—something I understand. Writer friends tell me it's difficult to get a novel published these days. The question almost becomes an accusation: *You haven't made it yet, have you?*

"Not yet," Tommy admits. "I do have an agent, though."

"Well, that's good. It's only a matter of time, then."

"Thanks," he says wryly. "You didn't have to say that, but thanks."

"No, I meant it. If someone believes in you enough to take you on, that's half the battle right there. You write full-time?"

"Pretty much. I mean, I do freelance editing for a living, and I've written some articles, mostly medical and scientific. That takes up about half my time. The rest I spend on my fiction."

"Well," I say, smiling. "Little Tommy Lawrence, on his way to becoming a bestselling author."

He laughs. "I guess I still have a few cliffs to climb. Which reminds me—I hear you write, too."

"Yes, but nothing as ambitious as novels. I have a column in the local paper. *Round the Town*. It's mostly chitchat about local events, laced with a bit of gossip." I shrug.

"No, don't put it down. I heard you worked for

the *San Francisco Chronicle* and were nominated for a Pulitzer once.''

I turn to him, surprised. ''That was years ago. A whole other lifetime. Besides, how do you know all this?''

''I don't know, I must have read about it somewhere. Is that why you and your husband are having trouble? Do you miss your work, all the way down here? It can't be much fun, after what you used to do.''

This is getting a bit too personal.

''You know, it seems odd,'' I say. ''You appear out of nowhere after all these years, yet you know so much about us.''

''Not everyone, just you.''

''And my husband, it seems. What's going on, Tommy?''

''I just asked around,'' he says, replenishing a plate with celery, carrots and dip. ''At the hotel bar, where I'm staying. La Playa. You know it?''

''Of course. It's the biggest hotel in town.'' I can't help wondering how an unpublished writer can afford to stay at the fancy La Playa, though. At least, for any length of time.

''I came in yesterday,'' he says, ''and had some drinks and conversation with the bartender.''

''Ah. *Jimmy-John.*'' My tone says it all.

''You know him?''

''I know he's a gossip,'' I say, rinsing out glasses.

''Well, he didn't say anything bad about you, just filled me in on some details.''

''And why would you want to be filled in on details, Tommy? Especially about me and my husband?''

''Because you were friends of Marti's. Well, you, anyway. Jimmy-John says your husband didn't like her much.''

Damn Jimmy-John. What else is he passing around town about us? A newcomer, he seems to thrive on gossip, especially about the Eastwoods and others in town who hold positions of fame and/or power. Twice, now, the hotel has threatened to fire him, but somehow he keeps hanging on.

''Is it true? Your husband didn't like Marti?'' Tommy asks.

''He didn't really know her,'' I say, turning back to him.

But the question raises more questions, like what did Jeffrey have against Marti, and why did he never want her around? It isn't the first time I've asked myself this. Jeffrey has always refused to talk about it.

''It might have had something to do with the fact that Marti stood up for the poor,'' I say, not even sure why I'm bothering to answer Tommy's question. Certainly he's gone way too far for a simple visitor, someone I haven't even seen in twenty years.

''The poor?''

''Children in third world countries, children in this country. Homeless women and men. Marti had a special spot in her heart for people without places to live.''

''And your husband? He doesn't have a similar spot in his heart for them?''

''I guess you might say that.''

The truth is, Jeffrey would run roughshod over a six-pound infant if it stood in the way of a real-estate or political deal.

"What does your husband do?" Tommy asks.

"He's involved in politics. He also fancies himself a land baron. Jeffrey thinks that when they set land aside in the twenties 'for future generations,' they were doing it just for him so he could build on it."

"And the politics?"

"Jeffrey worked for Clint Eastwood's advisors when he was getting together his campaign to run for mayor of Carmel. He got bitten by the political bug, and ever since he's been wheeling and dealing behind the scenes."

"Does he have aspirations of his own to run for office?"

"Not at all. For him, politicians are the drone bees he sends out to do his bidding. Jeffrey says that's where the real power lies. Look, why am I telling you all this?"

Tommy smiles. "Beats me. But hey, you know what? I doubt Clint Eastwood would appreciate being called a drone bee."

"Well, that was different. Jeffrey was just getting started in politics, and he was just another campaign worker then."

I put the glasses in the dishwasher and wipe up the mess on the center island. "Why are you so interested in us, Tommy?" I ask more seriously this time. "I doubt you're writing a novel based on our lives."

"I might," he answers. "Unless you really didn't want me to."

"That would stop you?"

"It might."

"Then I take back what I said earlier. You'll probably never be published, with an attitude like that. Tommy, writers have to develop shark instincts if they're going to write exposés about real people."

He doesn't smile, though my tone has been one of teasing.

"All I really want," he says, "is to know who killed Marti."

"Is that the real reason you're here?"

"That…and to bring the roses," he says. "I promised Marti…"

A small but heavy silence fills the air. "Tommy? You promised Marti what?"

He seems uneasy and begins to busy himself at wiping the counter by the sink.

"Tommy?"

"It was a long time ago" he says. "Just something I remembered from way back."

"But—"

The doorbell rings, loud and long, interrupting my thoughts. Moments later a hush falls on the crowd in the living room. Men's voices drift down the center hall from foyer to kitchen, sounding clipped and businesslike.

"I wonder who that is," I say, moving toward the swinging door between the kitchen and dining room. I have in my hand a tray of coffee cups, and I turn to ask Tommy to bring the tray holding cream, sugar and napkins.

"Tommy, would you—"

But, that quickly, he's gone. I glance into the pantry, thinking he went in there in search of clean cloths. He's not there, nor anywhere in sight.

Puzzled, I head toward the living room, nearly spilling the coffee as Jeffrey opens the swinging door from his side.

"Oh, there you are!" he says, as if surprised to find me here, working my shift at his party. "There are some, uh, people here who would like to talk to you," he adds carefully, aware of our curious guests.

"Oh?" I ask, puzzled. "What people?"

My first thought is that it's Ned, or perhaps even Sister Helen.

As I enter the living room, I see it's not either of them. Agents Mauro and Hillars stand in the foyer. I place the tray of coffee cups on the sideboard and walk toward them.

"This is not the best time," I say, prepared to usher them out.

"Sorry, Ms. Northrup," Mauro says dryly. "Much as we hate interrupting your party, we really must talk with you."

He glances into the living room. "Is there someplace we can go to talk? Alone?"

I look at Jeffrey, who seems tense and strained. I haven't mentioned my meeting with the Secret Service to him, but it's clear they have introduced themselves. Jeffrey, I am guessing, would as soon slip through the floor as have the Secret Service in his house at this moment.

"We can talk in my office," I offer, motioning down the hall to the room opposite the kitchen. "Jeffrey?" I wait for him to follow us.

"If you don't mind," Agent Mauro says softly but firmly, "we'd like to talk with you alone first."

My husband seems about to argue the point, sliding a quick look to me. Then his face takes on that meaningless smile. "I'll see to our guests, dear."

Dear?

When we're in my office I take a seat behind my desk. Agent Mauro indicates he prefers to stand, while the older man, Hillars, settles into a straight chair along the wall, in front of my bookcases. His knees are together, and in the stiff, dark suit he looks almost prim, more like a schoolteacher than a Secret Service agent.

"All right," I say, less nervous here on my own turf than at the police station, "we're alone. What can I do for you?"

"There is certain information," Mauro says, "that we weren't at liberty to share with you the other day. Since then, the situation has changed."

"Changed? How?"

"Ms. Northrup, we must have your promise that what we tell you will be kept strictly confidential."

"I...all right."

"Confidentiality is of the *utmost importance*," he emphasizes. "If the press were to learn we were here, and why, it could get in the way of our investigation. If we seem overly cautious it is only because you, yourself, are part of the press—"

"Oh, for heaven's sake! I write a column, I'm not the goddamned *Enquirer*. Are you going to tell me or not?"

Agent Mauro looks at Hillars, who says nothing. He turns back to me. "We're here at the request of the president, Ms. Northrup. President Chase has asked Agent Hillars and myself to personally look into the death of Marti Bright.''

"The president? I don't understand.''

Those flat, pit bull eyes assess me. "You didn't know Ms. Bright and the first family were friends?''

"No, I did not.''

"But you must know she accompanied them on their trip to Africa three years ago. Her piece in *Life* magazine brought her several awards.''

"Well, yes, but Marti traveled with a lot of people. That didn't mean she got close to them.''

"In this case, Ms. Northrup, Marti Bright and the first family became friends. The first lady, in fact, maintained ties with Ms. Bright, and I understand that she is behind the president's request to do all we can to uncover Ms. Bright's murderer.''

I am surprised, but not overly so. If Marti never mentioned a friendship with the first family, it's probably only because she never bragged, never thought of people in terms of celebrity. Marti had connections to movie stars, rock musicians, heads of foreign countries. No journalist in the U.S., except perhaps Barbara Walters, had more friends among the luminaries than Marti.

"So you're saying the president sent you here to question me?''

"Not directly. However, in our investigation, it turned up that you and Ms. Bright were close for many years. If anyone can give us some clue or insight into who might have murdered her, it might very well be you, Ms. Northrup.''

"Well, I'm sorry, but I haven't a clue. If I did...''

"Yes?"

It is probably best not to say that I would kill the bastard.

"I guess I've been in shock. I haven't really thought about the killer, not to that extent. If anything, I suppose I've been thinking that Marti was a victim of something random. Some nutcase."

"Yet, the coroner himself told you that Marti Bright may have been murdered by someone she knew."

And how did you know he told me that, Agent Mauro? The long arm of the law again?

"Random killings," Mauro points out, "are seldom as well thought out, or as ritual, as this one."

"No. I suppose they're not."

"Do you know anyone," he asks, "who might have had so much hatred for Marti Bright that he or she might have done this sort of thing?"

I shake my head. "I honestly haven't a clue. I can't remember her having said she was afraid of anyone, or that anyone was after her. Maybe it had something to do with a story she was on. You might start with the homeless shelters, the rape crisis shelters—"

"We've talked with them," Mauro says, interrupting. "The path keeps leading back to you, Ms. Northrup."

A flicker of fear runs up my spine. "To me? In what way?"

He smiles, without warmth. "In our work, we often feel like the crooked man in the nursery rhyme. 'There was a crooked man who walked a crooked mile.' You know that one?"

I nod.

"In the end," he says, "all things come together for the crooked man. He buys a crooked cat who catches a crooked mouse. They all live together in a little crooked house."

"Your knowledge of childhood literature amazes me, Agent Mauro. And this relates to me exactly how?"

"Only in that getting to the happy ending—or rather unhappy ending, in our work—often involves a morass of crooked sixpences and stiles. In this case, that would be you, Ms. Northrup."

"Lovely."

"Everyone we've talked to," he continues smoothly, "says the same thing, Ms. Northrup—they didn't know Marti Bright well. They loved her for the work she did with them, but they never got close to her. One person said it was as if she was hiding something, something she couldn't share with anyone."

"Well, then—"

"You didn't let me finish. I was going to say, with anyone but a very close friend. Ms. Northrup, we need you to tell us everything you know about the son Marti Bright gave birth to fifteen years ago."

I thought I'd gone beyond the point where Agent Mauro could surprise me. Now, however, I am shocked. I see Marti's face, suddenly, as it was the day her little boy was born—full of fear mixed with incredible love for the child she held close to her breast. *You've got to swear, Abby, swear you won't ever tell anyone about him. Not anyone at all.*

It takes all the strength I can muster to say firmly, "I have no idea what you're talking about."

Mauro stands in front of my desk, leaning his palms on it. "Ms. Northrup, all cards on the table. We know Marti Bright came to Carmel for the first time fifteen years ago, not fourteen, as you claim. We know she had a child, that you were there for the birth, and the child was named Justin. We know she gave him to people named Ryan to raise—"

I open my mouth again to deny all this, but Mauro sighs. "Please, let's not play games. Ms. Northrup. The boy has been kidnapped. Now tell us what you know."

I am on my feet, my hands covering my mouth. "Kidnapped! My God, no! What are you talking about?"

"Marti Bright was here on the Peninsula three months ago for only one reason—to help the Ryans find her son. When she couldn't find him she called the first family for help. The president assigned us to the case."

I lean forward and reach out to my desk for support. "I don't believe this! Marti never said a word to me. And what about the FBI? The local police? No one's said anything, there's been nothing in the press."

"No one has been told. At Ms. Bright's and the Ryans' request, only the president and Mrs. Chase know about the kidnapping. The first family honored this request when Marti Bright was alive. And now, given the way Ms. Bright died and the attention it's drawn, making the kidnapping public could work against negotiations for the child's safe return."

"Negotiations." I lick my lips. My mouth is so dry, it hurts. "There are negotiations, then? You know who took Justin?"

Mauro's eyes give the hint of a flicker, and Hillars leans forward.

"You know the boy personally?" Hillars asks in his Southern drawl.

"No, no, of course not."

This is not the entire truth, but I'm still not sure I trust the Secret Service any more than they apparently trust me.

"Do you know who took Justin?" I say again.

"We are not at liberty to answer that."

"But if— When did you say it happened?" I ask.

For a long moment it seems they won't answer. Then Mauro says, "As I told you, our information is that Ms. Bright began negotiations with the kidnapper three months ago."

"Three months! But that's impossible, we told each other everything! Marti would never have kept something like this from me."

Still, I am remembering that in the past three months she never answered my phone calls, never came by when she was here. I am hearing Ned say, "You're the one who killed her," and seeing Sister Helen's cold, unfriendly face.

What in the name of God has been going on?

"If indeed she told you everything," Agent Mauro continues, "then you must be able to tell us the name of the boy's biological father."

I shake my head. "No, I don't know. She never told me."

"Ms. Northrup, I can't emphasize enough that the boy's life is at stake. If you know—"

"I don't, dammit! She said it was only one night, and she didn't want the father involved."

"Did she give you a reason for that? Was the man in question abusive, for instance? Did she feel she had to hide the child from him?"

"I...no. I don't think so..." I hesitate.

"But?"

"She said she didn't think he'd make a good father. Wasn't father material, or maybe that he wasn't available. Something like that."

"Was he unstable?"

"I'm telling you, I don't know. That's all she said."

I don't know how much longer I can hold myself together. And where the hell is Jeffrey? Surely he isn't still out there hosting that damn party. Surely he sent everyone home.

In fact, I know I heard cars leaving. Why doesn't he come in here and throw his considerable weight around, demanding to know what's going on? Why doesn't he call Sol Lenquist, our lawyer?

Maybe he has. Sol will get me out of here.

But Agent Mauro has one more zinger under his cap. "You know a woman named Helen Asback?"

"Helen Asback. No...no, the name isn't familiar."

"You may know her as Sister Helen."

"Oh. Well, yes, of course, I know Sister Helen. I just don't recall ever hearing her last name." That was another thing my former teacher had refused to use, that and civilian clothes. "What about her?" I ask.

"Ms. Northrup, we spoke with Helen Asback, or Sister Helen, as you know her, before coming here. She and Marti Bright's brother—" he consults his notes "—Ned Bright. They both seem to think you know more about Ms. Bright's murder than you've admitted to."

"But that's crazy. I haven't seen Sister Helen in twenty years. And I never really met Marti's brother until today. I don't know how they can say such a thing."

"Perhaps Ms. Bright told them something? Something that might incriminate you?"

I might have given up a good job to marry Jeffrey and fritter my life away in Carmel, but I was not a working reporter beforehand for nothing. Every remaining instinct I have tells me Agent Mauro is fishing. Otherwise, he would not be telling me all this. And his questions would be more specific.

"Perhaps she did," I say coolly. "And perhaps they—and you, Agent Mauro, and you, Agent Hillars—can all just go to hell."

Gathering strength from my anger, I stand. "I'm sorry, but I don't see that this is getting us anywhere. I obviously don't know the things you want to know. And I am very, very tired. If you insist, I and my lawyer will meet with you in the morning. Meanwhile, I'm asking you both to leave."

I am rewarded by a deep flush filling Agent Mauro's face.

Agent Hillars is the one who speaks. "We apologize if we have offended you, Ms. Northrup. Please understand, we are only trying to get to the bottom of things. We would like to find your friend's murderer. Stephen? Shall we go?''

His back is stiff as he leads the way to the door. Agent Mauro turns as if for a parting shot, but Hillars, amazingly, grabs his arm and shoves him through the door, muttering, ''Not now, Stephen. For God's sake!''

As the door closes I sink back into my chair and bury my face in my hands.

Justin—Justin has been kidnapped. Oh, dear God, Marti, now what do I do?

Jeffrey is in the living room alone, slumped in his favorite easy chair and downing what looks like his favorite drink, straight scotch. He's been at it a while; his face is flushed and slack.

''God, Jeffrey, anyone would think you were in there getting the third degree, not me! And why the hell didn't you *do* something?''

I know I sound like a shrew, but I can't help it. My nerves are a-jangle.

He gives me a sour look. ''Do what, Abby? Charge in there and throw them out? That somehow didn't seem quite the way to go.''

''You could at least have called Sol.''

''I did.''

That takes some of the wind out of my sails. I slump in the chair opposite Jeffrey's in front of the fire.

''What did he say?''

''He's on his way.''

I make the snorting sound my husband despises.

"What did you do, wait till the horse was halfway out the barn to call?"

"No, my dear, I reached him on his cell phone in Santa Cruz. He said he'd be here within the hour." Jeffrey looks at his watch. "Which means any time now." He downs the rest of his drink in one swallow. "Well…what did they want?"

Aside from the fact that the Secret Service told me to keep Justin's kidnapping confidential, I am not ready to tell Jeffrey about Marti's son.

"I'm not really sure," I say. "They asked a lot of questions about Marti."

Jeffrey flicks a look at me. "What did you tell them?"

"Not much that they didn't already know."

"They've been investigating the murder?"

"They… Yes."

"You hesitated. Why?"

"Dammit, Jeffrey, I'm exhausted, and I don't feel like telling it twice. You can hear it along with Sol."

I get up and go to the sideboard, pouring myself a stiff drink. "You need a refill?"

He sets his glass down and stands, beginning to pace. "No. I should stay sober for when Sol gets here."

"A bit late for that," I say.

"You know, your mouth—"

"Will get me in trouble one day. Right. I apologize. It's just that it does seem you've been drinking more than usual lately. What's going on, Jeffrey?"

"What's going on? You have to ask? I feel like a prisoner here, locked up with someone who can't stand the sight of me and wants me gone yesterday, if not today."

The ice in my glass clinks as I whirl around. "Oh, and you think it's a picnic for me? This whole thing was your idea, for God's sake! If you want out, *get* out. It's as simple as that."

"You know it's not that simple."

"No, nothing with you ever is."

I study him, the Clooney haircut passé now, the bedroom eyes beginning to pale. Jeffrey is only in his fifties, yet in the past few months he seems to have aged quickly. The exercise isn't helping, and his trainer either hasn't the guts to tell him or can't afford to lose the income.

I sigh, remembering the early days and how much fun they were. The dreams still alive, promises not yet broken. "Oh, Jeffrey..." I say, "it's not you I can't stand the sight of. It's what you did. That night keeps coming back, over and over. If I sound bitter, I'm sorry. I can't seem to get it out of my head."

"Well, now I have a night to remember, too," he says coldly. "You and your little policeman friend. Christ, Abby, couldn't you at least have picked someone with more class?"

I am hot to the defense of Ben. "More *class?* You mean like Karen? Your little bimbo?"

"For Christ's sake, she's your *sister!* Show a little respect."

I laugh, but without mirth. "Like you did, there between her legs, gobbling her up like the last dinner of a condemned man?"

"Well, I felt like a condemned man."

"Jeffrey…" My sigh is heavy, loaded with both misery and guilt. "Let's not do this. Not again."

He falls silent. But the odd thing is, he's probably right—maybe I should try to show a little respect. Karen is, indeed, my sister. Unfortunately, she is also a tramp. If the word sounds harsh, I like it for its versatile definitions: hobo, walkabout…sleepabout. My parents did their best, but Karen never responded to anyone's best, only their worst. At sixteen she ran off, never wrote, never called, broke both my parents' hearts. When she showed up here in Carmel five years ago, she was a forty-year-old adolescent, a woman who had learned to make her way through the world by using people. She lived with me and Jeffrey for several months, during which time she slept with half the married men in Carmel in an effort to prove she was still young enough to attract them. When she ran out of marital fodder elsewhere, she started on mine. Part of Karen's problem is that she loves *things,* and when she saw what I had, she wanted it.

I got the last laugh, though. Jeffrey may have put her up in a million-dollar condo with an ocean view, but now she's stuck with him—while I've got Ben.

Ben and this house, so long as I put up with Jeffrey until after the election.

Chase's reelection. I wonder what my husband would say if he knew his golden boy had sent the Secret Service here tonight.

But then, he must have known this the minute they walked through the door. The Secret Service acts at the behest of the president, and no one—in private life, at least—is closer to the president than Jeffrey.

So why does he seem so nervous about their visit? Why is he drinking so heavily? And why doesn't he tell me he knows why they were here?

A car pulls into the drive, and moments later the doorbell rings. I go to the foyer to let Sol in.

"Sorry it took me so long, Abby." He looks around. "Your visitors leave?"

"You mean the federal ones? I chased them away."

"Well, if anyone could do that it would be you," he says, smiling. "What's going on?"

"Come in, Sol. Sit down. Can I get you a drink?"

He follows me into the living room, where he nods to Jeffrey but passes on the drink. Sinking into the sofa, he groans, putting a pillow behind his back to prop it. "I wish you'd get real furniture some day," he mutters, not for the first time. "This puffy shit is killing my knees."

Sol is short, dark and beefy. He looks and thinks like a mob lawyer, but his heart is pure. He's been Jeffrey's and my lawyer ever since we married, and he's always been absolutely fair with both of us. I'm one of the few divorced or divorcing wives in Carmel who didn't need to go out and get a shark of her own. It was Sol, in fact, who talked Jeffrey out of a prenup before the wedding. He held up his own happy marriage as an example and told Jeffrey it was based on trust. Nothing could work without it, he argued, and Jeffrey finally agreed to marry me without the agreement he'd wanted: that if we ever split, I'd leave with only what I'd brought in.

Which was virtually nothing. I was so in love at

the time, I didn't care. I'd have signed the prenup without a second thought.

"Okay, so tell me what this is all about," Sol begins.

I sit across from him and sip my drink. "This isn't the first time they interviewed me," I say. "I talked to them a few days ago, too."

Jeffrey looks startled. "You didn't tell me that."

"Well, you weren't here. After that, I forgot. Anyway, Sol, they were asking me questions about Marti. And they seemed to know everything about me, right down to the mole on my behind. They had obviously done an in-depth background investigation."

"Really? What kinds of things did they know about you?" Sol asks.

"They knew all about my school years," I tell him. "My grades from kindergarten on, they said, my friends through high school... They even knew that Marti and I were in the convent together and left together, that we've been friends over the years."

Sol's heard all this, so I'm not telling him anything new.

"Did you get their names?"

"The one who did all the talking was an Agent Mauro. Stephen Mauro. The other one was Hillars. I don't know his first name."

"That's okay, I can get it easily enough. What kinds of questions did they ask?"

"They wanted to know everything I could tell them about Marti. Specifically, who she saw when she was here in the area, and who she might have had close relationships with."

"You mean, like a boyfriend? A lover?"

I hesitate, tempted to tell him about Justin, that he's been kidnapped, and that because of this Mauro and Hillars were here at the request of the first family. I am stopped, however, by the fact that, first of all, Mauro emphasized confidentiality, and secondly, Jeffrey is here. Again I wonder: If Chase wanted Jeffrey to know about this, wouldn't he have called and told him? A phone call from the president warning us about a pending visit from the Secret Service wouldn't have been out of place.

Sol, I think, must be reading my mind. He rubs his face and seems thoughtful. "Jeffrey?" he says at last.

"Yes, Sol?"

"They didn't talk to you?"

"No. They did stop in here on the way out. Said they wanted to see me tomorrow morning at ten, at the Carmel police station."

"You didn't tell me that," I say.

Jeffrey gives me a dark look, as if I am personally responsible for this imposition.

I turn to Sol. "What do you think?"

"I don't know, Abby. Did they ask you anything you felt was unusual?"

"Any number of things." I summarize the conversation for him, leaving out only the information about Justin. "I finally told them they should question people at the different shelters Marti visited, that if she knew anyone here besides me, it would be them. They said they had already talked to people there, but no one had ever felt close to Marti. People said they had liked her, but that they never really knew her well."

"And that struck you as unusual?"

I look down at the ice melting in my glass of scotch. "Only because I'd come to feel I didn't know her very well, either."

"You weren't that close anymore?'

"I thought we were. But in the past three months, Marti changed. I never really knew where she was, and I tried to reach her several times but she didn't answer my phone calls. In fact, the last time I actually talked to her, now that I think of it, was one day about six months ago. I saw her here, driving down a street in Monterey. I remember the day because it was when President Chase was here to speak to that environmental group at the Monterey Bay Aquarium. You remember that, Jeffrey?"

He nods, but does not look at all happy.

"Foam Street was closed," I recall, "and as I turned down one of the alternate routes, there she was, going the opposite direction. I waved to her and we both pulled over and talked a few minutes."

"About anything in particular?" Sol asks.

"No, just that she was here to do that piece on the homeless, and I was on my way to a...luncheon." I must have sounded like a fool, I think. A rich, aimless fool.

"I never saw her again after that," I say softly. "Until the other day, that is. On the, uh...the hill." My eyes tear, and I look away.

Sol heaves his bulky frame up and groans again, stretching. "You got any soda water?"

"Sure. Your stomach bothering you?"

"Like a blazing oven."

"Sol, you should see a doctor."

"Doctor! Ha. The day I put myself in the hands of one of those shysters is the day I'm dead."

Sol saw his wife die from the wrong medication, prescribed by a doctor and administered in a hospital. I pour him a glass of soda water from the sideboard.

Jeffrey seems unusually quiet. Even Sol seems to notice.

"Jeffrey? You worried about something?"

"Of course I'm worried," he snaps. "This is the last thing I need right now, with the election only a month away. If voters get wind we're being investigated by the Secret Service, it won't matter why. The press will build it up into something Abby—or I—have supposedly done wrong, and by the time they're finished making things up, it could very well rub off on Chase. I haven't backed him for the past twelve years, from the time he was a raw-nosed congressman, to have him lose this reelection."

Gary Chase, with Jeffrey's help, climbed the ladder rapidly on the heels of a president who had been dragged through the mud for sexual "indiscretions" in the Oval Office. When squeaky-clean Chase appeared on the scene, he was a breath of fresh air for voters. A shoo-in.

"Jeffrey," Sol says, "I think you're exaggerating the importance of this visit from the Secret Service. They obviously want to know about Marti Bright, not you."

Jeffrey makes an impatient gesture. "You know better than that. Once you open a can of worms… dammit, Sol, I want you to get them off our backs. Throw a few bills at them."

Sol looks at me, and I shrug and walk to the window, staring out at the fairy lights over the arbor gate. We're getting into fantasyland territory now, I know. Jeffrey's fantasy—that money can fix everything.

"I promise you, Jeffrey," Sol says, "that would only make them want to question you more. Look, this will pass. They'll find a suspect. And if it ever does come out that you and Abby were questioned, you both say it was all part of a routine investigation. Which it was. Right, Abby?"

"Right, Sol."

But I can see from his eyes that he's not so sure.

"I don't care, I don't like it," Jeffrey says angrily. "I didn't even know that woman. Sol, I'm telling you, I won't talk to them. Let Abby handle it."

"My, how gallant of you, my husband."

"For God's sake, Abby, there's more at stake here than a little inconvenience for you! And it makes sense for them to question you, while it makes no sense whatsoever for them to question me."

But Sol is adamant. "You will have to talk to them, Jeffrey. This is the Secret Service, not the kinds of political clowns you're used to dealing with. I will go with you to this meeting in the morning, and you will tell them everything you know—or don't know, which is more to the point. They will be satisfied that you cooperated and that will be the end of it. Otherwise—" he shrugs, as if washing his hands of his client "—I don't see how I can help you."

There is a long silence as the fire crackles and Jeffrey considers his options. Finally he sighs.

"All right, all right. But I want you to be a buffer,

Sol. Like in a courtroom. Don't let them grill me or anything.''

"For heaven's sake," I snap, "what the hell are you so worried about? What could you possibly say that could incriminate you in Marti's death?"

It is a hypothetical question, one of those things you say when you fully expect the answer to be, "Absolutely nothing."

Jeffrey gives me a look I can only interpret as fear. It startles me, and after a moment I look away, confused.

"Sol?" I say. "Go home and tend to your ulcer. And thanks for coming. We'll be okay."

He nods. "I'll see you in the morning, Jeffrey. Meet me at the Carmel P.D. a few minutes before ten so we can get all our ducks in a row."

Jeffrey is already reaching for his coat and briefcase, which he keeps by the door. "Wait up, Sol. I'll walk you to your car. Abby? Don't forget to lock up. I'll be late."

Meaning, he won't be home at all.

"Right," I say, downing my drink. "Give my best to my sister."

After Jeffrey and Sol leave, I go into the kitchen to finish up with the cleaning and to think. This news about Justin has thrown me; I don't know where to go from here. *Speak to me, Marti. Tell me what to do.*

But my old friend is as silent now as she was for the last three months of her life.

I am at the sink, washing a plate, when I sense

movement behind me. *I should be alone. All the guests went home hours ago.*

Murph? No, Jeffery put Murph in the garage to keep him away from the guests. In all the turmoil, I've forgotten to let him out.

I go stiff, my hand gripping the sponge as my mind runs wild. I have a blue belt in Kenpo, but that doesn't even occur to me now. My fingers find a knife at the bottom of the dishpan, and I grab it, whirling around.

"Hey, easy! It's only me!"

The fight goes out of me, but not the fear. I lean back against the sink, breathing heavily.

"Tommy? What the hell are you doing here?"

He smiles a bit nervously. "Actually, I'm embarrassed to admit this, but I never left. See, you left me in here, and then I saw you go into your office down there in the hall with those guys, and I heard your husband sending everyone home. Then he was on the phone and I wasn't sure what to do...so I just went out and waited on the patio. When I saw you in here again, I came back in. I'm sorry if I startled you."

My pulse is still racing. "You were out there all this time?"

He nods. "Most of it. I came back in once to get a drink of water. Look, are you going to jab me with that thing?"

I am still shaky, but I drop the knife in the sink, dry my hands on a towel and collapse into a chair at the kitchen table.

"You sure have quick instincts," Tommy says, seating himself across from me.

"You scared the hell out of me," I say.

"I really am sorry. I know it's been a tough day for you. Can I get you something?"

I shake my head. "I'm just tired. I really need to be alone now. If you don't mind?"

"Sure. I'll go. Can I just ask you something first?"

"I suppose."

"Why do you stay with that jerk husband?"

My breath catches. "You were listening to us?"

"I only heard a little bit when I came in for that water. But it was enough. Abby, I always thought you, like Marti, would take the world by storm."

"I didn't even realize you noticed me, Tommy."

"Sure I did. You just didn't notice me."

To that, I have no answer.

"Can I ask another question?"

Oh, for God's sake. This is like dealing with a five-year-old. I rub my face with my hands, push back my hair and sigh. "Go ahead."

"Abby, how come you're not taking the world by storm? You were a really good writer. Still are, judging by that great piece you did for the *Chron,* about water rights. How come you didn't keep writing that stuff? Why are you wasting your time on some little column in a local newspaper?"

"It's not just 'some little column,'" I argue. "I enjoy it. That other stuff is behind me."

"You sound like your life is over, or you've given up, or something."

Again I sigh. "Tommy, I'm far too busy for my life to be over. I'm also far too busy to write *serious stuff.*"

"Too busy giving parties for your jerk husband, you mean?"

I shove my chair back. "That's enough! Where the hell you get off talking to me like this, I can't imagine. You come here, a virtual stranger—"

"It's because I'm a stranger I can talk to you like this, Abby. I haven't got anything at stake. You throw me out, I'm gone. It's over. But I hope you don't do that. You sure need somebody to talk to."

"I *have* somebody to talk to."

"The cop? You can't talk to him about everything. He's too involved."

Tommy is right about that. There are things I keep from Ben all the time.

"Look, I'm fine," I argue. "Except that I'm tired. Please leave, Tommy. I'll call you a cab to take you back to the hotel, or the airport, or whatever."

"The hotel," he says. "I think I'll stick around a while."

"Like I said, whatever." I am too exhausted to think what this means.

"Abby, I'll leave now. But may I come back tomorrow?"

He sounds like that five-year-old again, asking if he can have an ice-cream cone. I look at his earnest, thin face and give in. He, too, has lost someone this week.

"Yes, you can come back tomorrow. But I'll be busy in the morning."

"I know. With the Secret Service."

My voice turns sharp. "Dammit, no, Tommy, that must be something you missed. Jeffrey is the one they want to see tomorrow."

It is only now I realize I never told him about Ben, either. He said "the cop." How did he know about Ben?

"Tommy…" I stand facing him with my arms folded. "You are not who I thought you were. Are you?"

"Maybe not." His eyes are dead serious. "But you aren't who I thought you were, either."

6

When Tommy is gone, I call Ben. While it may be true that I keep things from him at times, my cup runneth over. I need to download.

I also need to know if Mauro and Hillars told him about Justin by now. If so, what is everyone—or anyone—doing to find him?

"Can you come over?" I ask Ben when I reach him. "I really need to see you."

"What about Jeffrey? I'd prefer not to have a repeat of the other night."

"He's with Karen."

"Oh. The bimbo."

I smile. "Thanks."

"Anytime."

Ben is one of the men Karen put the moves on, back when he was still married. He fought her off, and there's no love lost between them now.

"Give me thirty minutes," he says. "I need to shower."

"Make it fifteen. We'll shower together."

"Did I ever tell you you're the love of my life?"

"I can't believe you came here, after the other night."

We are on the floor before the fire, and Murphy is

wriggling under our blanket, doing his best to insert his very large body between us.

"You sounded like you meant it when you said you needed me," Ben says. "Ouch. Darn it, Murph. Go 'way."

"He didn't bite you, did he? Murph, go lie down." Murphy wiggles out from under the cover and plants himself by the hearth with a solid, unhappy thump.

"No, but his nails are sharp. Almost as bad as yours." Ben nuzzles my ear as I run my nails along his back, showing him just how sharp they can be. He comes inside me in a friendly, comforting way. We lie together silently for several moments.

"You feel good," he murmurs.

"You feel better."

He begins to move slowly, not rushing things.

"Oh, even better."

"Tell me about your day," he says.

"*Now?*"

"Sure, we can make it last longer that way."

I very much doubt that, but I try.

"Well, it's been a, uh, horrible day," I manage, wrapping my legs around him and pulling him closer.

"The funeral, you mean?" His breath quickens. "Or something else?"

"Something...something else. The Secret Service. Were. Were here."

He moves faster suddenly, and it's all I can do to think straight.

"Mauro and Hillars?" He pants. "What the hell did they want?"

"They...they were asking...dammit, Ben, slow

down, I can't...no, don't slow down, don't slow down, don't..."

"Questions," he breathes. "They were asking you..."

"Marti. About Marti." I roll us over till I'm on top. It won't be long now. I start talking faster. "They wanted to know all kinds of things about her, yeah, that's it, who she knew, if she'd had an affair, yeah, right there, and I'm pretty sure they know about the baby—"

"Baby," Ben breathes.

"Marti...baby."

"Baby," he breathes again, over and over, as we come together. Grabbing my hair, he brings my mouth down to his and moans "Baby, baby," against my lips. After a few moments he rolls us both onto our sides, staying inside me.

Finally he lets out a loud, "Oh, God," and falls back. "I don't think I've ever interviewed a witness like this before."

"You don't *think?*" I punch him on the shoulder.

So much for making it last.

"I don't get it," Ben says. We are in the kitchen, drinking fresh-squeezed orange juice. "What do they want with Jeffrey? He didn't really know her, did he?"

"No. He never wanted to. I always felt he was jealous of our friendship."

Ben shakes his head. "There's something else going on here."

It is at this point I would ask him, if I were going

to, if he knows about Justin's kidnapping. But something holds me back.

"You think maybe they're after Jeffrey for something," Ben asks, "and investigating Marti's death is a cover story?"

"That never even occurred to me," I say, surprised. "What would they be after Jeffrey for?"

"Hell, Abby, Jeffrey is involved in so much crap. Who knows? By the way, who was that guy I saw you leaving the funeral with?"

"His name is Lawrence. Tommy Lawrence. I knew him in high school."

"I thought you went to an all-girl school."

"I did. He had a thing for Marti and used to come over from St. John's and hang around. That's why he came for her funeral."

"That was a nice touch," he muses, "putting flowers on her grave."

I'm used to Ben thinking like a cop, but this time I look at him sharply. "You think it wasn't genuine?"

"I don't know, what do you think?"

"It seemed real enough to me. He came back to the house and helped me in the kitchen. We talked."

"Where is he now?"

"At the La Playa. Said he decided to stay a few days. Ben, there is one thing. He was here when Mauro and Hillars were talking to me. I thought everyone had left, but Tommy had just gone out to the patio, and at some point he came back inside. I think he overheard a lot of what we said."

"Did he tell you he heard?"

"Not Mauro and Hillars, but Jeffrey and I were

talking afterward, and it wasn't a pleasant conversation. Then Sol came, and he asked me a lot of questions. All this time I thought we were alone in the house, but Tommy was out there listening.''

"He admitted that?''

"He asked me why I stayed with Jeffrey. 'That jerk,' he called him. And he seems to know an awful lot about us. Even you. He says he asked questions at the hotel bar because he was curious.'' I shrug. "He's a writer.''

"You think that explains it?''

"It could.''

"Maybe,'' Ben says. "And maybe I should have a talk with this guy.''

"Ben…if you do, be gentle, okay? He was pretty broken up over what happened to Marti.''

"Maybe,'' he says again.

I look at him. "Okay, tell me.''

"Nothing I can put a finger on. I just have a feeling about the guy.''

As I've said before, I have come to respect Ben's instincts. I, too, have not been entirely at ease with Tommy Lawrence. Still, I can't help saying, "Ben, I know from these past couple of days what it feels like to be treated as a suspect. I just wouldn't want that to happen to him—not if he's innocent, that is.''

"Don't worry,'' Ben says. "And don't worry about yourself, either. I told Mauro and Hillars you were okay.''

"Okay?''

"Not a suspect, so far as the Carmel P.D. is concerned. I told him I've known you for years and you're pure as the driven snow.''

I smile. "Well, that might be a bit of an exaggeration."

"Actually, that's what Mauro said." Ben grins.

"And Hillars?"

"Stiff upper lip, no comment."

"Not likely. I've got a feeling Hillars is commenting all the time. He just doesn't do it out loud."

Jeffrey not only doesn't come home that night, he doesn't come by in the morning for clothes. When he also doesn't show for the meeting at ten with the Secret Service, an agitated Sol—followed by an even more agitated Agent Mauro—calls here, demanding to know where he is. I tell them both he's probably at Karen's and give Agent Mauro the number.

"I've already tried that," Mauro tells me.

"You know about Karen?" I say. "Why, of course you do. I'll bet you have a camera in her bedroom."

"Ms. Northrup, please don't test my patience," he responds with a sigh. "Not today."

"I'll do my best. So Jeffrey wasn't there?"

"She says he never showed up last night."

"Then I don't know where he is."

"No idea at all?"

"Look, Agent Mauro, I'm sure you've already checked his office in Carmel. So no, I haven't a clue."

"You don't sound surprised that we can't find him."

"I'm not. I've had a lot of practice at not knowing where my husband is."

"Ms. Northrup," he says in the tone a teacher uses

when warning a student to get his homework in on time, "it's my duty to inform you that if we haven't heard from your husband by noon, we'll have to consider him a suspect. I won't hesitate to have an APB issued for him at noon sharp. You might tell him that if you hear from him."

"An All Points Bulletin? Cool. I hope they have more luck finding Jeffrey than I ever have."

Agent Mauro hangs up on me.

I ruffle Murphy's fur and think about Marti, hanging there on that bleak, ungodly hill.

Marti, where is Justin? Who would kidnap him, and why? Is he being taken care of? Is he cold? Injured? Afraid?

Or worse?

Compared to this, nothing seems important enough to worry about—not Jeffrey, and definitely not the goddamned Secret Service.

After a while I make my way to the kitchen for a second cup of coffee. Taking a lined yellow pad and pencil, I sit at the table in the breakfast nook and begin to write.

Point one: Mauro and Hillars are working in the dark, despite all their surprising knowledge of Jeffrey, Marti and me. They wouldn't have questioned me last night if they really knew anything, or even had a good lead on Justin's kidnapper and Marti's killer.

Point two: They haven't told Ben about Justin's kidnapping. If they had, he would have mentioned it to me. I think.

Point three: I haven't mentioned the kidnapping to Ben. Why not?

And finally: How in the name of God are the Ryans handling all this?

A bright, white sun drifts through the tree over the patio, warming my arms with dappled light. The mental fog I've been walking around in since the day my friend was murdered begins to lift. It is almost as if Marti is talking to me: "You promised you'd watch over him, Abby. Don't let me down now."

Drying my hands, I leave a message on the answering machine for Jeffrey, telling him about Agent Mauro's call and about the APB. Then I throw a jacket over my jeans and sweater, grab my keys, say goodbye to Murph and give him the Beggin' Strip he always expects when I leave. In the garage I have a choice between a two-year-old BMW convertible and the car I've lovingly dubbed the Green Hornet—a '92 Jeep Cherokee I bought to beat around town in. Actually, I bought it in the first days after finding out about Jeffrey and Karen. For some crazy, obscure reason I wanted to follow them, catch them together as many times as possible, and the Jeep was more anonymous than the BMW. There are almost as many green Jeep Cherokees in this town as there are jewel heists, which is saying a lot.

Climbing into the Jeep, I pull out of the garage and check to see if anyone is watching the house or following me. The coast seems clear, but even so I watch the cars behind me all the way to Pacific Grove. When there's no one on my tail, I have to assume Mauro and Hillars are either too busy looking for Jeffrey, or Ben's done a good job at keeping them off my back for a while.

Even so, once in Pacific Grove I run a diversion tactic, turning right off Forest, then left and left again a few blocks down, which puts me back on Forest. No one follows me through the neighborhoods, and all the cars that were on Forest have long since passed by. Another few blocks and I turn right at Aberdeen, driving up the hill to Seadrift, an area of upscale homes sprinkled with a few graceful old Victorians.

I stop halfway down the block from a well-kept historical beauty, yellow with white lace curtains and gingerbread trim. There I sit in the Jeep for a few minutes, engine off, getting a feel for the neighborhood. I have seldom seen anyone out and about, as most home owners here work to keep up house payments. Still, I must be certain.

Just check on him now and then, that's all I ask, Abby. Don't intrude. Don't let anyone know you're doing it, not even the Ryans. Not unless you see or hear something's wrong.

"Well, something's wrong, Marti," I whisper. "It's damned wrong. Now tell me what to do."

Given the circumstances, it seems almost too quiet at the Ryans' Victorian. Shouldn't there be activity of some kind?

Mauro did say it had been three months since Justin was kidnapped. It wouldn't be unusual for the first hectic days of activity to have slowed down. And if the FBI and police were never told...

He said there were negotiations in progress.

I have never heard of negotiations in a kidnapping taking that long.

I have watched the Ryans and checked on them long enough—fifteen years, now—to know they are caring, loving parents. How could they stand to keep silent about their adopted son's disappearance for three months?

It has been more than three months since I've been here. And for that I feel guilty. In the past I have tried to check on Justin at least once a month. When he was younger, I volunteered to work in his school library, and as he's grown I've gone to swim and track meets, then basketball and baseball games, depending on his age and the seasons. Never once have I approached either him or the Ryans, nor would they know of my connection to Marti if they were to see me in the crowd. But I've watched as Marti's son greeted his parents at these events, as they praised and supported him, and I've never seen anything but love in the way they treated him.

My surveillance, however, if one could call it that, stopped six months ago. Since Jeffrey brought Karen into our home that day, I have been distracted by the final death throes of my marriage. Though I have tried to maintain a sense of humor and even admitted that my marriage was long over by then, the one thing I've been unable to admit to anyone is how the betrayal—both by my husband and my sister— rocked me. Even my work has suffered as I've thrown most of my energies into becoming absorbed with Ben, losing myself in him and in our affair.

I wasn't here when your son needed me, Marti. If I had been, I might have seen something. Someone hanging around, someone watching for an opportunity to grab a fifteen-year-old kid.

Desperately, I defend myself. *How could I have known? Justin is not weak. He's thin and wiry, but strong—like you, Marti. He's a star on his swim team and excels at track. How could I know someone could come out of the blue and take him away?*

My arguments aren't enough, even for me. Marti charged me with Justin's safety. I've let them both down.

When there are no other cars on the street for several minutes, I slide from the Jeep and cross to the other side, walking up the block to the Victorian. Taking the steps, I am thinking of what to say to Justin's adoptive mother, whom I have never met. How do I gain her trust? I need her to talk to me.

No one, however, answers the bell when I ring. After a minute or so I knock. Still no one, and though I strain to hear, there are no sounds of movement on the other side of the door.

I know Mary Ryan doesn't work. She might, of course, be out shopping, running errands, or whatever a mom might do when her kid has been gone three months.

There is no garage, and the Taurus wagon I've seen before in the drive isn't there.

Frustrated, I turn to leave. A voice drifts across the small, well-tended yard from the house next door. An elderly, white-haired woman stands on a porch lined with Halloween pumpkins. It's still three weeks till Halloween, and the pumpkins are starting to cave in on themselves.

"Are you looking for the Ryans?" she asks in a querulous voice.

"Yes," I say, walking to the edge of the Ryans' porch. "Do you know where they are?"

"Well, they're not there," she says. "They've gone away."

"Really? Do you know where?"

"They're in Europe," she says. "France, actually. They'll be gone a while."

It is not unusual for people on the Peninsula to travel abroad, spending only half the year in their homes here. But I've never know the Ryans to do that.

And why would they, when their son has been kidnapped? Wouldn't they want to be right here, in case he came home?

I shiver, as fear grips me. *Marti, this is all wrong. It's terribly wrong.*

I go down the steps and cross the yard, approaching the neighbor. "Did they leave an address? Or a phone number?"

"Who are you?" she asks, suspicious suddenly. "I probably shouldn't be telling you all this."

There is a Neighborhood Watch sign on one of her front windows, so I'm not surprised she's being cautious—though it might have been better if she'd thought of this sooner.

"I'm the mom of one of Justin's friends," I say. "From school. I have something for Justin."

"Oh. Well, I guess it wouldn't hurt, then. They did ask me to forward their mail, so I've got an address. Wait there a minute."

She goes inside her house and comes out a few

minutes later with a piece of paper. I go up the steps and take it from her, glancing at the address. It is on a street I can't pronounce, in Paris, France.

"Did they take Justin with them?" I ask. "We haven't seen him at school this fall, so we thought he might be sick."

"Oh, no, he's fine. A good boy, that one. Good to his mother and father, not like mine. Never call, never visit."

The corners of her mouth droop as she peers at me through eyes that are clouded with beginning cataracts. "You wouldn't know. You have to live a while to see what that's like."

"I'm sorry," I say. "I can only guess how that must feel. Did, uh, did Justin go with the Ryans?"

She nods. "They got permission for him to be out of school a while. Had to take his books, Mary said, and did he ever grumble about that."

"Did they say how long they'd be gone?"

For the first time she hesitates. "I suppose you could find that out from the school..."

"Oh, I'm sure I could. I was just out running errands and thought I'd drop by instead."

She nods again, as if that makes sense. "They didn't give me any notice at all the day they were leaving, don't you know, just took it for granted I'd be here to collect their mail. I always have, of course. And they collect mine, it works both ways. Not that I go away all that much, air travel being what it is these days. All you do is stand and wait, stand and wait, and my hip's not all it used to be, so just walking from gate to gate..." A look of disapproval tightens her lips.

"I know," I say. "It's getting worse every year. Mrs....?"

"Jeffers," she says. "Like Robinson Jeffers, the poet. No relation, though it would certainly be nice if he were. He built that nice stone house in Carmel, you know, built it with his own hands. I suppose if he had any children, they didn't mind visiting *him*, not there."

"Mrs. Jeffers, did you happen to see them leave?"

"The Robinson Jefferses?"

"No, no, the Ryans. Did you see them?"

"Land, no. Left in the middle of the night, without so much as a goodbye."

I see doubt working on her mind. Something she never thought of before, but it's been brought to the fore and given importance by my questions. Her eyelids flicker, and she looks hesitant again. "You know, it did seem odd."

"That they left in the middle of the night?"

"No, them taking their own car. That's how I know when they left, I heard them pull out. You can't leave your car for months at the airport, don't you know. Unless, of course, you're rich. It's a lot cheaper to take a cab."

"You're right, Mrs. Jeffers, you're absolutely right. By the way, when did they leave?"

"Oh, I'd say several weeks ago now. A couple of months, at least."

I don't know what to make of any of this. Thanking her, I say, "Well, I'm sorry I missed them. But it's good to know Justin's all right. My son misses him."

I turn to leave, but she is still talking. "Oh, they did, too," she says, "like the dickens."

I turn back. "They?"

"The Ryans. Missed that boy like crazy."

"I don't understand. You said they all went together."

"No, young lady, that is not what I said. People think I get confused, but I don't. The fact is, Justin left a full month before they did."

Now it's I who am confused. "I don't...how do you know this?"

"Well, Mary told me herself," she says. "They had their tickets all ready in July. But Paul—Mr. Ryan, he's a lawyer, don't you know—couldn't leave because of his work. So they sent Justin ahead. And by the time they got to leave, she was missing him like crazy."

"She told you that? About missing him?"

She shakes her head and makes a clucking sound with her tongue. "Poor thing, she didn't have to. I used to see her out my kitchen window. It faces hers, you know. I'd see her crying like her heart was broken. She was so close to that boy."

"But then why would she have sent him on ahead?"

"Because," she says patiently, "he had to be there on time to attend a semester at a special school. Didn't I say that?"

"No, no you didn't."

"It was some grant he'd won, they said, to study history or something. That's why he got excused from school here."

"So Justin actually left three months ago? In July? And the Ryans didn't leave until August?"

"That's what I said." She peers at me curiously. "I'm surprised Mary didn't tell your boy that Justin was gone. But then, like I say, they didn't give me much notice when they left, either. A bit rude, if you ask me."

I risk one more question. "Has anybody else been here asking for the Ryans?"

She shakes her head. "Not a soul. Well, the Jehovahs, of course, the two of them all dressed up in their Sunday best. Land, they've been around so much lately you'd think we might give them the mail to deliver. Save us poor taxpayers some money."

"Not a bad idea," I say with a smile. "And isn't it interesting, how they always come in twos." *Mauro and Hillars, or I miss my guess.*

Mrs. Jeffers narrows her eyes at me. "They asked questions just like you. I didn't tell them much. So whatever it is that's wrong with the Ryans, you don't have to worry."

I look at her in surprise.

"Hah. Thought you fooled me, didn't you?" she says with a sly cackle.

"Fooled you?"

"Well, it's pretty obvious something's going on. I didn't tell *them* that, though."

"Them? The Ryans?"

"Missy, will you please pay attention?" she says. "The Jehovahs. I didn't tell them a thing."

Back in the Jeep, I look at the address Mrs. Jeffers gave me.

Okay, so now what, Marti?

The Ryans are gone. Left two months ago, a full month after Justin disappeared. Their cover story to the neighbors and his school was that he'd been granted a scholarship to study in Paris for a semester. Then they left. For Paris. In their car.

Hope it has paddle wheels.

Remember, Marti, the time in high school when we took the paddleboat out on that man-made lake and the paddles got tangled in the tops of trees they'd flooded? You were more worried about hurting the trees than getting back to shore, and you...

Shut up, Abby. Stop dwelling.

I sigh. All right, then. Let me think. There could be any number of explanations for the Ryans having left in their car. They drove it to a friend's house to garage it while they were gone, and the friend drove them to the airport—either here or in San Francisco. If here, they would have had to take a commuter plane to S.F. There are no flights out of Monterey to Europe.

Unless, perhaps, you have a private plane.

Did the Ryans have access to a private plane?

But no, go back. The Paris trip was clearly a made-up story to cover Justin's disappearance.

So the parents probably didn't go there, either.

Where, then, are they?

If they left a month after their son disappeared, in August, does that mean they heard from him? Went to find him?

Did they have some clue as to where he might be?

And if so, did they tell anyone? Marti, for instance?

They did tell her the boy was gone. Mauro and Hillars said Marti was the one who told the first family that Justin had been kidnapped. She went to them for help when her own efforts failed.

The Ryans, of course, knew from the first that Marti was Justin's birth mother. I helped to set up the adoption, through Sol. Not that the Ryans or anyone else, even Jeffrey, knew of my involvement. And to my knowledge, Marti never went near Justin once she gave him up.

Funny how Mauro and Hillars didn't think to share with me that the Ryans were gone, too.

How long have they known?

And where the hell are they?

The Ryans, that is. I don't have to wonder about Mauro and Hillars, I think, glancing into my rearview mirror. They're in a spanking-new black Volvo, right behind me.

"This is not a good idea," Agent Mauro says, leaning into my car window. "We must ask you to stay away from here, Ms. Northrup."

"Well, then," I say in my best annoyed voice, "I must ask you to tell me why. And where are the Ryans?"

"I can't answer that," he says. "Please, Ms. Northrup, leave here now. Go home and forget about this."

"Sorry, I can't do that. I promised Marti I'd look after Justin."

"The best way to help Justin is to stay out of it."

"Out of what?" I say angrily. "What do you

know? Who are you negotiating with for his release? And why is it taking so damned long?''

''I can't tell you that.''

I turn my key in the ignition. ''Then I'll have to find out some other way.''

His expression hardens. ''Ms. Northrup, may I remind you that you could still be a suspect in the murder of Marti Bright? Your name was written into the ground where she died. Her brother thinks you are somehow responsible for her death. And, there are other things—'' He pauses, then clamps his mouth shut.

''Other things? Like what?''

''Suffice it to say we have not yet taken action against you out of deference to Detective Schaeffer, who has vouched for you. That could change at any moment.''

''You mean if I'm not a good little girl and do as you say, you'll arrest me?''

''No, I mean if I decide I have probable cause, I'll arrest you.''

''Agent Mauro, don't try a bluff with me. I did not kill Marti Bright, and there is no way you can prove I did.''

''Perhaps not at the moment,'' he says smoothly, ''but if your husband doesn't turn up soon, I could take you in for aiding and abetting a felon, obstructing justice, and/or harboring a fugitive. After a few days in a cell, who knows what you might admit to?''

''Now you're really stretching it. The only thing I'm harboring is my dog. Last I heard, that wasn't against the law.''

Agent Mauro's grip tightens on my open window. "Ms. Northrup, we've issued an APB and a warrant for your husband's arrest, and your sister—Karen Dean, that would be—claims you are the one person who would know where he is."

The little bitch.

"My sister," I say, "is crazy, and she's got it in for me. She wants to marry Jeffrey, and she thinks I'm the one holding up the divorce. If anyone's hiding him, it's her."

"And Marti Bright's brother, Ned Bright? He's crazy, too? Everyone's crazy but you, is that right, Ms. Northrup?"

"Of course not. But according to Henry Kissinger, even the paranoid have enemies."

"This is the way you want to play this, then? Junior G-girl running around town trying to solve crimes, getting in the way of our investigation?"

"If you don't tell me what's going on, you leave me no choice." But in truth, I am getting worried.

Mauro opens my car door, which I've forgotten to lock.

"Please turn off your engine and step out of the car, Ms. Northrup."

"I damn well will not."

"Don't make a scene."

"A scene? You haven't seen anything till you've seen—"

Dammit it to hell, I'm losing it. My face feels hot and my hands are shaking.

"Unless you have a warrant for my arrest, I'm not going anywhere with you," I say, steadying my voice till it's quiet yet firm.

"Dale?" he calls out to Hillars, who's sitting in the Volvo. "Come help me with this, will you? We're taking Ms. Northrup for a little talk."

"You can't do this," I protest as Hillars joins us. But to no avail. Mauro reaches in, turns off the engine and shoves my keys under the mat. I am pulled from the car and handcuffed faster than I can blink.

I have never been so afraid in my life.

They don't take me to the Carmel P.D., but to a hotel room at the Embassy Suites in Seaside. They take me up back stairs so that no one can see us. There is no one else in the room but the three of us, and they sit me in a chair at an oversize table. My hands are cuffed in front of me now, and there is a glass of water on the table, which I am allowed to drink from.

We have been here over two hours, and I get it now. These two have a mission, and they've been given carte blanche to carry it out. They are more dangerous than rogue cops; they have the power and they don't give a damn about rules.

If I thought I was afraid before, I am deep-down frightened now.

"Let's go over this again," Mauro says, pacing. "Tell us about your husband."

"What about him? If you'd tell me what you're after—"

"Where is he?" Mauro interrupts.

"I told you, I don't know. Jeffrey goes away all the time. He seldom tells me where."

"If your marriage is that troubled, why haven't you divorced?"

"That's none of your business."

"It's our business if it would give us some insight as to why he's disappeared."

"Aren't you being a bit melodramatic? Jeffrey is probably just off on one of his usual business trips. For that matter, he may be with your boss."

Mauro gives me a look.

"The president?" I say. "The man who sent you here?"

"Why would your husband be with President Chase?" he asks.

"Oh, come on. Don't tell me you don't know they're thick as thieves, you'll pardon the expression. Jeffrey's the man behind the man."

Mauro's eyes narrow. "What exactly are you saying, Ms. Northrup?"

"For heaven's sake, Jeffrey's a mover and shaker. The power behind the throne. When Jeffrey says jump, Chase jumps."

Mauro looks at Hillars, who shakes his head. Whether what I've said is news to them or not, this is clearly not territory they want to travel.

"There's one thing you told us the other day that doesn't fit," Mauro says.

"Only one?"

Mauro frowns, and for a brief moment I think he might like to strangle me. I catch Hillars watching him, and wonder if his main job here is as a restraint or balance for his younger and testier partner.

"You told us you don't know who Justin Ryan's biological father is," Mauro says. "If you and Marti Bright were as close as we know you were, you must at least have some clue."

"Well, I don't. She showed up at my house in labor. I never met the man."

"She would have had to file a birth certificate," Mauro insists. "And you were with her at the hospital."

Again, I am amazed at how much he knows. However, he apparently hasn't been able to find the birth certificate, doesn't know to look for it under "Maria Gonzalez," the phony name Marti used in the hospital.

Score one for our team, whatever good it does.

"As I remember, she listed the father as 'Unknown,'" I say truthfully. "She said he was someone she met while she was traveling, and she didn't want him involved. Look, why is this so important?"

"It's important if the father found out he had a son by Marti Bright and saw her silence about the boy as betrayal. If he was a bit off in the first place, that might have sent him over the edge. He might then have kidnapped the boy, and if this is the case, he might then have murdered Marti Bright in some sort of blind rage."

"That's a lot of ifs and thens, Agent Mauro."

"We have to consider all the angles, Ms. Northrup."

My patience, and fear, are wearing thin. I slap my hands down on the table. The handcuffs jangle on the dark wood.

"How's this for an angle, then? Marti traveled with a lot of people that year. One of them was a young congressman named Gary Chase. Why don't you ask him if he's Justin's father, and if that's why he really sent you here to look for Justin? Ask Mr.

Squeaky-Clean if he went into a rage on the campaign trail and kidnapped his illegitimate child, then crucified his mother on that goddamned hill!''

I can see I've hit a nerve. Hillars pales, and Mauro stops in his tracks.

Is this something they haven't considered? I myself haven't considered it seriously till now—though I must confess I've wondered. It was something I heard on television once, when Chase was on vacation—that he'd gone to his ''cabin in Maine.''

Marti spent the last three months of her pregnancy in a cabin in Maine. When I heard on television that Chase had such a cabin, I wondered if he was the ''friend'' who had loaned it to her. Marti did travel on press junkets with Chase back then, when he was still a congressman.

Good God. *Could* he have been Justin's father? He was married at that time—not available, as Marti said. He wouldn't have been able to help her raise her child.

And if he *is* Justin's father, and Marti revealed that to him, it might explain why he sent his Secret Service agents to help her find Justin. He wouldn't just leave an investigation like that to the FBI or local investigators. He'd send the best he had.

Does Jeffrey know about Marti's baby, then? And is this what he's afraid of? That Chase's secret might come out, creating a scandal just before the election?

Mauro clearly doesn't know what to say. Jamming his hands into the pockets of his dark suit he stares at the ceiling, clears his throat. When he begins again, his voice is under control. The subject has changed.

"Ms. Northrup, this trip to the Ryan house today. I understand it's not your first. You've done this before—often, in fact."

"I have never spoken to the Ryans," I say.

"That's not the point. You've sat outside their house and spied on them."

"I have not *spied* on them. I've been making sure Justin was all right."

"In fact, you've been making sure he was all right quite often, haven't you? Once a month or so for the past fifteen years. Ms. Northrup, you've never had a child of your own, have you? How do you explain this obsession with Justin Ryan?"

Obsession. The word hits me between the eyes.

You're obsessed with wanting a child, Jeffrey has accused me of, more than once. *Obsessed with wanting to adopt. Get over it, for God's sake, it's not healthy. It's an obsession.*

It is not an obsession, I have argued. *It's the healthiest desire in the world, wanting a child.*

But what do I tell these men, who have no concept of how I got to this place in my life, and wouldn't care if they did?

"Ms. Northrup, I asked you a question. You have not had children of your own, have you?"

"I need some food," I say, holding out my trembling hand. "I've got hypoglycemia, low blood sugar. You can't keep me here without food. I could go into shock, and you'd have to haul me off to the hospital. They'd ask questions. Is that what you want?"

Mauro sends me a look that tells me he doesn't really believe me about the blood sugar. Still, I will be out of here, eventually—I hope—and I could talk about abusive treatment at the hands of the Secret Service.

Sighing, he shoves back his chair and goes to the phone, calling room service. "We need three turkey sandwiches," he says, looking at me.

"And coffee," I say.

"Coffee," he adds. "Send up a pot."

When he's finished, he motions to Hillars, who stands and joins him at the window. They whisper to each other, now and then looking at me. I close my eyes and rest my head in my hands, thinking about that word again, *obsession*.

When I met Jeffrey sixteen years ago, I was twenty-three. I'd just gotten a good career rolling as a staff reporter on the *San Francisco Chronicle* and had latched on to a story that, as Tommy said, almost won me the Pulitzer. Then I came down here that fateful day and met Jeffrey. A few months later we married, and I "retired" to Carmel to live out my childhood dream to be a housewife and mother. I was young—and, about relationships, incredibly dumb.

Jeffrey and I never talked, beforehand, about children. When I became pregnant three months after the wedding, he was livid. I thought he just needed some time to get used to it. I realize now, however, that he wanted to be the only child in the family. When I was four months pregnant, Jeffrey took me out on the sailboat he owned, assuring me the water was calm enough even though we'd just had a major storm. "This is the best time to go out," he argued. "It's so wild and dramatic after a storm, Abby. You'll love it."

I can't prove my husband tried to kill our baby. In fact, over time I managed to convince myself that the entire thing had been an accident. That's how badly I wanted to hang on to my marriage back then.

The way I remember it is that Jeffrey swerved sharply and unexpectedly—to avoid a giant piece of driftwood, he told the Coast Guard later, part of the Carmel beach stairs that was dragged all the way to Santa Cruz by the storm's tide. A twenty-foot swell caught us at that moment. I tried to grab on to the rail, but was caught off guard. I went in, and the struggle to stay afloat in the swells and fend off other pieces of driftwood was too much. Eventually, Jeffrey pulled me out, reaching over the rail for my hand. I ended up in the hospital with broken bones, internal injuries and a miscarriage. I was told I'd never have another child.

Marti gave birth to Justin shortly after that, and the space in my heart that would have been filled by a child of my own was filled by Justin, by my promise to look after him always. I saw this as a sacred trust, one I would never break.

I doubt Marti meant for me to make her son a monthly quest. It simply happened that way—one of those day-by-day, month-by-month habits that develops. In this case it grew into a steady stream of years.

And now Justin is gone, disappeared into thin air—just like my child.

I am older and wiser than when I miscarried that first year of my marriage. With the twenty-twenty vision of hindsight, it does not escape me that the reason Mauro and Hillars are so interested in questioning Jeffrey is because they think he might have had a hand in Justin's kidnapping.

But why would Jeffrey have done such a thing?

It would have to be because a connection could be made between Justin and Chase. Everything Jeffrey does lately is either wrapped up in, affected by or affects Chase's reelection.

"Ms. Northrup? I asked you a question."

I come back from my thoughts and look at Mauro, who has taken a seat across from me again. Hillars is on the phone.

"Sorry, what was that?"

"I asked you to tell me everything you can about Helen Asback."

"You mean Sister Helen?"

"I suppose she might still hold that title."

"Still hold it? I don't understand."

"You don't know that Sister Helen, as you know her, has left her order?"

This stuns me. "You mean she changed orders," I argue, though that would still be unbelievable.

"No, I mean she dropped out. Sometime in the eighties. You didn't know this?"

I shake my head, bewildered and still shocked. "No. I told you, I haven't had contact with her in years."

"Exactly how many years?"

"At least twenty. Since Marti and I left the Joseph and Mary Motherhouse."

"But Ms. Bright did have contact with her?"

"I'm not sure. I think she might have, but if so, she never told me."

I still can't quite believe it. Sister Helen no longer

a nun? One might as well say the moon no longer comes up, or the sun has burned itself out.

"How do you know all this?" I ask. "Have you talked with her?"

"Helen Asback?"

"Yes."

"Ms. Northrup," Mauro says with exaggerated patience, "she's the one who sent us to you. Ms. Asback agrees with Ned Bright that you might have had a hand in Marti Bright's murder."

"That's ridiculous! I don't believe it! She was angry with me for leaving the convent, but that was years ago. And why would she say a thing like that? Marti and I were best friends."

"Not according to Helen Asback," Mauro says. "According to her, Marti Bright no longer trusted you. And Marti Bright's brother confirms this."

I feel as if I'm in some Kafkaesque drama where nothing makes sense. Marti no longer trusted me? That can't be true.

Hillars hangs up the phone and comes over to Mauro. They whisper again. Mauro makes a gesture of protest, but Hillars waves a hand as if to settle him down.

Mauro sighs, stands and comes over to me. He takes out a key and unlocks the cuffs.

"I'm afraid you'll miss lunch," he says. "We have to leave."

"And I was so looking forward to it," I say.

Standing, I flex my stiff knees and rub my wrists. Glancing at my watch, I add, "On the other hand, there's still time to see my lawyer about suing you both for false arrest."

"But you haven't been arrested," Mauro says smoothly. "No one booked you. There's no record anywhere of our little chat."

"You mean it's my word against yours? I don't know, Agent Mauro…with the climate of the country today, I have a feeling people will believe an innocent citizen over a couple of renegade Secret Service agents."

Hillars speaks in that slow, thick voice. "I must admit, you may be right about that, Ms. Northrup. However, you also might want to take into consideration the fact that Agent Mauro and I have perhaps the best chance of finding Marti Bright's killer. If you are indeed innocent, you wouldn't want to tie our hands in any way, would you?"

He reaches for my arm. "Come now, let us take you back to your car."

Despite the friendly Southern accent, Agent Hillars makes my skin crawl. "No thanks," I say, stepping back. "I'll take a cab."

They look at each other and shrug, almost in unison, then walk to the door and hold it for me.

As we're leaving, room service arrives. I grab half a sandwich off the cart and stuff it into my mouth, chomping down hard and wishing it were Agent Mauro's arm.

7

BEN

This isn't going as well as I'd hoped, Ben thinks. He sits across from Chief Peter Bridges in his private office and folds his arms. "I just don't feel good about this, Chief. I can't put a surveillance on Abby and not tell her about it. She's a friend."

"Friend? Ben, you think we're all blind around here? You think I don't know what's going on?"

Ben shrugs. "I've tried to be discreet, sir."

"Discreet!" The Chief thumps an inch-high stack of letters on his desk. Taking one from the top, he reads. "'Detective Ben Schaeffer was seen having dinner the other night with a woman many believe to be your chief suspect in the murder of Marti Bright. Not only that, but she writes the town's gossip column. What's going on?'"

He slaps the letter down and takes up another. "'Why aren't the police arresting Abby Northrup? Everybody says she knew Marti Bright, and her name, written in the ground where Marti Bright died, points to her as the killer. What more do the Carmel police need before they arrest her? Or is this just one more case of money greasing palms?'"

He picks up another letter, but Ben holds up a hand.

"You don't have to go on. I get it. But, Chief, we get letters like that all the time. Shit, Carmel's a town where people call the police when they find kids playing in trees. And you remember when somebody called in to report two black men standing on a corner? The caller said they looked suspicious. They were our own cops, for Christ's sake."

Ben leans forward. "You and I both know there isn't any real evidence that Abby killed Marti Bright. I'm telling you, they were best friends. And Abby is not a killer."

Chief Bridges sighs. "Ben, you want to be chief when I leave, or not?"

"You know I do. I very much want that."

"Then you've got to close this case. And you've got to beat those assholes from the Secret Service to the punch. I've got the city council on my back, the city manager's office and a committee of business owners, not to mention residents up the kazoo. This damned crucifixion has hit all the papers nationwide. It's been on *Entertainment Tonight*—did you see that? They're billing it as *Murder in Clint Eastwood-Land.* Some are even calling it the *Crucifixion Murders,* like there's a whole slew of 'em. Our own local *Herald* ran a headline the other day, *Crucified in Carmel.* Shit, Ben, every television station in the country is running this over and over in the news every day, and nobody wants to come here anymore. This damned thing is killing the tourist business, not to mention scaring Peninsula residents half to death. We've got to do something fast."

"The task force is on it," Ben argues. "Everyone's doing their best."

The chief stands, pointing a finger at him. "*You've* got to do something, Ben. You personally. You don't want to have to stand before that board when you come up for promotion and admit you were helpless in the face of the town's first truly gruesome murder. You don't want the Secret Service grabbing all the glory."

"I don't give a damn about the glory," Ben argues.

"No, I'm sure you don't. But for Christ's sake, man, this is a small town. You've got nowhere to go but into my seat. And I want you in it. You've done a damned good job over the years. You care about the people, and they like you. You're smart, and you've built trust and respect, the two primary qualities a cop needs to survive in this town."

Ben is silent.

"Look," the chief says, "put the surveillance on Abby Northrup. She's the best lead we've got."

"Chief..." Ben rubs a hand over his face. "I haven't been entirely honest with you."

Chief Bridges narrows his eyes. "What the hell does that mean?"

"I've been working on this on my own. In my spare time."

"Alone?"

"Well, I've had a little help."

"Lehman?"

Ben shrugs. "He's my right hand. You know that."

The chief studies him with narrowed eyes. "What have you found out?"

"That's just it. Nothing. I don't know why the name Abby was written in the ground out there on the hill. Maybe the killer wrote it. Maybe it's somebody who knows Abby and wanted to throw suspicion on her. But I'm willing to bet that, if Marti Bright wrote it, she was sending a cry for help to Abby, not fingering her as the killer."

Chief Bridges lights a cigar, ignoring the No Smoking sign on his own wall. "You're willing to bet that, are you?"

"Yes, sir. I am."

The chief puffs. He fixes his eyes on Ben, assessing. "You willing to bet your future?"

A small silence. "I hope it won't come to that," Ben says at last.

The chief stares at the stack of letters. "What are you planning?" he asks.

"Right now I want to talk to that nun, the one who knew Marti Bright and Abby years ago. I saw her at the church, then the cemetery, and there's something about her I don't like."

"A nun? You want to finger a *nun* as the killer? Christ, Ben, that's all we need. 'Carmel Arrests Nun in Crucifixion Murder.'"

Ben smiles. "As I understand it, she's not really a nun anymore. And she's bitter."

"Bitter, huh? She live here? She a resident?"

"That's the funny thing. I couldn't find her at first. I tried the motherhouse in Santa Rosa, where nuns from that order used to go to retire. It's been turned into a private school, and there are only a handful of nuns there, the ones that are teaching. One of them told me Sister Helen left the order years ago, back when the motherhouses were closing. I take it she had some problems with that.''

"Doesn't surprise me," Chief Bridges says. "I've got an aunt…'' He shakes his head. "Let's just say the Church would like everybody to forget that some of those old nuns had a rough time of it. What about this Sister Helen?''

"I don't have a complete picture yet, but I talked to Lydia Greyson, the woman who owns the estate where Marti Bright was buried. She and Sister Helen—Helen Asback, now—were at the funeral together, along with Marti Bright's brother. She told me Helen Asback lives out in the Carmel Valley now, at that place called The Prayer House.''

"So how's Lydia Greyson involved?''

"Well, she owns and runs The Prayer House. Other than that, I'm not sure. She is on the board of one of the shelters Marti Bright did some volunteer work at, in Seaside.''

The chief squints through his cigar smoke. "The Prayer House, huh? Odd name. You ever hear of it?''

"A few times lately. There's been some trouble about the food they prepare out there and sell to the public. Apparently some tourist got sick and claimed it was from something made out at The Prayer House. Now there's a lawsuit been filed to make them bring their kitchen up to code, put in all kinds of changes. Sounds to me like a nuisance suit, pure and simple. You know how it is around here. Some people can't even sell soup in coffee shops.''

"So what's this place do besides sell food? I can't say I've heard of it."

"Not many people have. It's a retreat of sorts for nuns and ex-nuns. Selling breads, soup, and stuff to support themselves. That, and private funding. They keep a low profile."

The chief falls silent, thinking. "What do you expect to get out of this woman?" he says at last. "The nun? Ex-nun, whatever."

"I don't really know, Chief. I just think there could be some connection between the people out there and the way Marti Bright died. I mean, a crucifixion…that's not your usual kind of murder. Not only that, but since it happened down there on the hill next to the Carmelite monastery, it could be some religious nut, somebody who's got something against the Catholic Church. Who knows?"

"So, you want to go poking around this Prayer House, stirring up trouble with these nuns, or whoever, and you want me to approve that."

"I'm hoping you will, sir. We haven't got much else." Ben clears his throat. "Leaving Abby out of it, that is."

Chief Bridges leans back in his chair, staring into space. Finally he grinds his cigar out on a clay-molded ashtray.

"You see this?" he says, pointing to the ashtray. "A kid made this for me. He was missing, and I found him myself when I was out on patrol. He was hiding up at the old Flanders mansion."

"I remember, sir."

"Not a chief's job, you know, going out on patrol.

I did it because I had a nose for it. Finding missing kids, that is.''

"I remember," Ben says again.

"I still got a nose, Ben. And my nose tells me Abby Northrup is up to her neck in trouble. I know, I know—you don't agree. And I've learned to trust those damned instincts of yours, maybe better than my own." He stands. "On the other hand, there's the fucking Secret Service. So what do we do? I'll tell you what we do. I'm giving you forty-eight hours. After that, I can't promise anything."

Ben stands. "Thank you, sir."

"Don't thank me. It may not matter, Ben."

"Sir?"

"Not if the Secret Service moves on her first. Word is, Abby Northrup's living on borrowed time."

8

ABBY

My first thought after escaping Mauro and Hillars is to talk to Ben, but when I reach Arnie at the station, he says Ben is out. Just "out." He doesn't seem inclined to elaborate on that, and at any other time this wouldn't worry me. There is, however, an odd note of caution in Arnie's voice when talking to me, and that does concern me.

Arnie says he'll have Ben call. While I wait, I check the messages on my machine, hoping he might have phoned while I was gone. There are twenty-two messages from this morning alone, all but two from newspaper reporters and television stations wanting to talk to me about Marti. One is from Dan Green at KSBW-TV, one of my favorite local anchors, along with Kate Callaghan. I make a mental note to call him back, and to touch base with Kate, too—but not until I have something I feel free to share.

One of the two exceptions is from my boss at the *Pinecone*, reminding me that this week's column is due in the morning. At least they haven't fired me yet.

The other non-media call is from Tommy Lawrence, whom I'd completely forgotten.

"Abby? I came by this morning around eleven, but you weren't home. I guess you forgot, huh? That's okay, I just wanted to check and see when you want to get together again." The number he leaves is one I recognize as the La Playa Hotel.

I sigh, not sure I can deal with Tommy Lawrence today. I delete all the messages, deciding to call him later.

Meanwhile, I make my way upstairs to take a shower in the big bathroom at the end of the hall, which has a heater. My limbs are sore from holding them stiff with fear, and I'm hoping some warmth will help.

While in the shower I hear a noise. "Jeffrey?" I call out.

No answer.

"Jeffrey?"

Still no answer.

For the past six months Jeffrey's been sleeping on a fold-out couch in his downstairs office. Often, he'll slip out the back door and be gone before I know it.

I debate whether to go down there after him. What decides me is that if Mauro and Hillars don't find Jeffrey soon, they'll be after me for "aiding and abetting."

Quickly, I rinse the shampoo from my hair and am wrapping a towel around it when I hear another noise. This time it's much closer, as if coming from the hallway just outside the bathroom door.

"Jeffrey, is that you? I'm in here."

When there's still no response, I wish I hadn't said

that. There's been more than one break-in around here lately. Grabbing a large towel, I wrap it around myself and stand quietly, listening.

Moisture drips down the shower door, clearing the fog away. Suddenly I know why they started making see-through shower doors—so you can know when Norman Bates is out there with his knife.

Unfortunately, the downside is that he can also see you.

There are footsteps in the hallway, closer now. *Get to the door, Abby. Lock it. Call 911 on the wall phone.*

The latch on the shower door clicks as I ease it open. To my ears, the small metallic sound is deafening. I step out onto the tile floor. My bathroom is large, a good nine steps to the door. Do I run to it? Will whoever it is hear and fling the door open before I get there?

There is no time to work it out. My antennae are up, and every instinct is yelling, *Lock the door, Abby!* I make a dash for it, pressing against the wooden panel with all my weight and twisting the lock at the same time. Then I turn to the phone by the sink.

Frantically, I dial 911. But when I lift the receiver to my ear, there is no sound of ringing. Have I hit the wrong buttons? My hand shaking, I dial again. Still nothing. I rattle the receiver, punch buttons and shake the cord.

It is then I remember the short in the wire. I've been meaning to replace this phone, but have put it off. It's dead.

I wonder about Murphy. Where is he? Why hasn't

he barked, or at least growled? Even if it were only Jeffrey out there, he'd growl.

Murph. Oh, God, no, Murph. Visions of the night he was brought home with the letter A etched into his skin flood my mind.

It is this that brings me out of the bathroom without another thought. Arming myself with the only weapon at hand, a can of hair spray, I unlock the door and throw it open, standing off to one side. No body hurtles inward, no bullets fly, and after a moment I risk a look into the hall.

Murphy sits quietly at the top of the stairs, where he's been ever since I got home and came up here to shower. This, in itself, is so odd it's alarming. While he wouldn't normally go after anyone unless they tried to hurt me, he will always bark to alert me when a stranger comes to the house.

Is it Jeffrey after all, then? And if so, why didn't he answer when I called?

There is a noise in my room, like the sliding of drawers. Tiptoeing down the long hallway, I stop a few feet from my bedroom door and pause. I look at Murph and he looks at me. Slowly he rises and comes over to me, pushing his body against my legs as if to stop me.

"What is it, boy?" I whisper. "Tell me."

He only pushes harder.

I have two choices. I can try to make it past the bedroom door, without being seen, and run down the stairs to the living room or kitchen phone.

Or I can see who the hell is in my house.

Anger outweighs fear and I flatten myself against the wall. "Hello, who's there?" I say loudly.

A small silence, then the sound of footsteps coming toward the door. Murph growls.

Rounding the door in a flash, I jam my finger down on the nozzle of the spray can.

"Ow! Ow, dammit! My eyes!"

My sister, Karen, comes barreling toward me, screaming curses like a banshee. She takes a swing and knocks me aside with one hand while rubbing her eyes with the other. "Dammit, Abby, I can't see!"

I drop the spray can, regain my balance, and grab her by the shoulders, shaking her. "What the hell are you doing here? Dammit, Karen, why didn't you answer me?"

I half drag her across the bedroom to the small master bath. Shoving her head over the sink, I cup my hands with cold water and flush the hair spray out of her eyes.

"What the hell did you do that for? Spray me like that," she says, shaking her short blond hair free of water and dabbing her face with a towel. "Jesus, Abby!"

"What are you doing here?" I demand. "And how did you get in?"

"I still have my key," she says, rubbing at her eyes with the towel. "You could have blinded me, Abby. Jesus, you're mean lately."

"Well, if I am, you've given me good reason. What were you doing in there?"

I go back into the bedroom and survey the mess she's made. It's clear she's been rifling through Jeffrey's bureau drawers.

Behind me, I hear her many gold bracelets jangling. "I didn't even know you were home," she says. "You scared me to death sneaking up on me like that."

"*Me* sneaking up on *you*? Karen, may I point out that this is my house?"

She gazes at me defiantly. Her hair, mussed from the toweling, sticks out in all directions. The dark roots are showing, and she seems older than the last time I saw her, five months ago. There are deep circles beneath her brown eyes, eyes that look so much like mine, yet so incomprehensibly different.

"I asked you a question, Karen. What are you doing here? Why are you going through Jeffrey's things?"

"He—he asked me to pick up some clothes. Some shirts, and one of his good suits."

"He did, huh? And when did he ask you to do this?"

"Last night." She gives me a mutinous look. "And, yes, he was with me last night. So what? Why do you give a damn?"

"Believe me, I don't—except that you're lying. I know you told the police, or whoever talked to you this morning, that Jeffrey never showed last night. No one knows where he is."

"Well, don't look at me." She sniffs. "I don't know, either."

Tossing the wet towel on my bed, she crosses to my dressing table, where she sits and calmly brushes her hair. She even has the audacity to start repairing her face with my makeup.

I stand behind her with my arms folded. "I think

you do know," I say. "And dammit, don't give me that look. Where is he, Karen? This is important."

My sister shrugs and continues to outline her lips, making them a quarter size bigger than they really are. As she moves her head, diamond earrings flash. A makeup gift from Jeffrey for his being away so much? He was always good at that.

"I have absolutely no idea where Jeffrey is," she says, pursing her lips. "I haven't seen him for a couple days."

"Then how did you know he wanted his clothes?"

She lifts a too-dark penciled eyebrow. "He called me, little sister. Ever hear of the phone?"

"Okay, he called you. And he told you to pick up some of his clothes. You must know, then, where to take them."

"Actually, Jeffrey didn't say. Well, you know him. He'll show up eventually. Or he'll call and let me know where he is."

"Don't bet on it," I mutter.

"What?"

"Nothing." I am silent, thinking.

"What?" Karen says again. "What?"

"I'm just thinking it's odd Murphy didn't let me know there was a stranger in the house."

My sister's mouth curves into a smile, like a satisfied cartoon cat's. "Well, maybe I'm not all that much of a stranger."

"It's been years since you lived here, Karen."

She gets up from the dressing table and turns to me. Fingering my towel, she flips an end of it and flounces away. "True. But I've been around. Maybe more than you think."

"What does that mean?"

She laughs, the sound so brittle it hurts my ears. "You didn't think that night you caught us together was the first time, did you?"

I can't answer.

She laughs. "Jeffrey and I were sleeping together when I lived here, Abby. We've been together for years—starting with right here in your bed."

It is all I can do to keep from slapping her. "What a little slut you are."

She grabs my arm. "Watch who you're calling a slut, Abby. Won't the good citizens of Carmel—all your socially acceptable friends, that is, not to mention your very devoted readers—be surprised when Jeffrey tells them about you and your little boyfriend."

"I don't give a damn what he tells anybody!"

Dropping my arm, she grabs her purse from my bed and takes out a cigarette, lighting it slowly and deliberately.

"Put that thing out," I say.

Karen grins and blows smoke into the air. "Oh, that's right. No one's allowed to smoke in your home. Really, Abby, you should learn to loosen up a bit."

I am allergic to smoke, and Karen knows it. Too much and my throat closes up. In fact, more than once I've landed in the hospital from second-hand smoke.

"Please, Karen, give that to me." I hold my hand out.

Her eyes are so filled with hate, it startles me. In

the next moment, she grabs my hand and jams the cigarette into my palm, lighted end first.

I scream as she grinds it in before I can pull back. Grabbing her hand with my free one, I twist away while my palm sears. By this time Murphy is in the room, growling and snapping at Karen's heels.

I run to the bathroom, spin the water faucet frantically and dash cold water over my burnt palm. The pain is almost unbearable, and I am shocked, hardly able to believe this has happened. Tears fill my eyes. How did it come to this? Dear God, what has happened to my sister?

When we were ten, twelve, Karen looked after me, made sure no one ever hurt me. She stood up for me against bullies in the schoolyard.

How did she get to be this monster?

When the pain in my hand diminishes a bit I dry it with clean tissue and look at my strained, pale face in the mirror.

Karen did not follow me into the bathroom, nor has there been any sound from her in my bedroom. Cautiously, I go back in there. She is sitting on the bed with Murphy holding her in place, his front paws planted firmly in her lap. Tears flow down Karen's cheeks. With the frowsy hair, the jewelry and the tears, she looks like an overdressed rag doll someone has tossed aside and forgotten to play with.

My first instinct—to call 911 and have her dragged away—subsides as I remember that she is still my sister, the one I lost and cried for when she ran off at sixteen. There is a flicker of caring left, overcoming my fear of what she might do next.

"It's okay, Murph," I say softly. "Come here."

He whines low in his throat, but gets down and comes to me, taking a position beside me.

"Karen?" I say.

She doesn't answer immediately, and I wonder if she's heard me.

"*Karen?*" I repeat.

"He's with her," she says in a hollow voice.

"Jeffrey? With who?"

She shrugs her shoulders, which seem frail to me now, and old, like the petals of a wilted flower.

"Who is Jeffrey with?" I ask, going over to kneel in front of her.

"I don't know. That's what I was looking for."

She's losing it, I think. "Karen, I don't understand."

She rubs at her tears with the heel of one hand, like a child. "He wrote her address down. It was in one of his jackets, dammit, some place in Brazil! I just want to see him. I want to face him with it!"

"You mean, Jeffrey's having an affair with someone else?"

She comes to life, then, that look of hatred back in her eyes. "Are you happy now? You said he'd do the same thing to me. Once a man strays, you said, he does it again and again."

"I know." I brush her hair back from her cheek. "I know I said that. But, Karen, I thought you and Jeffrey were happy together."

She shoves me away. Jumping to her feet, she runs from the room. "You don't know a damn thing about *anything!* Not anything at all!"

I hear the downstairs door slam, and after that it takes a few moments to get my legs back under me again. Finally I check to make sure my sister is truly gone. Satisfied there's no one in the house but me, I go back upstairs and dress as well as possible with one hand, in khaki slacks and a white T-shirt, no buttons.

In the kitchen again, I lean my injured hand on the counter to steady it. Pricking a vitamin E capsule with a fingernail on my other hand, I squeeze some onto my palm and rub it gently in. Then I put a pot of water on for tea, and sit at the table, thinking.

The water is boiling before I've managed to work anything out. Fixing myself a soothing cup of jasmine tea, I take it back to the table and think some more.

A late-afternoon sun pours through the window, and I get up and draw the blinds halfway to diffuse it. My instinct is to cocoon, to hide out, go back to the womb. Part of me wants to call my mom in Santa Rosa and talk to her about Karen, about Jeffrey, about Marti.

The other part says I'm a grown-up, and what could she do to help things, anyway?

Reaching my good hand over to the radio on the kitchen counter, I put KRML on for some quiet jazz. Sitting there, I sip my tea. My hand hurts like hell; it has reached the throbbing stage. Murphy sits beside me on the kitchen floor, so close against my legs I can feel his heartbeat. One thing about Murph, he sure knows how to comfort a woman.

I am more disturbed by this rift with my sister than I've been able to admit, and I wonder how much of it is my fault. I know I haven't always been as aware as I might be of her problems, or about what's going on in her life. I also know that she sometimes sees this as my being snooty, or too privileged to care.

What Karen fails to realize is that there can be an appearance of privilege that isn't always quite fact. While it's true I live in a lovely home and don't lack for spending money—a circumstance for which I am deeply grateful—California is a community-property state. Everything that's mine is Jeffrey's, and vice versa, since we had no prenup. So when Frannie advises me to sell, she does it without realizing that I haven't the right to do so without Jeffrey's agreeing to it. I must wait until he turns his half over to me after the election—and until then, I must keep up a good front, give the appearance that we're happily married.

I am not entirely proud of this arrangement, but I'm still living in the past enough that I don't want to be poor again. Despite the sacrifices my mother made to keep us going, there were times when my father's sales were down, times without enough food, and the rent was often late. The eviction notices, of course, came right on time. The wolf wasn't simply at the door; he moved right in.

Then, too, I have a long-standing love affair with basic amenities. I told Marti once that if God had wanted me to live in the 1400s he would have sent me there, not here. He would have said, "Here you go, little Abby soul," and plunked me down at an outhouse in a town riven with cholera.

Instead, he gave me Carmel. Which, on a good day, is close to heaven. On a not-so-good day, it can also be close to hell.

So this is where it stands: After the election next month, I get my freedom and my house. After that, it's anyone's guess. Jeffrey has always been a master at hiding his assets, and I've got a feeling I'll end up supporting myself.

Which is fine. I just won't be able to do it on the few dollars my column brings in every week. So, like most divorced women, I'll have to go to work—and like most divorced women who have been out of the job market for years, I probably won't rake in a lot of bucks, at least at first. So I'll end up having to sell *Windhaven*.

Which puts me ahead of a lot of women out there working to support themselves and their kids. The sale of *Windhaven* could keep me going quite a while. The thought of losing it, though, makes my home all the more dear to me now. "A woman without a house," my mom likes to say with that great crafty wisdom of hers, "is like a cat without a mouse. No power, no game."

Meanwhile, here I sit with my "privileged" life, and I know that inspires jealousy in my sister.

Beneath the half-drawn blinds I can see people walking by on Scenic with their dogs. I wonder again about the kid who brought Murphy home that day. Is he one of them? I would like to return his leash.

Sighing, I sip my tea. If it was important, he'd have come back.

And there are so many things, suddenly, so much more important than returning lost items: What about Karen's plight? Has Jeffrey really found another woman? Is he cheating on her?

The teakettle ticks as it cools, keeping rhythm to my scattered thoughts.

Karen came here looking for the address of "the other woman." It was on a piece of paper in one of Jeffrey's jackets, she said, though she obviously didn't find it, as she was looking through his dresser when I caught her.

I remember, suddenly, Frannie saying she takes some of Jeffrey's things to the attic now and then, to annoy him. Karen couldn't know that.

Is that where the address of the other woman is? In a jacket in the attic?

I could go up there, find out.

But why bother?

Maybe because Jeffrey has disappeared—conveniently missing an appointment with the Secret Service, an appointment to talk with them about the way Marti died and the way her son disappeared.

Mauro and Hillars thought it was important to find Jeffrey—so important, they issued a warrant for his arrest.

And so important, they are ready to arrest me if he doesn't turn up.

What the hell have you been up to, Jeffrey?

And how dare you leave me here holding the bag?

Setting my teacup down, I head for the attic, to find—I hope—a clue to my wayward husband's whereabouts.

This time I take a flashlight with me, as well as a good, high-voltage lantern. At the top of the attic steps I look around, nervously making sure I'm alone after my previous adventure here. I set the lantern down in the middle of the floor, near the stairs. The flashlight I sweep from side to side, examining every corner.

There's no one here but me, and a lot of memories: my old journals, a box of letters Marti wrote to me over the years—

It surprises me to see them. I suppose I've blocked the fact that I had them, thinking it would be too painful to read them the day she died. Picking up the small blue box, I put it by the stairs and look around for Jeffrey's clothes.

Right away, I spot them. It's not as if Frannie seriously tried to hide them from him—just put them here to annoy him, as she said. Jeffrey, she knows, is allergic to the dust in the attic. And our attic, largely ignored for years, is thick with the stuff.

There are a couple of his good suits hanging on a rod from the rafters, a blue blazer, three sweaters and a white silk shirt. I can't help smiling. Jeffrey thinks he looks exceedingly handsome in that shirt, as, indeed, he does. He must be going crazy without it—especially if he's with a new woman.

Score one for you, Frannie.

I begin with the blue blazer, the one I know he likes to wear with the white shirt. The pockets are empty, except for lint and an unused handkerchief. I start on the black suit. Again, empty pockets. Thinking I've struck out, I turn to the gray pinstripe. Jeffrey likes to wear the gray pinstripe for business. He wouldn't ordinarily wear it to a rendezvous.

In the left breast pocket of the pin-stripe, however, I find what I think Karen must have been looking for: a folded piece of paper with an address on it.

There is also a plane-ticket folder and stub—for a flight to Rio de Janeiro, Brazil. Holding the flashlight up to the paper, I see that the address is in Rio, as well—or more precisely, Sao Conrado, a nearby beach town. I remember it from a vacation Jeffrey and I once spent down there.

Jeffrey has always liked Rio. But why in the world would he have a girlfriend that far away from home?

Inside the ticket folder is an itinerary showing the date of departure to be this past August seventh. The return date was the ninth, two days later.

Puzzled, I slip the ticket stub and the address into the back pocket of my slacks and return to the stairs, picking up the lantern and the box of Marti's letters. Taking one last look around I head down the stairs and close the attic door.

At the kitchen table, I sit with the address and ticket stub in front of me and think back to August. Jeffrey went on a business trip in August. I remember it because we were having a rare heat wave in Carmel, and the air-conditioning broke down. I couldn't remember the name of the repairman we had a service contract with, and tried to reach Jeffrey in Washington to see if his memory was any better than mine. He hadn't checked into his hotel, and we had an argument later about where he'd been and why.

Not that I really cared by then—I just didn't want him to think he was getting away with anything. Since the day I'd caught him with Karen, it had come down to this: If I had to continue living with Jeffrey, I would. But I couldn't, and wouldn't, take the lies. There was no longer a need for them, I argued when he got home. If he was at Karen's all that time instead of Washington, why didn't he just say so?

Jeffrey had stomped out of the house without answering.

Now the answer seems clear: because he *wasn't* with Karen. He was with someone else.

The same woman Karen believes him to be with now? Is Jeffrey lazing away the days under a hot Brazilian sun with a new lady love, while I'm here taking the heat for him? Would he really just leave me here to be arrested for allegedly aiding and abetting his disappearance?

The only answer I can come up with is, *Of course he would, the bastard.*

I need time to think. Going to the laundry room, I sort out clothes, then start the washer. After that, I clean up the kitchen, rinsing out my teacup and scouring the sink with Comet. Finally I go into my office and sit at the computer, zapping out a column about the out-of-control raccoon problem and whether it's PC or not to wear T-shirts that say THE NEW WHITE MEAT—RACOON. I e-mail that to the Pinecone, then go back into the living room, figuring I've cleared my head enough to at least tackle Marti's letters.

There is nothing to tackle, however. When I open the box, I find with a shock that it's empty. Someone has taken the letters Marti wrote to me over the years—twenty years, in all.

There weren't a lot. Thirty or so, each of them written on the thin tissue paper Marti liked, the kind often used in overseas air mail, as it doesn't weigh more than a feather.

Those letters were all I had left of Marti.

And now they're gone.

Anger mixes with confusion—and even a bit of fear—as I realize what this means: that someone's been in my house.

As I'm thinking that, the phone on the table next to me rings. I've turned the answering machine off, and I hesitate to pick up, as it might be more reporters. On the other hand, it could conceivably be Jeffrey.

"Hi," Tommy Lawrence says when I answer after several rings. "I left a message, but I wasn't sure you got it."

"Hello, Tommy. Yes, I got it. Sorry, I've been busy."

"That's okay. I just wondered if you'd like to get together, and I thought I'd call again and find out before I make other plans."

"I don't know, I've got a lot on my mind right now."

"So I hear," he says. "Abby, I'm worried about you. There are all kinds of rumors flying around, and one of them is that the cops have a warrant out for your husband's arrest. They also say if he's not found soon, they might be arresting you. Abby, don't get me wrong—I know you couldn't possibly have had anything to do with Marti's murder. But are you okay? I can't believe your husband would just disappear like that, leaving you to handle things with the police."

I haven't known till this minute what I'm going to do next. Now, hearing Tommy echo my own thoughts, I look down at the ticket to Rio and the address there and say, "Actually, Tommy, I'm fine. But I'll be away a couple of days."

"Oh. I'm sorry to hear that." A small pause. "I mean, I guess I am. I hope you're going away to relax?"

"Something like that. How about if I call you when I get back?"

"Sure, that'd be fine. I've decided to stay here another week or so."

"Will you be at the La Playa?"

"Uh, yeah. I'm out a lot, though. Just leave a message at the desk."

"I'll call when I get back, then," I say.

"Okay. Abby? Take care."

He rings off, and I hang up.

An odd boy, I'm remembering. And an even odder man. There is something about Tommy Lawrence I can't put a finger on, something not quite right.

There isn't time to think about it, however. Karen thinks Jeffrey's with the girlfriend in Brazil, and a woman usually knows. If I do nothing else this week, I'll at least find my erstwhile husband's pale ass and nail it to the wall. Then I'll drag what's left of him onto Mauro and Hillars' doorstep. I've taken enough from Jeffrey Northrup, and I don't intend to take any more.

Briefly, I consider telling Ben where I'm going. But I need to do this alone. Bypassing my usual travel agent, I call the airline direct and book a round-trip flight from Monterey to Brazil via San Francisco, leaving late tonight and returning tomorrow at midnight, the first return flight I can get.

I prefer not to stick around down there any longer

than I must. When Jeffrey and I were in Rio a few years ago, he had business meetings nonstop. I was left to amuse myself in the biggest party town in the world. When Jeffrey found me in the hotel bar, talking to another man—just talking—he was furious. The rest of my memories about Rio are not pleasant.

Next I call Frannie and ask her if she'll take Murph for a couple of days. She's done this before when I've had to go away, and readily agrees.

"Billy will love it!" she says. "They can run on the beach, and maybe that'll get some of the energy out of him. Billy, that is. You know, I really love my kids. But I liked them a whole lot more before they got legs."

Between the connections and the early check-ins required, it is a long and tiring trip to Rio. On the plane heading south I let my thoughts drift to Marti and Justin.

Justin at six, on his first day at school. I remember how I sat outside the school in my car and watched Mary Ryan go in with him, holding his hand. By the time he was eight, I had the volunteer job in the school library. He would come to me at the research desk, asking me to help him find books.

It was heaven. A good student, Justin had Marti's dark hair and large, dark eyes. At thirteen he developed a sparse beard, and his deepening voice cracked when he accepted an award as the most popular student of the year.

I was there for him, Marti. For you—and yes, for me. The son I never had. He was so beautiful, so tall. His smile was like yours, too...and he had that won-

*derful sense of humor. I can't think I may never see
him again, Marti. Or you.*

*Hillars may have been right, Marti, when he said
he and Mauro were our best chance of finding your
son. I don't know anyone else who could do it better.
And if they need Jeffrey—for whatever reason—so
help me God, I'll find him.*

I arrive in Rio after eight in the morning, feeling
light-headed and as if my legs are stumps. My small
flight bag passes through Customs quickly, however,
and I'm able to hail a cab just outside the International Airport doors. I give the driver the address I
found in Jeffrey's pocket, and he takes me along the
Linha Vermelha, the Red Line, through the working-
class neighborhoods. Traffic is heavy, but eventually
we end up on the more luxurious South Side. Here,
the scenery becomes stunning, the beaches lively.
Wending our way through the traffic, we pass Leblon
and arrive at Sao Conrado, a residential area of Hol-
lywood-style mansions, golf courses and a sky full
of colorful hang gliders.

The cabdriver pulls up to a huge white house of
modern design, three stories of loops, arches and
curves. It stands on a cliff overlooking the sea, and
the palm trees surrounding it wave in a gentle breeze.
There are no other houses around; this one holds
court in glorious isolation.

*God, Jeffrey. Some girlfriend you've got here.
Must be a movie star.*

Or does he provide this for her? Is this one of
Jeffrey's little assets he's forgotten to mention?

Given community property, I can only hope.

The cab stops on the road, at the end of a long,

winding drive lined with burgeoning red shrubs. I ask
the cabdriver to wait a few moments while I collect
myself, running over the plan I rehearsed on the
plane:

*Knock on the door. When it opens, if it's a woman,
ask for Jeffrey. She'll deny he's there, no doubt.
Force my way in somehow.*

*Tell her his other girlfriend, Karen, is looking for
him.*

A flimsy plan, I admit. How do I force my way
into someone's house without getting arrested—or
shot?

Finally I ask the driver to take me to the door and
wait, paying him a sizable "deposit" in advance to
quell his protests. I tell him it's okay to keep the
meter running—just wait.

Stepping out, the first thing I notice is the quiet.
In Carmel, there's always some sort of construction
going on lately. In this place, a person could think.
It's a silent, beautiful retreat.

Lifting a large wrought-iron knocker, I rap four
times, loudly. Listening, I hear nothing on the other
side of the door. I rap again.

When no one answers the third time, I follow a
shell-lined path around the house to the left, thinking
Jeffrey and his lady love might be outside. Rounding
the corner of the house to the back, a breathtaking
sight greets me: a well-manicured green lawn rolling
down to a cliff, and beyond that a postcard perfect
sea, so blue it's hard to tell where it ends and the
sky begins. Overhead, the hang gliders swoop in the
soft, warm air.

In the center of the lawn is a swimming pool in a

natural shape, with chaise lounges surrounding it. There are three gaily striped cabanas off to the side, and music plays softly on a stereo somewhere.

So there is someone home. Now, where the hell are they?

At that moment I hear laughter coming from one of the cabanas, then a man's low voice, followed by a woman's.

Ah-ha, Jeffrey. Gotcha.

Tiptoeing through the grass to the cabana in question, I cannot wait to throw the canvas door back and expose my delinquent husband, otherwise known as Karen's footloose lover.

It is therefore a shock—one that rocks me back on my heels—when I lift the canvas and rip it back to see, in a warm and very nude embrace, Justin's adoptive parents, Mary and Paul Ryan. A Polaroid camera is on the floor beside them, and photos of Mary in half a swimsuit are scattered around.

I go back to the cab, settle up with the driver and tell him he can leave. Then I join the Ryans inside the house. Mary and her husband have dressed in shorts and lightweight shirts. She sits across from me in the immense white living room, her hands folded in her lap, while her husband stands behind her, clearly ill at ease. He, in fact, seems even more distraught at being caught half-naked in a seaside cabana than she.

I have chosen to ignore what I saw and focus instead on Justin. I've told the Ryans who I am and that I know their son has been kidnapped. They, in turn, have told me a story that scares me to death.

There is little hope now, I think, of Justin still being alive. I don't think the Ryans have come to that understanding yet.

"This is the first time we've even been out by the pool since we got here," Mary explains in the tone of someone justifying a sin. "The first couple of weeks here we did nothing but cry and worry about Justin. For the past six weeks we've walked and cried, walked and cried. Like zombies, half the time. I couldn't even tell you what time of the day it was. Then, Paul said we had to put out an effort to live a normal life. It could be months—" She bites her lips.

Paul Ryan paces like a caged animal. "It's been so damned long. Our lives have been on hold, and it's not like we can really do anything—"

He breaks off. "I mean, we just couldn't take it anymore. Mary was getting—" He pauses again and looks at her, his eyes tearing. "My wife is not doing well."

"It's true," she says, staring at her hands. "I've been getting bitter and withdrawn, I know that. You have no idea what it's been like."

I cannot hold back the note of accusation in my voice. "I still don't understand what you're doing all the way down here in this—this virtual spa. Why haven't you been at home where Justin could have found you if he came back? No normal parent—"

I shut my mouth on that one. What do I know about normal parents, and what they would do if their son was gone?

"We did wait there!" Mary says defiantly. "We waited a month, and then…then we agreed to come here."

"Because?"

"Because we were told it would be safer for Justin if we were out of the way. Where reporters couldn't get to us if the story came out."

If the story came out. That has a familiar ring.

And it's coming together now. Why Jeffrey had this address in his jacket, and why he came here in August and didn't tell me where he was. That was the month the Ryans left Pacific Grove.

"My husband brought you down here, didn't he? This is his house?"

Mary Ryan looks bewildered. "Well, yes, of course. I thought you knew that. Isn't that why you're here?"

I sigh. "No, Mary, it's not. I'm looking for Jeffrey. I thought he was keeping a girlfriend here."

"Oh, no, not at all! I'm sorry. We haven't seen him, have we, Paul?"

Her husband shakes his head. "We haven't seen Jeffrey since he brought us here two months ago. He's telephoned, of course, keeping us up to date on the search for Justin."

"Oh? And what precisely does Jeffrey say about that?"

"Well, that the investigators are still hard at work on it, that they've come up with leads but most have fizzled out. Even the negotiations...they, uh, seem to have fallen through."

Paul Ryan sounds less confident about Jeffrey's handling of things than he should be, given the fact that he and Mary have followed my husband's advice to desert their home and leave him to search for their son.

As for the so-called negotiations, I'm beginning to wonder if there ever were any. But why would Mauro and Hillars lie about that?

Because the government lies. All the time. About anything and everything. Lying to civilians comes naturally to agencies like the CIA, the FBI and the Secret Service.

The only thing one really needs to question is— why?

"We're so worried," Mary says tremulously. "Jeffrey keeps telling us he's sure Justin's all right and we must believe. I'm sorry, I don't mean to say anything about your husband, but it's getting more and more difficult—"

She breaks off and sits straighter, while her voice takes on a note of anger. "We would so much rather be at home. I keep thinking that any moment Justin could walk in and not find us there." Her eyes fill with tears, and she turns to her husband. "He wouldn't even know where we were, Paul."

It's my turn to pace. I stand and walk to the gigantic two-story windows that span the living room from wall to wall. My heels clatter on the marble floor, and the room is so large I'm tired just walking across it. Looking out over the lawn to the sea, I can only wonder at what I've discovered here and what to do.

"Let me see if I've got this straight," I say, turning back to them. "Justin disappeared in July. You contacted Marti right away in New York and told her about it, thinking he might have run off to her. That's because he had just found out she was his birth mother. Is that right?"

Mary nods. "I was out one night, and when I came home, Paul told me what had happened. Justin said he suspected all along he was adopted, and he wanted to know who his biological mother was. Paul had to tell him, finally—though that's the last thing we ever wanted to do. We planned to wait until he was out of school, keep him just to ourselves a little bit longer, you know, but—" She turns to her husband again.

"Justin was angry," he says, not looking at his wife. "He stormed off to his room and I thought he'd gone to bed. But then in the morning..."

He covers his face, and Mary looks at her husband and bursts into tears.

"In the morning, when Justin was gone, you say you called Marti," I continue after a minute, "to ask if she'd seen him. She hadn't, so she flew to Pacific Grove to help you look for him. Both of you thought at first that he might have just gone to a friend's house, but when you still couldn't find him, Marti contacted...who?"

Agents Mauro and Hillars said she went to the first family for help. But do the Ryans know that?

"She told us not to say anything." Mary twists her hands and looks uncertainly at Paul.

"You mean about the president?" I say.

Her face clears. "Oh, you know, then. Yes, Marti said the president and Mrs. Chase were old friends, and she felt she could ask them for help. She said the FBI might work harder on the case if they were under direct orders from the president—"

Paul Ryan interrupts. He is kneading his fists against his legs and looks as if he might break down completely at any moment. "You have to understand," he says, his voice thick with tears, "this all happened within forty-eight hours. Justin was so angry with us for not telling him sooner that he was adopted, we...we honestly believed he had run away. We didn't think he'd go far. In fact, we fully expected him to show up by the end of the first day. He's always been so good about things, more mature than most kids, and—"

He pales, and his voice begins to shake. "We didn't want to embarrass him by going to the police and having it all over the news."

"We spent a whole day on the phones," Mary says, wiping away tears. "Marti, Paul and me. And Marti even went out and talked to parents of Justin's friends, in person. No one had seen him. And then—" She chokes back a small cry. "Then, the note came."

"A note? When?"

"Not right away. Justin had been gone over three weeks. It said—"

She covers her face and sobs into her hands.

Paul seems to shrink into himself. "It said," he continues for his wife, "that if we called the police or the FBI, Justin would be murdered—and his head sent back to us. In a bag."

"Oh my God." I feel sick and chilled to the bone.

"But even before that," he says, "Marti called President Chase for help. We weren't sure it was the right thing to do, but Marti insisted. The truth is, she was crazed. We all were."

"Then we had a visit from your husband," Mary says. "He told us the president sent him to help us.

He said the FBI was working on the case quietly, and we shouldn't talk to anyone. He said he'd be a liaison for us."

"A liaison? Mary, are you telling me you haven't talked to the FBI yourselves in all this time? Only my *husband?*"

Mary looks uneasy. "Well, with the kidnapper threatening what he did…" She turns to Paul, as if for confirmation that they did the right thing.

Again, he doesn't meet her eyes. "Jeffrey said it was best if we remained apart from the actual search, and that everything be kept absolutely quiet."

"Are you saying we shouldn't have trusted your husband?" Mary says, her voice rising. "Jeffrey Northrup is well known in the community. He's respected, a close friend of the president."

I would like to tell them precisely what I think about their having trusted Jeffrey, but I don't want to frighten them any more than they already are.

"Was Marti all right with Jeffrey's being involved?" I ask. "What did she say about it?"

"To be honest," Mary answers, "she didn't like it at first. She wanted to go to the FBI herself, but Jeffrey said the president felt it would only put Justin more at risk."

Jeffrey said, Jeffrey said. The fear I felt before hangs heavier now.

"What about when you came down here?" I ask. "Was Marti all right with that?"

Mary looks at her husband. "We—we didn't really tell her. Jeffrey said—"

I cut in. "He said the less people who knew where you were, the better. Right?"

"That's…that's right."

I am so overwhelmed with anger, I can't help lashing out. "So you and your husband left town in the middle of the night, leaving your home and your missing son behind, and you didn't even tell Marti, his *mother?*"

"*I'm* his mother!" Mary flashes. "And how dare you come here accusing us? You don't know what it was like! You have no idea!"

"I know you two are sitting here in the lap of luxury while Justin's going through God knows what! His head could be sitting in a bag on your doorstep and you'd never even know it!"

I'm losing it, and the look on the Ryans' faces tells me I'd better get a grip or I'll lose them too.

"Look, I'm sorry," I say. "It's just that I'm worried about Justin, too. Marti and I were good friends, and I promised her I'd look after Justin's welfare if anything ever happened to her."

Mary looks bewildered. "You don't mean something's happened to Marti?"

For a moment I simply stare at her, wondering. "You mean you don't know? You didn't see it on the news?"

"What news?" Paul Ryan says. "We don't have a television here. Or a radio, just that CD player you saw by the pool. What are you saying? Something's happened to Marti?"

I sigh. "You'd better sit down. And have you got anything to drink?"

It's clear Jeffrey has deliberately isolated the Ryans by bringing them down here. I have no idea why, but one thing I do know is that knowledge is power. The Ryans need to know at least as much as I do. After that, they can decide for themselves how to exercise whatever power it affords them.

Paul fortifies each of us with a glass of wine, and I sit across from them. "This is all confidential," I say. "May I have your word you won't tell anyone what I'm about to tell you?"

Mary nods, but Paul looks unsure. "I'd like to hear what you say first."

I agree to it, as I think I can get him to go my way once he knows. "Jeffrey has disappeared," I say, "and there's a warrant out for his arrest. The Secret Service is looking for him, as well as the Carmel police. They think he might know something about Justin's disappearance…and Marti's death."

"Marti is dead?" Mary's hands fly to her face. "Oh my God! What happened? When did this happen?"

It is difficult telling them about the way Marti died. I make my way through it, leaving out as many details as possible.

When they've expressed their shock and sorrow, Mary says, "How is Helen taking this?"

I hesitate. "You mean Sister Helen? Helen Asback?"

"Yes, of course," Mary says. "She's come to see Justin often over the years. You didn't know?"

"No. Marti never told me that. How did this come about?"

"Well, we met Helen originally through Marti, after we adopted Justin. She had just moved to Carmel, and we became better acquainted over the years."

One surprise after another. "Sister Helen lives in Carmel?"

Mary nods. "It's a long story. Poor thing, she's had a terrible time. But she lives out at The Prayer House now."

I shake my head, confused. "What prayer house?"

"It's in the Carmel Valley, an hour or more past Carmel Valley Village. She's been there for years—"

Her husband interrupts, saying tensely, "I would like to get back to why the Secret Service think your husband is involved in Justin's disappearance."

"I don't know for certain," I tell him. "I came down here loaded with questions for Jeffrey, but since he's not here, I can't ask him any of them. I will tell you this—I think it's time you and Mary went home. Whatever Jeffrey's reasons were for bringing you here, they can't have been good."

I set down my wine after a couple of sips and lean forward, staring at my hands a few moments while I choose my words. "There's more," I say. "Mary... Paul...I don't know how to tell you this. But according to the Secret Service, the FBI doesn't know a thing about Justin's disappearance. And the Secret Service, themselves, never showed up till last week. I'm very sorry, but it doesn't look to me as if Jeffrey ever reported Justin's kidnapping to anyone at all. I don't think anyone's been looking for your son."

For a long moment, Mary seems speechless. Paul's reaction is something else. He covers his face again, while Mary comes to life suddenly and flies to her feet in a rage. "I told you we never should have trusted him! All this time we've been down here it never felt right, never once!"

"Don't blame yourselves," I say quickly. "I've lived with my husband fifteen years. It took me a while to know he couldn't be trusted."

"But I should have known!" Mary says, still furious. "Just because a man has a good reputation with locals, even local and national politicians, that doesn't—it doesn't—" She gasps, catching her breath.

"You're right. It doesn't mean a thing," I finish for her.

Paul stares at me, his eyes red-rimmed and bleary. "You live with this man?"

"Not anymore." It's a decision I've only now made.

Paul rubs his eyes and shakes his head. Mary touches his shoulder, becoming the strong one now. "You're telling us there's been no search?" she says. "None at all?"

"I can't say for sure, Mary. But let me ask you this. Paul said there was a note, right?"

"Yes."

"In the note, the kidnapper threatened you? He said that if you told anyone about the kidnapping, Justin would die?"

"That's right."

"But did you ever get a ransom note? A demand to pay something or do something for his return?"

She looks at Paul, her chin trembling now. "No. No, we never did."

"And you didn't think that was odd?"

"Of course I did. But your husband said—"

She pauses, looking at me with dawning horror. "It doesn't matter what your husband said, does it? Because none of it was true. It was all a lie."

She crumples over, burying her face in her hands. "My God, Paul! Where is our son?"

9

Statistics say that if a kidnapped child is to be murdered, he is murdered, usually, within an hour of his disappearance. Children who live beyond that point are believed to be dead within three hours. Once three months have passed, it can be assumed—in most cases, not all—that the child is gone and will not return. The police and FBI are looking for a body now.

The Ryans know this as well as I. Too much time has passed, and even if the FBI had been looking for Justin—which they have not—it would almost certainly be too late to find him now.

We have Jeffrey to thank for this. Jeffrey, who pretended to launch a search, while doing...what?

It's a question none of us can answer. A question that has filled the Ryans with bewilderment, grief and rage. I am not far behind them. What kind of devil did I marry? How did he come to this?

And what was Marti thinking throughout all this?

From what Mary Ryan said, Marti did not fully trust Jeffrey. What would she have done, then? If she went to the president and he asked Jeffrey to handle it, and Jeffrey only pretended to—how soon did Marti realize this? Did she uncover whatever Jeffrey was up to? Did she confront him with it? And if so, when?

The day of her murder?

Even I can't believe Jeffrey could be that evil. He couldn't have killed Marti. He *wouldn't*. Jeffrey has shown me a violent side, more than once—but it's been a long time. I've truly believed that with maturity, he'd changed.

Now I can't be sure.

When I leave the Ryans they're packing and booking a flight home. I don't know what they'll do there, but certainly their return will shake Jeffrey when he learns of it.

Will that bring him out of hiding? Or send him deeper underground?

There are several hours left before my plane leaves at midnight, and I am on tenterhooks, anxious to get home. Aside from Jeffrey, I have one more person to look for now—Sister Helen.

Before the Ryans and I parted, I asked them how they felt about Sister Helen's visits over the years; if it seemed she was keeping too close an eye on them. They said no, that Justin had always liked Helen and accepted her as simply an old friend of his parents. They said they understood that Marti would want to know for certain her child was safe and healthy.

All this time I'd been thinking I was the only one, when in reality, Marti's son had two guardian angels. Part of me is envious, the other part glad.

He had a good life, Marti. He was genuinely loved. Know that, at least.

Sister Helen's closeness to the Ryan family, however, makes me wonder even more about her hostility toward me at Marti's grave. Did they tell her of Justin's kidnapping, and did she suspect Jeffrey of not playing it straight when he said he was trying to find the boy?

Did she share her fears with Ned, Marti's brother? If so, that could explain a lot.

I should have asked the Ryans these questions. The shock of finding them, however, and their shock at Marti's death, wiped all but the most important matters out of my mind. I decide to find Sister Helen when I get back to Carmel and ask her myself.

As for Justin, in my heart I have begun to let go. I don't honestly see how he could still be alive. There are only two things I can do with that: I can grieve. And, I can do everything in my power to find his kidnapper. With any luck at all, I might be able to bring the monster to justice.

Meanwhile, I need food. The cab I've called picks me up and takes me to a terrace restaurant by the beach in Ipanema, where I can relax and have a meal before my flight. While I wait for my order I sip an ice-cold coconut water and lean back in my chair, thinking. A dark, handsome and very young man at another table gives me the eye, but I pretend I don't see him through my sunglasses. I'm sure he's just doing what men must do in Ipanema, flirting with the lady tourist.

Closing my eyes, I let my bones warm and my nerves loosen in the hot sun. When there's movement by my table, I assume it's my food coming, but don't open my eyes. I don't, in fact, feel like budging, even to lift a fork.

"Hey, pretty lady," a man's voice says.

I figure it's the guy from the other table, so I ignore him.

"Hey, aren't you speaking to me today?" the voice says again.

My eyes fly open and my mouth follows suit as I see it's not the *carioca* at all, but Tommy Lawrence. "What the hell? Tommy? I...what are you doing here?"

I am stunned at seeing him in these unfamiliar surroundings. And why am I feeling not pleasure, but something more like fear at his appearance? *What is he doing all the way down here? What does he want with me? Really want with me?*

He slides into the chair across from mine, not waiting for an invitation. "I heard you'd flown down here. Thought you might like some company."

I lick my lips. My voice is low, my throat dry. "You *heard?* That's impossible. I didn't tell anyone I was coming to Brazil." *How much does he know about my visit to the Ryans? Did he follow me there? And how did he find me at this restaurant?*

"Let's just say I've got my sources," he answers, grinning.

Sources. Obviously, he's not going to tell me. But this time he's gone too far.

"You should have saved your money," I say when I find my voice again. "I'm having dinner then going straight to the airport."

"You're flying back tonight?" He makes a small frown of disappointment.

"I am." I remove my sunglasses and look him in the eye. "So—you have business down here?"

"No. Abby, it's Rio, the city that doesn't sleep at

night. I thought you could use some company. How long's it been since you had some fun?"

"I haven't had a whole hell of a lot of time for fun lately," I say pointedly. "You might remember? A little matter of a good friend of mine being murdered?"

He sobers instantly. "I can't very well forget that. I know you can't, either. That's why I'm here. I sort of thought Marti would want me to boost your spirits a bit. Maybe take you dancing on lighted rooftops with a view of city and sea."

"I can't think of anything I'd like less," I say tersely. "And I don't mean to be rude, but I am so tired right now, I can't even fathom what that would be like."

I jam my sunglasses on and lean back in my chair again. *Maybe he'll go away.*

"Then let me show you," he insists with that ready grin. "I know Rio like the back of my hand."

With that, I lift my glasses and peer at him through narrowed eyes. "You've been here before?"

"Sure, I spent time here right after college."

"An unpublished writer," I say thoughtfully, "who can afford an extended stay at the La Playa in Carmel, round-trip air tickets to Rio and a night on the town? Hmm, let me think. What doesn't seem right about that?"

The grin widens. "Your suspicious mind, for one thing. I had an uncle who left me a small inheritance."

"Small?"

"Well, sizable." He shrugs. "You remember my uncle Ron?"

"No, I never knew your uncle Ron. Tommy, it occurs to me that I never really knew you, either."

"Hey, there's no time like the present. *Dance with me...*" He sings a few bars from the old tune that Fred Astaire danced to, *Cheek to Cheek*. "Let me show you heaven," he says.

His singing voice is so bad, I can't help smiling. But my food has arrived and I start on it, deliberately chewing slowly, which gives me a few moments to think. Around us, people are leaving, as it's late for lunch and early for dinner. The white umbrellas over the tables flap in a small breeze, and out on the sea sailboats are returning to dock. The sun is lowering over the western hills, the sky turning pink and gold.

"So, what do you say?" Tommy persists.

"I can't go dancing with you tonight," I answer between mouthfuls. "I've got to get home."

"What's at home?"

"My dog, for one thing. And I have to see some people."

"Can't they wait? What's so important it can't wait another day?"

I lay down my fork. "Tommy...what is it you want? Really want, I mean. I'm not in the mood to play games."

He spreads his hands in an "I give up" gesture. "I have some time on my hands and a few bucks burning a hole in my pocket. I just thought I could help somehow. Besides..." He sighs. "I miss Marti. I don't know what to do with myself."

"Tommy, how can you miss someone you hadn't seen since high school?"

He doesn't answer for a moment, and when he

does, there are tears in his eyes. "It's sort of like, when they're alive you think anything could happen, that one day things could change. Then when they're gone, it's so damned permanent. You know nothing's ever gonna go right, no matter what you do. You can't bring people back."

I push my plate away and fold my hands under my chin, leaning my elbows on the table. I may be a fool, but Tommy's tears have softened me. "I've been thinking the same thing," I say. "I don't know why Marti drifted off from me the way she did the past few months. I just wish she was back here so I could do things differently somehow. The only thing is, I don't know what things. And now maybe I never will."

"See, I knew you'd understand," Tommy says, leaning forward earnestly. "There's nothing we can do now, Abby. We can live with that every minute for the rest of our lives, or we can try to put it in the past. Not all the way in the past, just in some little drawer where we know we haven't misplaced it, just put it aside for a while."

"I don't know if I can do that."

"Sure you can! Come with me tonight. Let me show you Rio."

It's tempting. Not Tommy showing me Rio—I've done all that before. But my plane doesn't leave until midnight, despite what I told the enigmatic T. Lawrence about having to go straight to the airport.

So how best can I use that time?

By finding out what he's really up to. I am not a

total fool; there is more to his showing up in Rio than a desire to lift my spirits.

"Okay," I say, deciding suddenly. "Show me heaven, Fred. And make it good."

I pick up a dress at a boutique in Ipanema and change into it there. That leaves less than four hours before my flight, which is fine. It is, I'm hoping, all I'll need.

Rio, as I remember from previous trips, is everything Tommy promised—provided one doesn't look beyond the bright lights to the poverty and children on the streets. They are everywhere along our route, from the first nightclub to the tallest hotel in the city, where we have a nightcap and slow-dance to exotic rhythms.

The street kids keep getting to me. I begin to cling to straws, wondering if Justin is one of them in some city back home. What if he truly did run away, as his parents and Marti had first thought? What if the "kidnapper's" note was only a ploy of Jeffrey's, and Justin was never kidnapped at all? He could be wandering out there somewhere.

The thought drives me wild, though I know it is probably only wishful thinking.

As to Rio, we are going along just fine until the last stop, when, during a dance to "As Time Goes By," Tommy plants a kiss on me that takes me completely by surprise.

When I pull back, astonished, he says, "Was that a mistake? Shouldn't I have done that?"

"No, you should not have done that! Tommy, you know I'm involved with someone."

"With the cop, you mean? Ben Schaeffer? Is that serious?"

"Yes, it's serious." I frown. This is the second time he's mentioned Ben. "How do you know about Ben Schaeffer?"

He shrugs. "I have my—"

"Sources," I finish angrily. "Never mind."

We don't talk about it further, nor does he pump me for information about what I'm doing in Rio, as I've expected him to.

On the other hand, he doesn't give much up, either. I'd played along, hoping to find out just how long he'd been following me, if he knew I went to the house in Sao Conrado, and who I found there.

But if my oh-too-charming dance partner knows anything about the Ryans and why I came to Sao Conrado, I'm still at a loss to discover it when our cab deposits us both at the International Airport, just in time for the midnight flight.

At three in the morning I sit bleary-eyed and exhausted next to my travel mate, longing for sleep but unwilling to pass up one more chance to pump him for information.

The fact that he's paid for his own first-class ticket does seem to confirm that he has a trust fund. Beyond that, I'm still pretty much in the dark.

Then it begins.

"So, what were you doing in Rio, anyway?" he asks.

"I flew down there looking for Jeffrey," I tell him, adding the half truth, "I thought he was keeping a woman there."

"Ah. Evidence of infidelity? Are you getting a divorce?"

I don't answer.

"Did you find this woman?" he asks.

"No. I suppose I do let my suspicious mind run away with me sometimes."

"Well, if you ask me, your husband gives you good reason."

"I didn't ask you," I say, annoyed. I'm still thinking about that kiss. Is Tommy Lawrence transferring his obsession with Marti to me?

He changes the subject. "You asked me how I knew your cop. As a matter of fact, I had a visit from him yesterday, before I left for Rio."

"Oh? What did he want?"

"Wanted to know where I was from, what I was doing in Carmel and how long I planned to stay. Asked me some questions about Marti, said he saw me at the funeral. Wanted to know how long I'd known you, too."

"What did you tell him?"

"Just that I had nothing to hide. Said I was down from Santa Rosa, didn't know how long I'd be staying, and that I knew you and Marti from high-school days."

"Is that all he wanted?" It sounds like a routine interview.

"That's about it." Tommy grins. "See, *I* don't mind answering *your* questions at all. You know something, though? Don't be offended, but there's something about Ben Schaeffer I don't much like."

"What do you mean?"

"Well, he seems pretty uptight about his work. If

I did know anything, I don't think I'd tell him. If it was something I thought might hurt someone, that is."

"Hurt someone?"

"I'm not thinking anything specific. Just that he's not the type to keep a secret, is he? Not if he thinks it might hurt his career?"

"No, I suppose you're right. Ben takes his work very seriously."

"To the point where he'd haul you off to jail if he thought you'd done something against the law, right? Even though you and he are close?"

"I guess so."

"See, that's what I mean. A guy like that, he only goes so far for a woman."

Tommy leans his head back in his seat and closes his eyes, leaving me to think about that.

Five minutes later he pops back up and puts the light on for the flight attendant. When she comes he asks for coffee.

"Would you like coffee, too?" the flight attendant asks me.

"No, white wine," I say. "Wait. On second thought, make that vodka, rocks. A double."

Suddenly, I feel in need of a good stiff drink.

By the time we're on the commuter flight from San Francisco to Monterey, I would like to rid myself of Tommy Lawrence. It's impossible, though. He sticks like glue—even sharing my cab from the Monterey airport to Carmel. During the fifteen-minute ride he says, "I've been curious about Sister Helen—

the nun who taught Marti in high school? She was at the funeral."

"Yes, I know Sister Helen."

"That's right, of course, you'd know her, too. Anyway, I saw her at the funeral and got curious about her. She seemed odd. More angry than grieving."

"I noticed."

"And she wasn't with any other nuns from Mary Star of the Sea, your old high school. I thought at first that, if she came here because she used to be Marti's teacher, some of the other sisters from the high school would have come with her."

"Except for one thing," I say. "Sister Helen doesn't live in Santa Rosa anymore. Or so I've heard."

"You're right, I found that out. She's been living out at this weird place called The Prayer House, so far out in Carmel Valley it's practically to hell and gone."

"An interesting allegory," I say.

"Well, wait till you hear what I found out about it, and how Sister Helen ended up there. It's not a pretty story."

I must admit this grabs me. "Go ahead, I'm all ears."

"Well, you remember when Vatican II was held in the sixties? The conference that modernized so many things in the Church? Did away with the Latin, turned the Mass into your everyday boring lecture in English?"

"I remember."

"Well, the Church gave the noncloistered sisters

the freedom to go out in the world, dress like civilians, get jobs and rent their own apartments. Sometime after that, some of the motherhouses were closed because they'd become too costly to run. While that made sense financially, it was apparently tough on some of the older, retired sisters. A place they had thought of as home all their lives was suddenly gone."

"I remember that, too," I say, though I haven't really followed the Church and its machinations in years. "The motherhouses were huge, and as I remember, the Church—or maybe it was just the individual religious orders, I'm not sure—decided it could no longer afford to keep them running."

"The equivalent to once-wealthy families," Tommy agrees, "who had to sell their mansions and downgrade to condos."

I am recalling more details now, from news reports in the seventies or eighties. Traditionally, the motherhouses were the home base where young girls went to become nuns and then retired to when their life's work was over or when they were seriously ill. In between—in the active orders, at least—the nuns were assigned to smaller convents in towns and cities, next to the church schools they taught at or the hospitals where they were nurses. Sometime after Vatican II, however, many of the motherhouses closed, just as Tommy said. Whether the closures were due primarily to the changes in the Church after Vatican II, or whether they had more to do with financial conditions in the world at that time, I've never really known.

"How do you know so much about this, Tommy?"

"Well, like I told you, I've done some freelance writing for magazines. Also, I grew up in Catholic schools, and I've made it my business to know what's been happening in the Church over the years."

"So, what happened to the retired nuns whose motherhouses closed down? I know a lot of the younger ones welcomed the freedom to go out into the world, but what about the ones who were too old to work at jobs and take care of themselves?"

"I think it kind of depends on who you talk to," he says. "Some in the Church say they were taken care of just fine. Others say it wasn't always like that. Unfortunately, neither faction seems to like talking much about it. Reminds me of the rule of silence doctors and lawyers keep, when they refuse to talk about something bad going on in the profession."

"Well, that shouldn't surprise you. Churches are, after all, political organizations. And there's none more political than the Catholic Church. Unless, of course it's the Mormons. So anyway, what did you learn about Sister Helen?"

"I talked to somebody up at Joseph and Mary," he says, "who told me some of the retired sisters were sent to convents in California and neighboring states to live. Some tried to make it in the world with low-paying jobs, like the retired people who work at the fast-food places now. There's a fund these days to help the retired sisters, but when the changeover first began, things were a bit shaky. I take it Sister Helen got caught up in that transition period."

"And?"

"And somehow—I'm not sure how—she ended up in San Francisco, on the streets. Somebody found her and brought her to this place in the Carmel Valley called The Prayer House. At that time, she'd already been on the streets a few months. She was in pretty bad shape."

"But that's terrible!" Regardless of her attitude toward me lately, I still have a few fond memories of my former teacher and sponsor. Knowing she went through something like this disturbs me greatly. And what kind of long-lasting effect has it had on her? I wonder.

"How did you find all this out?" I ask Tommy.

"I drove up to Santa Rosa and talked to some people at your old Joseph and Mary Motherhouse. It's a private school now, and one of the nuns who knew Sister Helen still works there, as a teacher."

Our cab is pulling up to the La Playa, and I am silent a moment. Finally I say, "So, Tommy, you managed Santa Rosa and Rio, all in the twenty-four hours since you called me yesterday?"

He grins. "There you go again."

"Go?"

"Into that suspicious mode. Woman, you are one hard case."

"Remember that," I say.

Part 2

The Prayer House

Matthew 25:40: "Inasmuch as ye have done it unto the least of these my brethren, ye have done it unto me."

ABBY

It's midmorning when I get home from Rio. I call Frannie to tell her I'll pick Murphy up later in the day, if that's okay.

"No problem."

"How's he doing?" I ask.

"Billy's complaining he doesn't know any tricks," she says, chuckling.

"Well, that's Murph. He's pretty much a lay-around dog."

After that I call Karen to ask if Jeffrey's returned. The phone is answered immediately, as if she's sitting anxiously next to it.

"I haven't heard from him," she says in a bitter tone. "When I get my hands on that sonuvabitch…"

I don't tell her she doesn't have to worry about the "mistress in Brazil." To do so would require too many explanations.

I do wonder, however, if Karen's problems with Jeffrey go deeper than simply another woman. Jeffrey hit me that time in Rio when he was jealous because I'd talked to another man. I threatened him with arrest if he ever touched me again, and he never did—though there were times when he was under stress and I thought he might. It's one of the reasons I'd stopped loving him, and why—though my sister's betrayal tore me apart when I found her sleeping with my husband—I didn't grieve for my marriage as much as I otherwise might.

I make a mental note to talk to Karen about this. Her violence toward me, in burning my hand, could stem from her being abused herself. Stress has always escalated Jeffrey's mean streak, and if he's hurting her because of the trouble he's in now, she has to be convinced to leave him.

Checking my messages for word from Ben, I find only one. "I'll be pretty busy for a couple of days, Abby. I'll call you." *Click.*

Well, that's that, then. Nothing more to do but erase the several messages from the media that have all but jammed the machine, then shower, change clothes and head out to this so-called "prayer house" to see Sister Helen.

Dressing in jeans, boots and a T-shirt with a leather jacket over it, I'm on my way in an hour. I take the Green Hornet, not knowing what kinds of back roads I might run into. Both the Ryans and Tommy described the area surrounding The Prayer House as isolated, and I remember that Jeffrey and I became lost in the valley once, several years ago. He was looking for property to buy, and I went along for the ride, which became strained. We wound up on a road full of potholes that damaged Jeffrey's brand-new Mercedes, which did not add to the fun.

Between Carmel and the village of Carmel Valley there is more life than one might suspect. Off to the

sides of Carmel Valley Road a number of inns, restaurants, shops, homes, apartments and at least one
country and golf club nestle in the arms of the Santa
Lucia mountains. After one passes the village, however, signs of civilization begin to thin out. The
road winds east and south—the key word being
"winds"—through ranch and farming country. Depending on how well one navigates curves, it can
take an hour or two to get from the village to Highway 101 and Soledad. It is a route rarely traveled by
tourists, as there are faster ways to head south to L.A.
or north to San Francisco.

Rather than waste time searching for The Prayer
House, I stop at a real-estate office in the village—
End-of-the-Trail Realty—to ask directions. There is
only one agent there, a man with white hair, sitting
at a desk with the nameplate RICK STONE in front
of him. He is huge, broad-shouldered, his face weath-
ered, and he wears a cowboy hat. I feel I've stepped
into a Marlboro ad, the only difference being that in
this ad the Marlboro Man sports a significant belly
over his belt.

"Well, hello there," he says, looking me up and
down and smiling. "What can I do for you, little
lady?"

"I'm looking for a place called The Prayer House.
Can you tell me how to get there?"

His expression seems a blend of quizzical and cautious.

"I can tell you," he says, "but I don't know why
a pretty little thing like you would want to go there.
An awful lot of hills, valleys and curves."

The "pretty little thing" and "little lady" bother

me, but not as much as the way his eyes survey my own hills, valleys and curves.

"I'm visiting someone," I say.

"Oh." He lets out a loud, "Whew! For a minute there, I thought you were one of them nuns."

His gaze slides up and down again. "Not that you look like one," he adds with a smarmy smile. "No, indeed, not at all."

"Do you know where this place is?" I ask, restraining myself. "Do you have a map or something?"

He sighs. Groaning, he leans forward in his chair, opening a side desk drawer. The ample belly falls forward, and the chair squeaks under his weight.

Pulling out a map he opens it on the desk. "I'd like a nickel for everybody who stops in here wanting a map," he complains, smoothing it out with his hands. "All righty, look here now. You take this road till you get to this one."

He waits for me to lean over the desk and look at what he's pointing to on the map. When I do, he ogles my breasts, which push against the tight fabric of the T-shirt I'm wearing. A lock of my hair falls over my shoulder, and he reaches with a finger to touch it. "That's real pretty hair you've got there."

I'd forgotten about some of the characters who live out here. Pulling back safely out of reach, I fold my arms.

"What road, where?" I say briskly.

He points it out. "There's no road sign, so you have to watch your odometer. Call it maybe thirty-five-point-five miles or thereabouts. It's the only unmarked road off to the left. It goes into this canyon, here, then up over the hill. There's a lot of twists and turns, and no markers. You just have to find your way the first time, till you know where you're going."

He taps the map with his forefinger. "The place you're looking for is on this hill, here, and there's just one road into it, this one. You can't get to it any other way."

"Sounds pretty complicated," I say, wondering paranoically if he's sending me on a wild-goose chase, and if there'll be a gaggle of gangsters waiting for me at the pass.

"Well, see," he says, "most of the land around The Prayer House is ranches or it's owned by somebody and fenced off. In fact, this Prayer House, it's completely surrounded right now by other property. That'll change, of course, when the developers—"

He bites off his words and looks up at me, intently studying my face. "Say, don't I know you from somewhere?"

"I don't think so," I answer, taking the map, folding it and shoving it into my jacket pocket.

"Sure I do," he says as recognition dawns. "You're Jeffrey Northrup's wife. I remember you from when you came out here with him years ago, looking for property."

I do not remember Rick Stone, not at all. In fact, I barely remember stopping at this particular real-estate office before.

"That's pretty amazing," I say. "It's been at least six years. You must have a good memory for faces."

For a moment he doesn't answer. Then, "You're

absolutely right, Ms. Northrup. I guess that's it. I've got a good memory for faces.''

He stands and comes around the desk, putting a hand behind my back and ushering me firmly to the door. "You have a good visit with your friend now, hear? And thanks for stopping by."

The next minute, I find myself out in the small parking lot beside my car, wondering why I was given what my mom might have called "the bum's rush."

The chill began when he remembered that Jeffrey was my husband. But why? Bad business dealings?

This might well be one of the real-estate agencies that Jeffrey ended up buying through. I have no idea what he owns in the valley, only that Jeffrey was buying land here long before I met him. I've always assumed he's continued to either buy or sell, though that's a side of his finances he's never shared with me.

I shrug it off as unimportant and slide into the Jeep. Pulling my hair straight back, I fix it in a ponytail with a Scrunchee and head out into the valley. Tossing a CD into the player, I lose myself in some lively jazz and conflicting thoughts of the upcoming meeting with Sister Helen.

11

MAURO AND HILLARS

Half a block from the End-of-the-Trail real-estate office, a black Volvo sits well hidden by an overhang of live oaks. Mauro sneezes and reaches for a handkerchief. "Damn, I hate this place. Even this time of year, there's more pollen here than there are tourists in D.C."

Hillars folds his arms and sighs.

"I'd sure like to know what she's doing there," Mauro says, strumming his fingers on the steering wheel.

"My guess is she's carrying a message to Stone from her husband," Hillars answers.

"You're probably right." Mauro shoves the handkerchief into his pocket and slams a hand down on the wheel. "Damn, I knew we should have bugged this place."

"There wasn't enough time," Hillars reminds him mildly.

"She's not going back into town," Mauro notes as Abby comes out, starts the Jeep and turns east on Carmel Valley Road. "We should follow her." He reaches to turn on the engine.

Hillars lays a restraining hand on his arm. "No. Right now this Rick Stone is more important. If we crack him it could blow the whole thing wide open."

"I disagree. I'd bet the wife is right in the middle of it. She and that girlfriend of Northrup's, the sister-in-law."

"Karen Dean? Maybe. Regardless, I say we wait here and follow Stone when he leaves."

Mauro's expression conveys his disapproval. He doesn't say anything because Special Agent Hillars is his superior. *Shit, he's one of the highest-ranking agents in the Secret Service,* Mauro thinks. *Which is why the president put him on this case to begin with.*

There are times, however, when Mauro wonders.

Reaching into the back seat he grabs a book from a foot-high pile.

"The Rise and Fall of Western Civilization?" Hillars glances over and reads the title aloud. "That's a rather versatile collection you've got there. World history and *Ten New Ways to Make It Rich in Real Estate?"*

"It passes the time," Mauro says. "Not to mention, I believe in keeping up with what our suspects are doing." He reaches into the back again, and Hillars makes a face. *"Trepanning,"* he says, reading the title. "That's what killed the Bright woman."

"It's a fascinating subject," Mauro says. "Been around for thousands of years, they say."

Hillars shakes his head. "You like reading this stuff?"

"Like I said, it helps to study up on these people.

Gives some insight into how they think. You should try it sometime," he says.

"I'll pass."

Sure you will, Mauro thinks. *That's why you'll never be as smart as me.*

12

ABBY

Journeying to The Prayer House I feel the way pilgrims of old must have felt when, after trekking miles and miles through vast forestland on foot, they came upon their destination, finally: a dwelling, a haven with light, heat, food and water.

At least, I hope that's what The Prayer House ends up being for me. It's well after lunchtime, I'm tired and ravenous, and I haven't thought to bring water. I wonder if the good nuns might share a hunk of bread and a jug of H_2O with me.

Neither Rick Stone nor the map have lied. I find the left turnoff in almost precisely thirty-five-point-five miles. From there, the convoluted dirt roads leading from Carmel Valley Road to The Prayer House are narrow, so overgrown in places there is room for only one car. This hardly poses a problem as there are no other cars for the entire half hour of my journey in from Carmel Valley Road.

Rounding a final curve I find what I'm looking for: a magnificent old building of Spanish architecture that sits high on a hill overlooking the mountains and canyons of Carmel Valley. A carved wooden sign on a stone fence announces *The Prayer House* in small, discreet letters.

Inside the fence are flower and vegetable gardens, and there are a half-dozen women working in them, some in jeans and some in nun's long habits that are pulled up and tucked into belts, their white petticoats showing. At the top of the adobe structure of The Prayer House, in its precise middle, is an arched bell tower. Stained-glass windows tell me this tops a chapel, while low wings jutting out from either side infer living spaces.

Surprisingly, there is no gate. I follow a dirt driveway that takes me past the gardens to the left side of The Prayer House. In a backyard, visible from this angle, I see sheets and pillowcases on a clothesline, flapping in a light, sunny breeze. The pillowcases look heavy and thick, a vision that sweeps me back in time to my convent days, when we were taught to hang our undies inside pillowcases to dry, out of modesty.

It is a bittersweet memory that makes me want to sit in the Jeep for long moments after turning off the engine and think about how far, for good or bad, I've come.

There's little time for this, however. A sister approaches me from inside the nearest wing, coming across the lawn with swift strides, her black habit and white veil blowing, like the laundry, in the breeze. As she nears, I can hear the clatter of rosary beads dangling from her waist.

"Good afternoon," she says, leaning into my window. "I'm Sister Pauline. May I help you?"

She is a bit older than I'd first thought, though

probably not more than forty. Her face has a placid smoothness, like the faces of the more senior nuns I remember from the motherhouse.

"I'm looking for Sister Helen," I say.

"Helen Asback?"

"Yes. Could you tell her I'm here and would like to speak with her? If it's allowed, that is. I'm Abby Northrup."

The woman smiles. "Come with me, I'll take you inside."

I'm surprised at being accepted so readily, and it must show. As I slide from the Jeep, Sister Pauline says, "We're not cloistered here, you know. Just a bunch of women living out our lives."

We begin walking and I gesture to the gardens and the view of valley and hills. "Seems like a pretty good life. It's wonderful out here."

"Oh, we love it. All the sisters—and the others, of course—have worked hard to make it this way."

"Others?"

"The ones who aren't sisters anymore," she says softly.

"Oh. You mean like Sister Helen?"

She smiles. "Was Helen your teacher? It must be hard to break the habit of calling her 'Sister,' if so."

"Well, I haven't really seen her for years. But you're right, she taught me in high school."

We have reached the low adobe wing on the left, and I can't help but admire the riot of red bougainvillea that climbs most of a side wall and spills over the roof.

"It's incredibly old," Sister Pauline says. "It was

here when The Prayer House was founded twenty-five years ago.''

''Twenty-five years? I'd have guessed this building was here a lot longer than that.''

''Oh, much longer. It was the original home of the Carmelite sisters, a hundred or more years ago. Now they have the newer monastery in Carmel. Though new is a relative term.'' She chuckles. ''Even that has been around a while.''

''The monastery on Highway 1, you mean?''

''Yes, below Rio Road.''

The one beside the hill on which Marti was crucified.

Ted Wright said the site of Marti's crucifixion seemed to have been chosen deliberately, in keeping with the other ritual aspects of her murder. Is there some connection between that monastery and The Prayer House?

And why do I feel a touch of uneasiness as I follow Sister Pauline inside—despite her friendly welcome?

''Ah, here we are,'' she says, pushing through double doors at the center of the wing.

We are in a large reception area with white adobe walls and dark wooden trim around the doors and windows. It is much like the rooms in old Spanish missions I've seen throughout California, with the waxy scent of vigil candles carried over hushed air.

''We have lunch here at two,'' Sister Pauline says. ''That gives us a longer morning to work in the garden, before afternoon prayers.'' She pulls a pocket watch from her habit and glances at it. ''Helen should be in the kitchen by now. I'll take you to her, and then why don't you join us for lunch? We often have visitors from outside, and we like sharing the food from our gardens with them."

"I'd love that," I say, my stomach rumbling at the thought. "You don't maintain silence during mealtimes?"

"Only at dinner. Our lunch hours are for good conversation and planning."

She takes me down a long hall with floors that gleam the way they always did at Joseph and Mary. There the postulants buffed them once every three months, and I wonder aloud who does that sort of thing here.

"Oh, we all do," Sister Pauline says. "This is our home, and we're all very grateful to have it. We've taken great pride in keeping it well maintained."

I take it Sister Pauline is the "host sister," the one who greets outsiders and does the PR for the place. If so, she's doing a good job.

We enter a large, gleaming kitchen full of coppery pots and bubbling scents. In the middle of all this, Sister Helen stands at a stove stirring something in a large kettle. A deep, rich aroma of vegetables and herbs drifts across the room, and Sister Helen, to my amazement, is lost in her work, contentedly humming.

As we approach her, I note a slight smile tugging at her lips. I cannot recall ever having seen her look this happy. She is dressed in worn brown pants and a bright pink shirt, and her soft graying hair hangs over her forehead in damp curls.

"Helen?" Sister Pauline says softly, touching her

shoulder. Sister Helen turns. Seeing me, her eyes widen slightly. The smile fades.

"You have a visitor," Sister Pauline says.

"Can't you see I'm busy, Pauline?" she says sharply. "I don't have time to talk to anyone."

Turning back to her pot of soup, she continues stirring. But the humming has ceased, along with, seemingly, her peace of mind. My old teacher turns her back on me, but not before I catch a frown—or is it a look of fear?

"I'm sorry," Sister Pauline says quietly. "Ms. Northrup said she was a former student. I thought you would want to see her."

There is no response from Sister Helen, only a further stiffening of her back.

Sister Pauline looks at me and gently draws me away. When we're outside the kitchen door, she says, "You musn't mind Helen. She's had a very difficult time in recent years, and she may not have wanted to be reminded of her old life. I'm sure she'll come around once she's had time to think about it. Perhaps after lunch?"

I'm not so sure of that, but I follow Sister Pauline to a large narrow room with long tables that have chairs on either side. A few women sit talking quietly amongst themselves. One wears a white habit; the others are dressed in skirts and blouses. Two are white-haired, while another looks to be in her early thirties.

A crucifix hangs on the wall at one end of the room. At the opposite end is a large portrait of the woman I saw with Sister Helen at Marti's funeral.

"That woman," I say, nodding toward the portrait. "Who is she?

"That's Lydia Greyson, our founder. She reopened and refurbished The Prayer House in the seventies, making a home for many of the women you'll see here today. Others, such as myself, came later."

"Is Lydia Greyson a nun?"

"She was, long ago," Sister Pauline says. "But she left and married, and now she's a very wealthy woman. For the past twenty years, Lydia has provided this home free of charge to sisters and former sisters whose motherhouses closed. Our contract with her is to maintain the premises and to support ourselves, which we do in a number of ways. Some of the women grow vegetables and bake bread, much like in the abbeys of yesteryear. One sister writes spiritual books that have at times been on bestseller lists. Another—Helen, actually—makes soups, which are bottled and transported to Carmel, Santa Barbara and several small towns south of here, where they sell as specialty items in restaurants and gift stores."

"Sounds like Valhalla," I say. "Heaven on earth. But do you follow the same rules and restrictions as when living in a convent?"

She nods, crossing her arms and sliding her hands into her sleeves in a way I remember. "We do have certain rules that go way back to the days before the Ecumenical Council of the sixties. About other things we are much more free. We get to choose the work we do, for instance. And, oddly enough, there seems to be a job that fits each one of us. Something we enjoy doing." She smiles. "There is a wonderful synchronicity here about those things."

"Wow. So it really is Valhalla." But there is a question in my tone.

"Well, it's true we have our moments," Sister Pauline says confidentially, as if one girl to the other. "We have close to fifty women here now, and there are days…well, I probably shouldn't say." She rolls her eyes and chuckles.

We take seats at a long table next to the other women who have been talking as they wait for lunch. Sister Pauline introduces me to everyone, and one of the older women, Sister Gabriel, says, "You came here to see Helen? Well, good luck. Poor thing—she hasn't been herself lately."

"Not for a few months," another agrees. "Well, maybe it will do her good to see a former student."

Any former student but me, I think as a bell rings. Tables fill up with other women, both in habits and not. Large crocks of a creamy soup are brought to the tables by women wearing aprons, followed by huge plates of bread with fresh-churned butter. Crisp green salads are passed around.

When we've all helped ourselves and begun with soup, I say, "You mentioned that Sister Helen hasn't been herself?"

The woman who seems to be in her thirties, Louisa, pushes her short brown hair behind an ear and smiles. "She keeps forgetting to put the carrots in her soup. See—there's none in here today again. For Helen, that's a major faux pas. She's wedded to her soups."

"And did you notice she wasn't here at all the other day?" someone else says. "Never showed up until midnight."

Now, that's interesting. "That's allowed?" I say.

"Oh, sure," Louisa says. "It's not encouraged, but we aren't prisoners here."

"Things sure have changed in the Church," I say.

Sister Gabriel, the older nun, says, "You're one?"

"One?"

"Of the others. One that's left."

"What makes you think that?" I ask, smiling.

"Oh, it leaves a mark, don't think it doesn't." Her tone is sharp, and her eyes, behind thick Coke-bottle glasses, are unreadable.

"What mark do you think it left on me?" I ask.

"Mostly your table manners," she says briskly. "The way you broke your bread into quarters and buttered each piece as you came to it, and the way you took a little bit of everything that was passed to you—even the beans, which you obviously don't like, judging by the fact that you've barely touched them. Not many people have convent manners these days."

"You're quite a detective," I say, grinning. "But maybe I just took a course from Miss Manners."

"And maybe not," she responds, making a huffing sound. "I'm not so old I can't tell one when I see one."

"Well, you're right," I say, granting her the victory. "But that was long ago. I was eighteen."

She gives everyone at the table a look that says, *See, I knew it.*

For long moments we fall silent as everyone enjoys the fresh salad and Sister Helen's wonderful soup, carrots or no.

Just when I'm about to ask if Sister Helen will be

joining us, I see her coming through the door. She glances at us, but takes a seat at the far end of the room. Sister Pauline notices, but doesn't comment.

"See?" Louisa says. "She doesn't even sit with us anymore. And Tammy says that when she went to Albertson's in midvalley for groceries the other day, she couldn't believe Helen's list, she had so much chicken on it. She asked Helen later and she said she kept spoiling the soup and having to start over. I tell you, something's wrong."

"Hush, Louisa," the older nun says. "Helen's got a right to her privacy. And that friend of hers just died, you know. She's probably still grieving."

Louisa looks at me. "Did you know about that? A horrible thing. Right there in Carmel."

"Marti Bright, you mean? Yes, I knew. She was a friend of mine, too. Marti and I entered together. At Joseph and Mary, in Santa Rosa. Sister Helen was our sponsor."

There are several "Ohs" and nods around the table as if a last piece has fallen into place.

"I'm afraid we let her down when we left," I add.

"But she shouldn't be upset with you anymore," Louisa says. "Now that she's left, herself, I would think she'd understand. The Church was rotten to her, you know."

"Louisa!"

If I've been amazed at the openness and gossipy chatter of Louisa, Sister Gabriel is more like the nuns I used to know, whose job it was to reprimand the younger ones and keep them in line.

"Sorry," Louisa says, her chin rising, "but it's

true. All those years she gave to the Church, then to wind up on the streets when J&M closed—''

Sister Pauline interrupts in her quiet, gentle voice. ''It didn't happen in precisely that way, Louisa. Perhaps it is your own bitterness you speak of, not Helen's?''

Louisa's dark eyes flash. ''And why not? They wouldn't let me take a break from teaching, even when I was in chemo. Wouldn't even pay for my cure, for that matter!''

''Hush,'' Sister Gabriel says sternly. She slides a glance at me. ''You must understand, this issue is controversial, and there are many sides to it. Furthermore, there were many laypeople in the Church who came forward to help, within months of the motherhouses closing. They still do—help, that is. If that weren't so, Louisa wouldn't be here now. None of us would.''

''Why do you say that?'' I ask.

Louisa answers. ''She says that because the Church sold this abbey and the property for miles around to Lydia Greyson, virtually gave it to her for a song. Part of the sales agreement was that she would rebuild it—with her own money, of course— and provide a shelter for sisters who had lost their homes.'' She sends an angry look to Sister Gabriel. ''Or ones who got sick and didn't have any health insurance, like me.''

Jabbing at her vegetables with a fork, Louisa will not be hushed this time. ''You know very well, Gabriel, that when the motherhouses and many of the convents closed, they farmed the sisters out. That's what it amounted to, anyway, sending them hither and yon, all over the place. Most people don't know that, even to this day."

"That was then," Sister Pauline says quietly. "This is now, Louisa."

"Try telling that to Helen," she says darkly. "Things like that can leave a person with a lot of anger. I should know."

Sister Helen disappears from the dining room after lunch and is nowhere to be found. On the theory that any knowledge at all might help at this point, I let Sister Pauline take me on a tour of the gardens and surrounding grounds. Perhaps, I think, she will say something along the way that will help me to understand what's going on with Helen.

The grounds are far more extensive than as seen from the road. Behind The Prayer House and its quaint clotheslines we climb a low hill, with plots of vegetables and flowers on either side. Along the edge of the path are herbs, and the soothing fragrance of rosemary drifts my way.

"We have one sister who studies and grows herbs," Sister Pauline tells me. She breaks a sprig of rosemary from a bush and sniffs it, then hands it to me. "Rather than pay high premiums for HMOs— which aren't that available in Monterey County at this time, anyway—we've learned to use herbs for healing."

I sniff the rosemary and imagine I can feel my muscles relaxing. Though I often use rosemary-scented bath oils and lotions, I seldom have held the actual herb in my hand. Living here, I think, could bring a person back to the earth, make real a world in which so much is illusion.

A hundred yards or so away, I see Sister Helen walking up an adjoining hill to a cluster of older, dilapidated buildings. She carries a pail in each hand and seems to limp slightly.

Pauline follows my gaze. "She works so hard. Sometimes I worry about her."

"What are those buildings?" I ask.

"They're from the original days of The Prayer House, when it was a Carmelite convent," she says. "Those were outbuildings for smoking meats and shoeing the horses that helped them work the farm."

She sighs, shaking her head. "We don't use the buildings now, but Helen has a compost heap up there. Every day, despite the pain in her joints, she carries scraps from the kitchen—what some people call garbage—up that hill. It provides us with wonderful fertilizer for the gardens."

I watch my old teacher stumble under the weight of the pails, then set out again. Despite our differences, my heart goes out to her. "If she's in so much pain, why doesn't someone help her?" I ask.

Sister Pauline smiles. "Believe me, we've tried. Helen, I'm afraid, is quite territorial about her composting. It's almost as if she has some sort of sin to make up for, a penance to pay. Not that I can think of a single thing Helen might have done that was so terrible she'd have to go through all that."

I continue to watch as my old teacher circles one of the old outbuildings, to the plot of ground behind it. She has a noticeable limp now, and seems to stumble, then regain her balance. As she disappears, I, too, am wondering what awful thing she could possibly have done to lead her to this.

We reach the top of our own hill, and Sister Pauline points to another one toward the east, several miles away. "That's the edge of our property," she says, moving her arm side to side. "From there—to there."

I am surprised. "That's an awful lot of acreage," I say. "Hundreds, it looks like. And property is expensive out here. Your founder is a generous woman to have given you all this."

"Lydia is wonderful," she agrees. "Without her..." The soft voice trails off, and for long moments we stand quietly, enjoying the view and the scent of herbs and flowers that surrounds us.

But then a chill wind comes up, and I remember why I am here—because my friend is dead and her child is gone.

What must Marti have found in this place? I wonder. When Justin went missing, did visits here offer her peace and solace? Was she reminded of life at Joseph and Mary, as I am, and did she long to be back there where life was so relatively simple—though neither of us saw that at the time?

Of course, if we'd stayed in, our religious lives wouldn't have ended all that simply, any more than it did for these women here.

"Sister Pauline," I say, "I'm curious. There's Louisa here, who seems bitter about the Church. And I take it Sister Helen is, too. But then there's Sister Gabriel, who's more like the nuns I used to know—a stick-to-the-rules type. I don't know of many religious communities that would take in people with such differing opinions about the Church.''

''That's probably true, but the big difference here is that we aren't really a religious community,'' she explains. ''Lydia planned this as a home for sisters, who, for whatever reason, weren't able to cope with the changes after Vatican II. There are many who welcomed the new freedom, of course, especially the young, activist sisters who are helping the homeless in the cities, running businesses, investing in the stock market.'' She smiles. ''They support themselves and their orders in any number of ways, and most are happy to be doing so. Believe it or not, there are even sisters in their eighties and nineties who are thriving and still working, with no wish to retire.''

Her smile fades, and she shakes her head. ''Then there are the others...the ones who weren't able to cope with leaving their convents and going out into the world. Some were ill, and others...well, they needed care, a place to live that was more cloister-like, with fewer of the stresses people experience in the world. The Prayer House was founded by Lydia especially for them.''

With a soft laugh, she adds, ''You might say that those of us who came here are more like the cloistered Carmelites who used to live here than the teaching or nursing nuns we at first intended to be. I even imagine sometimes—though only in the dark of the night—that they've come back through us. To live again, you know.''

''Sister Pauline!'' My eyes widen. ''Reincarnation? Isn't that a bit New Age for a nun?''

''Good heavens, no! It's more Old Age. Reincarnation was in the Bible, after all, until the third century. It was man who took it out, not God.''

I shake my head. "I must say I'm surprised at the mix of women I've found out here. A former nun who rants against the Church, my old teacher, who hums while she makes her soups, like there's no other job in the world she would rather do, and now—someone who believes she could be a reincarnated Carmelite.''

Sister Pauline laughs. "If you come back here often, which of course you are welcome to do, you'll find that everyone here has had her own unique experience with both life and the Church. We do our best to honor each person's beliefs, whatever they are.''

"I'm impressed,'' I say, "and amazed that it works.''

Beside us is a small grotto with a statue of the Blessed Mother. A bench faces it, beneath a centuries-old oak tree. Sister Pauline sits, and pats the space beside her. I take a seat.

"It does take a certain amount of structure to make it work,'' she says. "For the sisters who want it, we have daily Mass, prayers throughout the day, silence in the evening hours. Even the women who have left their orders partake in much of that. It's not a habit one loses easily—but it also isn't required.''

I think back to my days before moving to San Francisco and working for the *Chron*. I attended Mass regularly, made novenas, took Communion. Sister Pauline is right; it's not something one loses easily. It took meeting Jeffrey to put me on a different path. Jeffrey, though born and baptized a Catholic, never practiced the faith after the age of fifteen. His parents were devout people who worked hard all their lives to eke out a living and finally acquired a comfortable, middle-class life. This they attributed to their faith in God, and when they died they stunned Jeffrey by leaving everything to the Church. He was fifteen at the time, on his own and penniless.

What his parents were thinking of, I'll never know. But kind-hearted lawyers took on his case and tried to fight the Church. They failed, and now Jeffrey speaks of the Roman Catholic Church in less than glowing terms. I know that much of his drive to accumulate money and property has to do with those early years.

In the beginning, I found it endearing to think of the wronged, naive adolescent going up against the huge and powerful entity of the Roman Catholic Church. Only later did I see the scars it had left.

"The sisters here who have left their orders," I say. "Are they the ones who no longer wear habits?"

"Not necessarily. Whether or not to wear the habit is a personal choice. Generally, the younger nuns like the freedom and comfort of civilian clothes."

She turns to me. "About Louisa. When one is thrown from self-sufficiency to dependency in the blink of an eye, and when that same someone is dealing with bad health and poor medical care, well, as Louisa said, it can do things to a person. She might turn to her faith and become stronger for it—or she might lose hope and become, at least for a time, bitter. Our prayers go up every day for our little Louisa."

"And Sister Helen. What about her?"

"Are you asking me if Helen is better or worse from her experiences before coming here?"

"Yes."

Sister Pauline smiles and touches my arm. "I'm sorry, but that's something you'll have to ask her."

Pulling out her pocket watch, she glances at it. "I'll be late for afternoon prayers if I don't go now. Would you like to sit here a while? Perhaps I can get Helen to come and talk to you after prayers."

I hesitate, thinking that it must be close to three, and the odds of Sister Helen talking to me today are not good. Besides, I still have a lot to do. Find Jeffrey, find Ben, put things together, figure them out...

It seems too much, suddenly, and I'm exhausted from Rio. "Tell you what," I say. "I'll give it an hour. Would you tell Sister Helen I'll be here, and I'd really like to talk to her?"

Sister Pauline assures me she will do that. As she hurries down the hill, the diminishing clack of her rosary beads drifts back to me, a poignant reminder of days gone by.

Rising from the bench, I stretch out instead on the ground a few feet from the tree, staring up at the open sky. There are no sounds now, only the occasional twitter of a bird. The grass beneath me pricks at my exposed arms; it is still dry and brown from the summer, as there has been little rain. But the sun feels good, and this is the first peaceful moment I can remember having since Marti died.

It is so odd, I think, when one loses a loved one. There are tears at unexpected moments, for no apparent reason. A feeling of being dead oneself, of the life force having left so that nothing remains but a numbness, an overwhelming sadness.

There is also an inability to believe it's really happened. *This person cannot be gone. It's not right.*

I know I have not been tracking well since Marti died. I haven't allowed myself to cry very often, fearing I'd lose myself completely in grief. In bed at night, however, there are moments of rage, when everything goes red. After the red comes the dark—as dark as I imagine the far reaches of the universe to be. I feel alone in the world, abandoned on a frozen star.

It is worse, I think, because of the way Marti "abandoned" me the few months before her death. Since Rio, I have begun to understand that. I still cannot accept it, but I understand it. Marti was searching for her son.

The Ryans told her that Jeffrey was negotiating for Justin's release, and that the FBI was involved. Marti, however, would never have sat idly by and let him run the show. She would have launched her own investigation.

And if that's the way it happened, she must have discovered pretty quickly that Jeffrey had lied about the FBI being on the case. That would have been easy enough to find out.

From there, would she have confronted Jeffrey with his lies?

Or did she pretend to believe him, while continuing to search for Justin herself?

I could see her doing that. I could also see her not telling the Ryans that Jeffrey had lied. Why make them worry, especially if she was on the kidnapper's trail herself, and believed that Justin would soon be safely home?

For that matter, she might not have completely trusted the Ryans with this information about Jeffrey. Since they were listening to and trusting Jeffrey so completely, she might have thought they'd tell him what she was doubting him.

Moments later I open my eyes as a shadow comes between me and the sun. My first wild hope is that it's Sister Helen. Instead, it's Lydia Greyson, the founder of The Prayer House and the woman who gave Marti a safe resting place in her family plot. She stands above me.

I sit up, shading my eyes from the sun. Here, I think, is someone who may be able to tell me many things.

But will she?

13

We sit on the bench beneath the tree, I in my jeans and Lydia Greyson in hers. She does not look like the stylish, wealthy woman who stood beside Marti's grave with Sister Helen and Ned. Here, she obviously works the land next to the other women. Her jeans are grass-stained at the knees, and I see that her hands, black-gloved at the funeral, are raw and chapped as if they have spent many hours in the ground, the laundry, the kitchen. I am guessing her age to be in the mid-fifties.

"Sister Pauline tells me you came here to speak with Helen?" she says. Her tone is distant, not at all friendly.

"I did, but she won't speak to me," I say. "Do you know why that is? Both she and Ned seemed upset with me at the funeral."

Lydia Greyson gives me an assessing look. There is more than a hint of anger in her voice. "I can't imagine that would be so difficult for you to figure out."

Irritated, I answer her in the same tone. "Well, I'm sorry, but it is. I'm not aware of having done anything to upset Sister Helen, at least not in the twenty years since I left the order."

"Not you personally, perhaps, but..." She hesitates. "Ms. Northrup, did your husband send you here?"

"My husband? No, of course not. Why would he?"

"You really don't know?"

"Ms. Greyson, I came here to talk to Helen about Marti. What would my husband have to do with that?"

A great deal, I now realize after speaking to the Ryans. But Lydia Greyson doesn't know about Justin.

Or does she?

Her sharp blue eyes study me and finally she nods. "I suppose I must believe you."

"I don't understand. Why wouldn't you?"

"Think about it, Ms. Northrup. Your husband has spent the better part of this year trying to persuade me—unsuccessfully, I might add—to sell The Prayer House and the land it's on to him. I thought perhaps you came here as his emissary. If that in fact is the case, I would like you to leave right now. I would also appreciate it if you would inform your husband that I have not changed my mind and do not intend to do so."

I am caught off guard. The only thing I've been thinking of since Rio is Justin's disappearance and Jeffrey's part in it, whatever that is. Lydia Greyson has thrown me a curve.

"Lydia—may I call you that?"

She nods, though a bit stiffly.

"And please, call me Abby," I add. "Lydia, I swear to you, I don't know about any of this. Why would Jeffrey want The Prayer House?"

"Oh, please. You have to ask?"

"Yes, I have to ask! What's going on?"

She points to a distant peak, as Sister Pauline did earlier. "You see that mountain? Our property extends to there, in the east. And to there—on either side. Beyond those boundaries, however, on all sides, lies your husband's property. We are surrounded by several hundreds of acres of land your husband owns."

I am startled. "Jeffrey's bought that much? I had no idea."

"Oh, he's been very clever, buying it up quietly over the years. There's only one problem, from your husband's point of view. We sit smack in the middle of land he wants to sell to developers—who, in turn, will put roads through, build golf courses, plant concrete. Even if I wanted to sell, which I don't, I will not allow them to do that."

Her jaw firms. "Some of us in the Carmel Valley have been fighting for years to keep development to a minimum here. The time may come when we can no longer hold out against those who are determined to turn this beautiful countryside into a cash cow. Meanwhile, I for one intend to stand my ground."

"And Jeffrey? You say he wants to sell to these developers?"

"Developers who won't buy until they have assurance that The Prayer House and its land is part of the package. When more water becomes available out here, they intend to build a major complex, including two hotels, several restaurants, a shopping mall and a country club. Your husband, I've learned through certain sources, already has developers lined up. Until he can promise them The Prayer House, however, they are dragging their heels.''

"My God. We're talking about millions of dollars here for Jeffrey."

"Many millions, I would think."

"Does Sister Helen know about this?"

"Helen has known for quite some time. She, Marti Bright and I talked about it frequently. Marti, in fact, is the one who brought this information to me several weeks ago."

Is this, then, the reason Marti and Helen turned against me? Was it not about Jeffrey's handling of Justin's kidnapping, after all?

"They must have thought I was in on Jeffrey's plan to take over The Prayer House," I say, "or at least supported him in it."

"Well, you do live..." Lydia pauses, giving me an arch look.

"A rather privileged life, you were going to say? Well, you're right. But why do people always see the wife as a carbon copy of the husband? Especially Marti. She was my closest friend. She must have known I'd never support Jeffrey in destroying something like this."

"Actually, I think she wasn't entirely certain. After what happened to Helen, Marti became a fierce advocate of housing for the elderly and the poor. She was outraged that your husband would try to take The Prayer House away from sisters who would lose their home, were they forced to leave here."

"As she *should* have been," I say, appalled. "I just wish she'd talked to me. I'd have helped her, dammit! She should have known that."

"There's more," Lydia says. "You might as well hear it all. Marti suspected your husband of manipulating real-estate prices here in the valley. She discovered that he'd bought undeveloped land at a low price when the market was right. Just a few months later he sold select parcels of the same land at inflated prices. Your husband's goal, according to Marti, was to increase the value not only of the first few properties he sold, but also the remaining acres he owned. That way he could sell the entire package to developers at an enormous profit."

"But property increases in value all the time. That's not illegal."

"No, of course not. It's the way he managed to inflate those prices. They went up quickly—far too quickly. Marti suspected your husband was involved in an illegal manipulation of the market. She wanted to expose him, bring him down, as she put it."

Lydia's voice turns bitter. "Unfortunately, she was murdered before she could come up with enough proof to take to the authorities. Convenient, wouldn't you say?"

I am silent a long moment. Finally I say, "You don't really believe my husband murdered Marti to keep her from exposing him?"

She just looks at me.

"I'm sorry," I say, "my husband has a lot of faults, but...a killer?"

Even as I argue the point in my mind, however, I know in my heart that for wealth and power, Jeffrey would do a lot. And if Marti stood in his way?

I stand and walk to the edge of the bluff overlooking Carmel Valley. The land here is some of the most beautiful I've ever seen. No high-rises or free-ways in sight.

Lydia stands beside me. "It's always been my dream," she says softly, "to build a center here. Nothing elaborate, and I'd see to it the trees and all our natural resources were protected. We already have enough well water to support such a center, and the gardens are providing most of our food. It's all organic, you know, so that runoff doesn't harm the surrounding land."

"What kind of center are you thinking of?" I ask.

"A place for women without homes, of course. That's always been my first love. I'd make this new center a home not for sisters, but ordinary women who have found themselves homeless for a short period of time—say, from the loss of a job, or extraordinary medical bills. It wouldn't be just a shelter. I'd offer them classes so they could learn new skills in work they enjoy, and there would be time for exercise and the creative arts, things that would build the spirit while they're rebuilding their lives."

She turns to me and smiles. "In the village of Brugge, Belgium, there once were houses for single women to go to live. The only rent they had to pay was prayer. I would like to provide a place for women going through difficult times, where their only 'rent' would be to attend to their spirit, in whatever way is appropriate to them."

"I like that idea," I say.

Her smile fades. "Well, then, talk to your husband. He's the only one who could ruin it for us."

"But you say you've refused to sell to him."

"Yes, well, that was bravado. Though I haven't

shared this yet with the women here, I'm afraid your husband has begun a campaign to run us out.''

''What kind of campaign?''

''The latest is a lawsuit designed to make me thoroughly gut The Prayer House and rebuild it according to code. It's an ancient building, and when I took it over twenty years ago I put in new kitchens, bathrooms, planted the gardens...''

She makes a gesture of defeat. ''Unfortunately, the kitchens are not up to code for selling our soups and baked goods to the public. I didn't foresee, when I originally remodeled them, that we'd be doing that one day. But the women here have worked very hard to support themselves, and the county has graciously looked the other way over the years—largely because they know our standards of cleanliness are the best. Recently, however, someone claimed to have become ill from our food. The ensuing lawsuit opened us up to all kinds of trouble.''

She sighs. ''You know, I've always prided myself on being a strong woman. But rebuilding The Prayer House over the years has eaten away at my resources, and now, having to defend this lawsuit—''

Her voice takes on a deep note of sadness. ''Rather than make the kinds of improvements they're demanding, I may be forced to close down The Prayer House. In fact, bankruptcy is not out of the question—not only for The Prayer House, but for me personally.''

''My God,'' I say, ''and wouldn't that fit neatly into Jeffrey's plans? He'd step in and gobble up The Prayer House in a hot second.''

''Including all the land he's been trying to persuade me to sell," she agrees. "Of course, I can't prove your husband is connected to this lawsuit, but that would be the ultimate effect."

She turns and faces me. "I must be frank with you, Abby. I went to the police about all this right after Marti was murdered. I told them what Marti had told me, that she suspected Jeffrey Northrup of illegally manipulating prices here in the valley. I also told them I believed your husband would not stop short of murder to keep Marti from unveiling his little scheme. I believe that's why they're looking for him now."

I am silent long moments, staring out over the valley.

"What are you thinking?" Lydia Greyson asks.

"That I have been a fool," I say. "Whatever else Jeffrey has done, I never would have suspected him of doing something like this."

"No, not a fool to love a man and believe in him," Lydia says gently.

"It's worse than that. A fool to believe in a man I haven't loved in years."

Sister Helen never shows, and I leave Lydia Greyson on the hill, contemplating the future of The Prayer House and her hoped-for new center. On my way back down the road, I have reason to wonder just how many ways and how often I have been a fool. On another lower hill facing this one, I spot a familiar car parked off the road. The vegetation out here is so brown I might not have noticed it, as Ben's unmarked police car, the Brown Turd, blends in so well as to be camouflaged.

Ben's been watching The Prayer House, I think at first.

Or it is me? Is he watching me?

If Ben follows me home, I don't see his car behind me. But then, it's his job to make sure people don't see him following them. To add to my distress, there has been no call from him when I arrive back at my house. When I phone the station, I'm told he "isn't available."

I put that on a back burner and call Frannie, asking if she'd like to bring her new boyfriend to dinner tonight.

"I know it's late," I say, "but I'd like to talk to Cliff about real estate."

I deliberately leave that vague, letting her think Cliff might be able to land me as a prospective seller at dinner tonight. Feeling a pang of conscience, I add, "I'm not really selling, I just want to know some things."

She accepts for both of them, and I tell her to come around seven.

Preparing chicken cilantro and vegetables, Frannie's favorite dish, I run through everything I learned at The Prayer House. It's not much, but some things are starting to come together in my mind.

When the food is in the oven I take Murphy for a walk along Scenic. While we're walking I look for the kid who brought him home the other night, thinking he might be walking his dog, too. I still would like to give him back his leash. There are plenty of people out with their dogs, but none of them is the kid.

The sea is wild today, the waves unusually high. Murphy loves this, and wants to go down to the beach and romp in them. I check my watch and see there isn't time before dinner. "Next time, boy," I promise. "Just cut me some slack for now, okay?"

He doesn't actually speak his answer, but the message is clear nevertheless. He's disappointed in me.

Ah, well. I'm disappointed in me, too. So many things I haven't known, so many things Marti was up against, things she never shared. What was it in me that told her she might not be able to trust me? Did I brag about my marriage to Jeffrey too much, caught up in my need to make myself believe I was living the fairytale? Did I seem too much in the ivory tower?

I always thought of Marti as my best friend; that was the way it appeared to me. But to her? Had I become someone not worthy of trust and friendship?

Standing on the path that runs along Scenic, my eyes tear as I feel I've lost her twice. I look out over the ocean and the drop-dead, half-moon coastline that stretches from Pebble Beach to the north and Big Sur to the south. The homes here run in the millions, and along this stretch there are no homeless—if one discounts those under the bridges.

How many times have I thought of the homeless, the way Marti did? The way Lydia Greyson is doing now? How many times have I used what I have to help those without homes?

Marti had so little…a tiny studio apartment she kept in New York for the few times she wasn't in some third world country helping everyone but herself.

I wonder if Ned has cleaned it out yet. If so, he can't have found much of his sister there. Marti was the type who threw newspapers out the minute she read them and paid bills the instant they arrived in the mail. She kept no clutter around, and wasn't the type to shop, at least in recent years. As she grew older, she became less and less acquisitive, probably because she worked day to day with people who had so little.

I can't help wondering how many homeless people I could feed with that BMW in the garage.

Murphy is tugging to move on, so I let him walk me back to the house. The chicken looks good, and Murphy has already eaten, so I put him in my study next to the kitchen. He's into silent begging, plunking himself down beside guests and looking soulful while they eat. I don't mind this, but it drives Frannie to distraction.

When my guests arrive, I have the table already set and the salad ready to serve. There's no time to waste with predinner cocktails; I am on a mission tonight. With any luck I'll learn how best to nail Jeffrey for his illegal manipulation of real estate in the Carmel Valley.

In so doing, I just may be able to get him off Lydia's back.

And I'll get him for you, too, Marti. I swear I will.

14

Frannie, her boyfriend, Cliff, and I sit at my dining-room table having after-dinner coffee. I have laid out for him what I learned from Lydia Greyson, as told to her by Marti, though I haven't mentioned their names or The Prayer House. Nor have I told Cliff that I suspect Jeffrey of having manipulated prices in the Carmel Valley. Instead, I've told him I'm working on a book, a novel, and need some information as to how this sort of scam might be carried out.

"You're working on a novel?" Frannie says, looking skeptical. "I thought you were a reporter back in the old days. And what about your column?"

It's always been difficult to hide anything from Frannie, but I tell her I feel in need of a change. "That happens, you know, when someone has gone through a loss."

There's not much she can say to that. She sips her coffee and watches the two of us as Cliff hands me a possible scenario and I take notes.

"Let's see if I've got this right," he says, ruffling his short blond hair, then making marks on the tablecloth with his fork as if drawing a map. "Your character wants to sell some property at maybe thirty percent more than he just paid for it. And what he just paid for it was the normal market value. Right?"

"Right."

"Okay, so first, he has to convince a prospective buyer that the price he's being asked to pay *is* the normal market value—even though the normal market value is really thirty percent less."

"I see."

"So, what he might do is pay off a local Realtor to show the prospective buyer a fake comp, or 'comparable.' I don't know if you know, but that's a study that shows a prospect what similar properties have recently sold for in the area. The price should be close to the one he's being asked to pay. In other words, it gives the buyer a sense of security about the sale price of the property."

"Okay." I write that down.

"A fake comp wouldn't be enough, though," Frannie chimes in.

Cliff sends her a smile. "That's true. To manipulate the value of property in the way you describe, Abby, your character would need a certified appraiser on the take, as well, to appraise this particular property consistent with the fake comps, so a bank would approve the loan." He scratches his chin. "And now that I think of it, banks usually pick their own appraisers, so the banker might have to be in on it, too. Otherwise, he couldn't very well justify giving the buyer a mortgage in that amount."

"You mean, a local banker?" My thoughts immediately go to Harry Blimm—Jeffrey's good buddy and president of Seacoast Bank.

But Harry Blimm, a crook? The man who danced wearing his wife's red hoop earrings, with my Spanish tablecloth wrapped around his waist? He's always seemed so harmless. Could he possibly be involved in Jeffrey's scam?

"A local banker would be best," Cliff is saying. "Someone your character knew well and trusted."

"That's a lot of people your *character* would have to trust," Frannie says, her emphasis on the word "character," telling me she knows exactly who I'm talking about. She doesn't say any more, however, and Cliff continues.

"She's right," he says. "Your character would have to have a lot more at stake than one piece of property, to take all these people into his confidence. On the other hand, by including everyone in the profits—the real-estate agent, the appraiser and the banker—he could keep the fraud in the family, so to speak. They'd each be breaking the law, so no one would be tempted to talk."

"And, speaking of the law, aren't we talking about bank fraud here?" Frannie says.

Cliff looks at her, surprised.

"Well, I'm not some dummy, after all," she says. "I hear you talking about this stuff all the time."

"Again, she's right," he agrees, smiling. "Which is why I'm saying your character would have to have a lot at stake. Hundreds of acres, at least. Something that would bring in a ton of bucks."

"Still, the beauty of it," I suggest, "might be that after the initial scam—that is, after my character sells three or four properties at, say, thirty percent over what he paid for them—those inflated prices would become the actual, legal comps for properties in that area. Right?"

Cliff nods. "For a while, at least. Your character's

remaining acreage could then be legally sold at this higher comp value, thus taking some of the risk out of the scam. He could sell it to developers at a price at least thirty percent higher than it would have gone for before the scam ever was perpetrated.''

"And are you saying no one, not even other Realtors, would get suspicious of this?"

"Well, other Realtors in the Carmel area, of course, might suspect something is up, because property typically doesn't go up in price that quickly."

He picks up his coffee cup and takes a deep swallow. "I don't think most Realtors would complain, though, because their own commissions are based on the price of the homes they sell. And this scam has made the prices of the entire area much higher, so those other Realtors win, too. Why would they want to rock the boat?"

He shrugs and looks uncomfortable. "Understand, I'm not saying other Realtors would necessarily *know* about your character's scam, or have any facts about it. Just that they'd be happy with the end result. You know—thank God for small blessings. Shoot, even the long-time Carmel Valley residents would be happy. Their homes would have just shot up significantly in value."

He looks at Frannie. "Abby's four cohorts could collect a king's ransom and retire for life. Boy, wouldn't that be nice! If it were me, I'd be rich by sundown."

"Don't look now," Frannie says mildly, "but it's well past sundown."

He makes a face, and she sticks her tongue out.

"What about you, Cliff?" I ask. "Have you ever

heard anything about an actual scam like this in the Carmel Valley?''

''Not here, but I just moved down from San Francisco, and I'm still getting to know the area. I've heard about it other places, though. Manipulating prices with fake comps, I mean.''

He looks around my dining room and through the windows, where he can only be imagining the ocean view, as it's dark by now. ''This place is really incredible. You sure you don't want to sell? As long a time as you've been here, I'll bet you could turn a nice profit right about now.''

''Well, let's put it this way,'' I say. ''When and if I ever am ready, you're the first person I'll call.'' Frannie's boyfriend has grown in my estimation tonight.

Cliff sighs, and I know his hopes for more than a dinner this evening have been dashed. Still, like any true dyed-in-the-wool salesman, I feel certain he won't give up.

Turning back to me, he says, ''One more thing I should add about that scam.''

''And that is?''

''If you want this plot to be credible, you should take into account that this kind of scam would be short-lived. Within a year after your character's first manipulation of prices, the comps of the surrounding homes would almost certainly begin to drift slowly back down, finding a more natural market level. I think he'd feel an urgency to find a developer before that happens.''

''I see. And if anyone stood in the way of his landing that developer in time to clean up? Say, for instance, someone caught on and threatened to expose him?''

Cliff smiles. ''Depends on what kind of story you're writing. If it's a mystery, and your character's greedy enough, he might want to kill that person off.''

15

Since Marti's funeral, I've been running on pure adrenaline. The minute Cliff and Frannie leave, however, I crash. Turning off the lights downstairs, I leave the mess in the kitchen for morning and trudge on up to bed, Murphy at my side.

My sleep is disturbed by dreams of Mauro and Hillars, Jeffrey and the Ryans, Lydia Greyson and Sister Helen. They all seem to come together in one big pot, at the bottom of which are Marti and Justin. Mauro is hollering, "Justin has been kidnapped, you idiot!" while Jeffrey stands with a trust deed in his hand, arguing, "I know nothing about any of this."

The symbolism of it being a "trust" deed doesn't escape me when I wake in the morning, more wrung out from exhaustion than rested.

A kind of change has taken place inside me, however. I feel that, since Rio and The Prayer House, I have traveled light-years from the person I've been to the person I used to be, BJ—before Jeffrey. Though I feel vulnerable and unsure of the next step I should take, I am beginning to understand that, from this point on, those steps must be more decisive. It's time I looked deeper inside myself and discovered what I'm really made of.

Somehow, finding out about Jeffrey's many manipulations has freed me in a way I've never felt free before.

To get myself mentally grounded for whatever's to come, I call Davis Bowen, a Kenpo black belt I've been practicing with on and off. I began studying Kenpo, a version of the martial arts, when I lived in San Francisco. Someone suggested I take a course in self-defense for those times when I was out at night alone, working on stories for the *Chron*. I found that Kenpo centered me, gave me a feeling of personal power that carried over into my work.

After Jeffrey and I married, however, I couldn't fit myself into the schedules of the martial arts schools on the Peninsula. I was too busy being Jeffrey's wife. Then one day someone introduced me to Davis. It was like going home. I'm only a blue belt, so Davis takes it easy with me. Almost as much as the Kenpo, I enjoy his conversation.

When I ask if he has time for a quick practice session, he says to come over at ten. I jump into the shower, don jeans and a sweater, tie my hair back and run downstairs.

In the hallway I pause, thinking something is not quite right. A quick check assures me I'm alone. My computer in my office, however, is on—and I definitely remember turning it off after sending my column in.

While this would ordinarily scare me, I do work with Windows 98. One of its many little idiosyncrasies is that, when my computer is in the sleep mode, it routinely turns itself back on and starts to "house-clean." When I first got Windows 98, this freaked me out. I'd be in the living room watching television in the dark, and all of a sudden I'd hear my computer turn on, as if someone were in here working on it. But no, it would be here all alone, busily scanning for errors like some overachieving housewife dusting in all the corners.

Now I usually just shut it down, instead of putting it to sleep. That way it stays put.

So, did I forget the other day and lapse into my old habit of hitting the sleep button? I suppose that's possible. I was in a hurry to get going.

I cross over to my desk and sit down, hitting Start from the desktop and then Shut Down. I watch while it does its thing, assuring myself that it won't pop back on while I'm gone.

Murph knows I'm leaving and is in the kitchen wagging his tail, already at the cupboard that holds the box of Beggin' Strips. Still shoving away an uneasy feeling about my computer, I get out the dog treats and give Murph two as a bonus for absolutely nothing other than being a good dog. Then I grab my car keys, dash through the pantry into the garage and set out in the Jeep.

Davis lives in a great house on the hill above Clint's Mission Ranch Inn. There's a view from there to sundown and a private patio with flowers and fountains. It's in the patio I find him, sitting on the ground meditating, legs crossed, a calm expression on his face. Soft meditative music plays inside the house, and knowing the program, I go in there, take my white *gi* and blue belt from the hall closet and go into the bathroom to change.

Out on the patio again I take a seat on a bench by a bronze Buddha, close my eyes and wait quietly for

Davis to finish. The sun beats down on my face till I feel like a lizard on a rock. My bones unbend and tension leaves through the tips of my fingers in waves.

"Don't get too relaxed," I hear Davis say. "I plan to give you a real workout."

"Shh. I'm about to levitate."

"Oooh, take me with you!" he says.

I laugh and open my eyes. Davis unwinds himself and crosses to one of the fountains, where he splashes his face with water. The fountain is an angel, with the stream of water pouring from a vase she holds in her hand. I have always loved Davis for his interest in, and openness about, all things spiritual—from Zen Buddhism, to Catholicism, to Protestantism and the world's most obscure religions.

"You ready?" he asks, preparing himself with stretches.

I join him in the stretches, loosening my muscles as we talk. "Ready as I'll ever be."

"You don't seem quite yourself today."

"Well, a lot's been happening."

"That woman who was crucified. She was a friend of yours, wasn't she?"

"Yes."

"That's really tough. But there's more, right?"

"Not much. Only that now I don't know who to trust."

"Oh, that." He grins. "I thought you'd come up with something new."

I glare at him. "And what exactly does that mean?"

"Only that you've been surrounded by people you

can't trust for a long time. Too long a time, if you ask me."

"Are we talking about Jeffrey? Again?"

He shrugs. "Think about it. You're a good person, Abby. Despite that tough attitude of yours, you like to believe in people. That gives them all the room in the world to take advantage of you."

"Yeah, well, that's over now," I say.

I take the starting position and we bow to each other.

"You think so?" Davis's expression changes in an instant, going from friend to foe. He grabs me suddenly in a bear hug from the front, pinning my arms to my sides. Instinctively, I make Eagle's Beaks of my hands and jab his lower rib cage. Both my arms circle under his to strike his floating ribs with an inverted punch. My right foot steps back to six o'clock, and at the same time I grab his head from behind. My right knee slams up to his groin. Planting my foot back to six o'clock, I drive his head down to my left knee.

When I'm finished, my opponent is stunned and even breathing hard. Not that he's hurt—most of my movements have been light practice ones, and for the rest he was wearing guards.

"Damn, Abby, you've been moving up on me," he says in an amazed tone when we step back from each other.

"Yeah, I could have done some real damage," I respond with some satisfaction. "May I remind you that Eagle's Talons is brown belt, two up from mine? But I got you, didn't I? I actually caught you off your guard."

"Well, that's what happens when we think we know someone," he says, grinning.

His expression turns serious. "It's something you might want to remember, Abby."

After our session I shower, dress in my jeans and sweater, then grab some orange juice at Davis's breakfast bar. He's still out on the patio, talking on the phone. The Kenpo has dusted off some cobwebs for me, and while in the shower I have remembered an old adage about journalism—that it's all about casting light into dark corners.

There have been far too many dark corners in this mess, and I plan to change that. Taking a pad and pencil out of my bag, I begin to write:

(1) Check out Tommy Lawrence, find out what he's really up to. He knows too damned much.

(2) Call someone or three someones—Mauro, Ben, Karen—and see if Jeffrey's turned up.

(3) Pay a visit to Harry Blimm, president of Seacoast Bank of Carmel.

If Cliff's suggested scenario is even close to the truth, Harry, I think, could hold the key to where Jeffrey is. My guess is that he and Rick the Randy Realtor—given how he cooled on me yesterday when he discovered I was Jeffrey's wife—could well be my husband's cohorts in the land scam out in the valley.

Or, if Harry is innocent, he could be just the person to help me nail Jeffrey. If I can do that, I'll have something to hold over my husband's head. Not only might that help The Prayer House, but if Jeffrey has been concealing Justin's whereabouts, or whatever happened to him, I might be able to force him to admit it.

From there, I'm not sure what will happen. I write down what little I know, hoping it will lead to other ideas:

(1) Justin was kidnapped by person or persons unknown, and for a reason we don't yet know.

(2) Marti went to President Chase for help—possibly revealing that he was her son's biological father.

(3) Chase appointed Jeffrey, his right hand (who also happened to live on-scene), to quietly launch an investigation to find Justin.

(4) Jeffrey decided on his own to *pretend* to launch that investigation, while actually hushing up Justin's disappearance—possibly out of fear that Justin's paternity would come out in the heat of what could end up being a nationwide search for the boy, thus tarnishing Golden Boy Chase's reputation.

Which leads me to an alternative theory: President Chase is not a golden boy. He's the one who told Jeffrey to keep Justin's disappearance and paternity quiet.

It's a reach, but, either way, the end result is the same. No official investigation, no real effort made to find Marti's son.

I now know that my husband is a crook. But is he diabolical enough to simply leave a fifteen-year-old boy in the hands of a kidnapper—one who has threatened to deliver the boy's head to his parents if they breathe a word to the police or the FBI?

And why was there no ransom demand?

Further, is Jeffrey diabolical enough to have killed

Marti simply to assure her silence about the Carmel
Valley real-estate scam?

And finally, on my list: Talk to Mauro and Hillars.
Tell them I know now why they're really here—and
why the Secret Service in particular is after Jeffrey's
ass.

When I walk through my front door again, my
phone is ringing.

"Hey," Ben says when I pick up. "Where have
you been?"

"Oh, out and about," I say coolly. I am annoyed
at his asking this, while I've been leaving messages
for him hither and yon for days.

"I met with your Sister Helen yesterday," he says.
"Out at this place called The Prayer House."

"Really?" *I saw your car out there,* I want to say,
but don't.

"Have you talked to her?" he asks.

"No, I haven't." Which is not a lie.

There is a small silence. He knows I was there.
Why doesn't he just say so?

"What did she tell you?" I ask him.

"Not much. She seemed skittish."

"Well, a visit from the police can do that."

"You sound sort of odd this morning."

"I can't imagine why."

He sighs. "She told you I was there?"

"No, I never talked to her."

"Then why—"

"Look, let it alone, okay? What did she tell you?"

"Only that she knows nothing about Marti or Justin. Says she hadn't seen Marti in a long time, and didn't know a thing about Marti having a son.''

Now that is a bald-faced lie. The Ryans told me she used to visit him regularly. So the inscrutable Sister Helen is keeping a lot to herself. But why? What does she hope to gain?

"I tried to call you yesterday," Ben says.

"I didn't get a message," I answer.

"I didn't leave one," he says.

Another silence.

"Any luck finding Jeffrey?" I ask.

"None at all."

"Well."

I hear him grunt. We're beginning to sound like him and Arnie.

"You have fun in Rio?" he asks.

"Sort of." If he has taken me by surprise with his knowledge of my travels, I don't let on. Neither do I tell him about finding the Ryans, remembering Tommy's warning that Ben would probably never keep anything of a professional nature to himself. It's an opinion I happen to agree with. And I don't want the Monterey County task force, or the Secret Service, breathing down the Ryans' necks till they've had a chance to get home and regroup.

"Well, guess I'd better go," I say. "I've got a ton of errands to run."

"Yeah. Guess I should let you go."

"Talk to you later, then."

"Okay."

Each of us waits for the other to hang up. I go first, taking only a small amount of satisfaction in having beat him to the punch.

*   *   *

Harry Wilkins Blimm, the sign says on the mahogany door. I push it open and am faced with a startled assistant in Harry's outer office. She's new and doesn't know me. It probably doesn't help that I'm dressed in old jeans and don't look much like a rich Carmel matron.

"Excuse me," she says, rising. "Do you have an appointment?"

"No," I say, continuing to walk toward Harry's inner door. Unlike some bank presidents, he doesn't sit up front where clients can see him. I've always wondered what he had to hide.

"Wait, you can't go in there," the receptionist says.

But I'm already in. Harry, as startled as she, is on the phone. In a low voice he says, "I can't talk now. Call me back." He hangs up.

I should tell Ben to check good old Harry's phone records for incoming calls, I think. Of course, if that was Jeffrey on the phone, he could have called from his cell phone.

But I doubt it. The crooks who slip up the most are the ones who feel so self-confident they don't think they'll ever be caught. And one thing Jeffrey has never lacked is self-confidence.

"How's he doing?" I ask conversationally, taking a seat across from Harry.

"Who?" he says, running a finger under his shirt collar. "How's who doing?"

"Jeffrey. That was him, right?"

A flush creeps from his neck to his chubby face,

ending at the bald head. He opens his mouth to speak.

"Don't even bother," I say. "For a bank president you're not a good liar, Harry. Now, look, I'll tell you what I know, and you don't even have to speak—you can just nod for yes or shake your head for no. That way there won't be anything incriminating on that tape recorder you keep in your desk drawer. How's that?"

I don't wait for a response. "Okay, so first off, I spent a few hours yesterday out in the Carmel Valley. A pretty little place called The Prayer House. You know it, Harry?"

When he doesn't respond, I say, "Nod, Harry. Just nod."

He nods.

"So okay, you know The Prayer House. You know Jeffrey's been trying to buy it, right?"

Again he nods.

"And you've been in on his scam to manipulate prices out there in the valley, right, Harry?"

This time he both shakes his head and stutters. "I—I d-don't know what you're talking about."

I stand and slam my hands on the desk, putting my face close to his. "Dammit, Harry, you're not playing by the rules! I told you just to nod."

His back stiffens as he pushes away from me and looks me straight in the eye. "I don't know what it is you want, Abby, but I am not now nor have I ever been involved in any scam, as you call it, with Jeffrey. Our relationship is banker to client, and it has always—I repeat, *always*—been aboveboard."

I study him a moment and wonder if he might be

telling the truth. Otherwise, I'm almost certain he'd have crumpled. I've had to call Harry on the carpet more than once at a party for getting too rowdy, and every time he's collapsed like a cold toasted marshmallow.

Easing back into my chair, I say, "Let's imagine you don't know what Jeffrey's been up to, then. Let's just say this is all fantasy. You know Rick Stone, End-of-the-Trail Realty?"

His tone is cautious. "Yes, of course I do. I know most of the Realtors around here."

"You know most of the certified appraisers, too. Right?"

He shrugs. "A few."

"Okay, good. Now we're getting somewhere. Still fantasizing, it wouldn't be all that difficult for you to set up a little meeting between Jeffrey, Rick Stone and one of those appraisers, would it?"

"You're assuming I would want to do something like that," he says, reaching into his drawer. I figure he's turning off the tape recorder.

"So let's say you wanted to do that. And let's say between the three of them, they come up with fake comps and fake appraisals for a few pieces of property Jeffrey owns in the valley. Not to mention a buyer who's willing to pay through the nose just because he believes the comps and appraisals are real. Are you following me, Harry?"

He doesn't answer, so I go on. "Jeffrey would be getting a huge amount over what he'd originally bought the property for, and he'd naturally enough share it with his pals. That'd be a sweet deal for my imaginary trio, wouldn't it, Harry?"

"I suppose it might. But—"

"But they'd need someone else—a banker, Harry, who would be willing to loan that much money on a property that he knew Jeffrey had bought for a third of that selling price months before. A banker who's a friend and who wouldn't ask any questions about how the property got to be that expensive so quickly—because he, too, was getting a piece of the pie."

Harry turns deep red and pushes himself up from his chair. His voice is tight with anger. "I see where you're going with this, Abby, and I must tell you I am profoundly offended. I would never go along with such a scheme."

"Not even for a piece of that pie, Harry? It might be a big piece. Half, even. You could retire and dance your way through parties the rest of your life."

"I cannot believe I thought you were a friend," he says. "I want you out of here—right now. In fact, if you don't leave of your own accord, I will call Security." He reaches for his phone.

"Not to worry, Harry," I say. "I already got what I came here for."

If he doesn't tell Jeffrey I know about his scam, I'll eat my hat, as my mom would say. Now all I have to do is wait and see if Jeffrey comes after me—the way he may, or may not, have gone after Marti.

Next stop, since it's only a few blocks away: Tom, Tom, the Piper's Son. Or whoever the hell he is.

And why am I not surprised when, upon asking for him at the desk of the La Playa, I am told he is not registered there and never has been?

I go into the bar and sit on a stool. Jimmy-John's not on today, so I ask the bartender on shift, who I know, if he's seen a guy named Tommy Lawrence in here. He says he doesn't recognize the name, but what does he look like?

I tell him tall, thin, brown hair, looks like a gangly kid.

"You mean the one that's always asking questions about locals?" he says. "Loaded with charm, like some con men in town I could name?"

"That's the one," I say.

"Sure, he's been in here having drinks. Haven't seen him today, though."

"Is Jimmy-John around anywhere?"

He shakes his head. "He got sacked."

"Really? What happened?"

"The boss caught him one too many times giving out too much personal information about guests. You know, you can give a guy a break, but if he doesn't make use of it..."

"When did this happen?"

"A couple weeks ago."

At least a full week before Tommy Lawrence hit town. Unless he lied about that, too, and has been here longer than he let on.

"You say you've seen this guy Tommy in here asking questions lately?"

"Last few days, yeah."

"Have you or anyone else given him any information about me?"

"Not me." He grins. "I like my job."

I take my notepad out. "Do me a favor?"

"Sure."

"When you see this guy again, give him something for me?"

"No problem."

I write on a clean sheet of paper, "I know the real reason you're here."

I sign it "Abby," then fold it, writing Tommy's name on the front of it.

The bartender takes the note and slips it into his pocket. I thank him and walk back out to my Jeep.

Mauro and Hillars I don't need to find. Predictably, they have found me.

"I take it my husband hasn't shown," I say, leaning into Mauro's window. "Any leads?"

"If I had leads, Ms. Northrup—"

"You wouldn't share them with me, Mr. Mauro," I finish for him. "So are you here to take me in?"

"As a matter of fact, the thought crossed my mind."

"And what did your mind have to say?"

"It said to let you dig a deeper hole."

Hillars sits next to him, his usual silent self. But his arms are folded, and his mouth droops in disapproval. I take it he doesn't like his young partner trading barbs with a suspect.

"How was your visit with Harry Blimm?" Mauro asks. "FYI, we already interviewed him."

"And?"

"And we feel you're barking up the wrong tree," he says. "However..."

"Yes?"

"Did you uncover anything useful, Ms. Northrup?"

"You know what, Mr. Mauro? FYI, I wouldn't tell you if I had. But I know now why you're after my husband."

That evening, I sit in my living room with Murphy, drink a cup of coffee and wait. I've drawn my blinds, an instinctive counteraction to those dumb movies where the heroine's being stalked and runs inside her house, locking the door but not bothering to close the curtains. It's black as pitch outside, and anyone could be out there looking in. She doesn't think about that, but blithely goes around the house flicking on lights.

Carmel is especially dark at night, since no streetlights are allowed in the Village, just as there are no mailboxes or addresses on houses—a throwback, some say, to the days when Bohemian artists and actors used to run here to hide out from frenzied media and fans.

I glance at my watch. Seven-twenty. I have now rattled the cages of a few select people, and I'm wondering how long it will take for at least one of them to show up.

Earlier, I have seen the storm coming in from the southwest, and it looked big. Still, the loud patter of rain on my chimney flue startles me. I am reminded that the Pineapple Express has roared up the Pacific from Hawaii more than once, tearing up trees on Scenic and lifting roofs. Out of habit I go around checking windows, making sure they are tight. When I come to the one in the kitchen that Tommy remarked upon earlier, there is little I can do. The broken hinge on the casement window leaves no way to lock it, so I settle for turning the crank and closing it as tightly as possible. Since it opens only to the patio and there is a high wooden fence surrounding it, I've never worried about the latch. This is Carmel, after all. A relatively safe little town.

Until now. Since Marti was murdered, anything seems possible.

Going to the fridge, I take bottles of ketchup, mayonnaise, tomato sauce and wine, lining them up on the windowsill. This makes me feel a bit foolish, but if anyone does try to get in, they'll at least have to make some noise.

Sitting beside Murphy again in the living room, I begin to feel like Snow White, waiting for my Crook to come. It's now after eight, and no one's shown yet. I'd expected Jeffrey or Tommy—even Harry Blimm. Did I figure this thing all wrong?

When the doorbell finally rings I nearly jump out of my skin.

Flicking on the porch light, I peer through the wet glass of the window next to my door and can make out only a huddled, dark figure. Not tall enough for Tommy or Jeffrey—nor fat enough for Harry Blimm. Who in the world have I snared?

My surprise couldn't be greater when I open the door to see, clothed in a black raincoat with a dark shawl over her head, Sister Helen.

16

I open the door wide and half pull my old teacher through. She seems numb, both unseeing and unfeeling. "Good Lord, Sister, you're drenched! Let me take that shawl."

I lift the sodden garment from her shoulders, but she barely seems to notice. I can tell from the way she moves that she's in pain. Sister Pauline mentioned arthritis. This weather, and the trip from The Prayer House, must have done her in.

"Did you drive?" I ask as I hang the shawl over a clothes rack in the foyer.

She doesn't answer, and when I turn I see her standing very close to me. A chill runs through me, and I don't think it's from the cold draft the open door let in. There is a fanatical look in Sister Helen's eyes that frightens me.

"Why did you have to meddle?" she says, her voice low and hoarse. "Why didn't you stay out of it?"

I back away. Looking down at her hands, I see them work into fists. My own rise in an automatic posture of defense.

"What is it?" I say. "What is it you don't want me meddling in?"

"Everything!" She takes a step toward me. "Haven't you done enough?"

I look around for something to fend her off with. But there's nothing here in the foyer, only the two of us. And there's no way I can Kenpo Sister Helen.

"Murph?" I call out, and immediately my protector is at my side, ears up and alert.

"I don't know what you mean," I say as calmly as possible to Sister Helen. "I'm only trying to find out what happened to Marti. And Justin."

At Justin's name, her angry expression turns to one of fear. Her eyes flick back and forth from one side to the other.

"Who's there?" she calls out in a strident voice. "Who is it? Who's here with us?"

I haven't heard a sound, except for the rain on the chimney flue and the crackling of the fire. "No one's here, Sister. Just you and me."

She whirls back to me. "I don't believe you! You are a vile, vile person. Almost as wicked as that husband of yours." Pulling her raincoat tightly around her, she mutters, "Spawn of the devil, that one."

Murphy growls in his throat, and I am at a loss. No one I've spoken to, either the Ryans or the women at The Prayer House, prepared me for this.

The woman who stands before me is someone I no longer recognize. My Sister Helen brought Marti and me peanut butter sandwiches in high school, when we had to stay late to retake a math test. She went down to the school kitchen and made the sandwiches herself, bringing them to us with a carton of milk. After we'd eaten, she stood over our shoulders and made "harrumphing" sounds every time one of us put down a wrong answer. She didn't give us the right answers—that would have gone against her code of ethics. But she steered us away from the wrong ones.

I'll never know how she justified that to herself. At the time I saw it simply as an inborn strain of kindness from an otherwise rigid, rule-dominated woman.

Where has that kindness gone?

She was homeless. On the streets.

Is that what did it? Or was there more?

"Come and talk to me," I say softly. "We'll work it out."

In small increments, I manage to get her into the living room. Inviting her to sit, I clean magazines and newspapers off the end of the sofa that's nearest the fire. She waves away that seat and chooses instead a straight-backed chair near the hearth. Sitting on it primly, she folds her hands in her lap and crosses her legs at the ankle, just as we were taught to do in the convent: *Proper decorum when out in public.*

It touches me that she does this. And if I didn't know better, I might think she's calmed down. But the shoulders are too rigid, the mouth too tight. I also suspect that the reason she's folded her hands is that they are shaking.

Even Murph is ill at ease, plunking himself down by her feet, between us.

I ask her if she'd like something hot to drink, coffee or tea. She shakes her head and narrows her eyes at me.

"I suppose you'd serve it in gold-rimmed cups."

"Well, no," I say, hiding a smile, "just an old blue mug. Would that do?"

"Don't be smart with me, young lady!"

Now, that sounds more like the Sister Helen I used to know.

"I'm not trying to be smart," I say. "Honestly. I just feel confused. I don't know why you're here, Sister. I don't even know why you don't like me anymore."

As I say those words, I am surprised to feel tears in my eyes. I can't bear the fact that this woman— this woman who once cared enough to feed me peanut butter sandwiches and help me pass a math test— is my enemy now. There have been too many losses of late.

"Justin could have had a good life," Sister Helen says bitterly. "He could have been with Marti all those years. That's the way it should have been. She never should have given him up."

"But he's had a good life—" I begin before she cuts me off.

"You don't know anything about it! You don't know what he's been through. And you come into it now with your meddling—"

She begins to sob—deep, hard sobs. Tears run unchecked down her face, and her mouth forms a wide O, as if frozen that way in agony. In one swift move I am on my knees, holding her.

"It's all right," I murmur over and over. "It's all right, it's all right."

Violently, she shoves me away. I fall back, stunned at her strength. Instantly, Murphy is on his feet, throwing his heavy body against her legs. Sister Helen seems not to notice.

"Nothing is all right!" she cries. "And it never will be now!"

Her face turns dark, and her breath comes in huge, harsh gasps. She clutches at her neck, as if having a heart attack.

Scrambling to my feet I try to grab her, to make her lie down on the sofa. But she's too strong for me. It's as if some strange force has taken over, the kind of adrenaline that makes mothers able to lift cars off their children.

"Get away from me!" she cries. "Get away!"

Rummaging desperately in a pocket, she pulls out an inhaler. Pressing it to her face she squirts it, inhaling shallowly at first, then more deeply. After a few moments her complexion and breathing return to near normal.

Asthma. I recall now that she has always had this.

"Sister, sit down," I say firmly. This time I do not take no for an answer, all but manhandling her till I've got her on the sofa. "Now, sit here. I'm getting you some tea. And don't argue with me, dammit!"

The look she gives me is inscrutable. Anger? Fear? I don't take time to think about it, but hurry instead into the kitchen and put the teakettle on. While it heats I take crackers from the cupboard and then a jar of peanut butter. This time, it's my old teacher who needs to be nurtured and fed.

The water boils, and I pour it over a jasmine teabag. Putting the cup, the food and some silverware on a tray, I carry it back into the living room.

"Sister, I want you to drink every bit of this—" I begin.

But I am talking to air. Sister Helen is nowhere in sight.

Dropping the tray onto the coffee table, I run to the foyer and see that her shawl is gone. I throw open the door, hoping to catch her before she can get to her car. The wind and rain drive me back, and at any rate there is no car—only the damned stupid fairy lights that come on automatically at dusk. They look sad, twinkling there in the midst of the storm. I flick the switch by the door, and they disappear.

All gone.

Like Sister Helen.

Marti and Justin.

And even Jeffrey now.

All gone.

Pretty soon, I think, I'll be in one of those Twilight Zone worlds where I'm the only one left except for— who? The alien, of course, who has come to impregnate me in order to create a new race.

I almost think that might be preferable to what I'm up against now.

But, no—as usual, I speak too soon. The one thing I should have learned is that things can always get worse.

When I go back into the living room there is something different, a slight change. Something that gives me pause.

What is it?

Glancing around, I miss it at first. Then my gaze fixes on the fireplace mantel. I cross over to it and stop dead in my tracks. Sister Helen has left me a gift—a photograph. It rests beside others I've accumulated throughout the years.

The photograph, a Polaroid, is of Justin. His pale face sags against his chest. He is gagged and tied to a chair.

My hands shake so much I can barely function, but I bring the photograph close to read the writing in the white space at the bottom.

"See what you have done?" has been written in my teacher's crabbed, familiar script.

17

She's crazy. A crazy old woman. I've done nothing.

That's my first thought.

My second comes rapidly on its heels. *Is he alive? Is Justin alive?*

There is no way of knowing from the position he's in. His head is down, eyes closed.

Oh, dear God, where is he?

What have they done to him?

And how did Sister Helen get this picture? Who sent it to her? And why?

I sit with the photograph on my lap, unable to cry, I am so afraid. Inside, I am screaming. I rock back and forth, numb with grief and rage. *Is it too late? What can I do?*

This time there is no answer from Marti. Nor is there word from the God of my childhood. It all seems a vast conspiracy suddenly, to have put us in a world where there's so much suffering and pain. Surely it can't have been planned.

Are we, then, only an eighth-grade science experiment gone wrong? Some kid thought us up, put us under a dome, then shoved us into his closet and went out to play ball? Years later he's packing to go to college, finds us in this god-awful mess and says, "Oh, shit," and shoves us back in there again?

It is the only explanation I can come up with. Which says something for the state of my mind.

I cannot think of any one direction in which to turn. Go to Mauro and Hillars with the photo? Show it to Ben?

They would want to know how I got it. They would go after Sister Helen, pummeling her with their questions, making her admit to—what?

Just what is Sister Helen's involvement?

Cast light into dark corners, I hear Marti say finally.

It seems the only thing to do. This situation needs more light, and I must move quickly now. If Justin is alive, if there's even a small chance of it, every minute counts.

I take the Green Hornet, driving through the storm to Sol's Carmel office. The streets are deserted; it is nearly ten o'clock at night. Sol has agreed to meet me here. With Mauro and Hillars so close on Jeffrey's tail, as well as mine, I no longer trust my phones.

For once, however, the D.C. Duo are not behind me. I suppose even the Secret Service must sleep, eat or take time for a beer in a pub now and then.

Sol's office is in a small courtyard surrounded by shops and a restaurant, near the Britannia. Parking on the street, I follow a brick walk through an arcade lined with flower boxes. The boxes are filled with rainwater, the flowers sodden and bent over. Their defeated posture reminds me of Sister Helen, and I wonder if she got home all right. Though I dread it,

I know I must talk to her again before the night is over.

Sol greets me at the door to his small office, a branch of the larger one in Monterey.

"I would have come to the house," he says.

"I know. I just thought this would be better. More private."

He takes me over to a chair by the fireplace. "I built a fire," he says. "Nasty night, isn't it? Coffee? I just made some."

I nod. When he brings it to me and seats himself, I waste no time.

"Sol, remember when you set up that adoption for Marti, with the Ryans in Pacific Grove?"

"Sure I do," he says. "That was…oh, fourteen, fifteen years ago, right?"

"Right. Refresh my memory, will you? How much did you know about the Ryans?"

"Well, as I'm sure I told you then, I knew Paul Ryan only as another lawyer at first. We talked several times at bar association meetings, and one day he happened to mention that he and his wife wanted to adopt a baby. He said they were having trouble going through the usual channels—not because of any problem personally, but because there weren't any infants available. I told him I didn't usually handle adoptions, but I'd see what I could do. It was only a few months later that you came to me and told me your friend had just had a baby and needed to give it up. I thought the Ryans were pretty good prospects."

He gives me one of his shrewd what-are-you-up-to looks. "Why, Abby? What's all this about?"

"I just wondered...have you noticed that Paul Ryan hasn't been around lately? That he's left his practice?"

"Now that you mention it, I think I heard that he'd taken a sabbatical and gone to France. I didn't think much about it. Why?"

"I'm not sure. Just casting about, I suppose."

Why I'm being cautious with Sol, I don't know. It's just a feeling I have that he's been keeping something from me.

"You hear from Jeffrey?" he asks.

"Not a word. You?"

"Nothing. Abby, I'm worried. It isn't like Jeffrey to run. He'd be more likely to assume he could bluff his way through whatever it is they're after him for."

"I agree, especially since he hasn't yet been charged with anything. Sol, have you any idea why the Secret Service would want him badly enough to issue a warrant for his arrest? Do they have something that ties Jeffrey in to Marti's murder?"

"If they do, they're not telling me," he answers with a distasteful grimace. "They wanted to question him and he ran, which is enough to make him a suspect in their eyes. I also take it they're pissed that he slipped through their fingers. Could be an ego thing. He made them look like fools, so they've brought out all the guns."

"Or maybe it's something else," I say, still fishing.

Sol folds his hands and looks me square in the eye. "All right, Abby. Give. What's going on?"

I figure I might as well get on with it; my fish is obviously not taking the bait.

"A place called The Prayer House, Sol. Would you know anything about that?"

His reaction isn't what I'd hoped. He seems genuinely bewildered.

"I believe I've heard of The Prayer House. Out in the Carmel Valley, isn't it?"

"That's the one. Have you by any chance filed a lawsuit against The Prayer House for Jeffrey, designed to shut them down?"

"No, I certainly have not," he says firmly. "What kind of lawsuit?"

"Something about food poisoning, I take it. And now they're being forced to remodel the place completely, at great cost. Enough cost that all those good women out there might lose their home, and Jeffrey would then be able to get his hands on it—something he's been trying to do for quite a while, I hear."

"Abby, I swear to you, I have not heard a thing about this. If Jeffrey is behind such a suit, he must have used another lawyer."

"That's what I've been thinking, Sol. Another lawyer like Paul Ryan, perhaps? Do you know what's going on between Jeffrey and Paul Ryan?"

Sol is silent for a moment, then he looks away.

"Hey. Old friend," I say. "Is there something you're not telling me?"

He heaves a great sigh, and leans back in his chair.

"I've been meaning to tell you," he says. "I've just had a hard time with it. It hasn't been easy, you know, over the years. It's a fine line I walk—representing both you and Jeffrey."

"I realize that, Sol. And I've always been grateful about the way you've looked after my interests."

"Well, I'm not sure your gratitude is warranted. Not anymore."

"You want to tell me what you mean, Sol? Before we travel any farther along that fine line?"

"I would rather cut off my arm than tell you," he says. "But I will. Abby, Jeffrey hired a P.I. to tail you six months ago, when you two first talked about divorce. The P.I. followed you to the Ryans' house several times in a three-week span, added two and two and came up with five. He figured you'd had an affair with the guy who lived in that house—Paul Ryan—and were hanging around like a jilted lover. He took photos of you sitting there in your car and gave this 'evidence' to Jeffrey. Jeffrey came to me with it, vowing to use your alleged affair in the divorce, to rake you over the coals."

I am stunned. "Jeffrey had *me* followed? When he's the one who's been keeping house with Karen all this time?"

"I'm sorry, Abby. This is dirty business, and I've already told Jeffrey I won't be handling the divorce for him. I'll do what I can to help you. But you should know, Jeffrey is adamant. He wants the house and everything in it. More than anything, he wants to hurt you. He intends to leave you penniless."

"But he can't do that—"

"He can try. That's why he persuaded you to let him stay in the house. Possession is nine-tenths of the law, and even with community property, it looks best if one or the other party doesn't 'abandon' the family home."

"Sonuvabitch! But Sol, he hasn't been acting as

if he's angry enough to screw me over. Not any more than usual, anyway."

"I'm sure his lawyer has been telling him to pretend everything's all right. Until after the election, that is. Then he can get as down and dirty as he wants, and the media fallout won't hurt Chase or his own position in the party."

I stand and begin to pace. "Hold on a minute. Are you telling me Jeffrey still believes I'm having an affair, or did have an affair, with Paul Ryan?"

He sighs. "I have good news and bad news."

I stop pacing and look at him. "Hit me with it."

"The good news is, he doesn't believe that anymore. The bad news is, he doesn't believe that anymore."

"Meaning?"

"Meaning, to calm him down, I had to explain why you were haunting the Ryans' house so many times."

For a moment, I don't get what he means. Then it dawns on me. "Oh, God, Sol! You didn't tell him about Justin?"

"I'm really sorry, Abby. I thought at the time I was acting in your best interests. I thought if I explained about the Ryans having adopted Marti Bright's son, and that you felt obligated to watch over him, Jeffrey would understand you weren't having an affair with Paul Ryan. I thought he'd drop his vendetta against you."

"But he didn't?"

"I thought at first he might. Then, right after that, you started seeing Ben Schaeffer. It seems Jeffrey has transferred his anger over your *alleged* affair to your real one.''

I stomp back to the chair and fling myself into it, folding my arms. ''Dammit, Sol! Jeffrey's the pot calling the kettle black, but if he thinks he can make me look worse than him, he's wrong! I'll fight him to the bitter end.''

Sol looks like a sad puppy who's displeased his favorite owner. ''Again, I apologize, Abby, for not telling you this sooner. I suppose I've been waiting for the right moment.''

''Well, there's no time like the present. You say he has another lawyer?''

Sol gives a shrug.

''Don't tell me,'' I say. ''Paul Ryan?''

''You got it. Ryan, it seems, has made some sort of deal with the devil. That devil being Jeffrey, of course.''

''Holy shit, Sol.'' Now I don't know what to think. Except that none of it can be good.

''Sol—what do you know about Rio?''

This time there is a small silence.

''What about Rio?'' he says at last.

''Big white house out near Sao Conrado? Land of champagne, caviar and dreams?''

''I can't say I've ever seen it,'' he says cautiously.

''Well, I have, so don't go all lawyerish on me. Do you know who's been staying there?''

''No, Abby, I do not. But since you know about the house, I suppose I can tell you I handled that sale. Jeffrey said he was buying it for you as an anniversary present next year. He asked me not to mention it to you.''

I can't help laughing. "You're kidding. We're getting divorced in a month, and that's really what he said?"

Sol makes a what-can-I-do gesture, turning his hands palm up. "Naturally, I didn't believe it for a minute. But that's what Jeffrey said, and I had no choice but to accept his explanation. Meanwhile, he's been renting it out, I understand."

"Renting it out?"

"That's what Jeffrey said. Why, Abby? What's wrong?"

"Hell, Sol, what's wrong is that he's been hiding the Ryans down there! He told them it was for their own and Justin's good, but it's my bet he doesn't want them around right now."

Sol looks both shocked and perplexed. "Why wouldn't Jeffrey want the Ryans around? And what do you mean about Justin's good?"

"Dammit, Sol, you don't know that Justin's been kidnapped?"

He swings forward, the chair hitting his desk with a thud. "My God, no! Where did you hear such a thing?"

"From none other than the United States Secret Service. And I didn't just hear it, my friend. I've been gifted with a photograph of Justin bound to a chair and gagged."

His face turns ashen, and the shock in his voice seems authentic. "Oh, Abby. Oh, that poor, poor boy. I haven't seen anything in the news, and Jeffrey never breathed a word. When did this happen?"

"Three months ago. July, to be exact."

"Three months ago? But that's impossible! I've never heard a thing about an investigation."

"Well, now, Sol—about that. Jeffrey convinced the Ryans not to tell anyone, even the police. He told them President Chase put him in charge of the investigation, and that he'd be a mediator between them and the FBI. Then he hustled them off to his little hideaway in Sao Conrado. Meanwhile, apparently, no one's been looking for Justin."

"But that's appalling! I don't understand why Jeffrey would do such a thing."

"Try this on for size, then. I haven't any proof, but I suspect Chase is Justin's biological father. I think either he told Jeffrey to hush the kidnapping up in order to keep the paternity question from coming out, or Jeffrey decided to do that on his own."

Sol rubs his brow with a meaty hand. "Abby, I'm very sorry, but I'm having a hard time with this. Let me think."

I give him a few minutes, and while he thinks, I am wondering how Jeffrey could have kept all this from his lawyer—and why. Was he afraid that if he told Sol about his machinations concerning the Ryans, Sol would have tried to talk him out of it? In fact, with an innocent child's life involved, did he think that Sol might well have turned him in—client confidentiality or no?

"There's something about this that doesn't feel right," Sol says at last.

"Hell, there's a lot that doesn't feel right."

"No, bear with me, Abby. I understand that if it came out just before the election that Justin was Marti Bright's and the president's illegitimate son, it could be an embarrassment. The media would jump on it. They'd have a field day—especially given that the boy's been kidnapped. But Abby, Chase's relationship with Marti, if there was one, had to be fifteen years ago. He wasn't president then, and he's never been charged with, lied about, or denied paternity. As I understand, Marti never revealed to anyone the name of the boy's father. Isn't that right?''

"It is, as far as I know.''

"So it's only supposition on your part that Chase is the boy's father?''

"Yes, but it makes a kind of sense, don't you think? Sol, when Marti was six months pregnant she hid out in a cabin in Maine, loaned to her by a 'friend.' Chase has a cabin in Maine, and Marti traveled with him that year. Furthermore, when Justin was kidnapped, Chase was the first person she called for help.''

"I suppose it does fit, at least on the surface. When you add to that the fact of Jeffrey's hiding the kidnapping, even quelling an investigation just before the election…yes, if that's what he did, it could fit. But shit, Abby, there has to be more. Chase's approval ratings are sky-high, even more so than Clinton's were at the height of his impeachment troubles. I don't think the public would be unduly upset if they learned about an illegitimate child. Especially if Chase never knew of the child and never denied him.''

"I don't know, Sol. Mr. Squeaky-Clean?''

"Even so, I know enough about politics to believe he'd overcome this somehow. No. There has to be something else.''

I sigh. "To tell you the truth, Sol, I don't much care what Jeffrey's done, or Chase has done, or why. I just want to get Justin back. Unless..."

"Unless it's too late," he says heavily.

"Yes," I say, steadying my voice. "And even then, I want to know."

"Abby, of course I'll do whatever I can to help," Sol says briskly. "Tell me what you need."

I pull the photograph of Justin from my purse. "You have a friend who's a photographer for the San Francisco Police Department. I want him to blow this up and tell me what he can about the background. Where the photograph might have been taken, whether he can come up with the specific kind of Polaroid camera that was used and when. Anything that might lead me to the kidnapper."

Sol takes the photograph, looks at it and pales. "Dear God, Abby. This does look bad. Where did you get it?"

"I'd rather not say."

He shakes his head, making a clucking sound with his tongue. "The poor kid. How could anyone—"

Breaking off, he looks at me. "You say the Secret Service is looking into this. Surely it's time to bring in the FBI and the local police, regardless of what that might do to the president's reelection."

"One would think so, Sol. Funny that no one's done that, wouldn't you say?"

"Actually, I would call it damned suspicious."

"Well, there is Jeffrey's explanation to the Ryans—that the kidnapper threatened Justin's life if anyone went to the authorities."

Sol shakes his head and hands the photograph back to me. "I'll call the photogropher right away."

"Thanks. And Sol? I'm not letting this picture out of my hands. I want to be there when he works on it. I'll fly up to San Francisco, and I want to do it as soon as possible. In the morning, in fact."

"I'll do my best. One question, Abby. How come you didn't ask Ben to do this?"

"Ben?"

"Well, he does have access to the same facilities as my colleague in San Francisco."

"That's true. But Ben's pretty busy these days."

"Even so—"

"Even so, can we leave it at that?"

He shrugs. "I'd feel better if somebody like Ben was helping you out with this."

"I wouldn't, Sol. And that's the hell of it."

Sol growls something unintelligible and picks up the phone. "I'll call you when I've got a time set up."

"Thanks. Or I'll call you if I'm not home, okay?"

He gives me a look. "And if you're not home, where precisely will you be on a night like this?"

"Following my nose," I say.

It's raining worse than ever when I leave Sol's office. He tries to get me to call a cab, but I've had too many bad experiences with cabs around here. Sometimes I'll get one that's great, but the next time they stand me up and I'm late for a plane.

Besides, I doubt a cab would take me all the way out to The Prayer House on a night like this.

But will the nuns let me in? How late do they stay

up at The Prayer House? And will Sister Helen even talk to me?

Well, there's no turning back. My only alternative at this point is to go home and just sit there all night, staring at that hideous photograph of Justin. I have to know how Sister Helen got it, and if she's had any other contact from the kidnapper. So far as I know, this is the only word anyone's had since Justin first disappeared.

There is a point in the road up to The Prayer House where it narrows and turns to dirt for a mile or so. When I come to it I throw the four-wheel drive on and let it carry me through the mud and small rocks that have fallen from the hillsides. The engine growls, but the tranny does its job. Tree limbs, now heavy with rain, scrape the sides and roof of the Hornet, and my headlights reach ahead only ten feet or so.

I try not to think what would happen if I got stuck out here in a flash flood. When El Niño hit, entire roads were washed away. Hillsides collapsed and minor creeks became raging floods. It wasn't unusual for cars, and their drivers, to be carried away.

Rounding a bend, I come within a few feet of crashing into a huge boulder that's fallen onto the road. Gripping the steering wheel hard, I press the brakes lightly and swerve. The Jeep's right-hand wheels climb a small embankment, while those on the left dig into mud only inches from the boulder. The Jeep turns partially on its side. It teeters, wobbles, and the right side raises into the air. My side window is now only inches from the boulder and in another moment will strike it. If the glass breaks, my face could be pulverized.

I grip the steering wheel harder, as if by sheer force I could make the Jeep revert to an even keel. My knuckles turn white, and my heart is in my throat.

"Dammit! Dammit! For God's sake, help!"

The Jeep sways another moment or two, then sinks back with all four wheels safely on the ground. I am past the boulder. The road ahead is clear.

I sit with my foot on the brake, dazed, wondering how I remembered that anger in a prayer always works best for me.

There are only a handful of lights on in the residential wings of The Prayer House. I ring the bell at the main door and wait. It takes Sister Pauline several minutes to get to the door, and when she opens it, expressing surprise to see me at this hour, I see she is dressed in a black bathrobe, with the kind of white, nighttime wrap around her head that I remember from Joseph and Mary. When Marti and I were postulants we swiped all we could find once from the laundry and hid them, just so we could see what the nuns looked like at night with their heads shaved. We hid in a corner of the hallway to watch them as they made their way to the bathrooms for their nightly ablutions—and after all that we were both surprised and disappointed to see that their hair wasn't shaved, as rumor had it, only clipped.

How young and naive we were, I think as I follow Sister Pauline down the corridor. Did Marti still have an element of that naïveté? Was she all too easily overcome and murdered?

I don't see how that's possible, and for the first time the thought comes to me: *It must have been someone she knew, then. She would have been more cautious, more self-protective with a stranger.*

Has anyone else thought of this?

Yes, of course. The police, and the Secret Service. That's why they questioned me from the first. *Marti was murdered by someone she knew.*

It fits. It all fits with Jeffrey having done it.

Sister Pauline takes me to a small room with a roaring fire and asks me to wait while she sees if Helen is up. "I can't take no for an answer this time," I tell her. "It's urgent. Could you please give this to her for me?"

I hand her a note I've written in the car. It says: *I know where Justin is.*

It's a trick, of course, and for that I feel bad. But I can't afford for her to snub me at this point.

Sister Pauline takes the note, and after what seems a long time, she comes back into the room wearing a raincoat and galoshes. "I'm sorry, but it took me forever to find her," she says in an out-of-breath voice. "You'll never guess where."

"Well, outside, I'd guess, from the look of you."

"Precisely! At this hour! She was picking vegetables for her soups tomorrow, she said—by flashlight, no less—and when I remarked that this might seem an odd time to do that, she snapped at me. 'I've got to get to them before the storm ruins them all,' she said as if I were a perfect idiot not to have thought of that!"

Sister Pauline takes her raincoat off and shakes it. Sitting on a chair, she removes her galoshes, which are thick with mud. "Poor Helen. I swear she's getting worse every day."

"Do you think it's her age?" I ask.

Sister Pauline shakes her head. "I don't know. She's only been like this since summer."

She holds the muddy galoshes up and looks at them despairingly. "Well, I shouldn't let her nightly meanderings get to me. After all the poor woman's been through, it's amazing she manages to get around at all."

"Being out in this rain can't be good for her asthma, though," I say. "Where is she now?"

"She read your note and said she'd be right in. The weather's getting worse by the moment, and it wouldn't surprise me if we lost some of our roof tonight, not to mention a road or two."

She looks at me worriedly. "I don't mean to alarm you, but I really don't think you should try to drive back tonight. We have a couple of guest rooms for people who need to stay over."

I'm not certain how I feel about that. It does occur to me, however, that I could keep a closer eye on my old teacher if I were here.

"May I decide after I've talked to Sister Helen?"

"Of course. I'm going to make myself some tea. How about if I get you a cup? I'll try to hurry Helen along while I'm in the kitchen."

"That would be great. Thank you, Sister."

She hustles off, taking the raincoat and muddy boots. I stand and walk to the fire, extending my hands for warmth. I can hear the rain, now, beating on the roof. If this keeps up, the hills will be green in less than a week.

And if the Carmel River rises too much tonight, roads could be out all over the valley.

It seems an interminable time before Sister Helen appears. Her old brown pants are wet to the thigh and caked with mud. Her gray hair is plastered to her skull, and she is wheezing.

"What do you want?" she asks belligerently. She holds up the note, waving it around. "What is this about?"

"It's about Justin," I say, matching her tone. "And that little present you left on my mantel."

"You said you know where he is." She narrows her eyes. "How can you? What do you know?"

"First, I want you to tell me what *you* know, Sister Helen. Or Helen, I suppose I should call you now. After all, you aren't a nun anymore, and you sure as hell don't behave like one."

She grabs the back of a chair, and her wheeze grows louder. "It's none of your business how I behave. I did more than anyone for that boy, more than you, and even more than his own mother!"

"You mean Marti?"

She falls silent.

"Are you talking about Marti," I press, "or Mary Ryan? What is it about the Ryans? What did they do to Justin?"

Her eyes narrow again. She looks at the note, which she still clutches in a hand that's grown blue from the cold.

"It's a lie, isn't it?" she says. "You don't know anything. You don't know where he is."

"No, to be honest, I don't. But I'm not going to give up looking for him, if it takes my last breath."

"Well, it could, young lady. It very well could."

She takes a step toward me, and the expression on her face saddens me. I see her as she must have been on the streets, raging inside at the Church she felt had let her down, determined not to let another soul harm her. She must have learned from experience to defend herself and even to attack if she felt threatened.

"Don't try to frighten me, Helen," I say, not backing off. "I want to know how you got that photograph, and I want to know if you've heard from the kidnapper."

"If *I've* heard?" She laughs, a dull, bitter sound. "*You'd* have been more likely to have heard from the kidnapper, not me."

"What do you mean?"

"Well, now, I'm just a poor helpless woman, stuck here in this house. Not like you, little Miss Fauntleroy. You can go flying around anywhere you want, at the drop of a hat. You do have all the money in the world, don't you?"

Rio. She means Rio. What does she know?

"Stop playing games," I say angrily. "Tell me what you're talking about. And for God's sake, tell me where that photograph came from!"

"Bothers you, does it?" she says waspishly. "Well, that's what you did—you and that evil friend of yours. You're the ones who strapped him to that chair! You're the ones who left that poor child to suffer alone."

"What evil friend? Are you talking about Marti?

She loved her baby! She gave him up because she loved him.''

"Then why did she—"

Sister Helen clamps her mouth shut.

"Why did she do what? What is it you think she did?"

"You have to *ask?*" Her hands form fists as she comes toward me again. "Fornicating like some animal with that...that man? Allowing herself to become pregnant, and then not taking responsibility at all? In my day we had rules, young lady! We had rules and we followed them. We didn't just do whatever we felt like doing, then turn our backs on the consequences."

"Marti didn't turn her back on Justin," I argue. "She found a good family for him, someone who could take better care of him than she could."

I say the words out of a habit of loyalty, though there have been times over the years when I, too, have railed against Marti—if only in my heart—for giving Justin up. When I knew I'd never have a child of my own, the one I held in my arms fifteen years ago became my lost child, a child I could have been godmother to and even helped to rear, if Marti had let me.

I did offer. But Marti turned me down. So I went to Sol, hoping that if he set up the adoption locally, I would always know where Justin was. I would be able to keep him, in some small way.

"Why are you so angry with me?" I ask Sister Helen. "I never wanted anything but good for Justin. I helped Marti with the adoption because I wanted to make sure he would always be happy and safe."

The look that comes over her face chills me. "You don't even begin to know what you did, do you? Off in your own little world, you don't know what happens to people, don't have a clue."

She turns away from me, her shoulders slumping. She is clearly exhausted, and my heart goes out to her. By not telling Ben about the photograph, I felt I was protecting her from an interrogation by the police. Now I've turned into the interrogator.

"I need to use the phone," I say, pointing to one on a desk against the wall.

She shrugs. I go to the phone and call Sol, reaching him on his cell phone in the car.

"Did you make that appointment for me?" I ask.

"Yes. Earliest he can do it, though, is around five tomorrow afternoon, at the end of his shift."

"Well, I guess that'll have to do. I won't be home tonight, but I'll call you in the morning to see if anything new has come up. Thanks, Sol."

Next, I call Frannie and ask her to pick up Murphy and keep him overnight, promising a bonus for going out in the storm this late.

"Storms like this spook him," I say. "I'd hate to leave him alone."

"I don't want any bonus," she says, "but I would like your recipe for that chicken dish."

Sister Helen looks at me curiously as I hang up. "You're staying overnight?"

"I thought I might. Sister Pauline advised that I not drive back in the storm."

My old teacher seems uneasy at the thought of having me under the same roof overnight. Well,

that's good. Up till now, I've felt I was playing a
losing game with her.

The guest room is one of the nun's cells, a white-
washed room about eight-by-ten with a cot, a small
dresser and a straight chair. There is a crucifix over
the bed and a statue of Mary on the dresser. I feel
I'm in a time warp, swept back to Joseph and Mary
Motherhouse, even to the rain drumming against the
one narrow window and the deep, deep "Grand"
silence in the halls.

"Meet me in the chapel," I hear Marti saying back
then. "I want to tell you something."

I see myself quietly opening the dormitory door,
peeking into the hall, slipping silently along it to the
stairs, then down to the chapel and into the choir loft.
By the time I get there, my heart is beating wildly,
out of fear of being caught. But Marti is beaming;
she loves all this intrigue.

"You ninny," she would say if I voiced my con-
cerns. *"What can they do? Line us up at dawn and
shoot us?"*

There were times when I wondered.

People think nuns are all sweet, kind and loving.
But I am here to tell you there are some who are
deep-down mean. Nuns, after all, are people, and
people are all different. Most enter the convent to
serve God and live lives of service and joy. A few,
however, are escaping something, and the things they
escape have a way of following them behind the
walls. One has only to note the expressions of pleasure on the faces of these women when engrossed in
the ritual of flogging themselves. Light, symbolic

"floggings" with a cloth whip were part of the life at Joseph and Mary. Self-inflicted, they were not meant to hurt but to keep us in a humble, sacrificial frame of mind.

There were always certain sisters, however, who got a kind of high from the floggings, who couldn't stop till they'd drawn their own blood.

The flogging Marti suffered was similar to that, though it had been taken to an insane extreme.

I think the new nuns, the young ones, may be more easygoing. They've had more freedom to think for themselves, and for the most part they come from stronger foundations of self-worth. The kind of order Marti and I were in was so old-world, so unbending, it sometimes took the fragile ones and shaped them into something they never would have been in the world.

Did they do that to Sister Helen? I wonder. She, I recall from gossip in high school, was raised by a mother and father to be both a fragile flower and an unbending perfectionist. Her father was a doctor, her mother a poet. Between the two personalities—the one scientific and the other off in another world half the time—Helen hardly knew which way to turn as a child. Her father taught her to be logical; her mother to be soft and giving. So at eighteen she entered the convent, seeking a life she hoped would complement both sides.

Religious life, she often told us in high school, gave a woman structure and rules; it kept her from being soft and silly. It also encouraged self-sacrifice, the ultimate form of giving.

How much painful sacrifice must it have required,

I wonder, of a woman whose mother raised her on Elizabeth Barrett Browning?

My thoughts won't quit, and after a couple of hours of tossing and turning, I decide to journey back into the past and make a visit to the chapel. Though I'm no longer religious, there's nothing like a dark chapel in the middle of the night to clear the cobwebs from one's mind.

Besides a toothbrush, toothpaste and a bar of soap, Sister Pauline has loaned me one of her black robes. So it really is déjà vu as I tread softly down the corridor toward the middle of the building, where I hope to find stairs leading to the chapel. I am on the second floor, and traditional architecture would put stairs at the outside end of each wing, plus a similar set of stairs in the middle, leading directly into the main structure.

The Prayer House is old, and despite its Spanish exterior, inside it is designed much like Joseph and Mary and other motherhouses that were built when nuns first began to come to this country from Europe. The stairs next to the chapel are just where I've expected them to be; they lead down to the first floor and up, presumably, to an attic.

On this landing there is a door, and on a hunch I open it quietly, hoping it doesn't creak and that it doesn't lead to a dormitory or private room. It doesn't, and even this is like Joseph and Mary. The door opens onto the chapel choir loft.

It's pitch-black in the loft, so I stand just inside it, letting my eyes adjust. After a moment or two I can see that there's no one else here. Ten rows of long wooden pews stretch from this side to the one op-

posite, and I tiptoe down the few stairs to the pew
in front. The wooden stairs creak, and as I reach the
last one I glance over the railing to see if I've disturbed anyone in the main chapel below. It isn't unusual for nuns to keep vigils at night in their chapel,
especially during special feast days or seasons. Usually shifts will be taken, and one or more will kneel
or sit in the dark and pray.

There seems to be no one about on this night, however. Everyone but me is probably tucked comfort-
ably away under their blankets, while the never-
ending rain pounds the roof. Wind howls, and I can
feel a draft from an open stairwell behind me, which
must lead up to the steeple. Below and along the
sides of the chapel are statues with vigil candles before them. The candles afford only a dim light, and
I can barely make out the statues. Mary, I think, and
Joseph with the Baby Jesus. Perhaps Saint Francis,
since The Prayer House is so into gardening.

Settling in, I take a position of meditation I've
adapted for myself from that of my Zen Buddhist
friend, Davis—feet flat on the floor, palms upturned
on each knee. If I were in a Zen chapel I would have
removed my shoes before entering and sat cross-
legged on the floor. The God I grew up following,
however, is more traditional than that. And when in
Rome....

Marti...oh, Marti. Why aren't you here?

The red sanctuary lamp glows dimly at the altar,
indicating the presence of the Host. Out of old habit
I make the sign of the cross, then quickly revert to
my meditation pose before God can spy me up here
and ask me what the hell I think I'm doing.

The truth is, I don't know what I'm doing. I have a carload of information now that I didn't have three days ago. What it all means is something else.

Harry Blimm, Tommy, Mauro and Hillars...I let them think I knew as much as they did, if not more. Then I waited, thinking they, and even Jeffrey, might show up and reveal something I didn't know.

My little plan, however, turned out to be a dud. The only one who showed was Sister Helen.

So, what does that tell me? Nothing happens by coincidence, I've always believed.

And what about Sol? He seemed completely innocent when I talked to him. But that could have been an act. Lawyers are good at playing emotional poker.

Sol did have one point, however. Jeffrey probably wouldn't go to such great lengths as sending the Ryans away just to cover up the fact that the president had an illegitimate son. There has to be something else going on, some greater motivation. But what? Is it somehow connected with The Prayer House, perhaps even Jeffrey's scam to take it over?

I can't shake the feeling that there was something odd about that whole setup down there in Sao Conrado. Though the Ryans' explanation made some sort of sense, I still have a problem with them being there all this time while their son's been gone. Then, too, there's Paul Ryan's having left his practice so long.

As for Tommy Lawrence—I can't for the life of me figure how he fits in. There are moments when I think he's only curious, and others when he gives me the willies.

And why all the lies? Where has he been staying, if not at the La Playa?

I sigh. There's only one more link to Marti I can think of: Lydia Greyson. I recall Sister Pauline saying, "Our contract with her is to maintain the premises and to support ourselves, which we do in a number of ways. Some of the women grow vegetables and bake bread, much like in the abbeys of yesteryear."

Abbeys of yesteryear... What about that phrase clings to me like a burr on a dog?

Lydia Greyson seems completely aboveboard, determined not to let The Prayer House fall into the hands of developers. Marti had the same goal. So, can Lydia tell me more, something she's left out? I'll have to track her down in the morning.

My "meditation" seems to be going nowhere; rather than emptying my mind, it's bringing up more questions. That's the thing about meditation when one is a beginner or doesn't practice all the time. The mind will not stop, no matter what.

On the other hand, there is a technique called observation meditation, in which one lets the mind flow and simply observes the thoughts. Theoretically, illumination comes from the observation. When I was a reporter, I found it to work a time or two.

Abbeys of yesteryear... I am thinking of that when a sound reaches me, a creaking, as of footsteps on wood. I turn around to see who has entered the choir loft. My eyes have fully adjusted to the dim light, but there seems to be no one there. Below me, then, on the chapel floor?

I lean over the rail, but can't see a thing down

there aside from the flickering candles at the feet of the statues along the side. Does it seem they are flickering more than before?

Suddenly I realize that I'm freezing. The draft, which I've assumed to be coming from the direction of the steeple, has grown worse. I wrap my arms around myself, tucking my hands beneath them for warmth.

A bad move. It leaves me defenseless when a dark figure, no more than a shadow at the corner of my vision, comes up behind me and bashes my head with something very hard.

I try to fight back, instinctively striking out. But everything turns black, and suddenly I feel my body going over the choir-loft rail. The last thing I see is the chapel's stone floor, a good fifteen feet below.

18

Lydia Greyson's face appears somewhere above me. "Abby? Abby, can you hear me?"

My mouth won't work, so there's nothing I can tell her. I slip back into the darkness, grateful for the oblivion.

Next I hear Ben's voice. "How could something like this happen?" he is saying. "You weren't supposed to—"

"Shh, she'll hear you," Lydia whispers. "I think she's awake."

Ben disappears into silence. I drift off again, only to hear someone else say, "I demand to talk to that nun."

It's Agent Mauro, and from the sound of him, I don't envy whoever "that nun" is.

On my cloud, I formulate a few things in my mind. One is that the cloud is salmon pink with streaks of gold. Secondly, angels are singing a Gregorian chant. I am in heaven, no doubt. Or on a bad drug trip.

Do I do drugs?

I can't remember.

I do have a vision of fighting off someone in the choir loft, with an elbow to the ribs. I tried to twist around enough to chop at the groin, but whoever had hold of me knew—I think—what I was trying to do.

He blocked me, and I wasn't in a good position to react with another defensive move. That's when I saw the chapel floor below my face.

I'd forgotten the first rule of self-defense—always be on your guard.

But the chapel in a nunnery is hardly the place to remember that.

One thing, this person wasn't from The Prayer House. And it wasn't a woman. At least, not one of the women from here. He was stronger than I, and I'm no weakling.

Unless—

My eyes fly open. Ben's worried face is inches from mine. "You okay?" he is saying.

"Abbey," I tell him.

"Yes, I know." He smiles. "I know you're Abby."

He turns to someone beside him. Lydia Greyson comes into view.

"She knows who she is," Ben says. "She's okay."

"No," I say, trying to shout, though my voice is no more than a hoarse whisper. "That's what she meant. She just didn't spell it right. *Abbey. Abbeys of yesteryear.* Not me."

Ben stares at me as if I've lost my mind. Then his face clears. "You mean the word Marti wrote in the dirt before she was killed? You think she meant an abbey? Like here at The Prayer House?"

I try to nod, but the pain in my head prevents any movement. "That's what it used to be. That's what Sister Pauline called it—'*Like the abbeys of yester-*

year.' Marti must have meant..." I lick my lips. "Ben, I think she meant to send us here."

This is all I can manage. But before I slip into unconsciousness again, I see Lydia Greyson's eyes turn hard.

"She can't be thinking straight," Lydia says stiffly. "It's the fall."

When I come off my cloud, I find I'm actually in a bed in what turns out to be the Infirmary of The Prayer House. There's a nun in a white habit fussing over me, taking my pulse and inspecting the tender lump on my forehead.

Ben sits in a chair next to the bed, watching. "Welcome back," he says, taking my hand. "How do you feel?"

"Sore as hell. All over."

"You must be incredibly flexible," the nun says, smiling. "Only yogis, drunks and cats can take a fall like that and not be hurt any more than you were."

"Kenpo," I say, remembering that as I went over I managed to twist myself into a diagonal position from right shoulder to left waist, bend my knees, land on my feet and roll.

"Like jumping with a parachute," I say. "What's the damage?"

"So far, no sign of concussion," the sister says. "This lump should go down in a few days, and, so far as I can tell, you haven't any broken bones. It's nothing short of a miracle." She smiles. "But then, we do have a few of them here. I'm Sister Anne, by the way. I was a P.A. before I came here."

"Physician's assistant?"

She nods. "We tried to get an ambulance out here when we found you, but Carmel Valley Road is washed out near Mid-Valley."

I look at Ben. "How did you get here?"

"You might say I was in the neighborhood."

"Is that right? Arnie, too?"

He shakes his head. "Just me. I was on a case."

I fasten my slightly blurry vision on him. "Are you going to tell me what case, or will you be taking it to your grave?"

"Not *my* grave," he says, sighing. "Local Realtor's—Rick Stone. Found dead behind his office a few hours ago."

"Dead?" I try to sit up, but my head hurts when I move. Sister Anne gently pushes me back down.

"You know him?" Ben asks.

"Met him. How did he die?" I'm thinking some local feminist whacked him.

"Bullet to the back of the head," Ben says. "Execution style."

It's his turn to fasten me with a look.

"Like Marti?" I say.

"Could be."

"Any suspects?"

"One. You'll never guess who."

"Don't bet on it. Jeffrey?"

"One and only. Spotted by a neighbor, hanging around the office earlier in the day."

This time I do sit up, despite the pain. "Somebody saw him there?"

"Mauro and Hillars, actually."

"No kidding. Why didn't they pick him up?"

"They decided to follow him, instead. See where he went and who he met up with."

"And?"

He shrugs. "They lost him."

"No way! Jeffrey managed to elude the Secret Service?"

"I guess he's better at eluding the law, in general, than any of us thought."

Ben looks embarrassed, and I fall silent, thinking.

"What were you doing out here at this hour?" Ben asks after a moment.

"I don't know, what hour is it?"

He glances at his watch. "After five in the morning now."

"God, what a night. I came out here to talk to Sister Helen."

"And did you?"

"A bit."

"Are you feeling up to telling me what happened?"

"I think so," I say, touching the lump and wincing. "I talked to Sister Helen, then I decided to stay over because of the storm. In the middle of the night I went to the chapel to think. Somebody came up behind me. I tried to fight him off. I wasn't ready for it, and he caught me off balance."

Ben's face darkens with anger. "You think it was a man, then?"

"Or a very strong woman."

I am remembering Sister Helen's almost abnormal strength at my house earlier. But that was in anger. Surely she wouldn't have pushed me over a railing in cold blood.

"What were you doing at Rick Stone's office yesterday?" Ben asks, obviously hoping to take me by surprise with his knowledge of my whereabouts.

"You mean yesterday when you were following me?" I say.

He has the grace to turn pink. "You saw me?"

"Hard not to spot the Brown Turd."

"Oh. That." He recovers, and his chin goes up. "So what were you doing at End-of-the-Trail Realty?"

"Asking directions," I say.

"That's all?"

"You mean, did I go there to kill Rick Stone?"

"No, that is not what I mean. Mauro and Hillars think you were taking a message to him from Jeffrey."

"Mauro and Hillars can go to hell."

For that, I get a mild glance from Sister Anne. "You must be feeling better," she comments in a dry tone.

"I am."

Despite her protestations, I sling my legs over the side of the bed. "I want to go home."

"You can't," Ben says firmly, reaching for my legs. He lifts them and shoves them under the covers.

"The road is still out," he says. "Besides, I've already arranged with Lydia Greyson for you to stay here today."

"*You've* arranged?" I say, annoyed. "And since when do you arrange my life for me?"

"Since Jeffrey's on the loose," he says calmly. "He still has a key to the house, and I don't want you there alone if he shows up."

"You know, I don't particularly care what you want." My head is splitting now, and I'm in too much pain not to be annoyed.

"In addition," he says, "we can't overlook the possibility that Jeffrey might be the one who pushed you over that railing."

Jeffrey?

I wonder. Do I remember anything that would give me a clue? Something seen out of the corner of my eye, or a scent? It seems there was something... A sound?

"Besides, like I said," Ben continues, "the road is still out. They won't have it fixed till late today."

"So where does that leave you? Are you staying out here, too?"

"No, I'm hitching a ride into town on the KION 'copter. They'll be out here looking at the floods."

"Well, they can take me, too, then," I argue.

"Can't. Not enough room—it's a small 'copter."

"I'll hire one, then."

He makes a grimace and stands, throwing up his hands. "Will you please stop arguing? God, Abby! You take a fifteen-foot fall and you're worse than ever. Anybody else would have had some of the piss and vinegar knocked out of them."

Sister Anne puts in her two cents' worth. "I'd really like to see you stay here in bed a few more hours, Abby. Just to make sure there's nothing I've overlooked. I do feel responsible for you."

She looks tired. For that matter, Ben does, too. And I'm only giving them more grief.

"All right, fine," I say without much grace. "Ben—do me a favor? When you get back to town, call Sol, my lawyer, and tell him I can't make that appointment today. Tell him I'll be in touch.''

"I'll think about it," he says, still annoyed. "What's up with Sol?"

I shake my head. "Nothing for you to worry about. By the way, how did I get up here from the chapel?"

"For some reason I'll never understand," Ben says, frowning, "I cared enough about you to carry you."

"I did check you out first to make sure it was all right to move you," Sister Anne assures me.

"So you've both been here with me for what—two hours, three?"

Ben shrugs.

"Your friend here," Sister Anne says, "is a very stubborn man. He wouldn't leave your side."

"I'm a cop," Ben argues. "It's my job not to leave victims of violent crimes unprotected."

Sister Anne rolls her eyes. "That's it," she says. "He was just doing his job."

When Ben leaves, Lydia Greyson takes his place. I am still fuming at my condition and the accompanying lack of freedom to move about, but Lydia sits beside me, seemingly unmoved by my grumblings. She doesn't talk, but is leafing through what look like legal papers, making notes on them. Small reading glasses perch midway along the bridge of her nose.

I remember Ben's and Lydia's words when they thought I was still out.

"What did Ben mean," I ask, "when he said,

'You weren't supposed to,' and you told him to hush, because I was awake and might hear him?''

She hesitates, then removes the reading glasses and says, ''I don't suppose it would hurt to tell you. He called earlier to ask if you were here. I told him you were staying the night, and he told me your husband had been seen in the area. He said Jeffrey was suspected of killing a local Realtor. I told Detective Schaeffer you were sleeping soundly, and he asked me not to let anything happen to you.''

''That's all?''

''That's it,'' she says. ''You're a lucky woman, Abby, to have someone care that much about you.''

''But how did you know I was sleeping soundly? I wasn't, in fact. I was awake for hours before I went to the chapel.''

''I suppose I thought you wouldn't want to be disturbed,'' she says, putting the glasses back on and turning back to her papers. ''Did I overstep my bounds in wanting to look after you?''

''No…'' I say, though reluctantly. I wonder: Am I really being protected here? Or am I a prisoner? How much can Lydia Greyson be trusted?

This is only a fleeting thought as I drift in and out. Sister Anne has told me I will probably sleep more than usual; a reaction to the emotional as well as physical trauma of the fall. She wakes me now and then to check for a concussion. Once satisfied I'm all right, she lets me slip back into the Land of Nod.

When I wake again, sunlight streams through the infirmary windows. Birds sing, and I almost expect a dove with an olive branch to perch on a sill. The rains, apparently, are over. The floods will go down.

There is a tray on the table beside the bed, loaded with orange juice, eggs, bacon and muffins overflowing with butter and jam. I would never eat all this at home, but this morning I am ravenous and wolf down every bite. My head no longer hurts so much, and the muscle pain in various parts of my body has eased up somewhat. Lydia is gone, and Sister Anne is with an elderly nun, who—she told me earlier—is confined to bed in the infirmary now. A condition has left her bones so brittle, they would break at the slightest movement.

I watch Sister Anne lovingly tend to this slight skeleton of a woman and see in her eyes and touch the kindness I remember from certain nuns at J&M, who had given their lives to God.

I remember seeing it in Sister Helen, as well, when she talked to students in high school who had a hard time making friends, or who had trouble at home.

I can't hold back a rush of pity for my old teacher, who began her religious life with nothing but a desire to serve God—only to fall on such hard times. When Sister Anne comes back to check on me, I ask her, "How did you end up here? Can you tell me? Did your motherhouse close?"

She takes a seat beside me and releases a tired sigh. "It did. And many of us were fine with that. After Vatican II we wanted to live in apartments, on our own. We felt we could support ourselves and work even better for God in the world."

"What happened?" I ask.

"Well, it was and still is perfect for many of the sisters in my order. For others of us...I don't know, perhaps we just march to a different drummer. I began to miss religious life as I knew it. I missed wearing the habit and living in a community. For me, that was one of the most important aspects of religious life." She smiles. "I guess I didn't really want to be in the world. That's why I entered to begin with."

"What about Sister Helen?" I ask. "I thought she'd never give up her habit, much less leave her order."

"You know Helen?"

"She was my teacher and my sponsor into Joseph and Mary twenty years ago."

"Really? No one told me that."

"I didn't last long there," I say. "I had a bit of a problem following the rules."

She smiles. "As did many of us, back in the old days. As for Helen, well, she's a special case. Joseph and Mary closed just as she was getting ready to retire. At one time she'd have gone back there to live and been taken care of the rest of her life. But the order couldn't afford to keep up the motherhouse, and the sisters were sent to various places for housing—some to a convent here or there, some to apartments or group houses. To make a long story short, Helen ended up having a hard time with this. She went over the edge and hasn't fully come back since."

"You mean she was having emotional problems even before she ended up on the streets?"

"I don't know if you'd call them emotional problems, but she did have difficulty coping." Sister Anne breaks off and looks as me curiously. "Did you know that Helen entered when she was eighteen, and her parents disowned her from that day on?"

"No...no, I didn't know that. I heard a few things about her parents in high school, but I certainly never heard that her parents disowned her."

"Well, they did. Both parents wanted *more* for her, as they put it, and were greatly disappointed that she decided to 'throw her future away' on a religious life. Her parents never once visited her as other parents did on visiting day, and she never had a single letter from home. Joseph and Mary became Helen's home, and the sisters there were her family. You may remember that the teaching sisters went home every summer—to the motherhouse, that is—for a month-long vacation and retreat?"

"Yes. It was a beautiful time, and they all seemed to look forward to it."

"Well, that was Helen's version of a family reunion, the only kind she'd ever known. It's understandable, I think, that when the one place she'd called home for more than forty years closed down, it felt as if her parents were disowning her all over again."

"But you say the sisters were relocated?"

"To a variety of places, yes. I think that was the problem for Helen—the fact that they weren't kept together. It must have been similar to growing up in an orphanage with all your brothers and sisters, then being split up for adoption. Helen lost not only her home, but her entire extended family. They sent her to a convent in Eureka, while some of her closest friends went to Southern California and even Arizona."

"How sad."

"I agree. Helen went where she was told to go, of

course. She's always been a great one for following the rules. At some point, however, she had a bad automobile accident, and following that she became clinically depressed. One day she disappeared, and months later she was discovered living in San Francisco, homeless. The people who found her brought her here."

"I just don't understand how that happened. Isn't there some kind of fund to help retired sisters with food and housing?"

"There is now, but some orders have more money in that fund than others. A lot depends on the wealth of the parish, and how much people are willing to donate. At any rate, I don't think that's why Helen ended up the way she did. My guess is she just wrote everyone off—her order, the Church, her entire past life as a religious. She wrote them off and disappeared."

"She must have been incredibly angry to do that."

"Angry, yes, but proud, too. I think, because of the experience with her own parents, Helen has very definite ideas about the way families should treat each other. Her families—both of them—had let her down. I don't mean this in an unkind way, but it strikes me that Helen has nothing but contempt for the religious life now."

"Yet she came here to live. And she's stayed."

"That's true, and she's nothing but kind to everyone. Makes her soups, grows her vegetables, keeps to herself. For the most part, she seems contented. Or did, until recently."

"You're not the first person who's mentioned that. Do you know what's bothering her now?"

"Truthfully, I haven't a clue. Some of the women here think it's because a friend of hers—and ours, too, for that matter—recently died. Marti Bright. Did you know her?"

"Very well."

"I'm just not so sure that's all that's wrong with Helen. I think she's been going through something rather difficult for a few months now."

Since the time Justin disappeared, would be my guess.

"You know," I say, looking at the clock on an opposite wall, "I'd like to go talk to Helen. Maybe just sit with her in the kitchen. That's where she'd be now, right? It's almost noon."

"Oh, I don't know…" Sister Anne says.

"I really am feeling better. I don't even hurt anymore."

Her look tells me she's not buying that. "Abby, I promised Detective Schaeffer that I wouldn't let you out of my sight until I was sure you were well."

"And I am," I insist.

Just to prove it, I slide my legs over the side of the bed and stand, trying hard not to wince when pain shoots up from my ankles. That was one hell of a landing, and in truth I feel like I jumped from a 300-foot-high bridge without a bungee cord.

"Look at me," I say firmly. "I'm fine now."

Sister Anne raises a brow. "I can certainly see that."

"Come on, Sister. I just want to sit in the kitchen instead of up here in bed. Maybe I can even sneak a bowl of soup out from under Sister Helen's nose."

She smiles. "I'd be surprised if she didn't force it

on you. Despite her gruff attitude, she's quite the little nurturer, you know.''

Taking her thin penlight from her pocket, she flashes it into my pupils. "Let me take one more look.''

Finally she nods and makes a satisfied sound. Standing upright she says, "Still no sign of concussion. I think you're pretty much out of the woods. I wouldn't do too much for the rest of the day, though. And promise to come back up here and let me check you out once more before you leave?''

"Absolutely,'' I say.

"Another thing. Get Helen to fix you some soothing chamomile tea. It'll help relax those leg muscles and keep them from tensing up.''

"Okay. And thanks. I mean that—really. I appreciate the way you've looked after me.''

"It's what we do here,'' she says. "The first rule of The Prayer House, from the time it was founded— 'Inasmuch as you do this for the least of My brethren, you do it for Me.' ''

In a bathroom next to the infirmary I wash my face and brush my teeth, thinking about Sister Anne's last words to me. *Inasmuch as you do this for the least of My brethren...*

My mind has begun to clear from the fall, and I am remembering thoughts I had in the chapel just before that, putting clues together that have been all around me, but that for one reason or another I haven't been clear enough to see.

I am now even more anxious to talk to my old teacher.

My clothes have been left for me on a chest of drawers in the bathroom, and moving with agonizing slowness, I manage to sit on the commode and slide first one leg then the other into my jeans. My back still hurts, and I can't seem to get my legs raised as much as I'd like without jabbing pains in my calves, hips and thighs.

Once dressed, I make my way down to the kitchen on the first floor—still a bit wobbly, but gaining.

Sister Helen is at a table cutting vegetables. She looks up with surprise to see me. Without asking, I take a chair from along the wall and painfully drag it over, sitting down and leaning on the table before I fall down. Behind Sister Helen I note a large refrigerator with a glass door. It is full of cleaned vegetables, some neatly wrapped in Baggies or Saran Wrap.

"That's some larder you have there," I say conversationally.

"Our gardens do well," she answers shortly.

"So what do you do, keep a good supply of them in there so you don't have to pick and clean them every day?"

"Something like that."

"You must have had your work cut out for you this morning, then," I say.

She just looks at me.

"Well, there aren't any that are still muddy from the storm. You must have been scrubbing all morning."

She doesn't answer that directly, but says instead, "You don't look well. I heard what happened to you."

"Sister Anne thought I was well enough to come down here, though. She said to ask you for some chamomile tea."

Sister Helen shrugs. "There's always a kettle of hot water on. Tea doesn't take much work, I guess."

I stifle a smile. "Do you want me to fix it myself? I will."

"No," she says grudgingly. "I'll get it."

This is more like the Sister Helen I remember. Everything is always "trouble," but she never really means it.

"Thank you, Sister," I say out of habit.

"Don't call me that!" she grumps as she takes a teabag from a box and puts it in a cup, pouring boiling water over it. "Here."

She thumps the cup down in front of me, leaving the teabag in.

"Sorry, it's a difficult habit to break," I say. "I don't suppose you have a spoon?"

"Little Miss Helpless now, are you? Or just used to being waited on?"

I can't help grinning at that. "I very seldom get waited on. I cook for myself, and believe it or not, I make my own tea."

"Huh."

She takes a teaspoon from a drawer and hands it to me. Taking up a potato, she begins to peel it. Her lips tug at the corners—not quite a smile.

"You're really happy here, aren't you?" I ask, warming my hands around my cup as the chamomile steeps. "You were smiling—even humming—the other day when Sister Pauline and I walked in."

"I suppose it's all right here."

"Hah. More than all right would be my guess. Right now, anyway. Helen, I've been thinking. You've been acting angry with me ever since you saw me at Marti's funeral. And you raged at me the other night. I've been trying to figure out why. At first I thought maybe it was because I'd had a fairly easy life, compared to the difficult time you've had. Then I thought maybe you were angry because my husband is trying to get his hands on The Prayer House and you thought I was in cahoots with him."

She doesn't respond.

"But you know," I say, "I've been thinking something else since I woke up from my fall this morning. Funny what a bonk on the head and a nose-dive into solid stone can do."

She makes a snorting sound that's surprisingly like the one I make myself, the one Jeffrey hates. I can't help wondering if I got it from her all those years ago.

"I'm guessing," I continue, "that it's really only Justin you're angry with me about. And I have to ask myself why that would be. Helen, you've been around Justin for years, so you must know I've never done anything to harm him. And I think you know Marti asked me to look after him, in the event something happened to him, that is."

She frowns. "You didn't even do a good job at that, did you?"

"As a matter of fact, I think I did, at least until a few months ago—"

"At which time you let your personal life take priority over Justin's safety," she snaps. "Oh, don't think I didn't hear about that. All of Carmel has been buzzing about your husband having an affair with your sister, and you prancing around with that police detective.''

"We are not prancing around!'' I say defensively, warping back to my teenage years.

Helen slams the potato down. "Young lady, Marti didn't just ask us to *watch over* her son, as if he were some expensive car parked in an alley somewhere! What she charged us with was nothing less than the safety of her child.'' Her voice lowers and breaks. "You failed her. And so did I.''

"I know,'' I say just as quietly. "And I regret that—so much, you will never know. I've loved Justin as much as you have.''

"Love! What do you know of love? Especially for a child? What do you know of the sacrifices it takes to give one's time and energies to a child, to be there for him even when you're not feeling up to it, to never turn your back on him, no matter what? What do you know—''

She breaks off, clamping her lips shut. Picking up the potato again, she begins peeling with sharp jabs, cutting huge chunks out with every slice.

I sip my tea, satisfied I'm on the right track. My thoughts roam back over the last days.

"You know what I think?'' I say, setting down my cup. "I think the person you've really been angry with is Marti, for giving Justin away.''

That elicits a sharp look.

"And,'' I say, "I think that goes back to the way you yourself must have felt when you entered Joseph and Mary, and your parents disowned you.''

Her eyes go wide at this breach of her privacy. "I never told you anything about that!"

"I know. I guess I must have picked it up somewhere."

"Somewhere! A bunch of old gossips in this place! Old biddies, talking about people behind their backs!"

"No, not gossip. Helen, that's the thing. They all love you here. As irascible as you may be at times—sorry, but you are—they love you. Some of that may just be their religious spirit kicking in, but I don't think so. I think they know you aren't an evil person, that below all the bluster, you are kind and good. Sister Anne even called you 'quite the little nurturer.'"

She makes the snorting sound again.

"So, anyway, this is the way I've got it figured," I say, "and I think I've done a pretty good job at this, at least. You remember how you used to make me think logically, one step at a time, in math? You taught me that there was only one way to arrive at an accurate answer, and that was to take what I knew and build on it—logically, no side roads, no errors along the way, or the entire problem would fall apart. That was a good lesson, one that helped me find the truth in stories I reported on later as a journalist."

The hand peeling the potato slows. I see I have my teacher's interest.

"See, what I think now," I say, "is that it's all about abandonment. When J&M closed down in the mid-eighties, there were those few months when they parceled all of you out to other convents and orders. That must have been incredibly difficult for you, losing the one home you knew. It wasn't as if you had the support of your parents during the first months before donations kicked in.''

"As if I wanted *donations*,'' she says angrily, jabbing the poor potato again. "Charity! Nothing but charity, just like before!''

Surprisingly, her eyes tear. But she straightens her back and says stiffly, "The order, you know, never gave postulants a thing. First of all, our parents were supposed to pay the order a dowry when we entered. Then they were supposed to buy everything we needed during our postulant year—uniforms, underclothes, shoes, stockings, soap, toothpaste...''

"But your parents wouldn't help you,'' I say. "Right? They abandoned you. That's what it felt like, didn't it?''

She sits heavily in a chair on her side of the table and studies her raw, gnarled hands. "The cloth for my first habit came from a Saint Vincent de Paul thrift store. It was cheap, heavy material, hot as a blister in summer. Rotted under my arms when I perspired and didn't clean up right, ever. Believe you me, young lady, by the time I took my vows four years later, I was sick to death of charity!''

Her chin goes up. "When I started teaching, I bought my own cloth. We didn't make much, mind you, but I put a little aside every month. I made my new habit with a washable material, and from the moment I put it on, I loved it. It was *mine*.''

"That's why you refused to give it up for so long. Sister, I can't even imagine how hard it must have been for you to go through all that at eighteen.''

She glares at me. "I was strong. Independent. I knew I could take care of myself."

"I'm sure you were strong, Sister. But it must have hurt. And you probably *thought* you could take care of yourself, but most eighteen-year-olds think that way. We always believe we can conquer the world. I know Marti and I did. But when we got into religious life, they did their best to strip us of that spirit of independence. Isn't that the way it was for you?"

"That's the way it was for all of us then," she snaps. "They took young women and separated them from everyone they knew and all they believed. Today that's called brainwashing. At least, by some. The younger sisters, the ones who like the changes, will tell you they turned us into mindless little servants of the Church. If you ask me, it was more like they kidnapped us and held us hostage somewhere."

Standing, she gathers up her vegetables in a large pan and takes them to the sink, rinsing them under running water. "Then one day they 'set us free.' Or so they said. We had no money and no way to take care of ourselves. So yes, I took their donations for a while. But it was still charity to me—and to a lot of the others, though they don't speak of it now."

She turns and fixes me with an angry look. "Don't go thinking we didn't appreciate what people were doing to help us! But we should have been paid properly in the first place for the teaching we did. We should have been allowed to put money away for our retirement. If things had been run right, we never would have had to take charity at all."

Dumping the rinsed vegetables into a large kettle, she slams a lid on it and lights a fire beneath it.

"You are quite an enigma, Sister Helen," I say. "You loved religious life the way it was, and you even loved living by the rules. Yet you were willing to end up homeless to be independent—which is part of the freedom the younger sisters were fighting for."

"It's not as if I chose to end up homeless," she argues. "I worked past my retirement for ten years, and I wanted to go on working, the way a lot of the older sisters have."

"But then you had a bad car accident, and you had to stop working because the pain was too severe. I know."

She sits down again and sighs. "No, young lady, you do not know. That might have been the reason I used for retiring, but the truth is—"

"You were tired," I finish for her. "Tired of all the changes, of your home closing down just when you were getting ready to live out the rest of your life there. You probably even had dreams of dying at J&M with all your old friends and sisters around, the way it used to be."

"I did love walking in the gardens," she says, her tone changing abruptly as her eyes look into the past and soften.

"I know," I say just as softly. "I loved it, too. Remember how we all made the rounds of the statues of Mary on May Day, singing songs to her and laying flowers at her feet?"

Her eyes close against tears, and the old chin wobbles as her mouth shakes. "It was beautiful...so beautiful," she says.

When she looks at me again there is so much sadness in her eyes, so much grief for a life she will never know again, I almost regret having to do what I'm about to do to her.

I lean forward and cover her hand with my own. "Sister? I was right, wasn't I? It's all about feeling abandoned. You felt abandoned, and you can't bear now to see that happen to anyone else."

"What are you getting at?" she says sharply, pulling her hand away.

"The primary rule of The Prayer House, Sister. It's a rule I would expect you, of all people, to follow."

The old eyes take on a wary light.

"'Inasmuch as you do this for the least of My brethren,'" I say, "'you do it for Me.'"

She looks away, avoiding my eyes.

"That's what you've been doing here, isn't it?" I press. "Caring for the 'least of His brethren'?"

She doesn't answer.

"I am so sorry for what happened to you," I say. "I'm sorry things weren't different. But they are different now, aren't they? Really good? See, it was the humming, Sister. That's what didn't fit for me, from the first time I saw you in this kitchen looking peaceful, content—and humming."

She pulls her hand away from mine. "What are you saying?"

"I'm saying that I couldn't help wondering. How could you be so happy, even here—when Justin, the boy you've loved for years as if he were your own, had been kidnapped and could even be dead?"

A shudder takes her body, as if a burden carried far too long has suddenly been dropped.

"You couldn't be that happy, could you?" I say. "That's how I knew."

Again, I take her hand, holding it firmly in mine. "I want you to take me to Justin, Sister. Take me to him now."

19

We trek up the hill side by side, each of us carrying a pail. Helen carries the scraps from her vegetables for composting, while I hold in one hand the pail with the extra chicken she's been buying at Albertson's the past two months. With the chicken, now roasted to crisp perfection, is a jar of hot soup and a loaf of bread—Justin's typical lunch for the past two months.

"You've just been pretending to make bad batches and throwing them out, haven't you?" I say, huffing a bit as I strain to keep up with her. "The other women were talking about that the other day at lunch. They said how unlike you that was. And when I thought about the way you come up here to these outbuildings every day, rain or shine, with your pails of 'scraps,' I realized finally that it wasn't like they thought, that you were making bad batches because you were getting old and forgetful. You just let them believe that. It was a good cover for buying all this extra food for Justin."

"You always did catch on to things faster than most," she says in a sour tone.

"Not really. I didn't actually put all this together till I got knocked on the head. It must have jarred something loose."

"Huh."

She keeps on walking, her limp getting worse, and as for me, my muscles are screaming to get there and have this Golgotha done with.

"That's why you won't let anyone help you with your composting, isn't it?" I continue. "And it's at least part of the reason you've been treating me the way you have. You were keeping me at arm's length, afraid I'd come to The Prayer House too often and find him here."

I stop a moment to catch my breath. "You know what? I'll bet that's why Ned, Marti's brother, was so cold to me, too. You turned him against me, didn't you, so we wouldn't put our heads together too much?"

She pauses, turns back, and gives me an irritable look.

"Ned's gone home already, hasn't he?" I say. "Not much to hang around here for with Marti gone. So you can't have told him Justin was kidnapped, and that you've got him now."

"You think you know so much," she says acidly, starting to walk again. "And I told you before—you know nothing at all."

"What do you mean?"

She won't answer that, and I am left to wonder what I'm getting into. Have I miscalculated this time? Is Sister Helen crazy as a loon? Will Justin be bound to a chair and gagged?

Or is he here at all? Is she leading me into a trap?

I don't honestly believe any of this, but these are the kinds of thoughts that run through my head as I follow my old teacher's stiff, arthritic footsteps up the hill to the old outbuildings.

Rounding the largest outbuilding, we come to a door at the back. Sister Helen takes a key from her pocket and opens a rusted padlock that looks as if it hasn't been used in years. The key slips easily into place, however, and I see there are traces of oil around the keyhole.

The sight that greets me when the door is opened shocks me. This is not at all what I might have expected.

Justin sits writing on a yellow pad, at an old wooden table in the middle of a room that has been dusted to a fare-thee-well and turned into a cozy, though rustic, studio of sorts. It is furnished with so many books, he virtually has his own library. They are stacked from floor to ceiling along a wall and piled on the floor by the desk. A battery-operated Coleman lamp sits on the table, casting light around the room, and there is a bed in a corner that is covered with a homey quilt. Several plump pillows lean against an old iron headboard, and there are piles of books scattered about the bed, as if Justin spends his nights there reading. The room smells like lemon-scented polish, and Justin himself looks like any student anywhere, doing his homework while munching on a candy bar.

Tears fill my throat and eyes. *I've found him, Marti. He's all right.*

Oh, dear God, thank you. Marti's son is all right.

20

"**Aunt Helen?**" Justin looks up, obviously nervous to see a stranger with her. He pushes up the sleeves of his "PACIFIC GROVE HIGH" sweatshirt and rubs his palms on his jeans.

"Good morning, Justin," Helen says in a reassuring tone. "This is Abby Northrup. She's an old friend of your mother's."

She doesn't specify whether she means Mary Ryan or Marti, but her hostility toward me disappears entirely in front of Justin. She clearly doesn't want to worry or frighten him.

"Hi, Justin," I say, willing my lips to stop shaking. "How's it going?"

He looks from me to Sister Helen and shrugs. "It's okay, I guess."

"We brought you lunch," Sister Helen says.

"I can smell it." He grins. "It sure smells good. Chicken?"

"What else? I hope you're not getting tired of it. I could try to get Tammy to buy a piece of pork or beef next time—"

"No, no I like your chicken. In fact, you make the best I've ever tasted. Honestly, Aunt Helen, it's great." He gets up and gives her a hug. "*You're* great."

The only way I can think to describe the expression on "Aunt Helen's" face at this moment is that she's beaming. Clearly, she is at her happiest doing "for the least of His brethren"—as children, I remembered earlier, have been referred to in the Bible.

I set the food pail down on the table and begin to unpack it. Sister Helen has put a large, blue-and-white-checkered napkin in with the food, and I lay it on the table and place the chicken, then the soup, on it. There is also a knife for cutting the small loaf of wheat bread, and two paper plates. I put one plate in front of Justin, who has taken a seat again. On the other plate I put the bread, and begin to slice it. My hands are still shaking from the relief of finding him here. If ever there was a miracle, I think, this has to be it.

Eyeing Justin closely, I say, "You seem pretty healthy."

He grins again, brushing his dark hair back from his forehead. "Thanks to Aunt Helen. You can see how she feeds me." He pats his tummy. "If anything, I've gained weight since I've been here."

"How—" I begin, but then fall silent. I want to ask him how long he's been here, but I don't want him to feel pressured by me.

"Almost two weeks now," he supplies, as if reading my mind.

"Two weeks!" Since Marti was murdered?

Picking up a drumstick he starts working on it, talking between bites. "It's been going by pretty fast, though. Did my mom send you here to check up on me?"

I am confused, and can't help showing it.

"Your mom? She knows you're here?"

He licks a finger. "No. I guess I just thought... Aunt Helen?"

She is behind him, tidying up the room, though it's relatively neat. Justin turns to look at her.

"Mary doesn't know," she says, giving me a look.

"Aunt Helen tried to reach her," Justin supplies, "but she couldn't find either her or my dad."

That's because they've been in Rio, dammit.

"Justin," I say, "I just saw your mom and dad. They had to go away, they thought, to protect you. It's a long story, but they thought they were doing the right thing."

His face clears. "Oh, so that's what happened. When I first got away, I went home, but the place was all locked up and dark. The car and a lot of my parents' clothes were gone, and finally I called Aunt Helen. She told me to come out here and she'd take care of me."

He looks at her and smiles. "Aunt Helen's great at spy stuff, you know. She sneaked me in, in the middle of the night."

"Did she, now?"

He nods and grins, as if proud of their caper. Then he sobers. "I've been real worried about my mom, though. I guess I just always thought my mom, at least, would be there."

"Your mom, at least? What about your dad?"

He looks at Sister Helen.

"You might as well tell her," she says.

"Well, see, the thing is, Aunt Helen wanted to make sure, first, that my dad would be gone."

I sit opposite him at the table. "Why gone?"

Again, his eyes flick to Sister Helen—dark eyes, full of questions, and so like Marti's.

"My dad..." he begins, his voice cracking as he lays down the piece of chicken, apparently losing his appetite.

"Paul Ryan," Helen interjects, reverting to her waspish tone, "is up to his neck in harassing The Prayer House into bankruptcy. He's the lawyer who filed the suit that could close us down. And guess who he's doing that for?"

I sigh. "My husband. I just found out about that tonight."

"Well, maybe you didn't know this," she says. "It's because of your husband's blackmail that Justin found out he was adopted."

I look at Marti's son, who never should have had anything but joy in his life. "Can you tell me," I say gently, "what happened?"

He shrugs. "I heard them talking one night. My dad and some guy, some guy he called Jeffrey. Aunt Helen says that was your husband?"

I nod.

"Well, anyway, this was back in July. This guy Jeffrey told my dad he knew I was adopted, and if my dad didn't do something for him, he'd tell my *real* dad where I was, and then it would be all over the papers and my real dad would take me away from him, plus I'd find out my dad wasn't my real dad—"

He breaks off, and his hand forms a fist. "I didn't know until that night. That I was adopted, I mean. I was pretty shook up, I guess, that they'd lied to me for so long. So I took off."

"You ran away?"

He swallows hard and nods.

"What about Mary?" I ask. "What did she say about your being adopted?"

"My mom wasn't home. She was at some prayer meeting at the church, and I didn't feel much like sticking around till she got home. Like I said, I just took off."

He falls silent, and I give him a moment, then ask, "What happened after that? Where did you go?"

"I ran. I ran as far as I could over 68 and then up Route 1. From there I hitchhiked to Santa Cruz and knocked about on the streets for a while." He shrugs, trying to sound tough about it, but his eyes tell me different.

"That must have been scary," I say.

"I guess so. But there were other kids out there my age. A lot of them, more than people think. So for a while it wasn't too bad. They helped me out, told me where to go at night to sleep, how to score some food. I could've gone on that way for a lot longer, but then this guy grabbed me in some alley one night and shoved me in his car. He took me to some cabin up around Felton, I think, in the mountains. I don't really know that's where it was because he had me blindfolded, but it was in the mountains, and it didn't take him too long to get there. Anyway, he kept me locked up in a room there for maybe a week."

I look at Sister Helen through tears that fill my eyes, and see that she is faring no better. Justin's chin trembles, and I know he is trying not to lose control as he retells this horrible tale.

"Did he hurt you?" I ask, dreading the answer. "This man. Did he...did he do anything to you?"

Justin shrugs again. "Not really. He wasn't there most of the time, just left me tied up in a room. He took pictures of me. I could hear the camera, and I figured he was going to send pictures to my parents with a ransom note or something. Most of the time I just couldn't sleep at night because it hurt, being tied that way. And he didn't feed me much."

He gives me a shy, embarrassed look. "But the worst part was not knowing. What he was going to do, I mean. I thought he brought me there to do things to me, at first. That's what some of the kids on the street said happens sometimes. But he didn't, so then I thought he must have changed his mind and didn't know what to do with me. I figured he'd probably kill me eventually, because if he let me go I'd be able to identify him. So I started to think about ways to get away before that happened."

"Oh, Justin..." I reach over and stop short of grabbing his hand, not knowing whether my touch would comfort or frighten him after such an ordeal. "I am so sorry. I had no idea these things were happening to you. Your mother would be so proud of you for being so brave."

He gives me an odd look. "Are you talking about Mary? Or my real mom?"

"Both," I say. "Mary is just as much your real mom. And she loves you a lot."

"But you said both. Do you know my real mom?"

"Yes. We were friends all our lives. She was my best friend, in fact. She was a wonderful woman, Justin, very brave. And you are just like her."

Helen gives an almost imperceptible shake of her head to me. But it's too late.

"Was?" Justin says, his eyes widening. "Did something happen to my real mom?"

I realize the mistake I've just made. *Helen hasn't told him. He's been here in this room with no television or radio for news, and no one to talk to. He doesn't know Marti is dead.*

But maybe that's for the best. This can't be the time to tell this poor kid, who's been through so much, that the woman who gave birth to him died a week ago, in a terrible way.

"I just haven't seen her for a long while, that's all," I improvise.

"But she's all right?" he says eagerly. "I can see her again when all this is over?"

"See her again? You've seen Marti?"

"She's been here several times," Sister Helen interjects. "I told her Justin was here the minute he turned up."

"I can't wait to tell her I've met you," Justin says to me, grinning. "She talked about you a lot."

"She did?"

"Sure. Mostly she told me how you helped her find a good home for me, and good parents. She said you were the best friend she ever had."

He looks at Sister Helen. "Well, next to Aunt Helen, I mean. She said she didn't know how she'd have gotten through life without both of you."

His face clouds over. "When I told her about the guy who kidnapped me, though, she said she'd find out who did that and she'd see he paid, if it was the last thing she ever did."

Oh, God. Is that what happened, Marti? Did you find him—and did he kill you instead?

My heart goes out to Justin, and I can't help it. I go around the table and enfold him in my arms. My love wraps itself around him, and it is almost as if Marti is here, holding him with my arms.

"Don't worry," I say. "We'll get him, Justin. We'll get him and make sure he pays."

I am anxious to know how Justin got away from his kidnapper and what he remembers about him. Before getting into that, however, I urge him to eat his meal. When it comes right down to it, Marti's son is just a kid. A kid who's been through more than most adults and come out of it with his spirit intact. For this, I give credit to Sister Helen. She's been with him since he got away, looking after him, an advocate for both body and soul.

It's been said that there are only two basic emotions—love and fear. Where one exists, the other cannot. Sister Helen, it seems, has been operating on fear since Justin disappeared and later showed up on her doorstep. Her focus has been on protecting him any way she can, so for her there have been shadows in every corner. At times they may even have driven her near the edge.

But she couldn't shut out the love. So she's been swinging back and forth, balancing both with the skill and now-and-again awkwardness of a tightrope walker.

She finishes her straightening up, then leaves me alone with Justin while she takes her scraps out to the compost heap. His appetite has returned, and I pretend not to watch as he eats the food we've brought. Still, I can't help smiling when, like any healthy teenage boy, he wipes the chicken grease from his mouth with his fingers, then wipes them on his jeans.

"You sure you don't want some of this?" he asks, pushing the plate my way.

"No, thanks. I'm not very hungry."

The truth is, my stomach is in knots. I still haven't fully recovered from the shock of finding him here, even though the idea began to form subconsciously, I suppose, the day I saw Helen stumbling up this hill under the weight of her pails of scraps. When she was up here for so long, I wondered why. Then, last night when she was out here in the storm supposedly "picking vegetables," that somehow didn't feel right. While Helen might have penances to pay, as Sister Pauline said, I really couldn't buy a woman with arthritis clumping around in mud and a driving rain just to save a few heads of lettuce.

More likely, I thought—especially when I saw that full larder in the kitchen—she was out here checking on her young charge, making sure he was warm and dry.

Even so, she might have gotten away with it if it hadn't been for the humming. It takes a lot to make a woman like Sister Helen hum.

When Justin is finished eating he scrapes his plate into a small bucket in a galvanized sink against the wall. Then he rinses it, and dries it before putting it back on the table and sitting across from me.

"May I ask you some questions?" I say. "I don't want to upset you, but—"

"It's okay. You want to know about when I was gone, right? That's what my mom—Marti Bright, I mean—kept asking me. You could sure tell she was a good reporter. She wanted to know every detail."

"I can imagine. Justin, could you identify the man who held you prisoner in that room?"

"I'm not sure. I mean, I never got much of a look at him, just the first night when he grabbed me. Even then, he wasn't anything more than a dark figure in back of me, and he got me blindfolded before I could even get a chance to fight him off."

"But you said you thought he might kill you to keep you from identifying him."

"I just thought he might be worried about that, but like I said, I didn't really see him." He pauses. "I did hear him, though. That might be one way."

"You heard his voice?"

"Just once, on the phone in some other room. He was saying something about somebody being after him, on his tail. I thought he might mean the police, like maybe one of the kids in Santa Cruz saw him grab me and called the police. That's what I kept hoping, anyway—that somebody got his license-plate number and they were looking for me."

"Is that all you heard?"

He reddens. "Well, no, there was something else, but it sounds pretty stupid now."

"That doesn't matter. What was it?"

"I just thought he said something like, 'Tell the president.' And then I heard, I thought, 'oval office,' but he might have said "in his office," or something like that. I mean, he probably just meant the president of some company, right?"

I close my eyes briefly. The picture is coming clear, too clear. "Justin...what about the man's voice? Did he sound the same as the man you heard talking to your dad that night about your adoption? The one your dad called Jeffrey?"

Justin shakes his head. "That's what my mom asked, but I'm just not sure, because he was talking so low. But the thing is, I heard that guy, Jeffrey, tell my dad, Paul, that night, that he thought he knew who my real dad was. He said if he was right, my real dad had lots of money and was in politics. That's why he said it would be all over the papers if word got out, and my real dad would come and take me away. So when I heard this guy talking on the phone in the cabin, I got this weird idea he was talking to the president of the United States. Pretty dumb, huh?"

I don't know how to answer that, except to say softly, "No, Justin, it's not dumb. Not at all. Could you tell me, do you think, what kind of car this guy had?"

"I'm not sure, but it must have been expensive. The engine purred like a kitten."

Or like a Mercedes? I wonder.

Jeffrey is on the run. The police are on his tail. And Jeffrey—could he possibly have kidnapped Justin himself?—might have been running some scam on Chase.

Or *for* Chase.

If Chase is Justin's real father, that is.

A bigger question: If Jeffrey is the one who grabbed Justin in Santa Cruz, what did he plan to do with him? How long did he plan to keep him hidden? Until after the election?

Or was this all about keeping Paul Ryan under his thumb? Did it have nothing to do with Chase's re-election, and all to do with Jeffrey's scheme to bank-rupt The Prayer House?

Either way, I doubt very much he would have let Justin go when either of these things were over. More likely, he'd have disposed of him when he was no longer of use.

My bones feel deep-down cold, and I pull my jacket more tightly around myself. "How did you get away from this man?" I ask.

Justin grins, clearly proud of himself. "I tricked him. It was the only way I could figure how to do it. I started to scream like crazy. He had my mouth taped, but I screamed in my throat, on and on. He came running in and tore the tape off. I told him I had a terrible pain in my gut. He didn't believe me at first, but I screamed so much and so long, I almost lost my voice. I told him I thought I was dying, and finally I stopped and just kept still. I acted like I was dazed, really out of it."

"You didn't worry that he might just kill you, if you were that sick?"

"Sure, I worried about it. But I figured the alter-native was just to wait till he killed me anyway some day."

I shake my head. "Justin, you are truly amazing. So what did he do?"

"Untied me so he could straighten me out and look at me better. He poked around at my stomach and muttered something like he knew something about medical emergencies, and there wasn't a damn thing wrong with me. That's when I popped him one in the eyes with my thumbs.''

The grin grows wider. ''Boy, did that feel good. I got him by surprise, just like he got me that first night. I didn't even take time to look back, just pulled my blindfold off as I was running to the door, then slammed it and locked it. There was a dead bolt on the outside, so there was no way he was getting out real fast. I saw a bunch of photographs of me on a table in the living room, and I grabbed one so I could prove what had happened to me. There weren't any keys to the car, though, so I figured he had them in his pocket. In fact, I couldn't even find the car. It was probably in the garage, but I just ran.''

I smile. ''Good thing you were a track star, huh?''

He looks pleased. ''You know about that?''

''Yes. I know about that.''

''You know, you look familiar to me,'' he says. ''Have I seen you at my school?''

''I've attended some events there,'' I say. ''I saw you run once or twice.''

''Well, you're right,'' he says. ''It's a good thing I could do that. But if I'd been smarter, I'd've at least looked at him before I ran off. I just didn't think I'd done all that much damage, and it felt like he was right on my heels till I locked that door. I ran all the way down that mountain to Santa Cruz, staying off the road and in the trees in case he came looking for me in the car. When I got to Santa Cruz I hitched a ride back to Pacific Grove and then out here, to Aunt Helen.''

''So, Justin, you were in Santa Cruz for maybe

three weeks, and then at that cabin for what, another week? And you've been out here at The Prayer House ever since you got away from this man?"

"That's about it." He looks around at the small room, so overflowing with books. "Aunt Helen's been sort of home-schooling me. She comes out here every chance she gets at night, when no one can see her do it. She sure is a good teacher."

"I know. She taught me."

"Really? Gosh, she must be pretty old."

I raise my brows. "Pardon me?"

He laughs. "Sorry, I didn't mean it that way. I just mean she must have been teaching longer than I thought. She's supposed to be retired now, you know, and it's a good thing, with that asthma—"

He breaks off. "Come to think of it, that's the other way I thought I might be able to identify that guy."

"Other way?"

"By his breathing. He wheezed a lot sometimes."

"You mean, you think he might have asthma?"

"Something like that. I heard him bringing in wood from outside one day, and then building a fire. It sounded like he could hardly breathe."

It is only now I remember that this is the one memory I have of the person who pushed me over the choir loft railing.

As I tried to fight him off, he was wheezing—the way I remember Jeffrey wheezing, when he's been up in the attic searching for his clothes.

21

I leave Justin in his "Aunt Helen's" capable hands and head home from The Prayer House late in the afternoon, my mind bending like crazy around all the things I've learned in the past twenty-four hours. Before leaving, I asked Helen why she didn't go to the police after Justin got away. Why didn't she take them the photograph Justin had brought home with him, as proof of what had happened to him?

"Who was I supposed to trust?" she said simply. From her almost paranoid tone, I realized that this was probably a hangover from her days on the streets. *Trust no one in authority.*

In addition, Marti had asked her to simply keep Justin safe until she herself could bring matters to a head.

"Why did you bring me the photograph, then?" I asked her.

"I was furious with you—and afraid for Justin, after Marti was murdered. I wanted you to know what you'd done by helping to place him with those people—that father."

Driving into Carmel, I realize my body is not doing especially well. I'm still sore all over from that nosedive, though not complaining. If not for Kenpo and a bit of luck, I might have died from a fall like that. All it would have taken was my neck twisting the wrong way when I struck that stone floor.

So the person who pushed me over probably wanted me out of the way, permanently—not just out of commission for a while.

Jeffrey? Jeffrey, all this time?

It's the only thing that fits. Sending the Ryans away, kidnapping Justin and hiding him out—even reporting to the president about it.

I recall now that Jeffrey's been disappearing more than usual these past two months. He claimed to have been traveling back and forth to Washington, but he could just as easily have been in the Santa Cruz mountains, holed up with Justin.

But when Justin got away from him—then what? Jeffrey must have died a thousand deaths, waiting for Mr. Squeaky-Clean's son—if that's who Justin is—to turn up and go to the police. Especially if he thought Justin could identify him.

But when Justin ran and then didn't turn up?

Marti's son, missing, must have been a sword over his head—a sword that could come crashing down at any moment.

And to make things worse, Marti must have confronted him. She had to have known, from the legal briefs that were filed, that Paul Ryan was the lawyer handling the suit designed to close The Prayer House and bankrupt Lydia, thus forcing her to sell. It would be only one more step from there to figure out that Paul wasn't the type to handle anything that dirty without some heavy persuasion—thus, Jeffrey must be holding something over his head.

What could that be, Marti must have wondered, other than Justin?

Unless I've got Paul figured wrong, and he did it for the money, then chickened out, and was only too happy to disappear to Jeffrey's little hideaway in Sao Conrado.

So let's say Marti confronted Jeffrey, who then got rid of Marti—and last night it was my turn.

Did Harry Blimm tell him I was on to his little real-estate scam? Was Jeffrey already in the valley killing Rick Stone when I drove to The Prayer House last night?

And why would he kill Rick Stone? Did the randy Realtor turn on him?

I can't know that. But Jeffrey was seen in the area of the real-estate office last night. That certainly put him in the right place to hop on over to The Prayer House and do me in. He wouldn't even have had to navigate the flooded roads from Carmel.

With all this in mind, I am more cautious than usual as I approach *Windhaven,* looking up and down Scenic for Jeffrey's car in case he's in the neighborhood watching for my arrival.

There seem to be only the usual tourists and locals about, either parked in their cars enjoying the scenery, or out walking their dogs. I pull into my driveway and press the garage remote, relieved not to see the Mercedes here, either.

Taking out my keys, I let myself into the pantry area through the connecting door in the garage. It's when I enter the kitchen that I sense something is wrong.

Standing stock-still, I look around, checking. What is it? What's not like it was before?

"Murph?" I call out. "Murph, I'm home."

No responding patter of feet, and I remember that Frannie picked him up the night before.

Then I see it—the casement window is open, not shut tight the way I left it, and the bottles I'd lined up on the sill are standing upright on the floor. A sound issues from my office, as if someone is moving about. It's followed by a click and the sight squeak of my desk chair.

Picking up one of the wine bottles by its neck, I move quietly down the hall to my office door. The hairs on my arms stand on edge, and I'm wishing I were in better shape. Whoever's in there can't be up to any good, or they would have shown themselves when I called for Murphy.

Karen again?

No. She wouldn't have any reason to loot my office.

Jeffrey, then. He could have parked up on the street above Scenic and walked the rest of the way. Isn't that what someone would do who planned to kill his wife? He wouldn't drive up to the scene of the crime in a Mercedes. And he wouldn't let himself in the front door with his key, in full view of the neighborhood. He'd have come the back way, through the patio.

By the time I reach my office, the fear is so heavy in the pit of my stomach, I feel ill. With Murph gone, there's no help there. And if Jeffrey is armed, I won't be able to get close enough to use my martial arts.

I stand to the side of the door quietly, listening.

Another small squeak of my office chair. I'll have to do something—no good just standing out here.

"Who is it?" I say in as firm a voice as I can muster. "Jeffrey? Is that you? I've got the cordless, and I'm calling the police."

No answer. I remember, too late, that I left the cordless phone on my desk the last time I used it. He knows I'm bluffing.

I hear the way the chair sounds when someone gets up from it. Footsteps come toward the door. I raise the wine bottle to swing.

But it isn't Jeffrey who appears. "Easy, Abby," says Tommy Lawrence, holding his hands palm out. "Easy."

He's in the hallway now, and I've still got the bottle raised. "Move back," I say, motioning with my head. "Get away from the door."

He raises his hands as if I have a gun on him. "Sure, Abby, sure. Hey, it's okay. I'm harmless."

When he's clear of the doorway, I step into my office. I see now that he's been at my desk, and my computer is on. I walk to the desk and ease myself around it, still watching the door. Tommy starts to step inside, and I tell him to get back.

"Do it!" I say when he doesn't move. He takes a step backward.

"What the hell have you been doing?" I demand.

"I...I was waiting for you," he says. "I'm sorry if I startled you. I thought you might not mind if I signed on as a guest, so I could pick up my e-mail on Yahoo."

"Bull!"

I look at the computer screen. Along the top of

the screen is a document name: *Dervish*. My shock is complete. "You've been going through my journals! My personal journals!"

He has found the way in, breaching the laborious subdirectories I set up to protect my privacy from Jeffrey. The page he's on is about Marti and my feelings about Justin and the way she gave him up. My disappointment with her decision lies on the page like an accusation, a reminder that I did not always understand.

When she was alive, that seemed reasonable. Now that she's gone forever, I feel like a traitor.

"How could you do this?" I demand. "What right have you to pry into something this private?"

My dictionary is on the desk, and I don't remember putting it there. I shove it aside and find hidden beneath it the slim packet of Marti's letters to me over the years.

"My God! It was *you* in the attic—maybe not the day I was up there, but the day Frannie heard something. Just how long have you been in Carmel? And how long were you stalking Marti *this* time?"

Tommy pales. "You don't understand. I wasn't stalking her, honest to God, I wasn't. I just still cared about her, and I thought if I could find out more about her, it wouldn't be like I'd lost her all over again. So, yeah, it was me your housekeeper heard that day. I figured you might have some old letters of Marti's, and I wasn't really meaning to break in when I came here, just talk to you. But then when you weren't home—"

"You just thought, oh, well, I might as well let myself in?"

He flushes. "Something like that, I guess."

I am starting to calm down and get my balance back. "You broke into my house," I say, "and stole private property. I suppose you know that's against the law."

"I was going to give the letters back," he argues. "That's why I brought them with me today."

"Yeah, right, and while you were at it, you thought you'd just take a little peek into my private files."

He gives me that embarrassed, barefoot-boy smile, but it's not working this time.

"I don't know who and what you really are," I say, "or what you're doing here. But I don't want you around anymore. I'm calling the police."

I grab the cordless phone from my desk.

He comes toward me. "No, wait. Abby, you really don't want to do that."

"Like hell. Get away from me!"

"Abby, put the phone down!"

I punch in the 911 number with one hand, still holding the bottle with the other, and move back.

"You're going to ruin it all," he says. "Everything I've been working for."

"I said, get away!"

He reaches for the phone, and I swing. The bottle glances off the side of his head, but it takes him down for the minute I need to run from the office and yell into the phone that I've got an intruder and need help.

The dispatcher starts to tell me to stay on the line, but by this time the police have already arrived.

"Well, that was fast," I say as Ben busts through the front door.

He stands there puffing and red-faced, as if from running.

"You know the Carmel P.D.," he says. "Always on the job. Now where is that sonuvabitch?"

Arnie, Ben's partner, has caught Tommy trying to leave by the garage door. He drags him in, handcuffed, reads him his rights and pushes him down on a kitchen chair. Tommy looks sullen, and in fact angrier than one might expect an arrested felon to be. I would have guessed he'd act more cowed, from what I thought I knew of him.

I stand by the table with my arms folded. "So I guess you two were following me again?" I say. "And when my call came through to dispatch, you were Johnny-on-the-spot."

"I hope that's not a complaint," Ben says, sinking into a chair. "We get enough complaints without yours, too. Kids in trees, somebody sitting in a car, cats on a roof..."

"No," I say. "Not a complaint. But we do need to talk."

"How about if we have a little conversation with your visitor first?" he says, looking at Tommy.

"Be my guest."

Ben takes out a small notepad and pencil, but before he starts to write, he reads from the notepad.

"Okay, let's begin, Thomas Jefferson Lawrence. This is what we know about you so far. You're up to your neck in debt and have not been staying at the La Playa at all, but rather pretending to. You make appointments to meet people there in the bar, telling everyone you're registered there, and even have an arrangement with the desk clerk to take your messages. In reality, though, you're staying at the Travelodge on Fremont in Monterey. And you're even about to be kicked out of there for not paying your room rent." He looks up at Tommy. "Have I got that right so far?"

Tommy shrugs, but flicks an uneasy glance at me.

"Point two," Ben says. "About that debt. You've been supporting yourself on credit cards, and they're about to run out—no thanks to your recent trip to Rio."

Ben casts me a look.

"Okay, so you know everything," I say, annoyed. "Get on with it."

"Point three, you do have the possibility of some rather excellent income in the near future—but only if you turn a certain book in to an interested publisher within the next month. And then, only if it's approved."

I break in at this point. "What book? And why do I have a feeling it's not one of those thrillers you mentioned writing, Tommy?"

He just looks at the floor.

"The book in question," Ben says, "is true crime. According to his editor, it's all about the crucifixion and murder of one Marti Bright. It includes, by the way, the reaction of her friends and family. Which explains—"

"Why he's been so intent on hanging around me," I finish for him, "even to the extent of following me all the way to Rio." I can't hold back the snort. "Just how much money do you expect to get for this book, Tommy?''

When he doesn't answer, Ben says, ''Enough to pull himself out of debt for a long, long time. For that matter, enough to have thought this all out way ahead of time.''

''Meaning?'' I say.

''Well, let's suppose he had it in for Marti for some reason—like maybe she's been rejecting him for years. So he kills her out of rage and in a monstrous way that's guaranteed to bring all the media out of the woodwork. Then he goes to his agent and says he's an old friend of Marti's and has an inside track with family and friends. It's a big story, not every day somebody gets crucified. Especially in a town like Carmel. So his agent negotiates a major deal. Seven figures, a Hollywood movie, all kinds of trash TV…''

''My God.'' I stare at Tommy, at a loss for words. This is something I never would have guessed, not in a million years.

''I didn't kill her,'' he says obstinately. ''I did not kill her.''

''You might want to hold off on any statements till you've got a lawyer,'' Arnie suggests, turning a chair around and straddling it.

''I don't need a lawyer! I'm telling you, I did not kill her. I loved her!''

''Love, passion…first and foremost on the list of reasons to kill,'' Arnie says.

''No, I *wouldn't*. I never could. Marti was everything to me!''

Ben looks at me.

"He was obsessed with her in high school," I say. "She hardly knew him."

Tommy sends me an angry look.

"It's true, and you know it. For God's sake, Tommy, you had to come here to my house looking for letters she wrote! That's how little you knew about her. And she never gave you a second thought."

He doesn't answer, but I can't help wondering when tears fill his eyes. What did he really feel for Marti? How deep could it have gone?

Deep enough that he killed Marti in some mad moment of revenge for not returning those feelings? Is Ben right?

And *did* he set it all up beforehand, to get out of debt? Is Tommy Lawrence, when it comes down to it, nothing but a cold-blooded killer?

"Well," Ben says, heaving himself up from his chair with a weary sigh, "it doesn't look like we're getting anywhere here. Let's take him in."

Arnie stands and pulls Tommy up. Tommy doesn't resist, but says, "You're making a big mistake."

"Yeah, yeah," Arnie says. "So sue me."

"Don't think I won't!"

"Shit, if I had a dime for every perp who's said that, I'd be rich right now," Arnie says.

He turns and looks at Ben, who says, "Go ahead, take him in. I'll be along."

"Hey, Chief," Arnie says on the way out the door, "you think I could write a book about all this?"

"If you do, leave me out of it," Ben says. "And easy on the Chief thing. I'm not there yet."

With Arnie and Tommy gone, Ben turns to me. "What do you think?"

I sit in the nearest chair, as my legs are not supporting me well. "Do you mean, do I think he killed Marti? I don't know. There's been something about him from the beginning that didn't feel right. Too many secrets. But, Ben, what about Jeffrey? I've been thinking he must have killed Marti."

I tell him finally about the real-estate scam, which makes him mad as hell.

"Why didn't you tell me about this at The Prayer House when I told you we were after Jeffrey for Rick Stone's murder?"

"I didn't think of it, dammit. I wasn't exactly in the best of health, you know."

"Even so, if you'd leveled with me about a lot of things from the beginning—"

I rub my face. "Look, are we really going to argue? *Now?* You just nabbed Marti's possible killer, which, if he's found guilty, will assure your upcoming Chief-dom. Besides, I'm still recovering from last night. I could use a good night's sleep."

He sighs. "Okay, but we still have to talk."

"Sure, right. We'll talk. When?"

"As soon as I've got a minute. First I've got to do a formal interrogation with Lawrence back at the station, and then there'll be reams of paperwork—"

"See?" I interrupt. "It's never that easy, is it?"

"For you and me, you mean?" He takes my shoulders, and I turn away. "Abby…hey, Abby, are you having second thoughts about us?"

"More like second, third and fourth." I am, in

truth, tired of men running off on me to take care of business.

Still, at his disconcerted expression, I can't help softening. "Go, Chief. Go do your thing, lock up your man."

"You know I'd stay if I could."

"Yeah, sure, wonderful. *Go.*"

"Just one thing," he says, hesitating. "As long as Jeffrey's running around loose, I'm putting an officer out front. I've got a sheriff's deputy from the task force at my disposal, and I'll call him from my car. I won't leave till he shows up."

"Fine. I can deal with that."

"And, Abby—I want you to be especially careful."

"I *will. Go.* Don't worry. I can take care of myself."

He looks at the open casement window and the bottles on the floor. "Yeah, you're a regular Jesse James, you are."

"Jesse James?"

"Detective novel I just read. Jessica James, a female crime reporter. You remind me of her."

"Really? Anything specific?"

"Well, the mean mouth, for one thing. And then, there's that ornery attitude."

After Ben leaves I call Frannie and ask if she'll keep Murphy until tomorrow so I can get some uninterrupted sleep. I'm beginning to miss my furry friend like crazy, but if Frannie were to bring him home we'd have to talk. She'd see the lump on my noggin, demand to know how I got it, warn me to sell my house and move into a gated condo... It'd never end.

Exhausted, I lock every door and window tight, then fix myself a tray with tea, crackers and a hunk of Havarti cheese, which I take up to bed. Hoping to be lulled to sleep I click the remote on the TV and find a presidential speech has taken over every channel. *Perfect.* That should put me out in no time.

Mr. Squeaky-Clean is polished and tan, like a fine copper penny. His graying hair makes him look distinguished, and his wife and fourteen-year-old daughter, whom the camera pans to every now and then, seem happy as clams.

I study Chase, and even his daughter, searching for some sign of resemblance to Justin. Is this his father? His half sister? I can't be certain.

Chase doesn't look, however, like a man whose illegitimate son has been missing for two months. In fact, neither does the first lady look at all worried that her old friend Marti Bright's son is still missing.

I wonder if Marti told them before she died that Justin had been found and was safe, swearing them to secrecy. The unhappy alternative would be that neither the president nor his wife have a caring bone in their bodies.

The first lady and the president are both consummate actors, of course. One has to be, to survive in politics. Right now, Chase is expounding on health care, which he did nothing about in his last term, but promises faithfully to fix in the next. Since health care will never be fixed in this country, at least not in my lifetime and not by politicians, I lower the volume and turn my attention elsewhere.

Munching on crackers, I let my thoughts roam back over the past few hours, including the surprises Ben brought me about Tommy Lawrence. I'd begun to like Tommy, in a way, and it's a disappointment that my instinct that he was hiding something, and wasn't who he pretended to be, was on the mark.

But then, I've learned that people will do a lot for money when they're broke and in debt. They'll do a lot for money, anyway. Look at me. I made a deal with the devil—Jeffrey—to hang on to my house. Maybe that wasn't all about greed, but it comes to the same thing. I wanted to assure my ongoing place in the land of milk and money.

And look at Jeffrey. What would he do to get his hands on The Prayer House and secure his future wealth? Despite the potential of Tommy being Marti's killer, I'm not writing Jeffrey off yet. Sometimes it comes down to who has more to gain. Tommy would have gained revenge for years of rejection and a seven-figure book contract. But for someone like Tommy Lawrence, would that have been more incentive than Jeffrey had, with his scheme to rule the world—or at least the Carmel Valley?

I am amazed at all the balls Jeffrey's had in the air, to tell the truth. The real-estate scam, holding Justin captive, dealing with the Ryans, with the president, with killing Marti—if he did—and now being on the run. I wouldn't have thought Jeffrey could handle all that on his own. Especially not with the Secret Service after him. That must have taken some clever planning.

Which reminds me. I haven't seen the D.C. Duo

for some time. And what kind of Secret Service men
are they, anyway, that they haven't been able to bring
Jeffrey in by now? My money is on Ben as the better
cop.

I wasn't bluffing when I told Mauro and Hillars I
knew "the real reason" they were here. Oh, Chase
might have sent them initially to look for Justin. But
I'm betting that once Jeffrey disappeared and they
started tracking him down, they uncovered the real-
estate scam. That's why they were outside the bank
the other day—not following me, but because they'd
been investigating Harry for bank fraud. Something
the Secret Service turns up for faster than one can
blink.

So, aside from all else, what does Mr. Squeaky-
Clean think about that? Mauro and Hillars must have
reported Jeffrey's illegal dealings to him by now.
He's probably furious at the thought of the headlines:
*President's Closest Adviser Arrested for Bank Fraud/
Land Scam*—just before the election.

In fact, that's probably why he called this press
conference about health care just now. It's a smoke
screen, something to take the public's mind off the
news about Jeffrey when it breaks.

One thing, regardless of what happens with Jeffrey, whether they find him or not and arrest him or
not, I'm going to Sol tomorrow and start proceedings
for a divorce. Just knowing what Jeffrey has done, if
only to The Prayer House, makes me feel dirty by
association. After I call Sol, if Jeffrey's still on the
loose, I'll get the locksmith over to change all the
locks, and then I'll have Frannie come and help me
pack up his things.

That settled, I let the president of the United States—whose son, quite possibly, is living in an abandoned shack not two hours from me—lull me to sleep. In the morning I'll take care of Justin, too. I don't know how, but I will.

"Why didn't you just stay out of it?" I hear through my sleep. *"You were never the type to meddle. Why now?"*

I struggle awake, but can't see. The room is too dark, the television off. Fear shoots through me, making me weak as I try to sit. A hand shoves me back down.

"We could have had it all. Why did you have to ruin it?"

"Jeffrey?"

Something cold and hard snaps around one wrist, then the other. "So you and Officer Friendly like to play, do you? Well, I've brought you some nice little handcuffs." His voice is hoarse, his hands rough. "You'll like these, wifey dear. Karen and I have already broken them in. We had a great deal of fun with them, in fact."

I feel cords tighten around my ankles. Before I can think and react, my legs are pulled apart and tied to each bedpost. I try to jerk a knee up. It doesn't move more than an inch.

"Sorry, no Kenpo for you tonight, my darling. I want you powerless—the way I would be if I let you tell them what I've done. I want you to feel what it's like."

I open my mouth to scream, but a hand clamps down hard. I manage a feeble bite. Jeffrey mutters

an oath, jerks his hand away, then slaps me, knocking
my head to the side.

Covering me with his body, he shoves his forearm
under my chin, keeping my head bent back so far, it
hurts. My jaw is locked by the position; I can't get
my mouth open to yell. I feel a hand yank my pajama
bottoms down, then jam itself between my thighs.
Tears of impotency and rage fill my eyes.

"How does it feel?" my husband murmurs into
my ear as he jams his fingers inside me. "How does
it feel to have all that power and not be able to use
it? Hmm?"

I flail with my body, but my efforts to throw him
off don't work. The most I can do is pull back a
fraction of an inch from the invading fingers. I get a
moment of relief, then Jeffrey thrusts himself inside
me. His arm still holds my head in place, so I cannot
scream except deep in my throat. He is ramming me
over and over, so mindlessly and rough I feel pain
everywhere. A grinding, excruciating pain.

"You know how sick I got of hearing how you
wanted a baby?" Jeffrey rasps. His breath comes at
me in short, laborious gasps. "You wanted pain
down here, some doctor, some other man, sticking
his bloody instruments up you? Well, now you have
it. Everything you ever wanted, *wife*."

A whole new kind of agony sears through me, rob-
bing me of sanity and will. I scream again, though
there is no sound. It's the last thing I know before I
awake on the hill.

22

Night air surrounds me, dank and chilling. The ground beneath me is wet. I have no way of knowing if the wet is from rain, or from the blood I feel trickling from inside me, oozing out onto my thighs.

I am blindfolded now, and there is tape across my mouth. But I know where I am, and that fills me with dread.

I know where I am not by sight, but by sound. Nails strike wood, and as the carpenter of my final resting place pounds them in, his breathing is labored.

Is this the way it was for you, Marti? Did you know it was Jeffrey? Did you know what he was going to do?

I wonder if she felt as much fear as I do now. Marti was brave, much braver than I. Even Justin is braver than I. He found a way to get free.

I am not able to move. None of my years of learning self-defense are working for me now. Jeffrey has what he wants—my impotence. I am stripped of power, just as he would be if I lived to tell what I know.

But, wait. He will have to take the handcuffs off, to put me on the cross. There may be time. A split second only, it's all I might need.

I begin to pray. I pray to all my lost saints, and to the God who seemed to abandon me, though I know, now, that it was I who went away, not he.

Take care of Justin, I pray. *Take care of him, please.*

My entire abdomen blooms with pain, and my head feels thick and heavy. There is an odor, one I remember vaguely from long ago in science class.

Chloroform. He must have chloroformed me to get me here.

I force myself to be awake, alert. At the same time, I lie unmoving, pretending to be unconscious still.

My moment comes sooner than expected.

"Time to say goodbye," my Roman soldier says, his voice coming from somewhere above me. "Sorry, no time for the flogging this time."

Jeffrey's voice sounds strange. Tight from allergies rather than emotion? The wheezing is more pronounced now.

I hear keys jangle. *Get ready, Abby. Don't flub this, it's your last chance to stay alive.*

A hand touches mine as he reaches to unlock the cuffs. They spring free, and the moment they do my left hand darts like a snake to grab a wrist. The fingers of my right hand form an Eagle's Beak and punch in the direction where his eyes must be. I know I connect when I hear a howl. In that instant, I kick with both tied feet toward the groin. When I don't connect this time, I know he must have sidestepped. Ripping off the blindfold, I jump to my feet and left-chop down on his neck while my right fist smashes up, striking him below the chin.

I am hampered by weakness, but the second he's

off balance from the punch, I slam my right fist into his groin. As he knifes over, I left-chop him again and watch as he falls to the ground.

He doesn't stay down long. Shaking uncontrollably, I step back for a breath as he struggles to his feet. We come face-to-face for the first time, and even though it's black as death itself out here, what I see shocks me so much, I lose valuable time. In the moment it takes me to recover, he's on me again, and this time I'm no match for the positions he uses—they are all black belts.

He gets me with a "Lion," several kicks to the body that end with a right chop to the throat. I'm down. Standing above me, my opponent says in that heavy, constricted voice, "Give it up, Abby. You can't win."

Ripping the tape off my mouth, I manage in a guttural whisper, "Go to hell, Agent Mauro. Go to fucking hell."

23

I am helpless as a kitten as Mauro drags me to the makeshift cross and lashes me to it, hands and feet. I have never been so frightened in my life, and I now know the meaning of "my blood ran cold." I can only pray, and I do, against the tape that once again binds my mouth.

"You're husband was right, you know," he says in that heavy, constricted voice as he searches through construction nails in a wooden box. The cross is still on the ground; he will have to lift me on it. I have no doubt he's up to it, even with the difficult breathing.

"You shouldn't have meddled so much," he says. "You had that nice little life going for you, everything a woman could want in the world, and you blew it. That wasn't smart."

He sits back on his haunches and looks at me. "I even told you. I told you to stay out of it, but you wouldn't listen. Funny thing is, I almost liked you."

He laughs, a low, evil sound. "*Almost* being the operative word. I couldn't let you go and blow everything I had going. I waited a long time for that deal to come together with your husband, out there in the valley. Ever since Hillars and I first came out here to look for Justin Ryan, in fact—three months ago. You think I wanted to be in the Service the rest of my fucking life? You think I want to go putting my life on the line for the kinds of jerks that pass through the White House now? Shit, none of 'em are worth it.''

My jeans have been pulled up around me, since Jeffery removed them, and Mauro plucks absently at one leg of material. ''All it took,'' he says, ''was one look at how people live here, and I was in. Bet you didn't know that. You poked around and you found the Realtor, even the banker. You just never found the appraiser. Or me.''

He takes up a construction nail and a mallet and stands over me. My bowels constrict, and my heart races. I can already feel the huge nail puncturing my palms, and I don't think I can take it. I will die before then.

Is this the way it was, Marti? Oh, God, Marti, help me.

Mauro seems to pause, thinking, then drops the nail and mallet, picking up a shovel. ''Guess I'd better dig a deeper hole this time,'' he says in a detached voice that is chilling. ''Let's see, now, you weigh maybe twenty pounds more than Marti, right? Tiny little thing, she was.''

He begins to dig in a hole he's already begun. ''Good thing the ground is nice and soft from that rain. Gotta make sure, though, the cross is deep enough so it doesn't fall over. Wouldn't want to deprive the press of a great photo op in the morning.''

I grunt against the tape, making a sound.

''What's that? You want to know how it all came down?''

He doesn't stop shoveling, but taunts me as he works. "Well, you gotta blink, then, Abby. Once for yes, twice for no. Isn't that what you did to poor old Harry in the bank that day? Made him nod? That was pretty cute. Oh, yeah, we heard it all on tape. Had his office bugged for weeks, but he didn't give anything up till that day you were there. Come to think of it, he didn't give anything up, anyway—it was you who said it all that day. In fact, if it hadn't been for you going to Blimm and laying the whole thing out, Hillars never would have had any real facts about the land scam. He wouldn't have started to put things together and get on my tail."

He kicks my leg hard with his boot. "You've got to pay for that, Abby. Okay? But you want to know how it all came down first? I can do that for you, Abby. Go ahead, blink."

I wouldn't give him the satisfaction, except that it might buy me time. I blink.

"Good girl!" he says. "Just like old Harry. Well, now, see, the way it came down was, the president, he sent me and Hillars out here to help find the kid, just like we said. But he wanted something else, too—your husband's head on a platter. See, his old pal Marti Bright didn't just tell him about her kid being gone. She told him something else, too—that his trusted personal adviser, Jeffrey Northrup, was running a big-time real-estate scam out here. She told him she was about to blow the scam wide open— which, of course, wouldn't be so good for Chase, given the upcoming election and his close ties to your husband. Understand?"

He pauses. "Blink, Abby."

I blink.

"So anyway, Marti, she told him she'd hold off on the story till after the election, but only if Chase threw his resources behind her and helped her find her kid. Chase agreed, but he knew she'd tell all eventually and it wouldn't look good for him. So like I said, he sent me and Hillars out here to find the kid. Plus, he told Hillars he wanted him to find out all he could about this deal of your husband's, then run some damage control."

He makes a sound of contempt. "Damn that Hillars, he's a real stick-in-the-mud, a pain in the ass. But like I said, our noble president, now, he ain't so innocent as he looks. Behind Hillars's back he offers me, personally, a bonus if I can get rid of your husband—and Marti Bright—for good."

He laughs that chilling sound. "You know, over the years I've known a lot of lying, cheating presidents, but Chase beats 'em all. He looks at you with that clear-eyed, boyish innocence, and you believe every word he says. Well, the public does, anyway. Me, I've had it up to here with all of 'em." He makes a gesture beneath his chin.

"So," he says, the shovel making thudding sounds as he lifts dirt out of the hole, "I cut a deal with your husband. Half the profits, and I wouldn't kill him. He could collect the cash from those developers, we'd split it, and we'd each disappear to someplace that doesn't have extradition."

He sighs and shakes his head.

"But there's this one little problem—this lady who owns The Prayer House, the one who won't sell. We need somebody to lean on her, and your husband

comes up with an idea to shut her down and wipe
her out. He knows this lawyer—Paul Ryan, you
know? Justin Ryan's father? Anyway, Jeffrey black-
mails him into filing a heavy-duty lawsuit that would
shut down The Prayer House for not being up to
code. He threatens to tell Ryan's kid he's adopted if
Ryan doesn't do what he wants. Only thing is, the
kid hears them talking about it and runs. At first it
looks like we've lost our leverage. But that's when
I come up with the perfect plan.''

He butts me on the arm with the shovel. ''It *was*
a perfect plan—or should have been. I go looking for
the kid and find him in Santa Cruz. I take him to this
cabin and hold him there. Now, Mary Ryan, she
thinks the kid's been kidnapped by a stranger because I send a phony ransom note, and I say if they
don't keep the kidnapping quiet, I'll send their kid's
head back in a bag. But Paul Ryan, he knows I've
got Justin, and he's willing to do anything to get him
back. He files the lawsuit and starts to lean on the
woman at The Prayer House in any way he can. Like
I say, the perfect plan.''

Mauro bangs the shovel into the ground, hard.
''Except that Ryan is a wimp. After a while he says
he's done what we wanted, and he wants the kid
back. We can't give the kid back, of course, not till
the valley deal's been finalized. We figure Ryan
would blab and ruin the whole thing once the kid
was safe, right? Oh, hey, I almost forgot. Blink,
Abby. Do it.''

I grit my teeth and do it.

''But that Lydia woman digs in her heels and the
deal's dragging on and on,'' Mauro says. ''Ryan

starts to go nuts. So your husband sends him and the wife down to Brazil, as far away as he can get them. Pays Ryan a huge amount of money to stay there and keep quiet. Even promises him the kid will be safe, so long as Ryan doesn't break down and spoil the land deal. Neat, huh?"

I try to wiggle my hands and feet loose, without him seeing it. But he's lashed me to the cross so tightly, it's stopped the flow of blood. My wrists and ankles both have lost feeling. I can't tell if I'm succeeding at all.

If only I could scream. That might waken the nuns in the monastery next to us, perhaps even some residents on another hill. But Mauro has covered all bases, keeping me gagged.

Well, he's had some experience at this.

"See, the thing is," he says, starting to shovel again, "this real-estate deal's been getting out of hand. Too many people were involved, and your husband had to close the deal fast. We couldn't let anybody rock the boat."

He shakes his head again. "But then guess what happens? The kid gets away. I let my guard down once, and the little sonuvabitch gets away. And faster than even you can blink, Abby, Marti Bright shows up at my hotel room and tries to kill me with her bare hands. She says she knows about the real-estate scam, and she's got proof now that your husband and I are running it. Not only that, but she says she's got her son, and he can testify we kidnapped him.

"Now, that one really got to me, Abby. I mean, it could've been true, since the kid had just got away from us. But on second thought, I figure she's bluffing, otherwise why would she even bother to tell me what she planned to do? Besides, it wasn't in the papers or anything that the kid had been found. So I tell her I know damn well she's bluffing, and if she ever wants to see her kid again, she'll keep her mouth shut. I run my own bluff, see? Let her think I've still got the kid. Then I let her leave—but I know by now there's only one thing I can do. I've got to kill her.''

He sighs, as if greatly disappointed at the way his perfect plan turned out.

''Of course, the method was a problem,'' he says matter-of-factly. ''I had Hillars on my tail already with supicions about the land scam, so I decided to make this murder look like something some religious nut would do, maybe even somebody from The Prayer House. That Sister Helen, for instance, or Lydia Greyson. Hell, we wouldn't even need the nuisance lawsuit anymore—we could put them in jail for murder. *That'd* close the place down!'' He chuckles.

''So I came up with the crucifixion. It seemed a nice touch, you know? Especially using that trepan. Back in the old days, priests used to open skulls to let evil spirits out. Did you know that? Oh, sure you did. The coroner told you that. So anyway, I figured that would throw even more suspicion on The Prayer House.'' He pauses and looks across at the Carmelite monastery, which is shrouded in darkness at this hour. ''I even picked this spot for that very reason. The connection, you know, between the two houses. Well, and it was closer than driving all the way out to the valley. See, I couldn't be gone that long.''

Mauro slams the shovel into the ground and leans on it heavily. "First, though, I had to know if Marti really was bluffing about the kid. After all, I couldn't leave him hanging around to talk about what happened. But the bitch wouldn't tell me a thing. I did everything I could to get her to tell me where the kid was, took it nice and slow with the scourging, making each blow count."

A smile reaches his voice. "Got that little S&M toy in a sex shop in Seaside. Nice touch, don't you think? Still, all I could get out of her was that she'd lied, she didn't know where the kid was." He sighs. "I couldn't help but believe her, Abby, all the pain she was in by then. So hell, I finished up the job— right down to a nice little last-minute touch. Found a can of red paint down by that house and painted the words 'I LIED' on her chest, sort of a Scarlet Letter for the lying bitch."

Mauro leans down, so close I can feel his breath. "But then you had to poke your nose into things. And it all got too complicated, Abby. That asshole husband of yours went nuts tonight and killed that cop outside your house."

I make a sound of horror and shake my head. *Not Ben! Please, not Ben!*

"Next thing I know he's raping you up in that bedroom of yours. Shit, his DNA was all over the place, and I couldn't just leave him there alive. He'd have been arrested, and he'd have blabbed about everything, including me. See, Abby, the land scam has been fading fast. But with any luck, I can persuade Hillars of my innocence, and I can still collect that bonus from Chase for getting rid of problematic right-hand man Jeffrey.''

I see his teeth flash white in a grin. "So I guess you know what I did," he says. "I shot your bastard husband in the back of the head."

Mauro holds something metallic up to my eyes that would probably be shiny, except that it's coated with a dark, dry material, like blood. It's in the shape of a long, narrow corkscrew.

"You know what this is, Abby? A trepan," Mauro says. "How about that? Same trepan I used on Marti, in fact. Got it at the sex shop, too." He checks the cloths around my wrists and ankles. "Tried to get loose, did you? Sorry, Abby. But you know, you shouldn't feel too bad when you're up there hanging. This trepan thing? I learned about it on the Net one day. When the skull gets opened up, it's supposed to bring back the same kind of bliss babies feel in the womb. You could go out singing."

The night is still pitch-black, no sign of a moon. I can make out his eyes, though, and they are so cold and flat they are barely human. I start praying again. It's all I've got left.

"Well, it really is time now," he says, standing. "I guess you know what I have to do, right?"

This time I don't blink.

His hand comes down on my wrist, fixing it in place. He holds the nail against it and lifts the hammer. I close my eyes, choking on a sob.

So many dreams, Marti, so many plans to do good in the world. You did that. Why didn't I? Where did I go wrong? Oh, God, where did I go wrong?

The hammer falls and the nail pierces my skin. I

scream against the tape. The iron digs in, and it's worse, I think, than childbirth must be. But then a loud clapping sound stuns my ears, over and over. Mauro stands straight and tall for a moment, and his hand goes to his head, as if saluting a flag. A dark, wet pool forms on his forehead and he wavers, totters and falls. The weight of him is on me, smothering me. I can't breathe. *Oh, God, help me! I can't breathe!*

I am blacking out when the weight is removed. I open my eyes and see Ben. He begins tearing at my wrists, cutting through the cloths, and gently, every so gently, he removes the tape from my mouth.

"I thought I was too late," he says, pulling me against him. There are tears in his eyes. "God, Abby, I thought I was too late."

Epilogue

Six months later

Ben found the sheriff's deputy dead in his patrol car that night, in front of my house. Racing up the walk, he beat on my door. When I didn't answer he broke through a front window and found Jeffrey on the floor of the bedroom. Just as Mauro said, he'd been shot in the back of the head.

That was long after Mauro had dragged me to that godforsaken hill, but someone had called dispatch to say he saw us leave the house and was worried. He told Ben he was out late walking his dog and thought he'd stop in if there was a light on in my house, to pick up a leash he'd left behind. He saw a man half carrying me to his car, as if I were drunk. The kid said he'd met me when he brought Murphy home one day and didn't think I was the type to be falling-down drunk. So he thought he'd call the police and let them know.

I will never make fun of Carmel's 911 calls again.

Going on the kid's description, Ben figured it must have been Mauro with me. He contacted Agent Hillars, who told him he'd been suspicious of Mauro for some time. Mauro, it seems, kept disappearing and not telling his partner where he was.

I figure he was in the Santa Cruz mountains, alternating with Jeffrey as they both kept an eye on their hostage.

Ben and Hillars put their heads together that night, and Ben, going on instinct alone, led the charge up the hill just in time to save me.

I don't suppose we'll ever know who killed Rick Stone, but my money is on Mauro. Jeffrey was evil, as evil as the day is long, as my mom would say. But he was also a coward in many ways. Karen told me he'd been beating her for months, and the beatings had escalated as he became more and more worried of late. I figure a man who beats a woman is usually too much a coward to kill a man.

Harry Blimm admitted to being in on the real-estate scam at first, but said he pulled out of it after he met Marti at the homeless shelter in Seaside where he's on the board. It was he who gave Marti the original information about Jeffrey's scam, once his heart was softened by seeing firsthand what it was like to be without a home. In return, Marti never turned him in. Harry is doing some time now for his part in the scam, but promises that when he gets out he'll make reparation to The Prayer House in some "financially substantial way."

As for the injuries Jeffrey inflicted upon me in his rage that night, I've healed, at least physically. I may never get over what my husband, a man I trusted for too many years, did to me. But life does have a way of going on. I've sold *Windhaven,* which Sol had made sure was willed to me, and I'm using the proceeds to build that center Lydia Greyson has always wanted on the property of The Prayer House. I'm also helping them bring The Prayer House itself up to code.

Frannie has been hired by Lydia to organize the new center and run it, and my sister, Karen, will live there for a while, helping with the new gardens and "rebuilding her spirit along with her life," as Lydia says.

Just to make sure the body as well as the spirit gets a fair chance, Davis and I will be teaching Kenpo to the women who come there. Most of them have been homeless and on the streets at some point, and they'll need a bit of bolstering in the self-confidence department.

When the center opens—which, by the way, we've named Marti's House in honor of Marti Bright—I'll have a small apartment there for myself. Something simple—almost like a nun's cell, in fact. I'm looking forward to the silence, and I can't wait to get my fingers in the soil.

Not that they've snookered me in again. There will be no Victorian rules about "no special friendships" this time. In fact, while I wait for the center and my apartment to be finished, Murph and I are living with one of those special friends—Ben. Chief Benjamin Schaeffer, if you please. No need to be discreet anymore in Carmel. Not that it ever did much good, anyway.

Oh, and the letter A scratched into Murphy's back? Ben caught some nutcase doing the same thing to another dog on the beach, this time a poodle. He'd read about the name "Abby" having been written in the ground on the hill and thought he'd get into the "fun."

Justin is back with his mom now, the only one he's ever known. Mary Ryan is relieved to have him home safe, though shocked and saddened by Paul's having covered up what really was happening to him. Meanwhile, Paul Ryan has disappeared. Seems he never returned with Mary from Rio, but left her waiting at the airport alone. Mary's theory about this is that Paul broke down and couldn't face what he'd done. Even though it started out with him knuckling under to Jeffrey's blackmail to save his son, she thinks the money Jeffrey gave him to go to Rio and keep quiet did a number on his conscience.

As for Justin, his real father—or biological father, if you will—came to me shortly after that night. He told me that he and Marti had one night together sixteen years ago. He had won her over in a vulnerable time, he said, and he knew it couldn't last. But that one night was everything to him.

He told me he didn't know until recently that she'd had a child, and that the child was his. Marti phoned him in July last year, at the same time Justin disappeared. She didn't tell him who she'd given their son to, or anything about him, including the fact that he was missing. She told him only that she wanted him to know the child existed, in case anything happened to her.

He was stunned, but thrilled to learn he had a child somewhere. And now, he said, he wanted nothing more in the world than to meet Justin and be a father to him.

I don't know if that will all work out, but I took

Tommy Lawrence to meet his son. The two of them hugged, but hesitantly, the way men will. Then they found some common ground, in books. It wasn't long after that before they were talking as if they'd known each other for years.

Tommy never was hanging around me for any dire purpose. While it's true he was writing a book about Marti, he was largely hoping I'd lead him to his son. That's why he took Marti's letters from my attic, and why he was looking through my journals on the computer—hoping for a clue about who his son's adoptive parents might be.

It's also why he followed me to Rio—though he never did put together what I was doing down there.

Personally, I think Marti didn't fully trust Tommy enough to tell him he had a son, after the way he obsessed over her years before. She might have been afraid he'd intrude on Justin's life. Once Justin went missing, however, she must have felt the only right thing was to tell Tommy a son existed. Perhaps she knew he'd be dogged enough to look for Justin if anything happened to her.

So, Jeffrey and I were both wrong about Justin being Chase's son. And that's what comes of assuming the obvious when the truth is as close as the nose on one's face.

Tommy finally admitted he'd had a small crush on me for a while; it's why he kissed me in Rio. His feelings are dissipating, though, as he works on the book about Marti and the way she died. The seven-figure advance, Tommy says, will come in handy now. He wants to set up a trust account for Justin, and looking for his son these past months wiped out his savings. That's why he was in debt.

As to why he lied about staying at the La Playa, it seemed to him that from the moment he came to our "land of milk and money," everyone he met was rich. He didn't think he'd be accepted as readily if people knew he couldn't hold his own in that department.

I must admit, he was half-right about that. There are people in this town who look askance at those who don't seem to be doing well. But that's "surface Carmel." Underneath, a lot of people are struggling, especially artists and writers who live in studio apartments because they love the town. Now that Tommy's getting to know some of them, he's more comfortable here. Which is good, since he's living here now, to be close to his son.

I can see why you cared about him, Marti. When all's said and done, Tommy's good people. And the book he's writing about you isn't just for money. It's a labor of love for Tommy, and a gift for Justin, too. It will include your good deeds and the way you loved everyone, especially the way you loved your son.

So, Marti, maybe some of our dreams have come true. Not the way we hoped they might, of course. Dreams seldom do. But your son has a home, he has a father, and he has good friends in Helen, Ben and me. We'll watch after him now that you no longer can. We'll see he continues to grow up honest, faithful, loving and strong.

Shining Bright, in fact—just like you.

According to Jayne Ann Krentz, "When it comes to romance,
adventure and suspense, nobody delivers like…"

CARLA NEGGERS

Three years after the sudden death of her husband,
Lucy Blacker Swift has finally got her life under control.
That is until a string of unexplained events threatens her
new life. Lucy turns to Sebastian Redwing, the man her husband
always told her she could ask for help. And they become caught in a
dangerous tangle of blackmail, vengeance and betrayal, with Lucy's
family—and Sebastian's troubled past—smack in the middle.

THE WATERFALL

"Carla Neggers is an irresistible storyteller."
—Susan Elizabeth Phillips

On sale mid-May 2000 wherever paperbacks are sold!

MEG O'BRIEN

66516 CRASHING DOWN ___ $5.99 U.S. ___ $6.99 CAN.

(limited quantities available)

TOTAL AMOUNT	$_____
POSTAGE & HANDLING	$_____
($1.00 for one book; 50¢ for each additional)	
APPLICABLE TAXES*	$_____
TOTAL PAYABLE	$_____

(check or money order—please do not send cash)

To order, complete this form and send it, along with a check or money order for the total above, payable to MIRA Books®, to: **In the U.S.:** 3010 Walden Avenue, P.O. Box 9077, Buffalo, NY 14269-9077; **In Canada:** P.O. Box 636, Fort Erie, Ontario, L2A 5X3.

Name:_____

Address:_____ City:_____

State/Prov.:_____ Zip/Postal Code:_____

Account Number (if applicable):_____

075 CSAS

*New York residents remit applicable sales taxes.
  Canadian residents remit applicable GST and provincial taxes.

MIRA

Visit us at www.mirabooks.com   MMO0600BL